A WINTER'S RIME

FORGE BOOKS BY CAROL DUNBAR

The Net Beneath Us
A Winter's Rime

A
WINTER'S
RIME

CAROL DUNBAR

TOR PUBLISHING GROUP
NEW YORK

A WINTER'S RIME

A Forge Book
Published by Tom Doherty Associates / Tor Publishing Group
120 Broadway
New York, NY 10271

www.tor-forge.com

Forge® is a registered trademark of Macmillan Publishing Group, LLC.

The Library of Congress Cataloging-in-Publication Data is available upon request.

ISBN 978-1-250-82688-6 (hardcover)
ISBN 978-1-250-82689-3 (ebook)

Our books may be purchased in bulk for promotional, educational, or business use. Please contact your local bookseller or the Macmillan Corporate and Premium Sales Department at 1-800-221-7945, extension 5442, or by email at MacmillanSpecialMarkets@macmillan.com.

First Edition: 2023

Printed in the United States of America

0 9 8 7 6 5 4 3 2 1

For
My Sistas

People are the miracles that emerge from
the ripped and worn pattern of your life
and help you stitch it back together.
—Richard Wagamese

PART

ONE

1

During the winter of her twenty-fifth year, Mallory Moe lived in a cabin in the woods with a woman named Andrea and worked overnights at a gas station store. Her shifts at the Speed Stop rotated—1400 until midnight, 2200 until dawn, or 0500 until the middle of the afternoon. She either left in the dark or returned in the dark to walk the dog around the frozen lake. She never knew what day of the week it was, whether morning or afternoon, day or night. She only knew that she needed to avoid being home.

Mallory had never been in a romantic relationship with another woman before, and it had been working out fine, until the government shutdown meant that Andrea was always around. It was a small cabin, a dark winter.

Mallory clipped the leash to the dog and pulled on her gloves, but Andrea had one of those fiddly leashes—a protracting reel with buttons and levers.

"You already walked her this morning," Andrea said, and Mallory jumped.

"Yeah." She'd thought that Andrea was on the couch, watching television. "But I'll just take her out again."

"She doesn't need to go out again."

Baily's little toenails clicked on the linoleum.

"I think she does," Mallory said. "I don't mind." She bungled through the back door, coat unzipped, hat jammed on her head, the protracting wheel spinning out as Baily zipped down the decking stairs.

When they'd first met, Mallory had been subletting a bedroom in her coworker's house in the bar district of Sterling, the blue-collar town on the Wisconsin side of the bridge. It had been the easiest thing, requiring the least amount of effort. But city buses rumbled along, the air smelled of cigarettes, and once, after working all night, Mallory had come home to see a woman peeing on the sidewalk. Her situation now was much better. The only place that made any sense to her was the woods. She needed to live someplace remote, without people and noise, where she could figure out her life. But ever since the government shutdown Andrea had been glued to the TV that blasted sound throughout the house—people gunned down in synagogues, in schools; stories of climate change, the end of life as we know it; bombs exploding in the streets.

Mallory pulled up her hood and stuffed her gloved hands in the pockets of her coat. They headed out down the middle of Riley Ridge Road, paved and plowed, but snow-covered and streaked with sand. From behind them, out on the back deck, the drone of the generator faded. She felt loosed from the center of herself, her muscles corded and tight. Above her a nearly whole moon rose in a sky amply pierced by starlight.

Baily trotted out front, a mystery terrier the size of a fuzzy slipper, with a red sweater and two ears alert on the top of her head. Her claws crepitated on the snowpack, collar jingling in the icy air. Usually they went about half a mile, until the road branched off and met up with another one. Normally, before the shutdown, Mallory would turn them around at that point to go back to the cabin, where it was warm. But lately, she'd been taking that branch because it looped around the lake, and sometimes, she lingered in front of the house of Landon James.

Landon, the only other full-time resident that winter at Mire Lake, split his own firewood and drove a banana-yellow truck. His house sat by the side of the road that looped around the lake, more than a mile and a half away. Once a week he came into the Speed Stop for his generator fuel and often the two of them would talk.

Mallory slowed and held out her hand. The last of a snowfall meandered down. Flakes tumbling out from a clear night sky glinted uncertainly, directionless, now that the source that had created them had moved on.

The last time Mallory had seen her sister and mom, they'd had a fight. That had been four years ago, the month before Mallory shipped out to Kuwait. She'd served a total of seven years in the army, joining at the age of eighteen, and that June she had come home. No one had been there. Her sister Laurel was living with their mom in Upstate New York and attending a private university. Her dad was someplace in the desert looking for Jesus. Mallory had been back six months—no, seven months now, she realized—but she still hadn't talked to any of them.

She veered to the right, taking the loop around the lake. Her boots creaked across the snowpack. She was not going to be one of those people who blamed every bad thing that happened to them on their parents. It wasn't their fault she didn't feel safe. It wasn't their fault she could never afford a place like this on her own. And anyway, things with Andrea weren't that bad.

"Once upon a time in the deepest darkest woods," her mother used to say, when she and her sister were young, and they would squeal with delight, beg her to tell them the deepest darkest bedtime stories. But those stories were just for fun. The people in them didn't act upon their deepest darkest thoughts, things always worked out, and nobody got hurt. They worried about things, what they feared they or others might do. But those things were never done. So, what scared them, then, what they only ever truly feared, was in the deepest darkest parts of their minds. It didn't get let out because it was never real.

Or it was never real because it didn't get let out.

That winter during her twenty-fifth year, something had been let out. Mallory could feel it in her gut, a disturbance that wouldn't go away. She heard about it from the news stories on the television that relentlessly played. People were acting on their darkest thoughts and doing things that, previously, they would never have done.

Mallory didn't know how to talk to Andrea about what was going on between them. She didn't know how to explain it, other than to say that it was her fault. Something was wrong with her—a character defect, a moral weakness. She wasn't just afraid of what Andrea would do; Mallory had begun to fear *who she was* whenever the two of them were alone. Images flashed through her head—memories, arguments, loud percussive sounds, and, more recently, her fight with Andrea.

They came fast around the bend, Baily leading the way, with the frozen lake to their left and the light of Landon's cabin straight ahead. Snow piled thick on his roof, his generator silent. A column of chimney smoke rose straight into the frigid air.

The brash, throaty bark of a dog broke into the night. Mallory startled and jumped, flinging out both hands and losing the leash. She dipped and picked it up, scooping little Baily into her arms and bringing her up to her chest.

"Shh shh, girl, it's all right," Mallory said, whispering into the dog's ear. It was Landon's German shepherd barking outside, a large dog that was never on a leash, and although she didn't think he would hurt Baily, Mallory didn't want her to be afraid. The little dog shivered and whimpered in her arms. The sound of the barking whipcracked through the night.

"Odin! Get back here! Odin!" Landon called from inside his house, the light from his open back door splashing into the woods. He was a hundred feet away, but in the cold stillness it sounded as though he were right there. Mallory lifted her face. "That's a good boy," he said to his dog. A hundred points of touch tingled in the soft skin under Mallory's chin. "Back inside now, old friend. There you go. That's a good dog."

Tingles rippling under her jaw as if feathers stroked her there, and her face softened, her eyes closed. The air seemed to bloom with the scent of fresh bread, and it made her want to cry, this feeling. Landon wasn't baking bread—unless of course he was. But she always got *the feeling*, as she called it, whenever she heard his voice. It was just the way her brain worked. Some voices didn't affect her— she felt nothing and didn't know why. Other voices came on so strong they activated multiple senses at once, like the wires of her brain had gotten crossed somehow. They had a name for it: auditory-tactile synesthesia. Sound touched her skin.

Her grandfather had been the one who explained it to her. He had synesthesia, too, after he came back from the war. She had his name, Mallory. German for "war counselor," French for "unlucky one."

From behind Landon's house came the soft thump of a closing door. Mallory opened her eyes. With Landon, it was more than just *the feeling*. It was the way he said things, the kindness in his voice. She had never heard a man talk the way he did.

It had stopped snowing.

Baily wriggled in her arms and Mallory set her back down.

"What is it, Baily Bales?"

The little dog stood alert and questioning at the end of her leash.

"Did that scare you?" Mallory asked, removing a glove. "Are you cold? We should go." The lever on the protracting reel had gotten stuck, and the little dog watched, then yanked the leash, slipping it from Mallory's grip as she wickedly ran off.

"You little shit!" Mallory hissed under her breath. The clunky protracting reel bounced out along the white tongue of the road and Mallory launched into a run, her hood falling back, the ends of her bloodred hair bouncing under a black beanie hat.

❄

The loop ended when it met back up with Riley Ridge Road, and Mallory could no longer see Baily. She heard the little dog barking, the splinters of sound echoing in the night. Mallory jogged to the left instead of going right, which would have taken them back to the cabin. Up ahead in the moonlight, the silhouette of Baily quivered.

Car parts scattered across the road caught Mallory's attention first. Particles of iridescence shimmered over the broken bits—reflector lights, plastic bumper shards. "You are a bad dog." Mallory dipped and swiped up the leash, breathing hard, lungs burning from the cold. The breath vapors rising from her mouth had formed ice in her lashes and brows. Baily yipped and hopped, hoarfrost clinging to the fur around her face.

A large brown mass lay across the road. A stillborn silence hung over the scene. Mallory never saw other cars out this far, out past the lake, and she'd never been on this section of Riley Ridge Road. This area was remote, Mire Lake not connected to the grid. Was somebody else staying there? Maybe for the weekend?

She wondered this, but it was only a fleeting thought. The deer was still breathing. A doe gurgling blood, eyes two glimmering slits. The muscle of her tongue hung limp and helpless from the side of her mouth, the fumes of her breath weakly white and forming tiny fronds of ice. Her legs were tangled below her body, disfigured with planks of protruding bone, the hooves shiny as summer plums.

A jolt fired through Mallory's body.

The memory played involuntarily in her head, a memory from childhood, and she could hear him and smell him like he was there. "Come on then," Dad said, home from Iraq for the holidays. "You want to go hunting so bad, wake up your sister up and get dressed." He moved through the dark of the house with a headlamp strapped to his head, his body lean and fit. She always admired the decisiveness of his movements, coiled and crisp. Whenever he did something, he did it right, and if he said he'd do something, it got done.

Laurel was eight then, which made Mallory twelve, although both girls were the same height. Bits of cereal still floated in their bowls as they hurried out to their father's waiting truck, rifles slung across their backs, exhaust curdling in the night.

They parked on the side of a county road and trekked out to the deer blind. Two sisters bundled together in a predawn stillness, crouched in a cheek-to-stock weld. Mallory wore an eye patch, a present from her father, to help align her sight—she never could wink or close just one eye. A slow-motion snow fell, the flakes tiny and iridescent in the limpid air. A quiet so still, she could hear the snow land with faint *tick-ticks* on the scraps of dried leaves.

A deer stepped timidly into the clearing.

Slender ears twitched and turned, she stepped forward, and in that movement, as if by secret signal, two smaller deer followed, creeping out from the duff. A mother and her young.

One for each of us, her father's look said.

The crack of gunshot. The blood invading snow. Mallory hadn't even known she was screaming until her sister punched her in the chest. "You ruined it, Mallory!" she said. "Why do you always have to ruin everything!"

Back on Riley Ridge Road, Mallory climbed over the crest of snow plowed in the ditch to tie the little dog to a tree. Taking a knee close behind the deer, she removed a glove, and sliding the knife from her boot, she thrust it quick and deep into the throat, wrenching it crosswise until two fountains of blood drained and light faded from the doe's eyes. Then, placing a thumb on the smooth plank of the glabella, she offered up an acknowledgment to the spirit passing, the way her friend Ottara had taught her when they served together in Kuwait.

She had cried all weekend after that hunt with her dad, not coming out of her room, staying in bed. She hadn't understood it, what hunting required. She'd begged to go because she wanted to be part of things, to have an experience with her dad, but it had devastated her, the thought of those two motherless deer. They'd tracked that mother doe for hours, her dad's bullet missing the lungs because she had cried and always, she cried. She was too sensitive, everyone said.

Wiping the blade clean, Mallory replaced her glove and stood. Breath vapors fumed around her face and she could smell herself—fight or flight, the scent of fear. It was an odor that had followed her from childhood, a smell that was real and pungent and able—somehow—to escape the mask of deodorant. She kicked at the car parts, knocking them off the side of the road. Her breath came shallow and fast, and saliva coated her tongue with the viscosity of blood.

"Tell her to quit being a pussy." She'd heard them arguing about her, later that night, her dad's voice coming through the thin bedroom walls. "She's weak," he said. "No mental fortitude." Venison was good meat, and deer were rats on legs.

A front bumper, the socket of a headlight, and what looked like the gray cover to a side fender—those she picked up and hauled off, tossing them into the woods.

The deer lay with her head facing the trees. Mallory lifted the back legs and pulled. The joints popped, part of the body stuck to the road. She yanked harder, ripping the fur as she tore it from the frozen ground. Walking backwards and averting her eyes, she dragged the deer, leaving behind a slick smear, the slosh and gurgle of fluids and the rank smell. She pulled it onto the snow piled in the ditch off the side of the road and left it there to get picked at by the crows.

2

One of the first Speed Stops to open had been in Mallory's hometown of Sanders, Wisconsin. Besides selling gasoline and potato chips, they also kept the store stocked with yogurt and onions and containers of cut-up fruit—honeydew, cantaloupe, grapes. They had restrooms with stalls that had real doors that closed all the way and actual doorknobs, divided by solid brick walls. Her sister, Laurel, had called them "apartments," and whenever they went in next to each other, they had pretended that they were living together and going to college, giggling while they peed.

Mom had taken them to the Speed Stop on the nights when she didn't work and Dad was deployed. "Let's go get shakes," she'd say, grabbing the keys. Her mom was different when Dad was overseas. They'd drive to the rural Speed Stop off the main highway that shot through their small town and gather around the new, state-of-the-art machine. Her mom watched as it churned the ice cream—you could choose your favorite flavors, add toppings like "whip."

Her mom wearing denim and sneakers, black kohl drawn carefully around her small hazel eyes—people always said they looked alike. Her mom had her girls when she was very young and was only five one. People always thought they were sisters. Three sisters, going out.

Mallory thought of her mom whenever she looked in the mirror, or smelled cotton candy, or saw other moms and daughters at the Speed Stop store. They were all over the place now.

Mallory pulled into the parking lot of the Speed Stop nearest Mire Lake, only thirty miles west of the town where she grew up. She talked to Noah while hauling out the freezer tote.

"Did you hear about that man at the Mall of America who threw a little kid over the third-floor guardrail?" Wearing her black work pants and a blue smock, she took out the plain cake doughnuts and lined them up in rows across a wax paper–lined tray. "The fall broke nearly every bone in the boy's face. And this man knew he would do it. He told the police that he *came* to the mall that day *looking* for someone to kill."

Noah Quakenbush, who worked with Mallory at the Speed Stop and was something of a genius, said that if you studied history, you knew things had always been this bad.

"We just didn't know it then," he said from the kitchen. "Now we have Internet, so we hear about everything." He wore a snug black hairnet over his acorn-shaped head, and Smurf-blue gloves. He set a timer for the oven and lined frozen puck patties across his industrial tray. It was easy for her to be around Noah—his voice had no effect on her skin. "Plus, there's the added problem of fake news, so you don't even know what's true anymore." He smiled, pushing his glasses up higher on his nose. Whenever he gestured, he did so smoothly, and he always kept the same pace, a relaxed gait with no sudden moves. He lacked the ability to hustle—something Mallory found comforting. Noah would have been a disaster in the military.

The kitchen filled with the smell of sizzling meat. Smells, to her, were a gift; they mitigated the effect of uncomfortable sounds on her skin. That plus earplugs was how she survived her time in the service, and why she worked that winter at the Speed Stop store— they all had bakeries and kitchens and brewed coffee twenty-four seven.

"Why doesn't anyone ever make fake news about good things?" She pummeled the clear plastic bag to make the icing mix and did a mock reporter voice: "Scientists find that penguins on the north pole are actually mating at twice the normal rates, populations are thriving, and their chicks are somehow learning to fly."

"Penguins only live at the south pole," Noah informed her. "And they can fly, through water. They have incredibly strong pectoral muscles and streamlined bodies."

"Thank you for the lesson in zoology." She snipped off the corner of the plastic bag and zigzagged icing across the doughnut tops. She dealt with bakery because the person who usually did it was out on medical leave.

"Gentoo penguins leap out of the water like porpoises," he added helpfully.

They talked together in the kitchen, and they talked all night over their headsets, especially during the dead zone between 0200 and 0330, when all the cops and truckers had gone—when all of life seemed suspended and they were the only two people in the world. Of course, Noah explained what dead zones really were: hypoxic zones in the earth's water systems that could no longer support life. And how those zones were expanding.

"Jesus, Noah. Don't you have any good news for me?"

"On Sunday there's going to be an eclipse of a blood moon."

The oven timer went off and Noah picked up the giant silver tongs and removed the industrial tray. Landon James had invited Mallory to a bonfire on the night of the blood moon.

"What day is it today?" she asked.

"Friday."

"Already?"

"When we started the shift, it was only Thursday." He set down the industrial tray. "You have to let those thaw first."

"What?"

"The doughnuts. Before you decorate them. They're going to expand as they warm and that will displace the icing." He picked up a platter of wrapped sausage biscuit sandwiches and disappeared through the swinging kitchen door.

Mallory looked at her doughnuts, covered now in sprinkles and already a glopping mess. The cakey sides were expanding, like they were breathing.

"Jesus, Noah," she said into the headset. "Why didn't you tell me this?"

"I was afraid you'd get mad."

"But they're already decorated!" She did sound mad.

"I thought you knew. You're the guest service leader."

Mallory flung the frosting bag and dropped to the floor, doing a set of push-ups there in the kitchen of the Speed Stop store. Nose to the ground, legs out straight, and her body a plank, she snorted out breath in percussive bursts.

Noah returned with his empty tray and dealt out slices of ducky yellow cheese.

"Statistically speaking," Noah said, while she did her push-ups, "good news doesn't get shared as much as bad." He made the sandwiches for the Hot Spot, a heated window filled with wax paper bundles of salty, cheesy food—breadsticks, burgers, and sausage croissants. "Bots spread fake news and real news equally across the web, whereas humans share fake news at an alarming rate, almost three times more. It's a proven fact." He pushed his glasses up higher on his nose. "Probably, I'm guessing, because it's titillating."

Noah wore thick-framed glasses and had taken all the AP classes at his school. He scored a 35 on his ACT, which is nearly perfect and could have gotten him into MIT. Instead, he worked with her at a rural Speed Stop as cashier/janitor/stocker/kitchen custodian earning twelve dollars an hour in a bizarrely overenthusiastic company culture with an obsessive adoration for the founding family—despite the fact that they were systematically wiping out all the mom-and-pop gas stations across the state. He did this because his mom was sick. He lived with her and paid the bills, kept the lights on and cupboards stocked while also taking classes at the state U.

Her mom didn't even know she was back from Kuwait. Mallory got to her feet, tossed the doughnuts in the trash, and went back to the cooler to haul out another batch.

❄

Landon James had come in earlier that week for his generator fuel. His truck had alighted at the pumps like a bright-feathered bird, and she'd twittered into the microphone, "Go ahead on pump three." For the suggestive sale, she'd dropped to her lower register, the one she reserved for hot guys in dimly lit bars. "Be sure to visit our Hot Spot, where we have pepperoni pizza on sale, tonight only, for $7.99."

Outside, Landon moved like a much younger man, his muscles rangy and his frame slight as a college boy. A photographer who freelanced for *National Geographic*, it wasn't that she had a crush on him—he was old enough to be her dad. Landon scurried and hunched, lugging out the fuel cans from his flatbed and filling them up.

"There's going to be a super blood wolf moon on Sunday," he said, when he came up to her register to pay. "Have you heard?"

She cracked a smile and weighed his spuds, ringing them up at thirty-nine cents a pound. "You're kidding," she said. "Super blood? Wolf moon? Sounds like a werewolf comic book strip."

"Yeah, it could be," he laughed, reaching back for his wallet. Landon was old school; he paid with cash. "Apparently a wolf moon is the first full moon in January."

"That so?" She gave him his change. "Only in January?"

"Only then."

She tenderly placed his bananas in a shopping bag. "What about the blood thing," she said. "What does that mean?"

"That one's a bit more on the nose. It's a full eclipse where the moon turns red. You'll be able to see it on Sunday around eleven at night. I'm having a bonfire with a few of my friends. You should come. Bring Andrea and some chairs, or pull up a stump."

She told him that she probably had to work that night and gave him his grocery bag. He left, but all she could think about was how she wanted to go to that bonfire. She wanted to sit outside under the light of the full moon and listen to Landon talk with his friends. It wasn't just the sound of his voice or because he was from California, with the rugged good looks outdoorsy men get when they age. It was the way he said "At any rate" to transition out of awkward moments, whenever he felt the attention too focused on himself. It was how the word "absurd" buzzed sophisticatedly on his lips—a windchill of forty below, "Absurd"; his nephew who warmed up pizza on the dashboard heater of his truck, "Absurd!" How when he smiled, his weather-beaten face crinkled and lit up like a meadow in summer.

She hadn't been this interested in someone from the male species in ten years. He didn't have that cavernous look so many of the boys she'd grown up with had; he wasn't wounded in the deepest, darkest parts of his soul. Andrea said the fact that he was fifty and living out here alone meant that something was wrong with him. But when he said her name, a warmth rose in her that made her want to, she didn't know, save him from that loneliness?

Which was absurd, considering that this winter she couldn't even save herself.

❄

Friday morning, Mallory came home from work and clipped the leash onto Baily for another three-mile walk. She kept her head down, hood up, and hands in the pockets of her coat. A winter rhythm beat inside her head: *boots and breath and boots and breath.* Her clothes smelled of beef burrito from working all night, and the cold ached through the tops of her thighs, but she didn't want to go home. Above them, halos of icy droplets encircled a nearly full moon in a double corona of yellow and blue. It shone down unblinking from a diaphanous sky and gleamed across planes of untouched snow.

All growing up, the woods had been her safe haven, a quiet place where she could go to recover some part of herself whenever her parents fought. She noticed the way nature handled adversity; how the trees bent under the weight of snow, making graceful arches and boughs; how the little birds fluffed up and huddled in the brutal cold. Mallory had spent an entire childhood avoiding home, and now that feeling had followed her here, to her adult life, and she wanted it to be some else's fault.

That night back in November when she and Andrea had that fight, it had been because of a bonfire at Landon's house. They had gone together but left at different times, Mallory staying after Andrea had gone home. That fight had gotten violent. Now she wanted to go to another bonfire. Mallory knew that she shouldn't go. She knew this: she should *not* go.

And yet she also knew that she probably would.

Something in her veered toward the reckless. An impulse to just do things. Her body moving out ahead of her thoughts to make things happen, make things different. Maybe, like Andrea, she was addicted to drama and needed to be in control. Maybe she really did have ADHD, like her teacher and therapist had said. Or maybe she wanted to feel the pain, wanted to get hurt.

Mallory stopped in the middle of the road. The leash went slack as the little dog Baily sat. Landon's chimney puffed shreds of smoke and the pines near his house stood like wardens all around.

She could picture him in there, in his kitchen, back where the light shone. It was the only part of the house that she'd seen other than the bathroom. She waited for a glimpse of movement behind the window blinds, the flutter of a shadow, a figure rising from the chair. Landon didn't watch television—he read books. He also cooked—scrambled eggs with vegetables served on a thick crockery plate, Mallory felt sure. She could picture him in there making breakfast, the gentle scuff of his slippers against the worn linoleum floor; how he would reach down and gently rub his dog, saying something encouraging; the scent of coffee drifting out. Holding herself there, erect and watching from the middle of the street, her face hidden under her hood, Mallory felt separate from the warmth of that house. She kept herself apart from it because that house and the kinds of things in it were unattainable, not meant for her. She believed this, privately, unconsciously. She had decided that she belonged on the outside of the life she really wanted, unable to let herself in.

Back at the cabin she hung up the dog leash and slid the knife out of her boot, placing it in the duffel bag, under her clothes. In the living room, she did a series of sit-ups on the floor, arms crossed, elbows twisting to her knees, before slipping into bed next to Andrea. The sun refused to appear, the clouds clearing only at night. Dawn prodded at the horizon as though lifting a heavy lid, and morning came gray and feckless through the trees.

3

The voice woke her later that day.

"Mallory," it said.

Fifty-seven hours before the night of the blood moon.

She came to, pulled from sleep. Red sheets over the windows swelled with crimson light, and the sound of a woman's voice droned from the living room. Andrea maintaining her vigilance by the TV. She had tacked maroon sheets over the bedroom windows so that Mallory could sleep during the day. Whenever the sun came out from behind the clouds, they glowed bloodred.

"You wouldn't think this kind of thing could happen out here, in a place of such wilderness and beauty," the voice on the television said, *"but it's happening everywhere, in both urban and rural communities."* The news story drifted through the bedroom walls. Mallory wore earplugs so she could sleep during the day, but one of them had fallen out. *"Some of these girls are as young as eleven years old."* The light went out, blocked by clouds, and the sheets fell dark. Mallory lay back on the pillow. It was an older woman's voice. *"Missing girls, invisible girls."* She sounded solemn, concerned. Mallory drifted back to sleep.

"Mallory!" The voice called her again.

"Andrea!" Mallory called back. She thought it was Andrea calling her, and she wanted to go back to sleep. A high-pitched ringing landed in her ear, shrill and exact. *"They're seen as teen prostitutes and not as victims. They're considered bad girls, dirty girls."* The ringing crescendoed, the curtain glowed bright red.

"Did you need something?"

Mallory jumped as if she'd been electrocuted in bed. Her arms spasmed and twitched and everywhere her skin tingled and itched. Andrea stood in the doorway and smirked.

"Didn't mean to startle you awake." Her bangs fell over to one side, coal black and frosted lavender to bring out the violet in her large, distrustful eyes. The other side she kept shaved close to her head, revealing planes of alabaster cheekbones high and sharp.

"Why are you calling me?" Mallory said.

"I didn't call you. You called me."

The voice had been a man's, Mallory realized, hearing it on replay from memory inside her head. The ringing in her ear waned but didn't go away. She gave up trying to sleep and got out of bed. Wearing shorts and a tank top, she dug through the duffel bag on the floor, which served as her clothes bureau.

"What are these red bumps all over your skin?" Andrea reached out to trace them with her fingertips.

Mallory flinched. "Nothing." The tiny bumps had spread like ants from her stomach to her back and all along the tops of her thighs. "I just get hives sometimes." She got them whenever she was stressed. "Have you seen my work pants?"

"Laundry room."

Jeans were forbidden at the Speed Stop, and the black pants made for women didn't have pockets deep enough to hide a phone, so she wore men's pants with long black sweaters or cardigans that hung down. Mallory tugged on socks and padded into the laundry room. The voice had been a man's, so it must have come from a dream, she thought, digging through another pile of clothes, this one on the floor in front of the clothes dryer.

"Did you have another bad dream?"

Mallory jumped and banged her knee on the open dryer door. "Jesus, Andrea. Why do you keep doing that?" She swatted the door closed.

"I walked into a room. Don't make that my fault." Andrea used to do the laundry for her when she first moved in—before they had that fight about Landon James. Now Mallory was being punished. "This isn't healthy, you always on edge." Andrea's breath shoaled across Mallory's bare skin. "I think you should see my therapist." She gently moved Mallory's hair out of her face. "I'll pay for it. Someone has to take care of the little cowbird."

The sound of her rich, cello voice erupted into a delirium of tingles against Mallory's cheeks, and it did this even when fingers weren't near her face. Mallory had once thought that she would do anything for Andrea because of that voice. She thought Andrea was better than her, educated and with a degree in chemistry, a minor in biology. She'd studied ornithology and said that Mallory was like a cowbird because she didn't have a stable family home. Cowbird mothers left their eggs in the nests of other birds because they didn't have the resources to properly care for their brood. That had shamed Mallory. She hated the way Andrea crowed and criticized her parents, and now Mallory wished she had never told Andrea anything about her life.

"No thanks." Mallory put on a cardigan to cover up the hives. Her pulse quickened, she could feel it throbbing against the skin of her neck, her armpits sticky and hot despite the goose bumps on her flesh.

"I was thinking about making lasagna tonight," Andrea said, which meant she would unwrap a frozen package that was vegan and gluten-free, then sprinkle it with cayenne pepper. "You like that, right?" Andrea thought she had to be mothering, but it didn't come naturally to her, and technically it wasn't accurate to call Mallory a cowbird. Her mom hadn't left until Mallory did.

"Sure. Whatever. You know I'm not picky." The ringing in her head had cut out. The voice hadn't felt like it came from a dream, or in her head, but it wasn't from the television either. She shook out her work clothes, the entire load covered in dog hair because Andrea had dumped it out onto the floor. Last week, Mallory had come home to find a load of her clothes tossed outside and furred over with snow. "You know," Mallory said now, feeling her heart beat harder in her chest, "it's not that hard to put my clean clothes on the bed."

"It's not that hard to walk into the laundry room and get them out of the dryer yourself."

Hearing the word "walk," Baily lifted her head.

"You next," Mallory said.

"She doesn't need to go out again," Andrea said.

Mallory could smell herself, the scent of fight-or-flight, the scent of fear, and it was stupid, she told herself. Why should she be afraid? Mallory knew that, physically, she was the stronger one.

"Is that it then?" Andrea said, still looming over her. "You're not going to talk to me?"

"It's not you."

"What is it then?"

Mallory braced herself. It was Andrea's house, Andrea's washing machine and dryer. Even half the clothes piled on the floor Andrea had bought for her at the mall, like the expensive lacy underwear. "She didn't have stuff like this growing up," Andrea had said to the salesclerk when paying. "She still wears Fruit of the Loom." Always getting in a cutting remark, even when she was being nice. Mallory didn't feel it. She'd let herself go numb. And anyway, things weren't that bad and soon the shutdown would end.

She leaned in and gave Andrea a kiss.

Before she could pull away, Andrea bit her hard on the lower lip.

Reflexively, Mallory raised a fist. Andrea caught it, held it in mid-air. Their arms tensed and eyes locked. Mallory had a temper, and Andrea was testing her, egging her on; a dark gleefulness played in her violet eyes. Metal zippers clicked and scratched inside the dryer drum and static crackled in the air. Mallory weakened even as she tasted her own blood.

"Pathetic," Andrea said, dropping Mallory's arm.

"These girls are particularly vulnerable to predators because of their history of trauma and abuse."

Andrea went back to the couch in front of the flat-screen, wide as a coffee table and taking up one whole wall of the living room. Wireless speakers mounted in the corners of a high-beamed ceiling pumped sound throughout the house.

"In most cases these girls believe that they have a boyfriend, that they're in love."

Even with the zippers ticking round and round, Mallory could still hear the TV.

"That's what makes it so hard for them to get out, because they don't have, in many cases, a stable family situation to go back to, and so the first time it happens, they don't even believe that's what's going on." Suddenly Mallory realized what she'd been listening to, her body flooding with nausea and heat. A roaring filled her head.

She marched out to the living room, punched the power button on the side of the flat-screen, and killed the TV.

"Hey!" Andrea barked. "What the hell did you do that for?"

Head down, hiding her face behind her hair, Mallory went back to the laundry room and shut and locked the door. Pulling down the box of Bounce dryer sheets, she pressed several to her face, closed her eyes, and sank to the floor, inhaling the heady scent.

"Mallory!" Andrea squawked from the couch. "Mallory!"

Andrea that winter had just turned forty. The summer they met, her house in Duluth had been vandalized, robbed, all her stereo equipment stolen. Whoever did it had urinated on the bed. And that was the part that disturbed Andrea the most, that haunted the darkest part of her mind.

"Mallory?" she called again. And Mallory wanted to reply, she wanted to feel close to Andrea again, wanted to be emotionally stable and worthy of all the things Andrea had done for her, wanted most of all to understand what was going on. Sweat pooled in her armpits and glazed the crevices of her neck. She didn't know how to explain it, why she felt so keyed up and displaced. When they said each other's names, that was supposed to be a call to presence, a self-awareness exercise Andrea's therapist had taught her so that they could learn how to better communicate their feelings. They had a lot of feelings that winter, both of them did, and that was always the problem.

Mallory never knew where to put them.

Tossing aside the dryer sheets, she got to her feet. Jumping up, she fell into a squat, knees on the outside of her elbows, then shot back into a plank, did a push-up, then sprang into another jump. Without speaking, without thinking, Mallory pushed out the memories with the burn of muscle pain, doing a set of thirty-five burpees there on the laundry room floor.

✻

Mallory and Andrea had met that June at a Speed Stop in Sterling, a port city with an oil refinery, sprawled on the northwest coast of Wisconsin.

"Do you have these in gluten-free?" It was the sound of her voice. It gave Mallory *the feeling*. A delectation of shivers rose through her cheeks and weakened her knees.

"We might have some in the back."

"Those are exceptionally straight bananas."

Mallory looked down at the bananas she was unloading from a box.

"So, would you mind checking for me?" The woman's hair was bluish black and cut artfully short, fringing elegant bone structure and a Grecian nose. On the ends of her fingers, black nail polish shone.

"Yeah, I can do that." Mallory didn't smile or engage. Her own body blunt and square, with the fit posture of ex-military, she continued to unload the exceptionally straight bananas from their box.

"That'd be real nice of you." That rich, deep voice, with just the hint of a snag at the back of the throat—it buzzed pleasantly in Mallory's cheeks and made her mouth water, not from hunger but from a sudden flushing of saliva in the space between her molars and cheeks.

"Don't get your hopes up." Mallory flicked the stepladder closed and hauled away the empty box. The sound of Andrea's voice tingled a certain way, just like the voice of Jarrod, her boyfriend from high school. She had grown up with him in Sanders—they had known each other since they were just kids—and the way his voice had stroked her cheeks, like the tickling of a cat's tongue, felt so much like Andrea's. It was impossible to overestimate just how dopey she could get from the sound of a voice. In the kitchen she inhaled several lungfuls of waffle batter and then stepped back out through the swinging doors.

"Here you go." She handed over the bubbled six-pack of gluten-free muffins in its bakery box.

"Well, aren't you sweet." Clearly the woman was being sarcastic, but also flirtatious at the same time. "Where did you come from?" the woman asked.

"I'm from here."

"I've never seen you before. I'm the Muffin Monday Lady."

"Congratulations."

"Want to get some coffee sometime?"

It took Mallory so much by surprise that she said, "Sure."

❄

In July, they met at an outdoor rifle range off County Road Z, twenty miles southeast of Sterling. Mallory stopped by the storage facility where she'd stowed her things while overseas and arrived with a duffel of rifles slung over one arm. Andrea worked at a water testing lab in Duluth, on the Minnesota side of the bridge, and played saxophone in a jazz band. After the change in administration and her house being broken into, she'd gotten her own gun. They shot at paper targets from high wood tables and later moved to their stomachs out on the grass, propping their weapons with sandbags. The sound of their gunfire popped against Mallory's thighs like hot-oiled kernels of corn, but Mallory was used to it by then and wore earplugs inside her hearing protection.

"Did you enjoy that?" Andrea asked as she cleaned out her gun with her slender, jazz-playing hands.

"Yeah." It was Mallory's habit to lie and then feel bad. But she'd decided on the flight home from Kuwait that she would be more conscious of this and stop lying by default. She raised her eyes, the temperature cooling off now as the sun dropped below the tree line. "Actually, guns aren't really my thing. I'd rather shoot photographs."

Andrea had looked at her.

"These belonged to my grandpa. He was a fighter pilot during World War II." Mallory zipped the sides of her duffel closed. "He taught me how to make the world's fastest paper plane."

"Are you a fighter pilot?"

"No. I didn't see much combat in Kuwait."

"What did you do?"

"Mechanic."

Andrea's nose twitched like it'd caught a whiff of allergen. "You must have gotten a lot of attention from the guys."

"Not in a bad way. They were like my brothers."

"Yeah, I got one of those." Andrea also came from a dysfunctional family, but hers had money and was from Chicago. She screwed on the cap to her vitamin water and rolled up her sleeves. Both arms were tattooed with angels clad in battle armor, wings with shining swords. The artwork, in its realism, reminded Mallory of her grand-father's tattoo—a black raven inked across his chest.

"Do you believe?" Andrea said, noticing where her gaze went.

"In what?"

"Angels."

She looked away. The fuchsia in the sky bled through the trees. I wanted to. "My parents were religious; we went to church all the time. But it seemed like hypocrisy to do whatever you want, knowing that, as long as you go to church and pray, you'll be forgiven."

"You don't believe in forgiveness?"

The conversation was making her uncomfortable. "Do you?"

"I have to. Forgiveness isn't about them, it's about you." It was one of the first of many profound things that Andrea would say, and Mallory had been attracted to that, to the idea of becoming more evolved. "I believe in angels because they're available to everybody," Andrea explained. "People get them mixed up all the time with their religious propaganda, but angels are older than religion. They've got nothing to do with Christianity or churches or man-made rules. They are their own powerful beings." She wriggled her nose. "Why do you smell so good? What is that—vanilla?"

Mallory nosed the black sweatshirt she wore to work. "Oh, sorry," she said. "It's cappuccino powder. From the machine at work. I changed the powders out today."

"Bonus." Andrea leaned over and inhaled. "Yum." She smiled. She was older than Mallory had originally thought, but she was lonely, and the angels had seemed like a sign.

❄

In August, when they drove out to the cabin at Mire Lake, Andrea told her, "I'm thinking of moving out here full-time." An excited Baily danced on her lap. It was hot, and Andrea drove a Prius, unselfconscious about the way her dress rode up, exposing the pillars of her thighs. When they arrived and the hybrid engine eerily turned off, Andrea's voice lodged itself in the pouches of Mallory's cheeks. "Ever since the Carrot got elected and my place got robbed, I don't trust anybody," Andrea said. "Plus, all this drama with the band—the budget cuts to the EPA mean none of us knows if we'll still have a job in six months. So we're taking a break." Mallory had never known a woman who played in a band or owned a second home, let alone a first. "Don't be too impressed," Andrea had said. "I bought it for the woods."

The woods had always been Mallory's favorite place. The town of Sanders bordered a national forest, but the woods of Mire Lake were the same—maple, popple, birch, and within an hour's proximity to the Great Lake. Once the sacred ground of the Ojibwa tribes, a place where food grew on water, Mire Lake was now a wilderness area with hiking paths and off-grid cabins tucked back on ten-acre lots, where hunters went to shoot deer and bear with their hound dogs and bait. Andrea strode up the cedar decking in her beaded sandals, pulled on the cord of a Honda generator, plugged in an extension cord, and invited Mallory in. A toaster oven sat out on the counter, a gas fireplace sparked with the turn of a switch, and raked windows offered views of the trees—the place so remote no curtains were needed.

Immediately, Mallory felt at home.

That fall a rafter of turkeys came to roost in the woods behind the house. At dusk they flew up into the trees in twos and threes to tuck in for the night, their chortles and coos echoing through the woods as though they were wishing each other good night. Andrea did their voices—"Good night, John-Boy. Good night, Jim-Bob."—explaining to Mallory about *The Waltons*. She bought DVD classics that Mallory had never seen and fed her miniature foil-wrapped peanut butter cups while they watched together on the couch. When Mallory found a giant turkey feather—brown with white stripes—she left it for Andrea under the wiper blade of her Prius.

When Andrea asked her to move in, Mallory said yes.

❄

In September, Mallory transferred from her store in Sterling out to the Speed Stop near Mire Lake, and they celebrated during Andrea's last gig. The orange globe of a harvest moon blazed through the picture windows of a bar overlooking Lake Superior, and after dinner they sat together, drinking with the band. They treated Mallory like one of them, letting her in on all the jokes. When it was time for their set, Andrea wrinkled her nose, downed the last of her sparkly water, and strapped on her nickel-plated horn. Up there on that stage, under a sultry light, she rocked and wailed, her body digging into the music, her fingers flying over the keys. She stomped and riffed and wagged her head. The crowd loved her. During one of her solos—a big, buttery sound that vibrated in Mallory's hips—Andrea began to change. She shed years from her skin—the worry lines, the eye bags, gone, sloughed off. This inner light shone through, and Mallory saw who she really was, how she must have looked when she was twenty-five and filled fresh with an innocence and hope that she could make the world a better place.

Mallory felt that same innocence rising inside of herself—maybe she could get close to someone again. She thought how beautiful Andrea was, not in a sexual way but in a purely human-beingness kind of way. Her spirit, that's what she saw. She fell in love with her as a person, a friend. She wasn't pretending in the beginning. She really did have these feelings.

That night, Mallory decided to tell Andrea about what things were like for her at home and what she and Jarrod had done to escape it. She felt she owed it to her because they were getting close, and because Jarrod had gone to prison. Mallory worried about how her past would affect her chances for a future and getting into a good college. Andrea had listened, and in a boozy haze of nightlife golden glow, Andrea told her, "I am going to take care of you."

And Mallory believed her.

4

The average customer spends two minutes and thirty-four seconds in a Speed Stop store, so they were always on headset, ready to spring to the registers. Mallory wore an earpiece that connected all the team members—any one of them could hear everything that any other person said—so they usually kept their mics on mute while they worked. They had a list of jobs that had to be done before they went home, no matter how packed it got with customers, even during a busy Friday night, forty-eight hours before the night of the blood moon.

The door buzzer indicated another valuable customer had walked in. Mallory hustled over to her register. Overnights during third shift it was just the two of them, and the most important job was the kitchen, so she always tried to be on the floor so that Noah could stay behind the scenes. "I have Asperger's," he'd told her during their first shift together. "It's on the spectrum; therefore, I struggle socially." Noah's favorite word was "therefore." He concluded things definitively and with logic, pushing up his glasses with the eff-you finger of his left hand. She appreciated the straightforward efficacy of his communication.

"Orange Juice Guy is here," she said, unmuting the headset mic—basically a walkie-talkie with an earpiece. She rang up a bag of Doritos and some dental floss.

"Is he there with you now?" Noah's voice crackled in her ear.

"Negative." Orange Juice Guy was their favorite trucker. Most people at her new store didn't get her sense of humor, but Noah did. Plus he never judged her for dropping to the floor to do push-ups in the middle of the night. Therefore, he made overnights tolerable.

"We have a visual," she said. "He's coming in."

Orange Juice Guy, with his French accent and bouncy, six-four frame, reminded Mallory of her friend Ottara, who served with her in the military. Ottara was now stationed in Bahrain, and that was the thing about military culture—you were always losing your closest friends.

Orange Juice Guy made eye contact, gave her a ready-to-go smile, and snagged a veggie tray and Simply Orange from the refrigerator case. She authorized a Trendar purchase for another trucker, whose gas was being paid for by the fleet, and helped an elderly woman who had dropped her cane. Then the ringing came back. It landed sharp and exact in her right ear, shrill and high-pitched. Mallory went back behind her register and got a strange, existential feeling that she'd better pay attention, but she didn't know to what.

"Ask him does he lift his feet up when he's in the shower to scrub the bottom of them," Noah said. "It's for my survey this week."

"Not going to ask him that." Last week his survey had been *Do you put conditioner in your pubes?*

Orange Juice Guy came up to her register. "How are you doing today, mademoiselle?" The luxuriousness of his French accent pressed into the backs of her thighs like warm sand.

"Are you going to ask him?" Noah said.

"With a customer." She grinned at Orange Juice Guy, peeling open a plastic bag.

"Oh, come on, Mal," Noah pleaded in one ear, the ringing in the other, and the sand tingling against her thighs.

"Any fuel for you today?" she asked, although she knew he had fuel on pump eight. She wanted to feel his accent when he said, "I do," the deliciousness of his *ooh,* and it took everything in her not to wiggle and smack her thighs.

Noah kept bugging her. "Ask him for me. Come on, Mallory, you owe me."

She handed Orange Juice Guy his purchase. "See ya next time," she said. All Speed Stop employees were required to end purchasing agreements with the phrase "See ya next time." It had a startling effect. He smiled, his teeth radiant against the backdrop of swarthy skin.

"Have a good night," he said.

She almost melted, wagging her head.

"Well?" Noah's voice clicked back into her ear. "What did he say?"

"He said to have a good night." The ringing was gone. She held on to the counter and the tingle of warm sand.

"You didn't ask him."

"I told you I wasn't going to."

"You're just a disappoint to me overall."

"Oh my god," she laughed. "Do you lift *your* feet up?"

"Of course I do. How else can you get them clean?"

She rolled her bakery cart out onto the floor and pulled on a pair of Smurf-blue gloves.

"Last week," Noah said, "I weighed myself before and after my shower. And guess what? I lost five pounds."

"Lost five pounds how?"

"I don't know. After my shower, I got out, I weighed five pounds less. Muscle mass weighs more than fat. Boys have thirty-five percent muscle and girls have nineteen percent. I have stopped working out. Do you think that could be it?"

"Dummy," she said, arranging the new doughnuts for display. "It means you had five pounds of dirt on you."

Most people lost weight during basic. She gained. They trained every day at 0500, out in their shorts and T-shirts, lining up in flights on the pad for PT. They did curl-ups, push-ups, running with sandbags or oxygen apparatus strapped to their backs. They trained for ninety minutes and then hit the showers before breakfast.

Mealtimes they had three glasses of water and three glasses of Gatorade, eight ounces each, and they had to drink them all before being allowed to leave. Everyone got their liquids. She went down the line for the food and told them what she wanted, they put it on a tray. She never chose more than two options. She didn't want to not finish—they didn't want to see any waste—and there were all those liquids to drink.

Most of all, she didn't want anyone to see her face.

"Don't sit with her," the other trainees joked. "She'll be done really fast." They sat in groups of four and didn't talk. She spaced herself apart and wore earplugs, keeping one arm up at all times by her face. She concentrated on the smell of noodles and canned meat paste to mask the sound of the sergeant's voice and the click and scrape of cutlery and trays.

The last two who finished had to bring up the trays.

When you brought up the trays, you passed in front of the tech sergeants, who sat there in their BDUs with boots crossed, watching the newbies' every move. They called the trainees to the front of the room before the entire mess hall and drilled you with questions about military history and protocol. It wasn't that she didn't know the answers; it wasn't even the sound of their voices. It was having to stand in front of the others, the attention, the exposure, knowing they could all see her face.

She kept her head down, shoveling in the anonymous mush. People next to her slammed their liquids. They gagged or snorted and sometimes puked, eating so fast it leaked in rivulets from their noses and mouths. But during the entire training period, she never brought up the trays. Not once.

❄

"Mallory," the voice said again.

Her heart blundered like a trapped bird. She stopped with her mop in the middle of the restroom floor.

"Noah?" She clicked on her mic. "You there?" It was the bewitching hour in the middle of the night.

"Yeah," his voice crackled back in her ear. "Where else would I be?" It was a dumb joke; they did it all night.

"Did you call me? Just now?"

"You called me."

"Right. Tell me, do you make a dent in your pillow at night so that your ear has room?"

"Why are you asking me that?"

"For your survey next week?"

"That's weird."

"They always are." The caster wheels of the mop bucket thudded across the divots in the tiled floor as she wheeled into the vestibule and propped open the men's room door. "I just want to hear you talk," she said. "Say something. Can you, please?" Normally, guest service leaders didn't clean the bathrooms, they assigned it to somebody else, but Noah was handling food in the kitchen, and Speed Stops were known for their tidy latrines.

"Who put the turd in Saturday?" Noah said.

The ringing in her ear came back, it flooded her head.

"Get it? Sa-turd-ay."

She set up the WET FLOOR sign, rolled her mop bucket in.

"There's a turd in the word. Hey, that rhymes. Sa-TURD-ay—"

"Yeah, okay, got it, thank you." She banged her mop bucket into the handicap stall as the ringing continued its shrill whine.

"Don't you think it's funny?"

"No, I do. I just . . ." She plunked the mop out on the floor and scrubbed. "I didn't know it was Saturday." The ringing stopped. She worked the mop into the floor, paying special attention because it was a handicap stall. The last thing a disabled person needed was a dirty bathroom, she thought, so she focused on that and tried not to think about the bonfire on Sunday or the voice that was calling her name. Her mop bumped into an empty blue and yellow can behind the toilet tank. "Oh my god," she said, picking up the can. "The Guzzler struck again."

"What was it this time?"

"A twenty-ounce can of Twisted Tea."

"That's a lot."

"Did you see him come in?"

"No."

"Probably happened during second shift." She put the can on the floor and stomped it with her shoe to compact it before tossing, then went back to rubbing at a sticky patch of urine on the floor. There were no cameras in the stalls, so they couldn't prove it, but the Guzzler was a large, ginger-haired trucker, and whenever he came in, they found empty cans of beer or Twisted Tea left behind in the toilet stalls. Meaning he smuggled the cans in under his coat and didn't pay for them; meaning he hid in there and drank alcohol where people shat and peed.

"My dad would never drink and drive," she blurted. "My boyfriend Jarrod did because his dad did. A lot of the guys in the town where I lived drove while stoned or drunk. But not my dad." She didn't know why she was talking about her dad. Noah's dad had died when he was young. "Sorry," she said into the mic.

Noah set the timer for one of the ovens—she heard the beeping through the mic. It was her dad who had taught her how to recycle cans, how to use a knife.

"Do you ever get a loud ringing in your ear?" Normally, she wouldn't have talked about it, but it was the bewitching hour in the middle of the night.

"Yeah, sometimes. Why?"

"I've been getting it a lot lately, but only in one ear. Is that normal?"

She heard another oven timer go off; they had both unmuted their mics. That existential feeling came over her again. Everything popped with importance—it was all supposed to mean something, if only she could figure out what. Her senses were dialed up, the mop handle extra glossy, its fibrous tentacles splayed out in gorgeous whorls.

"It could be tinnitus," Noah said, "for which there is no cure. Or, if it's only in one ear, it could be a brain tumor."

"Great."

"Maybe go see a doctor?"

"Yeah, thanks." Her military health insurance would expire at the end of the month. She had to decide: reenlist or go to school. She had to decide soon. She rolled out of the stall with her mop.

She thought maybe it was about college, the existential feeling. She thought it was about that because she didn't know if she should go or what she would study. Andrea had helped her to focus, sitting down with her to navigate the FAFSA for financial aid and to proofread her essay. Andrea in the beginning, so patient and generous, not putting any pressure on her, so the first time they made love wasn't until after Mallory had moved in. That was when she knew the experiment had failed and she didn't feel for Andrea what Andrea felt for her.

"My mom would say that a ringing in your ear means an angel is talking to you." Noah again. "I don't believe in angels, but that's what she would say."

Mallory stopped with her mop and stood very straight and still. With her hair pulled back under the hairnet, her ears stuck out, and her eyes, even with the black eyeliner, were small and watchful and sad. She thought about her grandfather, her father's dad. She had this memory of being outside at his house while Grandma was inside yelling at her dad. Grandma was saying terrible things, banging around the kitchen cupboard doors.

"The birches are releasing their spinners," Grandpa said. Tiny helicopters whirled down from the trees, pink as the half-moons in her fingernails. Mallory was kicking herself in the heels. She liked the way it felt, putting the pain on the outside of her body instead of keeping it in. She kicked both heels until they were bloody and swollen, ripping off the old and blackened scabs.

"Mallory." Grandpa put a hand on her arm. "Stop that."

Him. The voice. Certainty landed inside her like a plane. She touched down into a different reality. Grandpa was dead.

"Do you ever feel," she spoke into the headset cautiously, "like someone or something is out there watching over you?" She looked down at the mop. "Like, someone other than us?"

"You mean aliens?"

"No. That's not what I mean."

The oven timer went off—she heard it through Noah's headset. She moved the mop back and forth.

"I think I know what you mean," Noah said after a moment. "I feel that way about my dad sometimes."

"What does it feel like?"

"It feels like he puts certain thoughts in my head. Like, I talk to him more than I talk to God, and sometimes he talks back."

"What does he say?"

"I know it's just me trying to imagine what he would say, I know that. But sometimes it feels like the words come from somewhere else."

She stopped moving the mop. After his dad passed, Noah's mom had raised him and his two brothers all by herself on a schoolteacher's salary. But now that her boys were grown, she'd stopped taking care of herself. "Noah?" In the silence she heard him breathing. "Hey, you all right?"

"My mom is getting worse." He spoke quiet, his voice low. In the background she heard another kitchen timer go off. "She didn't pay the gas bill, although I deposited the funds. She spent the money on painkillers, because the ones the doctor gave her didn't work, she said. So now I'm worried that we'll lose our heat again like we did last fall." Again Mallory heard an oven timer go off. "It got so cold inside the house, I could see my breath."

"That sucks, Noah. She okay?"

"Yeah. She was asleep when I left. Her forehead was warm. I wonder if that means she has a fever. Probably it does."

"I'm sorry."

"Yeah. They have a cold weather rule during the winter months so they can't shut off your heat now, but if you get behind on your bills, they don't even have to turn it on. I didn't know what was going on last November, and then when I did, we owed eighteen-hundred dollars. I'm probably going to be working a lot of overnights." During overnights, they got paid two dollars an hour more.

"They have programs, if you want to look into it—government assistance that can help with the heating costs." Mallory returned the mop to its bucket and rolled it against the wall. It wasn't her dad's fault they'd had to go on government assistance. The economy had crashed and there were no jobs. He never got a break. "You know you can't save her, right? She has to want to save herself."

Noah didn't say anything.

Mallory swirled blue crystals into the toilet bowls. "I have to leave Andrea," she said. The blue crystals dissolved and aqua filigrees pinwheeled through the water. She hadn't admitted this yet to herself, was surprised to even hear the words out loud. That was the thing about overnights—during the dead zone, when no customers came in and the store hummed with its own kind of life, they said things they wouldn't normally at any other time say. "At first, I found it flattering, her jealousy," Mallory said. "But now it's getting weird and I'm not okay with it." The white crystals sank to the bottom of the bowl.

"It's not a normal jealousy?"

"What's a normal jealousy?"

"Well, who is she jealous of?"

She told Noah about Landon James. She told Noah what happened on the night of the first bonfire. What they said in the middle of the night they never talked about during the day. It was understood that these conversations were private. "I don't know what a healthy relationship looks like, is the thing."

"Do you ever hold hands?" Noah asked helpfully. "My parents would. They would sit on the couch and hold hands, or when they walked across a parking lot, or when they took Holy Communion at church."

"That's sweet."

"Yeah," he said. "It was.

※

On the night of the first bonfire, back in November, Andrea and Mallory had arrived together. Landon had invited them as a neighborly gesture, so it was just the three of them sitting in chairs sunk low in the snow around an aluminum fire ring dug into the ground. The snow had melted around the ring, but everywhere else was draped in white, and the sparks rose to break apart the night. It seemed darker in the areas just around the flames, and she thought how maybe the past didn't matter. They were all like sparks breaking up the dark, existing in a brief illumination of time. She'd smiled to herself, thinking that.

Andrea had kicked her chair. "Oopsie," she said, recrossing her legs.

Mallory knew Andrea had kicked her chair on purpose—it looked like Mallory had been smiling dreamily at Landon James. A little warning pinged in her chest. But it flattered her, the attention. It made her feel beloved.

Later, when she went inside to snoop around Landon's bathroom, he caught her examining one of his photographs—a rusty anchor photographed in such close-up that she could see rainbows in the striated hues.

"Are you a photographer?" he asked.

"Oh, no. I just take pictures for fun." Usually, she never told anybody about her pictures. "They're nothing like this. I'm only just messing around."

"Well, that's how I started."

They moved to the back door, where he held open the screen.

"I don't even own a camera," she said. "I just use my phone."

"That makes it really difficult to get a good close-up."

"Yeah, it does!" She turned to face him while moving backwards out the door, but she bumped into Odin and lost her balance. He reached out lightning quick and caught her arm. She would have fallen had he not caught her, his muscles rangy and hard as wood—he was built like her dad. And it wasn't that she was tipsy; it was the gentle encouragement in his voice.

"You two were gone a long time." Andrea's voice came from a dark pocket of night.

"Mallory here was just telling me how she wants to become a photographer."

"Oh my god, I did not!"

Mallory had snapped a photo of Andrea in front of the lake that fall. With the blue water behind her and the sunlight washed over her face, it had brought out the freckles across her nose and the lavender in her eyes. Andrea said it was the best picture anyone had ever taken of her. She said she had felt seen.

Instead of sitting back down, Mallory moved to put more wood on the fire. A fire was a personal thing, she knew; whoever built it felt a kind of ownership toward it, a kind of pride. She had her gloves on and arranged not one but two logs among the glowing embers. She felt Landon watching as she did this, heard the warning of her father's voice, "That which fuels can also smother." But her logs on that night fed the flames.

Almost imperceptibly and from across the dark, Landon raised his beer in acknowledgment of what she had done. Mallory flushed with pride, a deep pleasure and warmth. It was such a tiny thing, a stupid thing, really. It was nothing. And yet it was everything, because he had noticed, this man who was old enough to be her dad. He had noticed something half decent she did, a man who wasn't in competition with her, or like her in any way, and so she got this feeling that a girl gets from knowing her dad sees her as an individual with talents and abilities—it was that.

But then Andrea had to go and ruin it by making it all about sex. "A bit old for you, don't you think?" she whispered, when Mallory sat down. The firelight crackled and blazed in her eyes.

After that, Andrea left, but Mallory had stayed.

Nothing happened that night at the bonfire with Landon James. They sat outside and drank beer and talked about photography until he stood and said he had to go to bed. He threw snow over the fire and offered to drive her home. She told him no thanks, she'd enjoy the walk.

And she did. She buzzed home hardly noticing the miles. He had told her things about photography she hadn't known before, things about lighting and composition, how to pay attention to texture and shoot in thirds. It shouldn't have surprised her that Andrea was waiting up for her that night when she got home.

It shouldn't have surprised her, but it did.

5

Saturday morning, Mallory drove home with a fat moon squatting grandly on the horizon. Her car rattled and shook in the highway wind.

She'd been frugal with her military pay, only bought things used or broken, because they could always be repaired. That's how she'd been raised, and it was her policy to always give broken things a second chance. Only the driver's window opened; the back windows were nonfunctioning, one of them stuck partway down and sealed with duct tape. The key fob was useless because it had been left out all night in the rain, and the fan belt squealed no matter how many times she changed it out, no matter what brands she tried. She couldn't blast music to cover it up, either—all she had was a radio, and pop songs had too many sound effects that resembled car parts going wrong.

Baily must have heard the car coming from way down the street; she stood in the window, paws on the back of a chair, furry ears alert on the top of her head. She dove off the side of the chair and dashed to the back door as Mallory pulled into the driveway, pea gravel and packed with snow, speckled over with pine needles.

It was early, the light reclusive behind bands of clouds, and yet Andrea was up. The generator rumbled out from its corner on the cedar deck, and in the living room the television played. Privately, in the back of her mind, Mallory wanted her own place. Nothing fancy, just a house in the country, somewhere in nature, away from the city noise. But she'd never be able to afford a place like that on her Speed Stop salary alone.

"That you?" Andrea called. "I made soup."

"I can smell it." Baily greeted her at the back door. "How long have you been up?"

"Since four. The electricity went out so I had to start the generator, and then I couldn't get back to sleep." The stench of fennel and boiled cabbage hung in the air. Mallory finished petting little Baily and flicked on the venting fan. Kicking off her work shoes, she tucked them next to her boots on a waterproof mat and went into the living room to hang up her coat. Andrea, swaddled in her kimono and black leggings, sank into the carved groove of the couch, her feet wrapped in Smartwool and propped on the coffee table. Her toes poked out among a crowd of used tissues and a big bag of organic popcorn. "Help yourself," she said of the soup. "It's homemade." "Homemade" for Andrea meant she'd opened a can and added plant-based sausage, but Mallory was starved—they were never allowed a dinner break at the Speed Stop.

Back in the kitchen, she got down a bowl from the cupboard while Baily danced back and forth by the back door, claws clicking on the linoleum.

"Has Baily gone out this morning?"

"Sit down and eat first. She can wait."

Mallory opened the refrigerator door and looked at the beer. A slow, mournful wail, like the call of a wolf from some lonely hinterland, howled down through the venting pipe of the gas fridge. That sound poured sugar down her back. It happened every time they opened or closed the fridge. Andrea had said it was specific to that winter only; she'd never heard the sound before. Something to do with the way the snow piled up around the venting on the roof.

"I'm doing a *Sopranos* marathon," she said now in her bassy cello voice. "Come sit with me. I'll rub your neck."

Mallory took out one beer—it was after work; she had earned it. Her father never had more than one or two beers—he was disciplined, strong. She stood in her socks and cracked back the tab, watching on the television as a man pounded a staple gun into another man's chest. Andrea laughed, shoving popcorn into her mouth.

"I'm just going to eat out here," Mallory said.

She didn't understand why watching someone get hurt was entertainment. It gave her a feeling of vertigo in her chest—a sensation in her diaphragm like she was about to fall off the edge of a cliff.

She ate standing up at the stove. She could have asked Andrea to change the channel. She could have requested the best sound on television: Bob Ross from *The Joy of Painting*, with his crushed-velour voice that stroked the tops of her hands and feet and made her feel like dreams really could come true.

Baily ran into the kitchen again and barked. Mallory finished her soup and thought it was because Baily wanted to go out. She thought the dog was barking for her walk.

"Will you be quiet!" Andrea from the living room said.

Mallory turned, and her bowl hit the floor with a pop. Shards of crockery exploded across the linoleum.

A man stood across from her. He'd come in through the back door—just walked right in—a young man in a blur of flannel and smoke.

"What did you break now?" Andrea called out from the living room couch. From the television came the sound of rapid machine gun fire and a woman with a high, nasally voice yelled, *"Christopher! Christopher!"*

"Dude, where's Regan?" The man sniffed and contorted his face, hacking mucus in the back of his throat, ducking into the pantry and pacing around, as if Regan might be in there, as if there were nothing at all unusual about him walking into their house. His face was an almond shell, pitted and sharp, with patches of facial hair in a sparse goatee; his movements were evasive, trailing the scent of cigarettes and tire rubber thick in his clothes.

Mallory pressed her back against the counter, her hands balled in fists, keeping her head down and face hidden behind her hair. She'd changed its color on purpose, dying it black, streaking it red, so it didn't look anything like it had when she was a kid. The floor was littered with shards, and she was in her socks. She thought about the knife in her duffel bag in the bedroom, or how she could use one of those shards.

"Yo, I'm a friendly," the man said, hitching up his pants. "Where's my stuff?"

Mallory lifted her eyes, keeping her head down. A single chain snaked from his pocket to his belt and he wore a sweatshirt, sneakers, a knit beanie on his head. A dust had settled over his skin, a dull film that coated the faces of a lot of boys in the town where she'd lived, his eyes two black pinpricks even in the dim light.

He knows, she thought. A *whomp-whomp*ing came from her heart, and when he dragged his gaze toward hers, a flicker of recognition rippled across his face—or so she thought.

Mallory lunged, springing forward from the counter like a snapped rubber band. Grabbing his clothes, she kneed him in the crotch and took him down, releasing the smell of rubber and smoke. One knee bent, cocking her fist, she punched him, his skin slippery with heat. Mallory disappeared into a black hole inside of herself until her knuckles connected with the bone of Andrea's arm. It was an accident; Andrea had come up behind her, shrieking hysterically in the voice she used for the dog.

"Stop it! Mallory! Stop it!"

Mallory jumped back and the man rolled away, scrambling to his feet.

"Crazy bitches!" He hopped to the door, the screen banged, and in a hitching walk he escaped to his car. Baily was barking so hard she sneezed.

"What is wrong with you?" Andrea said.

Adrenaline fired through Mallory's veins, pumping heat through her limbs, muscles corded and tight. She felt outside of her skin.

"You could have seriously hurt someone," Andrea said, rubbing her arm. "You could have hurt me!"

Outside, the man gunned his engine, exhaust hurtling into the graying air. He peeled away in his car, and if it had been damaged by a deer, Mallory couldn't tell. Andrea slid the dead bolt across the back door. They usually left the back door unlocked, except at night, and nobody ever dropped by unannounced other than FedEx or

UPS—and they always knocked. Baily was barking so hard her feet came up off the floor.

Mallory went into the pantry for the dustpan and broom. Her fingers were twitchy, her insides hopping, the knuckles of her right hand bruised and swelling up hot and red.

"Let me look at your hand," Andrea said, picking up her dog.

"It's fine," Mallory said, working the broom. She didn't feel it, her hand. It was a balloon on the end of an arm that raked in the pottery shards. "He just . . . came in."

"Yeah, it happens. This guy Regan who owned the place before me used to deal, and his friends still think he owns the place." Andrea leaned against the counter, stroking the dog. She watched Mallory sweep and the hint of a smile played across her face. "Were you protecting me?" The lilt of pride in that rich cello voice.

Baily wiggled down and sniffed a trail into the pantry and then out again, zigzagging across the kitchen to all the places where the man had been.

Mallory slid the pottery shards with a scraped jangle into the trash. It humiliated her, how she had behaved. This wasn't who she wanted to be.

"You should ice that hand," Andrea said, opening the fridge, "otherwise, it will swell." The wolf howled down its lonesome wail through the venting pipe of the fridge. "Here," Andrea said, holding out a gel pack for the top of Mallory's hand.

"No, thanks," Mallory said, reaching for the leash. "I'll just take Baily out for a walk." She slid on her coat, fished out her boots. "Sorry about your arm," she said as she left.

❄

Mallory had learned from a garden gnome that her dad had sold the house. A bearded figure with a pointy hat clutched a sign between knobbed hands. "Bethany's Garden," it said. A profusion of flowers shot out from under the dogwood tree, a brick-lined path curved alongside garden beds. Whoever Bethany was, she'd been busy.

The leaves rustled overhead, the trees had gotten bigger—maple, popple, birch. June in her hometown of Sanders. Mallory stood out front in her army fatigues with a duffel slung across her chest. Hair cut short to collar length—he'd never seen it that way, pulled back into a stub with bobby pins tacking in the strays. He'd never seen her in uniform. Her ears stuck out from the sides of her head—just like his.

The taxi behind her beeped its horn. She jumped and reloaded her bag, asking the driver to take her back to Sterling.

She'd flown into Duluth International Airport and paid an outrageous sum for a cab to drive her out to Sanders. The area had changed during the seven years she'd been away. Six Speed Stops had opened in Sterling alone, the older gas stations frantically competing, offering BOGOs and punch cards and free pizza with the purchase of gas. In the end they all folded, every single one, run out of business, the empty shells of their pumps littered like dry sockets along the main streets of town.

She checked into a Holiday Inn Express, tossed her duffel on the bed, and took out her phone. She didn't know why she thought Dad would be home—it was just a feeling she had, as if her returning would summon him. He didn't respond to her texts, never returned her calls. She probably didn't even have the right contact information. The last time she saw him was high school, when he came to her graduation, but she didn't remember the moment or even what he had said. During training, when she came home for holiday breaks, she visited Mom and Laurel in their new apartment in Sterling, but by then he was in Florida, renting out the house.

Dad sold the house? she texted her sister.

Ru back?! Laurel responded. *He bought a motorcycle and drove out to the desert to find Jay-sus. Didn't Mom tell you?*

Mallory sank to the bed. She hadn't known. She never read Mom's letters, hardly ever texted her sister. It'd been four years since she'd seen any of them.

Serving had been the hardest thing she'd ever done, and yet it made life easier in so many ways. The duties were cut and dried, she always knew where the money was coming from, always had a place to live. They had a commissary and an exchange where goods were cheap. If she had an injury, she went down to the clinic on base and everything was covered. If she had a problem, there was a chain of command, a person to talk to.

The shouting and gunfire had ended after basic, and during her classes and training, her hives had cleared up. But the stomachaches and diarrhea never went away. She woke most mornings with her teeth grinding hard, her jaw clenched so tight she could hardly open her mouth, and when she did, her jawbone clicked.

And yet she would have reenlisted, for him. She'd have gone back in a second if he'd said, the person she looked up to, his approval the prize she held like a trophy tight to her chest. She just wanted Dad to see her in uniform. She wore it like he did, like Grandpa did. She just wanted him to be proud.

⁂

They took the three-mile loop that went around the lake, her hand burning hot under her glove. She didn't stop to linger in front of Landon's house. The sound of his generator rumbled in the parboiled air thickened with clouds, and she kept her head down and hood up, striding out past trees rising from giant pads of snow.

As a kid, she had thought that violence was contagious, like a disease. Whenever her dad got upset and yelled or hurt her mom, Mallory would feel sick afterwards, as if it had infected her, and she would want to break something, or—and this shamed her the most—she'd lash out at Laurel. Once you got it, she thought, the virus sort of lay dormant in your bloodstream, waiting for someone or something to wake it up so it could become active again. It attached like a parasite to your nerves—it *wanted* to be activated, like it had its own will to live.

Then she wondered if maybe violence was hereditary. She'd heard the way Grandma said cruel things to her dad, and so she wondered, did it pass through the family bloodline, moving from mother to son, father to daughter, infecting generation after generation and going back further than she even knew, because once it was there you had no choice but to repeat the motions born inside you?

Now, as an adult living on her own, she felt the energy of it living in her body like a black hole. Without warning it would collapse and swallow her down. She wouldn't even be aware of what triggered it, but it would take over like she wasn't even there, and she would say things and do things that were not like herself. Or she would think things, cruel things, on a track set to repeat in her head. Once she slipped into this rut without even knowing, it was hard to get back out. Because when violence was part of your normal, your everyday, since childhood, since before you knew how to talk or think or express a thought, it became your way of handling life. Because you had no other way. You knew of nothing else.

You even got to the point where you saw nothing wrong with it.

6

Sunday, the day of the night of the blood moon, Mallory slept five hours, showered, and drove to work. She hadn't heard the voice when she woke, and she told herself that everybody gets a ringing in their ear sometimes. She was just tired, or overly sensitive, or both.

Her right hand throbbed as it vibrated on the steering wheel, still puffy and slightly warm from punching that man. The hives were creeping in from the sides of her face—she glanced at the little red bumps in the rearview mirror, gathered at the edges of her cheeks. She pressed on the gas, pushing the car harder—sixty-five, seventy-five, eighty miles an hour. The serpentine belt jangled and whined. On the frontage road, when she slowed and turned, a scrum of black birds lifted from a bloodied patch and flew scattershot over the woods.

Second shift at the Speed Stop was from 1400 until midnight, which meant she wouldn't get to work with Noah and instead had to endure the presence of Asshole Craig.

Asshole Craig had a voice like a cheese grater against her back—not pain, exactly, but not pleasant. There was no cadence to it—all the words slapped out at the same pitch, a loud blare, every word puffed with importance as though not to be missed. At her old store in Sterling, she'd gotten spoiled by an all-female management. They trusted employees to be discreet with their phones and handle their private affairs in private, so phones were allowed and not a problem. But at the Mire Lake store Asshole Craig micromanaged everything they did. He made this big announcement about how if he saw them with a cell phone it was an automatic write-up added to their permanent file. Mallory left her cell in her locker the first time they worked together, respectfully following his rules, but then he wrote her up anyway for failing to offer a suggestive sell during the last five minutes of a ten-hour shift.

She'd been so mad, she'd gone out to his car at the end of her next overnight shift, carrying the utility knife they used to break down the boxes.

"What are you doing?" Noah had followed her out there, found her crouched by the wheels of Asshole Craig's car. "You do not want to do that," he said. "That's an eight-hundred-dollar prank."

"It's not a prank. I'm teaching this guy a lesson." She slid out the blade and thought how he treated her that way because she was a woman, and she'd been promoted young. She'd been promoted because of her military background—she knew what she was doing, at least in the store, more so than Asshole Craig, not that he knew or even cared.

"There are other ways to teach people a lesson," Noah said.

"Not without getting under the hood."

"Why not just let the air out from one of his tires?" That was when she understood just how brilliant Noah was. While he stood guard, she unscrewed the cap from the valve stem and held it down, pushing hard until enough air had released to render the tire flat. Then, as an upsell bonus, she threw away the cap.

That night, when she'd come on early for her next shift, Asshole Craig was still at the store, waiting for a tow truck—he didn't even know how to change a tire. His wife was holding dinner, his three kids were waiting up. Mallory couldn't stand it. She went out and showed him how to put on a spare, and he'd been grateful, although still an asshole.

After that, she and Noah became fast friends.

Mallory parked in the lot surrounded by woods, locked her car the old-fashioned way—by turning the key—and pulled up her hood. They'd gotten about three feet of snow that January, and then it had rained. Water packed down the snow and temperatures dropped. It had frozen the whole landscape into one giant marble block. Because the sun never came out, the snow that the plows couldn't scrape off stayed frozen to the asphalt, so walking anywhere was like walking on glass. Customers slid out to their cars with arms out, balancing their bags. Record numbers of people were in the ER with broken bones, and rental agencies were all out of cars—this according to the stories she heard on the news. Mallory skated out over ribbons of ice, hardened and yellowed as an old horse's hoof.

Around noon, a woman with four kids in a minivan was having trouble with the prepay at the pump. Mallory put on the safety coat with its reflector tape and went out to help her. The air was so cold that her fingers turned bright red, and the little hairs inside her nose stiffened and froze. But she stayed outside while the woman's tank filled and washed her windshield and headlights—they were crusted with salt and grime, it was a safety issue, and you just never knew how hard it was for some people to do life.

An hour after that, Landon came in for his fuel.

"Are you still having a bonfire tonight?" she asked him casually, weighing his bananas on the scale.

"I am." He slid out his billfold and plucked out cash. "Just me and a few friends."

"Too bad I have to work."

He seemed distracted as he took his change, wishing her a good night. She should have left it at that, but something in her couldn't.

"Hey," she said. "Will you still be up when I get off? At the bonfire?"

He turned back. "When will that be?"

"Midnight." No one else was waiting in line.

He took out his phone. "If you want, send me a text before you head over."

Asshole Craig was still hiding in the office. She took out her phone and slid it across the counter so they could exchange numbers. "Cool," she said. "I didn't know you had friends."

"At any rate." He grinned.

After he left, she waited for something to happen—her phone to crack, her ear to ring, a disembodied voice to call her name. He started his truck and exhaust churned white from his tailpipe as he drove away, turning left out on the highway and into the shapeless gray air.

She didn't know what she was doing or what she expected, but an unnamed anxiety shook deep in her chest.

Later, at the Hot Spot, she was changing out condiments, refreshing the pickles, lettuce, and tomato. They prepped them in the kitchen, where they kept the produce items in plastic containers called Cambros for easy access. The containers were deep and clear so she could see how full they were, and they were made of rock-hard plastic. From the back of her pocket, she felt the buzz of an incoming text. She looked around for Asshole Craig and pulled out her phone.

Spaghetti or tacos? It was Andrea.

Mallory thumbed back. *U pick.*

Thought bubbles appeared on the screen. She was there. She was always there.

I asked u.

Don't care.

Andrea sent a kissy face.

Mallory sent a thumbs-up.

Andrea sent a picture of a taco.

Mallory sent a slice of cake.

Andrea wrote: *You're naughty.*

Mallory didn't want cake. She wanted to watch the super blood wolf moon at the bonfire with Landon James. She knew it was reckless behavior, but she couldn't stop herself. She texted Andrea about the bonfire and how they were invited. *I want to go,* she thumbed quickly, and hit Send.

Thought bubbles appeared on her screen, then went away. No text arrived.

The door chimed, a husband and wife ambled in, he in a ball cap, she in a puffy vest. Mallory fit the lid of the Cambro over the pickle relish, with the little spoon coming out the hole in the edge, and put the emptied containers on her cart. The couple discussed their options in low serious tones over the doughnut display. Did they need a whole box? The grandchildren were visiting. They wouldn't want the doughnuts to go stale.

Mallory took out her phone and texted Andrea again. *I'm going,* she typed quickly. Then, just to be clear, *To the bonfire.*

❄

Twelve minutes to eclipse time and Andrea still hadn't texted back. Asshole Craig had finally left—a record for him, staying that late. The store had emptied out, no cars at the pump. Mallory checked in with the other employee and then put on her coat to drag a tote of cardboard boxes outside to dump. This store had its dumpsters in a brick enclosure separate from the main building, which made it harder doing the garbage in the wintertime, but it also gave employees a bit of privacy, if you knew where to stand.

Behind the dumpster she took out her phone. It was ten degrees out, but she removed her gloves and lifted her phone to the sky. Framing the moon glow over the woods, she scrutinized the image, reframed it to capture more textures, and took several photos. When she felt satisfied, she sent Landon James her first-ever text.

Mallory here, on break. Did your frenz come?

She waited, the cold freezing the hairs inside her nose. Bubbles appeared like magic on her screen—he was there, words, coming from him!

Yeah. Moon is incredible. Should start changing soon. Can U see it?

She found his uppercase *U* endearing. She peered up at the moon where it sat perched near the apex of sky, its shape slightly skewed, as though it'd gotten squashed. She didn't see any red. She took another picture and then examined it. The moon's gray mottling was maybe more pronounced, but other than that, she saw nothing incredible about it. She texted back.

I see it. U must be drinking.

He sent a thumbs-up.

She sent him a jar of jelly and waited, but nothing came back.

"Who are you texting?" Noah in his parka and knit hat rolled out a receptacle filled with trash. Mallory startled and put away her phone.

"What are you doing out here?" she said, unlocking the gate. "I didn't see you arrive."

"I came on early so I could help you with the garbage and maybe for once you can leave on time." He looked like a russet potato, humbled and padded and beige.

"Bullshit. You came out here so you could see the moon." She lifted the heavy lid on the dumpster and helped Noah pull out the bags of trash. He lived in a neighborhood where the glow of porchlights "obfuscated the moon."

"But Mallory"—he tipped his face up—"it's the last full total eclipse of this decade, a rare cosmic event and the convergence of three lunar phenomena at once. The moon in its super phase is fourteen percent bigger and thirty percent brighter . . ." He breathlessly regaled her with lunar trivia as they broke down cardboard and emptied receptacles and rolled them back. They picked their way across the snaked ridges of ice and emptied more bins while the wind caught up loose paper wrappers that flipped like wings into the night. Ever the good Samaritan, Noah went chasing after them.

He had what Landon had, she thought—an enthusiasm for life, an anticipation about what lay ahead. He expected good things and there was no question of his deserving them. Noah returned with the wrapper and his face beamed like it was its own moon.

"It's changing," he said.

They stood side by side in the parking lot behind the Speed Stop near the dumpsters in front of the woods. They tipped their heads back and watched the moon. It had swelled to a purplish red with banded circles around it, a giant's eye, bruised and plucked and punched. The tide of red slowly crept over it and a crown of white shone from the top. It made her think of a swollen breast, red and dripping with milk. It made her think of her mom.

"What's wrong with your face?" Noah said.

Noah said things like that, blunt and inappropriate, saying what he thought, without filters. Mallory found it refreshing. "This is how I look," she said, locking the gate. They rolled the empty receptacles back. "Why do you always think there's something wrong with my face?"

"I don't know, I'm just trying to learn social cues."

"Well don't learn them from me. I'm not a good example." She opened the back door and they went in. At her locker she peeled off her coat. "Landon invited me to another bonfire," she said. "To watch the eclipse. He invited us both." The ringing started up again in one ear.

"He invited me?"

"No, Andrea. Although I'm sure you could come if you wanted to." She closed her locker door. The ringing shrieked with the insistence of a teapot full of steam. "God," she said, "it's really loud this time."

"What is?"

"The ringing."

"Which ear?"

She had to think about it, the shrill reverberating in her head. "Left," she said. "Why?"

"That's a warning," Noah said. "I looked it up for you in one of my mom's angel books." He closed his locker door. "A ringing in your left ear means that an angel is warning you."

❅

The first time Andrea hit her they had been in the bedroom. It'd been playful, a light smack across the cheek, but Mallory overreacted and whacked her back. It had surprised them both—Mallory didn't think of herself as a violent person and would never want to hurt Andrea or anybody else. But that darkness in her had uncoiled itself like a snake. Things evolved into a kind of wrestling match, with hair-pulling and biting. It had been pleasurable at first because something about it was familiar, and though Mallory didn't know what it was about, she knew that, whatever it was, she deserved it. In a way it was a relief, like scratching an itch. They didn't beat each other bloody or anything. Andrea just liked it rough in bed. And Mallory returned it.

That next morning, after that first time, Andrea had said something along the lines of "You okay?"

Mallory hadn't known what else to say. "Yeah, I'm fine."

"You seemed to like it rough in there. Am I wrong?"

"You're not wrong." Her skin had flushed like she'd taken too much vitamin C, all the pores on her body sharp with a hopping kind of anticipation. She had no idea where this would lead, but she trusted Andrea, and letting out her pent-up anger and frustration felt good.

But on that night back in November when Mallory had stayed out too late at the first bonfire with Landon James, things had escalated. They weren't play fighting then. Mallory came home to a dark house, all the lights off, the television dead. Moonlight bounced back across the snow and shone in through the single window above the kitchen sink.

She was taking off her coat when a fist slammed into her chest and pinned her against the wall. Her shoulder popped, a hand smacked her face, and flames of pain shocked her awake. Andrea loomed over her, words spitting from her mouth. She didn't look like herself, more like a demon possessed, the dim light carving out the sockets of her eyes and the bones of her face. Mallory hadn't expected it—she'd been feeling peaceful, light. Her back thumped against the wall. She tried to get away—she didn't want to fight, didn't want to hurt anybody, least of all Andrea—but Mallory kept getting shoved against the wall.

It was that—the sound of her back thumping against the wall.

It happened then.

Mallory was no longer in the room with Andrea; she was somewhere else—in the black of a memory brought on by the soundtrack that had played mercilessly for the first fifteen years of her life. The sounds coming from down the hall, the thumping and thudding and cries of pain; her mom begging for him to stop, the pleas, the polite way she would speak. But he never did stop, and Mallory never could make him. She would run screaming from her bed, throw her body between them, clinging to her mother's skin. He would peel her off and carry her back, where he told her to stay because—he said—once you see a thing, you cannot unsee it.

That was true. But her dad didn't think about the sounds. He didn't know that this was also true for the things she heard.

In the kitchen, Mallory reached out with her good arm and grabbed the first thing she could find—a water glass that she pitched across the room. It shattered with a wet pop behind Andrea's head. When she turned, Mallory got away, grabbing the rotary phone and throwing that in a warning arc across the room. She didn't remember what she said, wasn't aware of everything she did, but she knew that she would do anything, say anything, to make the sounds stop. Saltshakers, coffee mugs, chairs—she pitched whatever she could find, until Andrea fled the kitchen, kimono flapping in her wake.

Mallory had never identified it before, how certain sounds triggered her, and why. She'd thought for the longest time that it was normal, how her family had lived. Her dad wasn't a drunk and he didn't do drugs. He served his country; they were a military family, proud. Mallory had thought she was supposed to follow orders and do what he said and stay there like a good girl in her bed. Even when she finally did figure it out and realized that something was wrong, really wrong, she'd lied to protect him. They all had.

Because it was true, what her father had said, no matter how much she didn't want it to be true. She was weak. She'd accepted violence like a baton he passed to her, too innocent to know better and too weak to pass it back, and so she went on holding it because it was from him and what he gave her.

After a while Andrea crept back into the room and sat with Mallory on the floor. She said she was sorry; they both did. Andrea held her and they sobbed in the rubble on the kitchen floor. It felt good to talk with someone who understood, someone who was also stuck in their pain. They made a pact with each other that night. They promised never to hit each other again.

Andrea was seeing a therapist and Andrea kept her promise—she hadn't struck Mallory again after that night. But Andrea did other things that made her feel worse, and sometimes Mallory wished she had the bruises to prove to herself that things weren't right.

7

The porch light was on but all the windows were dark when Mallory turned off the engine in front of the cabin that belonged to Landon James. It was too late to go to the bonfire but too early for bed. She'd gotten stuck doing the doughnuts again—their bakery person was still out on medical leave. It wasn't normal to sit in the dark in front of someone else's house. She should have just gone home. She should have never mentioned the bonfire to Andrea.

Mallory started up the engine but kept the headlights off. She didn't want to shine them into Landon's house. It was well past midnight, sometime after 0100, and under the moonlight the pines rose into a luminous sky. The tops of the pines nodded slightly like bowed heads, their boughs loaded down with snow. That was how she imagined angels, if they existed. She thought they'd look like this—giant pines standing watch with wings folded and gleaming white.

She put her car into Drive.

As a kid, when Mallory got dropped off after basketball practice, she wouldn't go inside her house right away. She'd walk down the street until she got to another house in the darkening twilight, where she would smell the neighbors' dinnertime smells and hear the faint sounds of clanking pots and pans. Movements of happy children bounced inside behind the windowpanes, along with the wagging tails of dogs and snatches of conversations, voices calling to each other. *Hey, honey, did you see this?* Such sweet things they said. *Who wants ketchup?* Just regular families doing ordinary end-of-the-day things. They seemed a marvel to her, the ease of it, the peace.

Mallory's headlights spilled out over the pea gravel driveway packed with snow. They illuminated the pine needles freckling the yard and the jagged pockmarks haloed blue from the salt and yellow from where Baily had peed. Mallory turned off the engine and sat with both hands squeezed into fists.

Laurel never woke up. Mallory never understood why. Laurel was only four years younger, and yet the sounds coming from down the hall didn't seem to bother her. Laurel never cried or screamed or begged for it to stop. Never fought or stole or received less than straight As. Laurel got a scholarship to attend a university in Upstate New York. Laurel hopped like a bunny across the driveway when they unloaded groceries from the car. Sometimes, Mallory wondered if her sister had a completely different childhood. Their dad had been overseas a lot when Laurel was small; when she was ten, the economy crashed and he couldn't find work, so he'd reenlisted and deployed again. When Laurel was thirteen, Mom finally left and moved to Sterling. Maybe Laurel never saw the violence, never heard the noises through the walls. Mallory always hoped this was true.

She pulled up the hood of her coat and got out of the car.

Inside the cabin, a shaft of moonlight passed through the kitchen window and illuminated the clean dishes drying on the drainboard by the sink. The floor was swept and the generator silent. On the stove, a note with her name sat on top of a cellophane-wrapped plate. The only other light in the cabin was the blue strobe flickering of the TV.

From the couch in the living room, Baily's collar jingled. "You stay put." Andrea spoke in low tones to the dog. "Let her eat."

In the dark, Mallory peeled off her coat. She thought she should apologize. She pulled a beer from the fridge and then put it back; she didn't deserve it. The howl came down from the venting pipe of the fridge. Mallory shivered.

She thought it was a peace offering, the food, the dinner with her name on a note. She thought if she accepted it, that things would be all right. She had come home. She hadn't gone to the bonfire or seen Landon James.

She unwrapped the plate. Loud music vamped from the show playing in the living room, but Mallory couldn't see the TV. She ate standing up, without even turning on the light. She was hungry and wolfed it down, not even tasting the first few bites. In her mind she expected spaghetti, and so that's what she tasted, moving her fork around the noodles until it bumped into the soft sack and skeletal claws of a rodent's body.

She flung the plate and her stomach heaved and vomit erupted. Over and over in the sink she retched, her body convulsing in hard spasms that curved her back. Dark slime spattered against the sink walls as she gripped the counter and retched. It went on for a while, long after her stomach had emptied out. Finally, she stood back from the sink and wiped her mouth with her hand.

"What did you do?" Andrea stood aghast in the middle of the kitchen, holding her dog. "You didn't *eat* that, did you?"

Acid bile burned in Mallory's nose and throat. Her eyes watered and the bones of her eye sockets felt sore.

"That was meant to be a *joke*." Andrea glanced nervously around the room. "I never in a million years thought you would be stupid enough to eat it . . ."

The kitchen walls pulsed with the blue strobe light flickering from the TV, and Mallory reached for Baily's leash. The little dog wiggled down out of Andrea's arms. Without a word, without a sound, Mallory slipped out of the house.

❄

The moon shone fierce and whole above the trees as they walked along the middle of the street. Mallory's breath whited in the frigid air and beads of moisture froze in the fine hairs around her face. Their footsteps scraped like knife blades across dry toast. Mallory pulled her fingers into the palm of her gloves and squeezed them into fists.

Baily tugged at the leash when they reached the road that looped around the lake, but Mallory pulled back. She kept them going straight. She did not want to think about Landon James tonight.

Once upon a time in the deepest darkest woods, a girl who was twenty-five got into an abusive relationship with a woman who was forty. She'd trusted Andrea because she was older, with a house and a job and a cabin in the woods. She'd trusted her because she had an education and a pet and cupboards filled with food—the signposts that said you were a bona fide adult. Mallory thought this was how she would escape it. Thought that if she trained like a soldier and crawled with oxygen tanks strapped to her back, if she worked nights and slept days, if she never got married and never had kids, she would end the cycle. She would stop the abuse. She would never become her mom.

They stayed on Riley Ridge and passed the other end of the intersection that looped around the lake. Baily tugged excitedly at the leash—they didn't normally go out this far. A billowing of shadows flapped across Mallory's face and she pulled back, looking up, the hood of her coat falling. A predatory bird rose up from the deer carcass on the side of the road. It flew through the trees, winging between the shadows and soaring out of sight.

Sound travels differently in the woods, as if the trees carry it from one to the other, reverberating in the heartwood, so that sometimes sounds coming from far away will land close. It came like that—like a whisper in Mallory's ear. The snap of twigs, a gasp of breath.

"Help me," a voice said. "Please can you help me?"

A girl came out of the woods, walking perilously across the frozen snow, hands held out to either side, exposed, no gloves. A young teenager, she wore only a man's shirt and a pair of too-large sneakers on her bare feet. They rocked across the snow, carried her in a careening momentum, her long hair swinging. "I'm lost," she said. "I don't know where I am. Please, I need help." A welted bruise on one side of her head wetly glowed and her nose appeared crusted with blood.

The sight of her pulled Mallory up inside of herself.

"Yeah, of course I can help."

Baily lunged forward, barking, and Mallory reeled the dog in, wrapping the leash around her fist.

"He's coming back," the girl said. "He's going to be back real soon." Her voice was like nothing Mallory had ever felt before, a tiny weight in the middle of her tongue, as if a small pebble rested there.

"Hold on to me," Mallory said, helping to steady the girl as she climbed down from the ridge of frozen snow. The girl stumbled and almost fell. Baily hopped to get out of the way, and her collar jingled, the sound of it echoing behind them on the road.

"What's that? Who's there?" The girl whipped around.

"Nothing. It's okay—just us."

"He's coming back." She was jittery, shaking, and not just from the cold. "He took my clothes and went to get gas. We have to be gone when he gets back. I have to be gone." She shuddered violently and moaned, bunching her hands inside the ends of her shirt. "Where do we go?" She turned in the road, her eyes wild and searching. Their footsteps rasped.

"Come with me," Mallory said. There was only one place. It was more than a mile back to Andrea's, and that was too far, too cold. "I know a place." Mallory shrugged off her coat and wrapped it around the girl's shoulders—her shirt smelled strongly of gasoline.

They hurried the other way down Riley Ridge Road, the girl's outsize shoes, with spaces around her ankles, filled with snow. She looked to be around fourteen, fifteen years old. They were the same height, her face even with Mallory's, eyes doggedly focused on the road—a young face, smooth and plump. They were so close, Mallory could see the force of the girl's footsteps vibrating in the flesh of her cheeks.

"How far?" the girl asked. "Where is it?"

"Take a left up there." She passed the girl her gloves as they came around the bend. "Just ahead." Baily stretched out, tugging on the lead. The lake opened out to their right, wide and white and hung with a winter moon. Across it, about a quarter of a mile away, a thin stream of cabin smoke rose straight as a piece of twine. It rose from the house of Landon James.

"That's it," Mallory said. "Over there."

"That's so far!" Her wail rose up like the smoke in the air and fresh blood appeared under her nose. She brought a gloved hand to her face. "I can't." She sniffed and cried. "I can't, I can't, I can't." With a series of small, hyperventilating bleats she turned in circles in the middle of the road.

Mallory went to her, putting her hands on her shoulders and fishing out the tissues from the pockets of the coat now worn by the girl. "You can do this," she said, keeping her voice calm and low. "Just hold this here and pinch your nose like this." She pressed the girl's face with the tissues and showed her what to do—medic training from the army kicking in. "You can do this because you have to do it, and I'm right here with you."

"But it's so far."

"Can you run?" Mallory said. "Let's run. It will keep you warm." She took the girl's arm and they trotted down the middle of the road.

"Motherfucker," the girl said, sliding in her too-big shoes. "Motherfucker, motherfucker, motherfucker." She chanted and sloppily jogged in her giant shoes. That made her laugh, jogging and dragging in giant shoes. It became comical and nearly hysterical as the girl sobbed and shrieked and laughed and moaned. She was euphoric from getting away, terrified of getting caught, and exhausted from the night she'd had. Mallory held on to the girl's arm and kept up a jog down the middle of the road. The girl couldn't stop laughing, gasping as she sobbed, "Motherfucker, motherfucker." She pinched her nose, alternating between spitted vehemence and heartsick tears.

Mallory felt it all with that weight cradled on her tongue; if she pressed too hard, she thought the girl would break. She'd never felt a voice like this before and thought she never would again. The girl slipped and cried; Mallory held her up. The cabin seemed to get farther away no matter how hard she pushed, a destination they couldn't reach, a nightmare that wouldn't end. All her life Mallory had felt this, the dread of what might approach from behind and herself incapable of moving forward, of getting away.

Any minute, she thought, a car would come up behind them. Any minute.

But one never did.

8

This is it," Mallory said. "Here."

They entered the mouth of a driveway plowed free of snow and Mallory led the girl to a shoveled path behind the house. She'd only ever been inside Landon's house that one time and they'd come in through the back, so that's where she took the girl now. The path led them by the remains of the bonfire, and the smell of woodsmoke, and the foot holes left by Landon and his friends.

The girl hunched and moaned, no longer laughing.

"I can't," she said as they approached the back door. "I can't, I can't." Her hair and lashes were frosted white from the moisture of her exhales, and she shook with tremors brought on by more than just cold. She took her hands away from her nose, the wad of tissues crusted black and slushed with blood.

Mallory pounded on the door.

"You already did it," she said. "You're here." Her fists felt like glass jars about to shatter, so she kicked at the door with her shoes until Landon's dog barked. "Landon!" Mallory called out. "I need your help! Please! It's Mallory! Let me in!" The barking intensified and the girl stepped back. "It's okay," Mallory said. "He has a big dog, a nice dog. He'll keep you safe."

A light came on in a bedroom window.

"Hey," she said to the girl. "What's your name?"

The girl didn't respond.

"I'm Mallory, and this is Landon's house." Baily, by her feet, hopped and barked. "Oh, and this is Baily."

"Shay." Her breath lurched in a flutter from her throat.

"Shay," Mallory repeated, as the light came on in the kitchen window, "it's going to be okay."

Landon's sleepy face appeared in the small window above the door. His eyes flew open like a pair of window blinds being raised, seeing Mallory standing out there with this girl in the middle of the night.

❄

The dogs had gone together into the corner of the living room, where Landon had banked a fire in the woodstove for the night. He and Mallory brought Shay in, and he cranked open the cast-iron doors and fed logs to the glowing embers inside. Shay moaned, with her arms crossed tight, as firelight lapped her bare legs.

"You're going to be all right," Mallory told her. "Okay? You're here now. You're safe." She wrapped a blanket around the girl's shoulders and knelt by her side. "Let's get you out of these." Snow had caked the laces of the giant white sneakers, which were creased and smeary. Mallory scraped and dug out the ice around the girl's ankles; the feet were raw and red as if burned. Landon brought towels and Mallory swaddled her feet, patting them dry. Mallory knew the pain would hit Shay harder as her skin thawed and the adrenaline waned.

A volley of flames shot up between the smoldering logs, and both of them flinched and jumped. She caught Shay's eyes then. Understanding moved between them like a wounded animal in the shadows.

"Hopefully, these will fit." Landon set a stack of folded clothes on the ottoman—sweatshirt, flannel shirt, sweatpants, and a roll of wool socks. "They're warm, at any rate." Without questions or intrusion, he left the two of them alone and went into the kitchen to brew coffee. He understood the nature of the situation without anyone having to explain, and Mallory was grateful for that. Her mind was doing its thing, reeling around the giant bakery bun of his voice that made her feel inappropriately beloved, and this girl who brought the sensation of a tiny weight in her mouth.

"Do you want to sit closer to the fire?" Mallory asked, moving the clothes and pulling up the ottoman. She felt an aggressive awareness of her own mouth, the soft pat of her lips, the precise touches of her tongue. The girl sat on the edge of the ottoman, holding the blanket around her narrow frame, folded into herself. "Pants first," Mallory said, hearing the voice of her mom in the cadence of her words. She held up the sweatpants, sliding the fabric over the girl's feet, around her knees, and up to her waist. She had to do most of the work; the girl barely moved, the stench of fight-or-flight coming from her body familiar—the sweat mixed with the fear.

"Okay, now your shirt." Mallory undid the buttons of the gasoline-soaked shirt, averting her eyes to give the girl privacy, but she couldn't help appraising for further injury. The bruise looked worse up close—the cut seeped and jellied, spreading underneath her dark hair. Shay kept her eyes turned away, her face shiny from melted ice. She had nothing on under that shirt; she was completely bare. And yet sweat glistened in the valleys of her back and in the little pool between her collarbone at the base of her neck. Her pulse throbbed visibly in her throat and the firelight flickered and popped. Mallory noticed the tattoo stamped on her shoulder, just under the collar bone, a cartoonish heart with an arrow shot through, inscribed with the initials J.T.

"Nice tat," Mallory said.

"My boyfriend gave me that." She sounded almost proud, pulling her arms into the sleeves of the sweatshirt.

"He the one who took your clothes?" Mallory asked, freeing the hood as she pulled the shirt carefully over Shay's head.

"That was Andre. He's a smooth talker." Her body barely filled out the fabric. She hugged the blanket around her shoulders and slouched on the ottoman, finally dressed. "It was his house and his party. J.T. brought me."

His house, his party. Mallory stood with the stinking shirt in hand. It felt heavy, and she didn't know where to put it, or where to stand. *His house, his party.* She felt herself shrinking, sliding back into that hole inside of herself. When she was fifteen, her boyfriend Jarrod had brought her to a party, and after that night, she had split into two. One part of her went on talking and walking, performing what was expected of her. The other part, she didn't know where she went. In a tomb somewhere? Underground in a dark room? Years of her life she'd spent in a fugue.

Mallory reached out for the back of the futon sofa and named the items in the room—she'd never been in Landon's living room before, so she focused on that—a light pine futon sleeper, big picture windows covered in blinds that glowed vanilla from the light of the moon. An end table in matching pine, lamp shade dressed in plaid, a set of moose coasters stacked conveniently to one side. A tidy space with just a hint of Northwoods kitsch.

"For her face." Landon handed Mallory a bowl of warm water with a washcloth and a Ziploc bag filled with ice. "You okay?" The concern created a fresh loaf of bread that bloomed under her chin. She turned away so he couldn't smell her.

"I'm fine." She still wore her Speed Stop clothes, the blue smock and black pants, and she still had vomit on her breath. It made her self-conscious of standing too close. They were in the archway in the middle of the room, with Shay on the ottoman in front of the fire, a few feet away. "Thank you for letting us barge in." She shivered and couldn't stop shaking. She held the bowl up and went over to Shay.

"Let's get you cleaned up." Mallory knelt by the ottoman and wrung out the cloth.

Shay lifted her chin, the ice pack pressed to the side of her head. She held her face in a dignified way, queenly, even with the makeup smudged in dregs under her eyes. In her nose a diamond stud glinted.

"Has he hit you before?" Mallory asked. Shay's eyes, a luminous brown, dark and guarded, furtively moved away. "Sorry," Mallory said. "You don't have to say anything."

From the kitchen came the smell of coffee, and Mallory focused on that, washing the girl's face. When a few drops of water trailed down the side of Shay's cheek, the girl reached up to wipe them away, and then deftly tucked her hair behind her ear, revealing the unblemished side of her smooth, young face. And Mallory knew what that felt like, to tuck hair that way, a gesture automatic and familiar, one she'd performed a hundred times, a thousand times without even thinking about it, that tickle of fine hairs, how satisfying it felt, moving the hair back from your face. She hadn't done that in years.

"Let me know if this hurts." Mallory daubed at the girl's forehead, but what she wanted to do was to hold her and tell her that she was important and good and that whatever had happened to her that night wasn't her fault. She wanted to wrap her in a warm embrace and keep her safe. Mallory never knew before how extraordinary young people were, how they were light-filled and possessed of so much power; how they were beautiful and capable and filled with potential, and yet so innocent of it. Maybe that was what made them so vulnerable to predators.

Landon was standing at the stove when Mallory brought the bowl into the kitchen.

"Coffee?" he asked.

She kept her eyes level at his throat: the haphazard cant of his shirt, the soft curve of his disheveled neck. He'd thrown a flannel over the T-shirt he'd probably slept in, and the smell of him was an actual smell and not one in her head: salt-vinegar chips, laundry soap, and the faint sourness of beer. She left the bowl in the bottom of the sink, letting her hair fall to obscure her face. She heard the slosh of coffee pouring into a cup and accepted, her face still turned away. She couldn't look at him. If he saw her, she would break.

"Somebody is probably looking for her," he said.

"Yeah, this guy Andre who took her clothes."

"Took her clothes?"

"She was at a party. Her boyfriend brought her there."

"Jesus," he said.

She'd never seen him upset before. She cradled her mug. "This guy is coming back. She said he just went out to get gas." Her throat tightened; she felt it closing at the back. "She's really scared, Landon, and she wants to get away."

Landon swallowed, set his mug down, and flicked off the lights. He moved into the living room, turned off the lights in there, and went over to the front door.

"What are you doing?" She followed him.

"If he goes looking for her," he said, "this is the first place he'll come. There's smoke in the chimney, my driveway is plowed. This place is lit up like a Christmas tree and it's right by the road."

"What do we do?"

"We call the police."

"No!" Shay stood from the ottoman, her eyes dark sparks. "No police." She'd gathered her blanket. In the corner of the room, the dogs stood and growled, the sounds low in their throats. Landon already had his phone in hand. He stood across from Shay in the living room, the two of them in a kind of stalemate.

"I left the light on in the bedroom," he said, and disappeared down the hall.

The firelight wavered and chuffed.

"Shay, do you want to call somebody? Someone who can come get you?"

The girl bolted. The blanket slipped from her shoulders and the ice pack fell to the floor, and then she was in the kitchen at the back door.

"Shay? What are you doing?"

"He's calling the police." She grabbed the too-large shoes, struggling to put them on, losing her balance, and falling against the door. "I need shoes," she said. "Please, I need shoes!"

Mallory didn't know what else to do, so she gave the girl her shoes. They were black work shoes, stinky and worn-out. She tried to reason with her. "You can't go back out there," she said. "That's stupid. Where would you go?"

"Don't call me stupid. I'm not stupid."

"Sorry." Mallory held out her coat.

"The police don't do shit. They never do." Her face contorted as she jammed her arms into the sleeves. "They put us in lockup because they think it's our fault. Even if we're hurt, if we're fucking bleeding, they still don't believe us." She tried to hook the zipper of the coat. It wouldn't catch. Her hands were still raw from the cold.

Without speaking, Mallory went in and carefully fitted the metal slot over the toothed rails and tugged it up.

"What happened to your eye?" Shay said.

"What?"

"You have blood in your eye. In the white part." Shay pointed to the side of her own head.

Mallory self-consciously put a hand there, to the side of her face.

"Does it hurt?" Shay asked, her voice pressing with its gentle weight.

"No. I can't even feel it." She swallowed and felt the rawness of her throat, the vomit creased in her skin. But standing next to Shay, she felt grounded, held in place.

Impulsively, Mallory took her hand.

"Let's get out of here," she said. "We'll go together. Do you want to? Let's just go." The hand in hers was smooth and small, and Mallory noticed again the wound on the side of Shay's head. "Does your head hurt?" she asked.

"No. I don't even feel it."

"That's the adrenaline. When you come down off it, you'll start to feel the pain. It'll hurt like hell then."

Landon came back into the kitchen. Both girls startled and Shay broke away. "What's going on?" he said. The girls were bunched on one side of the room, by the door, and Landon stood by the stove, the kitchen table between them.

"She thinks you called the police," Mallory said. "And they won't help her, so we're going to leave."

"Why? What did she do?"

"Fuck you!" Shay spat, giving him the finger. "You don't know shit about me."

Landon held up both hands. "Whoa, look, I didn't call the police, okay? Let's just take a minute and chill." He swallowed audibly, his Adam's apple bobbing in the low light. "That was probably not the best choice of words."

The dogs came into the kitchen then, Odin thumping a tail against the hollow metal box of the stove.

"Is there someplace we can take you?" Mallory asked. "A place where you'd feel safe?"

"I don't know where I am."

Odin stopped wagging and sat. The room hung with a dead-of-night silence.

Landon glanced at Mallory.

"Where do you live?" she said. "Where's home?"

"Milwaukee."

"Is that where you want to go?"

"No."

Mallory waited, trying to beam encouragement from her eyes.

"I want to go to my brother's," Shay said.

"Okay," Mallory said. "Where does he live?"

"Bemidji. On a lake." It was in a town in northern Minnesota, more than three hours away.

"Okay," Landon said. "I'll get my coat." He left again.

Mallory looked to Shay. "If we can't call the police, I don't know what else to do," Mallory said. "I'll go with. I'll be with you the whole time."

Shay's eyes dipped to her feet. "Do you want your shoes?"

"No, no, that's all right. I'll borrow a pair of Landon's." The dogs converged at the food bowls near the kitchen sink, and Mallory noticed Odin's water bowl was empty. She refilled it for something to do, the water piercingly cold. "Do you have a dog?" she asked Shay, trying to make conversation.

"No."

Mallory set the water bowl on the floor.

"My auntie had cats," Shay said.

"My mom and sister had a cat."

Their eyes locked. Shay almost smiled.

Landon came back wearing his coat and handed Mallory the keys.

"What's this?"

"The keys to my truck."

"Why are you giving them to me?"

"So you can drive," he said. "I'm inebriated."

"You're what?"

"I had a few beers at the bonfire. It'll wear off." Noticing that

Mallory didn't have any shoes or a coat, he went into the hall closet and started pulling things out. "You can take the first shift, I'll take the second. It's two hundred miles to Bemidji." He found a pair of flattened canvas sneakers and an old green duffle. "I took some Advil," he said, returning to the kitchen. "Any minute it'll kick in." He handed Mallory the shoes and the coat. "These were my sister's; they should fit. And this old coat, it's tattered but warm, and I can't be held responsible for what's in the pockets."

He handed her these things, and that plus the sound of his voice put her in full-blown bakery mode with frosted cakes and glazed doughnuts filled with cream. Her arms and legs felt honeyed and puffed with light. They were going on a road trip. In the banana-yellow truck. Holding the keys up, she looked at Shay and grinned.

9

Landon's truck was a hybrid like Andrea's, with a push button to start the ignition and a dashboard with controls that glowed vibrantly like a spaceship braced for the moon. Blue numbers, yellow lines, red warning symbols all populating the nook behind the steering wheel. A screen above the heat controls displayed moving energy silos to monitor how much the battery had charged. Mallory pumped the lever to raise her seat and then held down a button to close the gap between the pedals and her feet. It hummed ardently as it mechanically moved forward.

"Are you okay to drive?" Landon said from the front seat next to her.

"You think I can't drive because I'm short?"

"No, I'm asking about your eye."

She'd forgotten about that. She glanced in the rearview mirror, saw blood darkening the white of one eye. "I'm totally fine." She tested the windshield wipers, headlights, and the brights, and glanced at Shay sitting behind her in the back. "I can see perfectly and it doesn't hurt at all." She settled herself in the cockpit of the banana-yellow truck.

"The button for the garage door is up here," Landon said, reaching over and pulling down the visor. His arm crossed in front of her and his shirt smelled faintly of hamburger pickles—for real, the kind with the ridges—and she wondered why. It intensified the tingling under her chin. Behind them the door stuttered up. She put the truck into Reverse and the screen from the backup camera switched on.

"Oh my god," she said. "This truck puts me in a whole different century."

"Why? What do you drive?"

"A piece of crap from 1999."

She took it slow around the lake, her hands at ten and two on the leather-wrapped wheel.

"You know the speed limit is forty-five, right?" Landon said.

"I didn't know you were a backseat driver."

"Just trying to be helpful."

"Get down, Bales." The dog stood alert on her lap, feet pressing sharp divots into her thighs. They'd left Odin at home, but Baily insisted on coming with. Mallory nudged the dog to the side and glanced at Shay in the rearview mirror. The windows in the back were glossed black, so all she could see of the girl was the side of one shoulder where the seat belt pinned the ends of her hair. "It'll warm up soon," she said, the heater blasting through the truck. "You okay?"

If Shay responded, she didn't hear. Baily's collar jingled as she turned in circles and dropped, settling into the space between the front seats. They neared the end of the road that circled the lake.

Headlights from a vehicle on their left bounced into view.

Shay, from the back, let out a muffled gasp, unsnapped her seat belt, and shot down to the floor mats. Mallory's stomach flipped and that small pebble pressed on her tongue. The interior of Landon's truck flooded with light—whoever it was didn't even bother to turn down their brights. She stopped at the intersection where the two roads met, and the cones of their headlights crisscrossed, cutting into a low fog that had settled in the trees.

The pickup glided past. Its windows were tinted, its body large and shined a deep royal blue. It rolled by in the moonlight and Mallory saw nothing of who drove it, but she imagined him and how he saw them: a yellow truck out on the slickened road, the dead of winter, the middle of night, no other vehicles around. This truck hewed to the path as it drove past, branding itself in her mind.

"Shit," she said, letting out her breath.

Landon said nothing.

Mallory took a left and watched as the lights of the pickup receded in her rearview mirror. Its tail lights flushed coronas of pink as it disappeared around a bend not far from the place where she'd found Shay. Unapologetically, she hit the gas.

Up ahead on the left, the brown box of Andrea's cabin came into view, its uncurtained windows all aglow. Mallory's stomach lurched with the burn of acid reflux. Andrea was still up on the couch, watching TV, in full view of anyone out on the road.

"Maybe we should call her," Landon said, "tell her to turn off the lights."

Mallory reached for her phone and the truck eddied, fishtailing across the snow-slickened road.

"Let me do it," Landon said. "I'll pair it with my Bluetooth. You drive." She heard the soft bleat as he plugged her phone into a charging cord. "Just give it a minute."

She flicked her eyes to the rearview, watching for signs of the other truck. In the back, Shay had gone quiet, still on the floor. Baily was going berserk as they neared the cabin. The dog ran in figure eights, hopping from the back to the front with a barking that didn't stop. Usually, Baily's barking didn't bother Mallory; it only slightly itched the bottoms of her feet. But in that proximity, with her stomach emptied out and tensions high, her feet began to burn. She rolled down her window, just a little bit.

"It's okay, Baily Bales." She inhaled the fresh air as the dog clambered onto her lap. "Stay in the back." She slid a hand under the dog's belly and dropped her into the backseat. They passed the cabin. Baily yipped and scrambled, returning to Mallory's lap, claws ripping through her thin work pants. The dog was pawing at the window and barking frenetically. Landon reached over to grab her, but before he could, the little dog slipped through the window gap like a coin through a slot.

"Hey, where are you?" Andrea's voice came on over the dashboard on speakerphone.

"Baily, no!" Mallory shouted because the dog was trotting out down the middle of the road, making her way back to the house. They were about two hundred feet past the cabin. Mallory slammed on the brakes and shifted into reverse.

"What are you doing?" Landon said.

"Getting my dog."

"Who is that?" Andrea said. "Who's with you?"

In the rearview mirror glammed the headlights of the other truck.

"Turn out your lights!" Mallory hit the brakes and shifted gears again, her view of the dog blacked out by the glare of the approaching lights.

Andrea's voice squawked over the phone, "Why? What's going on? Where's my dog?" Mallory gunned it and their tires spun out, her phone sliding to the floor and disconnecting them as the cord came unplugged. She'd been blinded by the truck's high beams and didn't see Baily in the road anymore. But now, checking in the mirror again, she saw the truck was farther behind than she had thought.

"Take it easy," Landon said. They came down the other side of the hill, pushing sixty. The headlights of the other truck disappeared. "The highway is just ahead."

"I know where the highway is." Mallory rolled up her window. She'd driven that tract all winter, a hundred times or more, knew every dent and hill and bend. "I should have gone back for Baily," she said. "Fucking dog."

"I tried to grab her."

"I know."

"Just focus on driving."

"I thought they were right behind us."

"They're close enough," he said. "We'll lose them on the highway."

"How? You have a freaking yellow truck."

Tires thudded on the snowpack, and the headlights from the pickup bobbed back into view, behind them now by a good three hundred feet. The road curved to the right. She let up on the gas, fishtailed, and corrected, hurling up snow from the side of the road. It sprayed out pink in the glow of the brake lights and the rearview mirror went black, the bend concealing the headlights of the pickup again. Mallory knew they had about thirty seconds before those lights would blip back.

Two things happened then. The ringing came back in her ear,

shrill and piercing, followed by that voice landing sharp and exact. "Turn left," he said, as if her grandpa were sitting right there next to her in the truck. Her headlights shined on a snow-covered sign, white letters spangled in the high beams—a plowed dirt road she'd passed a hundred times without knowing where it led, but in that moment and without thinking, she lifted her foot and slammed on the brake, jamming the wheel hard to the left.

"Jesus!" Landon yelped. They fishtailed as she pumped the brake and slid toward the ditch, listing hard. The truck tipped but hung on. Adrenaline pounded through her head and cold air coated the back of her throat. The new road curved immediately to the right, and she went hand over hand, turning the wheel and pumping the brake as that ringing shrieked in her ear. They fishtailed again. The truck had new tires and front-wheel drive—it handled way better than her old clunker, which would have gone gliding into the ditch—and she was kind of enjoying herself, ringing be damned. The bend in the road hid the trail of their exhaust and the dust of the displaced snow. The ringing waned and her rearview mirror went dark. Mallory watched for several minutes, her heart a thumping lump near her throat.

"I might have to puke," Landon said.

"Should I pull over?"

"No," he gripped the door handle, looking peaked. "Keep going. You're fine."

"You okay?" she said to Shay in the back.

"I'm okay." Her voice sounded different. She sounded like a kid.

"I don't know where this road goes," Mallory said. They drove past chained gates and driveways walled in by snow. The fog had thickened and dispersed over the road.

"It meets up with the highway south of here in about eight miles," Landon said. "We'll have to backtrack, but it's a good way to lose them. Well done."

His compliment spiked Mallory's adrenaline with pride—it was intoxicating and freeing and she felt punch-drunk, high. Nothing hurt anymore; she wasn't nauseous or cold. She told herself that Baily would be fine and that Andrea had let the dog in. Another mile passed. She was with two people she hardly knew, driving a truck that wasn't hers, less than ten miles away from a house she didn't own, where she lived with a woman she didn't love. Her family lived a thousand miles away and she was starting to think that an angel was talking to her.

She didn't know who she was or what she was doing with her life, but she understood this girl—or thought she did—this girl who had come improbably out of the woods. She understood her motives and fear and the exact ways that she was alone, this girl who was braver and tougher than she'd ever been, and Mallory understood something about the kind of night she'd had, and she wanted more than anything to help her, to save her, no matter the cost.

A pair of headlights flickered through the trees ahead. Mallory stomped on the gas. The front wheels bucked hard into a rut, her butt flew off the seat, and they all bounced down like a handful of dice rattling in a cup. Mallory laughed—she couldn't help it—the tension of the last twelve minutes coming out in a donkey bray. It had just been the headlights of their own vehicle, reflected back at them from the windows of a vacant house.

"Okay," Landon said. "Time to pull over and let me drive."

"But you're drunk," she said, laughing. "And the highway is right there."

"I'm sober now," he said. "Quite." He gave Mallory a look that she would think back on for a long time.

It was a look that saw past her exterior, beyond her skin. A look that touched some raw place inside her. What it was: familial love. Not a blind love, not one that didn't see the faults, but rather a deep and abiding affection that saw everything and accepted her anyway, the faults, the idiosyncrasies—found them endearing, even, because that's what made her the person she was. It was a simple understanding that passed between them in that moment, and it gave her something to hold on to, something to move toward: the way he saw her, who she might become.

PART

TWO

10

They'd been driving north out on the highway for about fifteen minutes before Landon spoke. The clock read 3:21 and it was nine degrees outside, the information glowing in colored lights on the dashboard.

"We should take her to a hospital," he said, his eyes remaining on the road as he drove. "One in Minnesota. They're a safe harbor state." With the heater blasting, Shay couldn't hear what they were saying, but they kept their voices low just in case.

"What's a safe harbor state?"

"It means the state has passed laws to protect kids who find themselves victims of crimes like this."

"Crimes like what?" The air in the footwell had turned suddenly cold, but tentacles of warmth spread out from under her thighs. "Oh my god . . ." She figured it out. "You have heated seats!" She leaned back and laughed. "Are they heated in the back, too?"

"No. Only in the front."

"Oh. Too bad." She avoided his eyes but felt him looking at her.

"I think that Shay needs professional help," he said. "She needs medical care and treatment, maybe a counselor. They'll have people there at the hospital who can talk to her."

"Maybe she doesn't want to talk to anybody. Did you ever think of that?" Mallory fiddled with the heat controls, pointing the nozzles, angling the vents. She'd never felt peevish around Landon before. "Maybe we should just take her down to Milwaukee, you know, bring her home."

"No. If it was good for her at home, she'd already be there."

Now Mallory felt scolded, even if he hadn't meant to scold her, and her younger self—the girl she'd been at the age of fifteen—rose out from wherever she'd been hiding to join them there suddenly in the truck. It was being scolded and the fear she always had of not doing enough; it was riding in a truck with someone old enough to be her dad; it was being around another girl who was fifteen and also afraid of going home; it was the night and the cold and the heat that purled like warm water on her skin. Mallory felt the vitality of this younger self and she seemed happy to be in the world again, curious about life, although wiggly and self-conscious, and Mallory didn't know what to do or say next. When the sign for her Speed Stop came into view, she nearly bounced out of her seat.

"Let's get road snacks!" she announced to everyone in the truck. "You guys hungry?" She turned to Shay. "This is where I work. They have hot food—sandwiches, pizza, soup." She couldn't see Shay's face in the dark. She turned to Landon. "How about it?" She was hyped up, childlike, and it was hard to keep the rowdiness from her voice. "I'm starved. And I bet we could all use some coffee." They were an hour away from Duluth. Not counting Andrea's special dinner, she hadn't eaten in more than twelve hours, her last "meal" a fistful of trail mix they kept stashed behind the registers at work. Now that the danger had passed, her stomach was gnawing on itself. They hadn't seen any sign of the other truck out on the highway, and she thought Shay might also be hungry.

Without saying a word, Landon crisply flipped his blinker.

❉

They entered from the frontage road and curved around the brick building set back from the highway. Mallory told Landon where to go and they slid into the spot behind the back door, where the semis parked when they came in with deliveries from Rice Lake. That way, they were shielded on two sides by the store and a brick outcropping, with a wall of woods to the right. The trees stood ghostly under veils of moonlit fog.

"What do you want?" Landon asked.

Now that they were stopped and at a familiar place, Mallory felt she might settle down. "A waffle sandwich, please." She turned to Shay. "What do you want? Hot food? Coffee? Cold pop?"

"A water'd be Gucci."

Landon turned to Mallory, confused.

"She wants a water."

A blast of cold air filled the cab when he left. Mallory felt relieved. Ever since they'd gotten out onto the highway, he'd been serious and tense. A police car had passed them from the south; they'd been driving maybe five minutes when its siren wailed out from behind them and Shay in the back had stirred. They'd pulled over and watched it barrel neatly past.

Mallory took out her phone. It had exploded with text messages from Andrea. *Where RU? The hell is going on? U all right?* She scrolled through to the end and then read the last one: *Landon hit my dog!!*

"Oh my god." Anger perforated her chest.

"What?" Shay said from the back.

"Nothing." Mallory quickly texted Andrea back. She knew better than to ignore her and didn't want to get Shay involved. *Baily ran off,* she thumbed. *I'm so sorry, it wasn't Landon, is Baily okay?!?* Heart, heart, heart emojis. She waited, but Andrea didn't respond. *I'm all right. We're going to Bemidji,* she texted again. *It's not what you think!* Lamely, she added an emoji kissy face and put down her phone. Outside, the moonlit fog cast everything in a film noir glow. She hadn't meant to be abrupt with Shay. "That asshole driving that truck ran over my dog," she said. It seemed easier to call Baily *her* dog, and anyway, that's how it felt.

"Oh no," Shay said. "Poor doggo."

"Yeah. Hopefully, she's okay." Mallory had trained herself to not cry, to not let her emotions show. She'd overreacted to the headlights of the other truck; she'd panicked and hit the gas when she should have followed through and gotten Baily out of the road. Mallory clamped down, clenching her jaw and pressing hard.

"Is this really where you work?" Shay said. It was the first time she'd spoken without being prompted.

"Yeah. I usually work nights." Her words caught like hot sand in her throat. Shay sat right behind her, so they couldn't see each other, but Mallory could hear the trustfulness in her voice. "You sure you're not hungry?" She turned her body around. "We can get you some food, you know, a hot meal. Maybe some chicken tenders? Or egg rolls?"

"He your boyfriend?"

"Landon? No." Shay seemed chatty. "You should probably stay awake," she said. It had just occurred to her. "In case you have a concussion. I don't think you do, but just in case." Mallory could see the light glinting in Shay's eyes, and the regal way she held her face. "Do you feel better?"

"I'm really hot."

The heater gushed between them, and Mallory turned it down. She thought Shay was probably on something but didn't know how to broach the subject or what to do to help.

"Do you like him?" the girl asked.

"No." Mallory answered without thinking, falling back on her habit to lie and protect what was important. But she wanted to be truthful with Shay. "I do like him," she said, craning back around. "Landon isn't like anybody I've ever known. I admire him as a person, you know, as someone who I want to be like someday. Not as a boyfriend." She couldn't read Shay's expression in the dark, but the girl seemed satisfied, so Mallory turned again to the front. She thought of Jarrod and how she had once looked up to him. Jarrod's voice had stroked her like a cat's tongue on the sides of both cheeks, and just the thought of him still sent a certain sensation through her body.

"You know, when I was your age, I had this boyfriend," she heard herself saying in the dark, her younger self, the Mallory at age fifteen. "And this one night he brought me to a party." She'd never told anyone this part of the story before, how he had brought her there. Nobody knew the truth—not Andrea, not her high school therapist, not even the police. But it was coming back to her now with the tactile clarity of snow on skin.

"It's hella hot," Shay said, shrugging out of her coat. The sounds of its vinyl whispered behind Mallory as the girl folded it up and pressed it to the window, where she leaned her head.

"Stay awake," Mallory said. She thought they would have all day together to talk, so she didn't push the girl to say anything more. She just wanted Shay to feel safe, to feel that she could trust her and not be judged. They sat together in the silence of the truck with the engine running and the heater gushing, and when a blue hand reached out from the dark and rapped on the hood, Mallory yelped and dropped her phone.

"Mallory?" Noah wore his black hairnet under a knit cap, with his glasses and a shapeless beige coat. He looked like a russet potato. "Is that really you?"

She slid her window partway down. "Hey," she said jauntily from her perch way high up. "What's poppin'?"

Noah blinked, looked around. "What are you doing here?"

"We're going on a road trip to, uh, Bemidji." She felt self-conscious of the two Mallorys, her face doing things much more energetically than usual. "We came to get snacks."

"You came *here*?"

"Yeah." She adjusted her body position; her instinct was to protect Shay. Mallory didn't think he could see her there in the back, but she didn't want to have to explain. "What are you doing out here?"

"I'm on my break. I came out to check on the moon." He pushed his glasses up. It felt like ages ago that they had stood outside together, watching the moon. "What happened to your eye?" he asked.

She'd forgotten about that. She pulled down the visor flap and saw in the mirror where her right eye had flooded with blood, a patch of red filling in almost the entire white. "Jesus," she said, "I look like a freak."

"It shouldn't hurt."

"How do you know?"

"It's a subconjunctival hemorrhage," he said handily. Having a smart person around could really be nice. "It happens when tiny blood vessels break in the sclera of the eye. It's harmless. It'll disappear on its own."

"When?"

"I don't know, about two weeks? My mom got one once from coughing too hard. It's brought on by strain." He peered up at her. "What were you doing tonight that caused you strain?"

"Nothing."

"Are you feeling sick?"

"I'm fine." She slapped the mirror closed, smelling the vomit on her breath. It must have happened then.

"Where'd this truck come from? Did you hot-wire it?"

"Oh my god, Sherlock, take a break. I don't know how to hot-wire a truck, okay?"

"I don't know what you know."

"This is Landon's truck."

"Oh! Landon that-guy-Andrea-is-jealous-of Landon?"

"Yeah." She gritted her teeth. "I've never hot-wired anything." She said this for Shay's benefit, in case she was wondering, although probably she was not. "And anyway, hot-wiring is irrelevant because of the computers now, so you just swap out the ECUs." She didn't know why she was so talkative.

Landon came back. She rolled up the window and said good-bye to Noah. Landon brought coffees and a water, with a white paper sack. The smell of the food intensified her hunger, and she smiled at Noah, giving him a childish wave. They turned back out onto the highway, the two steaming coffees in the cup holsters by her side.

She was ridiculously glad that Noah had seen her on that night, with Landon James, in that truck. It was like high school—she felt better about herself because of who she was with. This would embarrass her later. Noah didn't care about being with the cool kids, but that's where her mind went on that night. Sometimes, the marble falls into the lowest spot.

11

Things took a turn about thirty miles north of Mire Lake. They had the radio on, tuned to NPR. They came to a rise in the road where the fog had cleared, and the cold lights of the Twin Ports grid glittered on the horizon in the distance below. The smokestacks of Sterling churned out steam in the moonlight, and behind Sterling, across the bay, rose the elongated hillside of its sister city, Duluth. The two towns watched each other from across the Saint Louis Bay, one of them flat and scarred with industrial silos and dilapidated homes that were some of the oldest in the country, the other award-winning and shining, with constant vistas of Lake Superior. Mallory turned to the back and checked on Shay.

"These waffle sandwiches are really good," she said. "You sure you don't want one?" Her days in the service had done nothing for her table manners. She took large bites and talked with her mouth full. "I will never, *ever* eat gas station food anywhere else again," she said. "Not after working at Speed Stop. I swear, it's gross. I mean, these other places leave their food out there all day, and I mean, *all day*. We rotate our stock, you know, every three hours, so nothing gets old." The food revived her, brought her back into her body. She was hyped up, alert; it was the bewitching hour in the middle of the night. "Whatever doesn't get sold to the consumers gets sold as slop for the area hogs. We have this great big kitchen out at Rice Lake where all the food gets made, and then everything gets packed up and shipped out to the stores in these reusable totes, so it's very environmental. Not that I'm a spokesperson for Speed Stop or anything." She took another bite. "They're kind of bourgeois, really," she laughed, swallowed, took a sip of coffee. "Sorry." She apologized for talking so much.

"Did you talk to her?" Landon asked. He kept his voice low, eyes on the road, the heater still blasting in the front of the truck. "About going to the hospital?"

Mallory lowered her sandwich. "No."

The radio buzzed low between them. She could feel every single one of her arm hairs, attuned as though receiving a signal from elsewhere.

"Could you?" he asked. "She seems to trust you, and it might be the only way we can get her help."

Mallory wrapped up her sandwich and put it away. Then she unfastened her seat belt and slid carefully into the back. It smelled of wet dog and sand, and she got a glimpse into Landon's life. She had the intruding thought, What if she got her own dog? And why didn't she drive a truck? These thoughts briefly flashed through her, the idea of rejoining the daylight world, but as soon as she thought them, she kicked them out and put all her attention on Shay.

"Hey," Mallory whispered. The girl sat against the corner by the door, head leaning on the folded coat. Lights from an oncoming car briefly slid across her face. Her eyes were closed, and Mallory saw the soft rise and fall of her breath. "Shay?" she whispered again. "Hey, you have to stay awake." She wanted to stroke her hair, tuck it back behind one ear. She wanted to hold her and rock her and tell her that she was brave and strong, that she had done nothing to deserve this, that she wasn't alone or a bad person, and that there were people who cared about her and would help her to get to wherever it was that she wanted to go. She wanted to say all the things to Shay that she'd wished someone had said to her. "Can I talk to you a sec?"

Shay opened her eyes. She was right there. In that moment on that night Mallory had the opportunity to say these things, but she didn't. Something inside her held her back, and so instead she said none of them, and felt only the ache.

"What is it?" Shay asked.

The truck thudded over a series of breaks in the road and the tires vibrated under their seats.

"We want to take you to a hospital in Minnesota," Mallory said.

"They have these programs there and people who are trained to get you some help."

"They won't help me."

"No, they will. That's what these programs are for."

"No, they're not. They lie. They send us back into the foster care system because they don't give a shit about me or girls like me." She turned away and put her head on the coat pillow by the door.

"Shay, please stay awake."

"Fine," she teeth-sucked, blowing air as she lifted her head. "But I'm not going back into the system. I'd rather die."

Mallory glanced in the rearview mirror at Landon's face. She tried again. "Shay?"

"What?"

"Can you at least think about it?"

"They're not my family," she said.

The shattering rattle of a semitruck passed them in the dark. Lights flitted through the cab, glinting on the jewel in Shay's nose. She lay her head back down on the coat pillow. Landon glanced up in the rearview mirror, and red and blue lights rippled across his face.

Mallory turned around.

Behind them, a police car approached with its lights swiveling but without sound. She thought it would pass—she thought it was the same cop car that had gone out to Mire Lake, because they were north of there now. But then its siren let out a single bleat and more lights ricocheted through the car. Shay lifted her head and her eyes thundered with betrayal.

"We didn't call them," Mallory said. "I swear."

"Let me out!" Shay yanked on the passenger door—it had automatically locked. "Let me out! Motherfucker." Red and blue ribbons swirled through the car and the police siren bleated again, Shay jerking wildly as she yanked at the door, "Motherfucker, motherfucker."

"Shay, it's okay." Mallory tried to calm her as Landon put on his blinker and coasted to the shoulder of the road. "We'll handle this."

The locking mechanism clicked and her door swung open. All the strands of her hair spiked up around her head. Her body leaned out over the moving tarmac, her feet still on the seat, hands gripping the door handle; her body turned like a hare on a spit. Then she let go and fell away, sucked down by a highway wind.

The door canted and flapped on its hinge.

12

More than half the seats in the hospital waiting room were filled, and everyone had someone with them. The companions resembled the individuals they were with in some way—Mallory could tell they went together, were part of a matched set. Mothers had the same facial features as their kids; the guy who needed a haircut had an equally hairy friend. Mallory sat alone. An aquarium burbled across from her, against the wall. One lone fish zipped back and forth in the tank above a raked landing of blue stones. Nothing else was in the aquarium. She felt a kinship with that fish, as if she and it were part of a matched set.

"Ima Hogg?" A young nurse in salmon scrubs stood with a clipboard at the edge of the room. "Ima Hogg? Ima Hogg?" she said again.

A gangly teenage boy chuckled from across the room. "It's Irma Hoeg," he said, standing from the chairs. His mother, presumably, rose shakily next to him.

"You did that on purpose," the mother said, taking his arm.

"I thought it would be funny," he replied, escorting her slowly and with earnestness across the solemn waiting room of the ER.

Mallory wondered at the ease of their relationship, at the son's ability to make a joke in a hospital in the middle of the night just to bring a smile to his mother's face. He had to be around sixteen, seventeen years old, the same age Jarrod had been when he brought her to that party. *I'm a hog.*

Mallory had decided a long time ago that she would never have kids. She was too afraid she'd mess them up. She looked down at the hands in her lap. They'd had to chemically restrain Shay. Mallory could still hear the sound of her body falling out of the car, hitting the ground like a dropped melon, her body a bundle of clothes lying on the side of the road. When the police officer tried to help her to safety, she'd refused to get into his car. Shay had screamed at all of them, with blood in her teeth, a highway wind stripping back the tears from her face. She'd groaned with deep and lonely sobs.

Landon had to go with the police. They'd gotten pulled over, there were charges of a hit and run involving a dog, so Mallory had to drive to the hospital herself. The police officer and medics had been very professional. They did all the right things, Mallory thought, though she wouldn't really know otherwise. As far as she could tell, they did what they could to get Shay the help anyone in her situation would need, and the ambulance had taken her over the bridge to a facility in Duluth. But it didn't look good. Shay was underage, found in the middle of the night with physical injuries and an older man and a woman who weren't her family. Mallory felt from them this unspoken attitude of *What did you do?*, rather than *What happened to you?* Or maybe it was her own judgment, the inner voice in her head. A fierce protectiveness had risen inside of her, and she had vowed that she would do everything she could to advocate for Shay.

"Mallory Moe?" a nurse called, and Mallory stood. She had given them her name at the check-in desk, asking if she could talk to someone about a patient who had just been brought in. She followed this nurse in aqua scrubs into a small, cluttered room the size of a walk-in closet, with a glowing space heater. The nurse sat in a roller chair with wheels and scooted with her sneakers across the floor, over to a computer. Mallory took a seat.

"I have some information about a girl named Shay," Mallory said, squeezing the edges of the chair. "I don't know her last name."

"Okay." The nurse moved away from the screen, took out a small spiral notebook with a Bic pen. "What's going on?"

Mallory fumbled and dropped her phone. It fell by the sneakers that weren't her own. She picked it up, slipping it into the pocket of the coat that also belonged to Landon James. And then she remembered that she had blood in her eye.

"It's okay," the nurse said, noticing her eye and the way Mallory's leg shook. Her right foot was pumping up and down, and she couldn't seem to stop it. "Everything you tell me here is confidential." The nurse rolled sideways with her chair and offered Mallory the tissue box.

Mallory took one—her nose wouldn't stop running, as if she had a perpetual cold. "I think . . ." She blew her nose, wiped her face. "*We* think . . . that this young girl, Shay, may have been trafficked." The word felt sharp and wrong, an awkward way to explain what was going on, what she had seen, but it was all she had. The nurse listened as Mallory described how they found the girl, how she didn't have any clothes and didn't know where she was and how scared she had seemed. The nurse used her notebook and pen to record what Mallory said, a notebook that she must have bought herself, instead of using the hospital computer. Mallory found that comforting, how she used these low-tech, personal items. It was easier to talk to the woman than it had been to the police. The nurse had pale skin with dry cheeks, and she wore earrings, and her eyelids were brushed in shimmering eyeshadow. When she blinked, the mascaraed fringes of her lashes shook the hairs of her carefully separated bangs.

"Okay," she said, when Mallory was done. "Thank you for bringing this to our attention. We'd already flagged this for a consult with the psych team. They'll probably want to talk with you themselves, if that's all right. Mind if I take down your contact information?"

"Sure." Mallory sat up straighter in her seat and gave her number.

"I'll have one of them reach out to you tomorrow." The nurse's voice felt like the roller ball on a stick of antiperspirant—damp, but not unpleasant. "Anything else?" They were surrounded by three computer terminals, a printer, a copy machine, and a phone that kept lighting up with red and white call lights, but the nurse gave Mallory her undivided attention.

"Will Shay be all right?"

"She'll be okay," the nurse said. "We have a locked ER with two secured areas. She's in a private room under a police hold. She won't be discharged until we get a solid plan in place."

Mallory nodded.

"You did the right thing," the nurse said, "bringing this to our attention. She'll be safe here. She'll be in good hands."

"What's going to happen to her?"

"Well," the nurse put her notebook down on her desk and slid back in her roller chair. "Our team will do an investigation from a physical and mental health standpoint, and it depends on what Shay says when she wakes up. Kids have more rights than you might imagine. We'll have to ask her about what happened, and depending on what she tells us, we'll find an appropriate placement for her."

Mallory squeezed her hands into fists. When she spoke again, her words came out as if coated in flour. "But . . . what if she doesn't know what happened to her? What if she doesn't understand?" Mallory tucked her legs tightly under her chair.

Some kind of professional shield lifted away from the nurse's eyes. Mallory felt as though she was addressing her as a person, then, and that she was letting Mallory see who she was as a person, and that they were both on the same side, in solidarity, as sisters. "That's very common with these cases," she said gently. "Especially if it's the first time, they usually have no idea what's really going on."

"She thinks she has a boyfriend."

"We have people here who will work with her."

"She doesn't want to talk to the police."

"That's also common with these situations. It's very difficult to talk about something so deeply personal with law enforcement." She lifted a hand and brushed a stray hair out of her face. "She'll be okay," the nurse said, rolling back in her chair. "Shay is a survivor in this case. We're here to help." The nurse looked tired. "Anything else?"

Mallory didn't know what else to say. She had expected more. It felt like a big deal to her—the biggest possible deal. But for the nurse, this was her every day.

"Okay." The nurse stood and it was time to leave.

They moved back into the oblong waiting room and Mallory tried to figure out what day of the week tomorrow was and what time she worked and when they might call and how she might visit Shay. Behind her, the nurse called out the next person's name, while the fish in the aquarium no longer zipped around. It hovered motionless as though stunned. It stared out through the glass, alone.

andon's truck idled in front of Andrea's cabin. The time on his dashboard read 8:17 and the energy silos glowed green, indicating his engine had charged the battery during the hour drive back to Mire Lake. The sky had gradually gotten lighter as they moved out into the country, illuminating a winter landscape of white trees. Mallory hadn't noticed and felt only a rising dread. She didn't want to go back home. In the kitchen of the cabin a light shone. Andrea was up.

"Look at that," Landon said, his attention turned outside. It was the first either of them had spoken since leaving Duluth. She'd picked him up from the police station after visiting the hospital. It was Andrea who had called the police, reporting his truck after finding Baily dead in the street. It was Andrea who had accused Landon of intentionally killing her dog, a Class I felony under Wisconsin law. Landon had to explain the situation, and he'd been the one who told Mallory that Baily was dead. "I'm so sorry, Mallory," he'd said. After that, they had driven in silence for the rest of the way.

"That's not hoarfrost," he said now. "You don't see that every day. The conditions have to be just right."

Mallory followed his gaze to the trees. With the light just up over the horizon, it was a landscape unlike any she had ever seen. The trees weren't white because of the snow in the branches, or because a rain had fallen and then turned to ice. This was different. This was something otherworldly.

"What is that?"

"Rime ice. It happens when a winter fog fixes to a supercooled surface. The moisture freezes instantly, creating individual barbs of ice. I haven't seen this since I was a kid."

She could see the crystals on everything, every branch, even the smallest twig, flocked with thousands of white shards. It formed a city of ice over every surface, delicate barbs rising on all sides. With the sun low behind the clouds, a citron light filled the sky, flushing the trees in a crystalline glow so clean and cold she was almost afraid to breathe. Even the snowflakes that had collected along the edges of the windshield were changed.

"Every snowflake has six arms," Landon said, noticing where her gaze went. "You can see them, six arms called dendrites, because they branch out like trees. And each tree grows the same, the exact same design replicated six times, even though it's a new design that has never appeared anywhere in the world before."

"They do look like trees." She could see the arms of the snowflakes that stuck to the car, entire worlds with dendric designs intricate and visible even as they piled up against each other. "How do you know this?"

"I read it in a book.

"What book?"

"A novel called *About Grace*."

"What was it about?"

"A man looking for his daughter who he thought had died." He swallowed, and his Adam's apple jogged. "At any rate," he said, "don't forget your coat." He was pulling it from the backseat and she heard the vinyl whispers and thought of Shay, how she had used the coat for a pillow to rest her head, how she had been concerned about Mallory's eye, as if they were sisters, comrades fighting the same fight. She'd thought they were going on a road trip; she'd thought they would have all night.

"Don't worry about the duffle," he said, handing over her coat.

"Thank you for everything," Mallory said.

"Someone should be thanking you. You were amazing tonight, what you did."

Her body softened; she wanted to cry. "I didn't do anything."

"You did all the right things."

"Then why do I feel so crappy?"

"One of the side effects of being an adult," he said. "Sometimes doing the right thing doesn't feel good."

Suddenly she wanted to talk to him, to ask what to do and how he had known so much about safe harbor states and what came next. They were sitting together in a car after being up all night, surrounded by the most inexplicable beauty, just absurd beauty, and she felt exalted, expanded somehow. He was the one person in the world who might understand this, and it was ironic how all during the drive she hadn't wanted to talk, couldn't think of one single thing to say, and now that their time together was over, she didn't want to be alone. She'd thought they were going on a road trip!

"Did the dad ever find her?" Mallory asked, searching for a way to stall. "The daughter in the book?"

"You'll have to read it and find out." He held his hands at ten and two on the wheel, his face ashen, drained of light. "At any rate," he said again, and their time together was at an end.

The shock of the cold roughed her up as she took the cedar deck stairs. Of all the scenarios she could have cooked up involving Landon James giving her a ride home, nothing even came close to the night they'd had. When she tapped her shoes at the back door to knock off the snow, she saw the dendrite arms in the snow crystals at her feet and bent to lift a handful of the flakes. As she put her other hand on the doorknob to go in, she looked over her shoulder.

Landon was there, waiting like a gentleman to make sure she got in.

❈

"You came back." Andrea slumped at the kitchen table and pulled a blanket around her shoulders. She sipped from a can of Diet Coke, though she didn't normally let herself have caffeine—it was a stimulant, and the acidity stained her teeth. "I wasn't sure you would." The television was off, the kitchen scrubbed, all traces of vomit cleaned from the sink. Even the plate of food Mallory had thrown across the room was gone. In the silence, the chatter of bubbles evanesced from the can.

"Landon drove," Mallory said, no expression whatsoever on her face. She stood in the middle of the kitchen hugging her winter coat.

"Of course he did."

The sound of Andrea's voice made her nauseous, and she just wanted to go to bed.

"So, are you going to explain?" Andrea strained Coke through her teeth and avoided Mallory's eyes. "I've been waiting up for you all night, running through all kinds of different scenarios in my head." Mallory could hear the sucking of her breath and smell the saccharinity in the can. Her heart jackrabbited. She didn't want to tell Andrea anything about Shay, didn't want Andrea to use it against her in some way, shaming her like she did whenever the situation with her family came up. But Baily's dog collar lay there on the kitchen table.

"I'm sorry about Baily," Mallory said. "I feel terrible."

"Cut the crap."

"Landon wasn't driving. It was me."

"You killed my dog?"

"No," Mallory was taken aback. "No, we didn't run her over. Baily was on my lap, I rolled down the window, and before I could stop her, she jumped out."

"Why were you driving Landon's truck?"

"We called—"

"What's all this 'we' shit?" Andrea lifted her can, smacked it down; Mallory jumped.

"Sorry." It was automatic. "It's not what you think."

"What the fuck am I supposed to think? I look out the window and see Landon's truck backing up with Baily out there in the middle of the street." Andrea became suddenly animated, gesturing wildly with both arms. "I get on my coat and go into the kitchen, you're on the phone screaming at me, you sounded deranged. I get on my boots and go outside to get Bales, and when I come down the stairs, I see her sweater lying out there in the street. And I think, 'What's her sweater doing in the street?' I actually have the thought, 'How did she take her sweater off?'" Her eyes shined. Andrea never got emotional.

But Andrea never even saw the other truck. She thought her girl-friend had run off with her neighbor after deliberately running over her dog. She had called the police and then sat alone in the dark, too afraid to turn on the lights. "You weren't answering your phone, so I called Ripley." Ripley was the ornithologist ex-girlfriend who came before Mallory. "She stayed on the phone with me until the police got here. They helped me bring Baily into the garage. Her body is out there now, lying on a piece of cardboard."

Outside, the rime ice clung to all the trees. A city of white, a stacking of crystals, a lacing of ice over every branch, every twig; tiny barbs with dendritic arms reaching courageously into the cold. And all on top of three feet of snow. They couldn't even bury her.

"I'm really very sorry," Mallory said. She felt queasy and weak from being up all night, sensitive to every little sound. But also, some part of her felt different, like one of the trees described in white. "I never meant for any of that to happen," Mallory said. "I loved Baily. She was my friend."

"What the hell happened to your eye?" Andrea said, and Mallory kept forgetting how freakish she looked.

"I bloke a foo . . ." She was so tired, she slurred her words. "I broke a few blood vessels from strain."

"Strain from what?" Andrea didn't flinch. "Are you going to tell me why you're dressed in that baggy old coat?"

"You want to talk about that dinner you made me?"

"No. Is that what this is? I make you dinner and you kill my dog?"

"I didn't kill your dog."

"Then who did?"

There was no getting around it. She had to tell Andrea about Shay. In the cold stillness of a winter dawn, the blush of light crept out from behind the trees in white, and Mallory saw it again in her mind's eye. "A girl came walking out of the woods," she said, her gaze pinned outside. "Fourteen, fifteen years old. She just came walking across the snow on the other side of Riley Ridge, wearing nothing but a man's shirt. She had no clothes. She was hurt. She'd been beaten—there was blood on her face."

She tried to describe it, that moment, how a girl had suddenly and improbably come walking out from the woods, the sheer guts of it, her determination, this girl who had propelled herself forward into that still and frigid night. It had moved something fundamental inside of her. It had meant something, everything, to Mallory, seeing a girl so young and so lost, trying so hard to be found.

"This really happened?" Andrea asked. She squeezed and dimpled her can, scraping the aluminum back and forth across the table.

"Yes. I brought her to Landon's. We were trying to help her." Mallory tried to explain everything, how they were driving to Bemidji but then ended up at the hospital. The scraping frazzled her nerves and she gritted her teeth. "Are you even listening? We just heard that story on the news about the exploitation of young girls."

"So . . . what?" Andrea lifted her face, eyes roving around the room. "Are you saying that this girl was out here at a cabin in these woods, at a party, working as some kind of sex slave, and now, what, you're going to save her because of what happened to you when you were fifteen?" She snorted a laugh. "Girrrl, you don't have a clue."

"Fuck you."

"Just leave."

"I don't understand your complete lack of compassion."

"And I don't understand what you're doing to me. All of this means nothing?" She held out her arms. "I open my home to you, my life. I buy you things, help you plan for college. Baily gets killed—*my dog*—you go running off with Landon James. And all you can talk about is some girl? I mean, I get it, your traumatized past. But what about this?" She pointed to the space between them. "What is going on with you and me?"

Mallory felt the membrane holding back her anger stretched to the edge. "I don't love you, Andrea. I'm sorry, but this relationship isn't working out, and this is the truth that we need to work with going forward." She swayed on her feet and grabbed onto the back of a chair. "And for the record, I don't think you love me, either, not who I really am. You're in love with a version of me that's only in your head and not who I want to be."

The quicksilver light in Andrea's eyes snuffed out. She planted both hands on the table, pushed off, and stood as though the night had added pounds to her body. At the kitchen sink, she drew a glass of water, her kimono rippling as she moved. Mallory heard the swishing as she rinsed and spit into the sink.

"I'm sorry," Mallory said again. "I didn't know how to tell you before."

"Well, you've certainly figured it out now. This is the most you've said in weeks." Andrea spoke in a low, gravelly voice, and when she turned around her eyes were puffy and bloodshot. "Being with you used to make me feel so beautiful. Now, I have never felt so ugly."

Mallory held on to the chair, the air between them ripe and soiled with emotion. "I'll move out," she said, putting down the coat. "But can you please just give me some time? There are no hotels anywhere near here. I just want to go to bed. I worked a ten-hour shift and then we drove—"

"Why didn't you call *me*?" Andrea said. "I'd have been there like *that*." She snapped her fingers and Mallory flinched. "I'd have been totally down for a road trip. Of course I'd want to help one of our sisters in distress. Of course I'd have taken her wherever she wanted to go. But no, you had to go running off to Landon James." She held her arms out and did an unflattering imitation of *Help me, help me.*

"Stop it."

"Truth hurts."

"This is not about Landon."

"You're lying to yourself."

"It's about the girl. I want to help this girl."

"You can't help her," Andrea scoffed. "A girl like that doesn't get saved; she gets knocked up."

The membrane snapped and Mallory shoved the chair. It clattered to the floor, and with that sound, Mallory was no longer there with Andrea in the room. She was in that place, that blinding, blazing, hateful place, with that burn, that careening, chemical burn just behind her eyes, and she could say anything, do anything, inebriated with rage.

They screamed and shouted insults, holding nothing back. When Andrea left the house, sobbing, Mallory finally came to and staggered back, dazed and abraded. Around her in the kitchen lay the shattered evidence of her rage—Andrea's favorite mug, the one with the little orange birds, and her iPhone in its sporty blue case, irreparably cracked.

From outside in the winter stillness came the pitiful hum of Andrea's Prius, driving away.

14

In her sleep, Mallory saw Grandpa. It didn't feel like a dream, more like a visitation, all the colors sharp and exact. His eyes the blue of winter skies, his gaze, a hand on her shoulder when he called her name.

"Mallory."

She came awake. She lay there in bed and saw him in her mind's eye. He looked the way he had the last time they spoke, that spring, at the house of someone she didn't know. She had been eight or nine. Someone had died. It wasn't anyone that Mallory knew, and it was after the funeral, and a dog barked stupidly in the kitchen. Mallory had kept interrupting her mom, she wanted to go outside, but her mother had said no, it was time to eat, and the dog kept barking, until finally Mallory blurted, "But it's itching me!" She had cried. "His barks are itching me, Mom!"

It was Grandpa who had taken her outside. They stood out on the porch, where the sun sparkled absurdly in the meltwater; springtime in the northland, all the snow melting from all the roofs, gleaming and glinting like diamond drops. He took off his rumpled suit jacket and laid it over the rail of the porch, rolled up his shirt sleeves, and took out a cigarette. He smelled of Old Spice and the cuffs of his shirt looked artificially white against his olive skin, the tattoo on his chest creeping out from the V of shirt. It was gruesome ink, a black bird he called a Nachtkrapp, German for "night raven." She had seen it whenever he took them fishing at Bony Lake—a raven clutching a ripped and bloodied hand in its talons, feathers ruffled around its fierce head. It had always scared her, that bird.

"Do you feel better now?" he'd asked, holding the cigarette in the side of his mouth.

"Yes." She watched him cup a match, and they stood facing the alley lined with parked cars and detached garages.

"Can you still feel the voice of the dog?" Grandpa wasn't looking at her, he was puffing the cigarette. The dog in the house still barked.

"Yes, but it's not itching me now because I'm outside."

"So, being outside helps?"

She nodded. They both looked out across the alley while he smoked. Broken toys and bits of colored plastic lay across the matted grass, among the dog turds and dirty patches of snow. A brick path led to the detached garage for the house.

"Tell me something," he said. "When you look at the address on the side of that garage, and you look at that number seven there, does it appear distrustful to you?"

She peered at the number seven slanted there under the shady eave.

"Definitely," she said. "Sevens are shifty."

"That's what I think too."

"Not to be trusted."

"And what about fives?" He looked at her with a twinkle in his eyes. "Fives are nice guys." There were two fives on the side of the garage, and they did seem like nice guys.

"The three is nice, too," she added.

"Maybe." The cigarette bobbed out the side of his lips. "But threes have some intelligence to them. The fives, they're not the sharpest tools in the shed."

She smiled because she understood, and Grandpa smiled, too. He had tobacco stains on his teeth and garlic-paper skin. His hands were splotched and freckled and they knotted up whenever he clenched the pads of his chair before he stood—a lawn chair with green straps and aluminum rails. He had that chair in his living room. But that day he had been dignified and kind, possessed of a wisdom that he'd never shared with her before. His eyes shone keenly with a gentle light, the sun pulsing in the water drops falling from the eaves, his hair so white it circled his head in a haloed orb.

"Let me ask you something else," he'd said. "What color does that three look like to you?"

"Black."

"And the seven and the five?"

"All of the numbers are black, Grandpa."

"Yeah, that's what I thought."

"Why did you ask me that?"

"Because when I see a number three," he said, "it's always red."

Melting snow sparkled everywhere—under the gutters, along the rooflines, through all the bare branches in the trees.

"Always?" she said.

"Every time. But I know that's not right, because I've lived here all my life."

"What color is the seven and the five?"

"The seven is dark blue and the fives are this kind of muddy yellow." He inhaled on his cigarette and took it from his mouth. "Nice guys, yellow." He looked to her and smiled.

It was the most they had ever talked, and Mallory didn't move. She held herself the way she held her hands under the candy dispenser of those little machines after she put the quarters in, not wanting to drop a single piece.

"It happened to me when I got back from the war," he said. "It has a name: grapheme-color synesthesia. There's over six hundred different kinds." He explained how it was nothing to worry about, that it happens to millions of people. "The doc said it was a manifestation of PTSD. It's just the way my brain works now, and I wonder if that's what's happened to you." He put the cigarette back in his mouth. "Don't be ashamed just because it's different. It means you can know things the rest of us can't. That's what I think." The cigarette dangled from his lips. "We Germans always think we're unworthy.

"Your father . . ." he said, and his face changed. Mallory leaned in, both ears open wide on either side of her head. "I wasn't there," he whispered. "I was gone a lot. But I did whatever she wanted to keep the peace. I did things." A blackbird rose from a tree, cawing aggressively overhead. He didn't look up. "She was always on him about something. She was merciless, ever since he was a baby. Nothing he did was ever good enough. It never stopped. She wanted him

to be someone else, or maybe she wanted *me* to be someone else."
The sunlight in the water drops winked all around. He pulled the
cigarette from his mouth. "We broke him. That's what I think. But
that don't mean we don't love him," he said. "That don't mean that."

❄

The sharp *ping* of dog kibble hitting a metal bowl pulled Mallory
from sleep, despite the earplugs she wore. Her body lay under a blanket, wedged between the couch cushions. Andrea, in the kitchen,
dramatically shuffled around. She wasn't even trying to be quiet. She
slammed the bowl against the garbage bin, dumping out the dog
food she'd probably automatically poured, and then Mallory remembered that Baily was dead.

Andrea's stereo clock across the living room said 9:30 p.m. Mallory
had slept all of Monday and into the evening, and now Andrea had
come back. Mallory reprimanded herself—the hospital had probably
called, and she'd been asleep. She lay there, wanting to check her messages and call them back, wishing she wasn't lying there so exposed.
When the whisking of Andrea's pants approached, Mallory tensed
and held herself still as an egg, but then Andrea left, the back door
closing, the stealthy hum of her hybrid quietly whirring away.

She didn't even wonder where Andrea was going. Mallory checked
her phone—the hospital *had* called. They had left a voice mail, a
male nurse asking her to reach out during daytime business hours.
Mallory sat up. She didn't have to work until second shift on Tuesday, so she set an alarm with a plan to call first thing in the morning
and got up to pee, promising herself she wouldn't screw it up again.
She went right back to the couch, knowing she didn't deserve to
sleep in Andrea's bed.

When she was young, Mallory used to fly in her dreams. She'd
take off from the windows of her bedroom and fly all night, soaring
out over the tops of all the houses and trees, far away up into the
starry night sky. The windows of the living room now reflected only
black, and she no longer flew in her dreams. Whenever she tried, her
stomach dragged across the ground, no matter how hard she flapped

her arms. No amount of effort could lift her heavy body, and this meant something to her now.

She rolled over onto her side and brought her knees up to her chest, pressed her hands between them for warmth, and mourned.

❉

The high lonesome wail of the wolf fluttered down through the venting pipe of the fridge and Mallory woke from the feel of sugar pouring down her back. She removed an earplug and the refrigerator door thunked. Andrea's voice shivered in her cheeks, but she wasn't talking to Mallory; she was on the phone. From the television Mallory learned that the government shutdown was over after a record thirty-one days, and all employees would finally be headed back to work. A few minutes later Andrea shut off the TV. From the silence came the secretive hum of her hybrid driving away.

Mallory's head throbbed, her hives itched, and her armpits felt sticky and hot. Her phone said 0730, Tuesday morning. She'd slept all night despite having slept all of Monday. Mallory turned off her alarm and rolled over onto her back. She thought of the moment when she'd broken Andrea's phone. She thought of Shay in the back of the truck, polygons of light shifting over her face. Mallory wondered if she had ever been that innocent, that young. She hadn't felt young when she was that age. It didn't seem possible that she had ever been innocent at all.

Mallory called the RN from the hospital. He answered right away, his voice hurried and brusque. When she told him who she was and that she had information about Shay, he immediately warmed. They set an appoint for later that morning and in a lift of optimism she showered and washed her hair.

Steam rose from the red bumps on her skin when she patted herself dry. They hadn't gotten better but they weren't any worse. Toweling her hair, she stood in front of the propane stove, swinging her head and raking it dry with her fingers because using a hair dryer hogged too much electricity and she didn't feel like starting the generator. It didn't matter—she'd spend half the night in a hairnet anyway.

She dressed in layers, pulling on a black thermal shirt under her blue work smock, and carefully drew eyeliner around one eye. She examined the other eye, its white part still flooded with bright patches of blood. It looked vicious and otherworldly, but it didn't hurt, and she could see fine. Still, she knew Asshole Craig would make a squawk about it, so the best solution was to just keep it covered.

She took three Advil for her headache, pulled on her jacket, and went out to the garage.

The first thing she saw when she walked in was the sheet of cardboard where Baily must have lain. Patches of body fluid and dog hair stained the sheet, her body now gone. Andrea must have made arrangements. It was a heavy sorrow, one that didn't go away, because Baily's affection for them had been so pure and constant.

Rummaging through the boxes, unstacking and restacking, Mallory hugged down the cartons until she found the one marked "M. Bureau." One of the perks of moving in with Andrea had been getting her stuff out of storage, but she hadn't gone through any of it. Ripping open that box, a kind of assault hit her at the sight of her things, this Mallory from another life: her journal, her unicorn stickers, a picture of she and her sister holding a giant muskie. She'd forgotten about the collection of shiny postcards from all the places Dad had been—Kenya, Holland, Egypt, France. She'd forgotten how he wrote to them when they were young, when he was out on deployment, how he got them the good kind of cards that shape-shifted with special effects.

When she found the eye patch, a slippery heat moved through her and she heard her father's voice in her head, "Come on then. You want to go hunting so bad, wake up your sister and get dressed." Her breath changed and her skull buzzed as the memory of it played moving pictures in her head. Two sisters slinging rifles over their backs. Vehicle exhaust churning from the back of the truck. He must not have gotten them permits, Mallory thought now, because they weren't even old enough. He must have been planning to use his for whatever they shot, although it turned out they got nothing. She was aware of how shallow her breathing had become, how her throat had tightened and gotten hot.

"Mallory." He'd called her around to the other side of the truck. He had parked on the side of a county road, near a logging trail that led into the brush. "I got something for you." His eyes glinting metal bits, they saw everything, but that morning they seemed easy, relaxed.

"I found it at an outdoor market in Kohistan." The dark knit of his cap folded down in a band and the light from the cab shone through the flesh of his ears, the cartilage thin and translucent, glowing orange. "I thought it might help you align your sight." He unfolded a square piece of cloth in the center of his hand.

Mallory never could wink or close just one eye. She took the patch from him, its smell exotic and mildly miraculous, the cloth oddly weighted in her hand. She looked up at him.

"Go ahead," he said. "Give it a try." He seemed earnest in that moment, childlike, young. His ears stood out like trophy handles on either side of his face.

She fit the elastic band over her head, pulled down the patch.

"Arh, matey," he grinned. "You look like a pirate," he said. He elbowed her lightly in the arm. She'd felt giddy and delirious, the top of her head buzzing and tingling from the praise. In the wing mirror of the truck, she'd caught a glimpse of herself and liked how the eye patch made her look tough, how the fabric kept her warm. Most of all, she liked that it was from him.

"Come on, girls, let's go." The crunch of leaves under boots, the air damp just before a snow.

Mallory cuffed the box, closed the flap, and got out of the garage before the rest of the memory could come back.

❄

In the kitchen she poured a bowl of cereal, made a fresh pot of coffee, and saw the note from Andrea. *Baily's pet remembrance ceremony is on Wednesday at five thirty. You may come,* it read. *You have until the end of the month.*

Mallory looked at the calendar where she had her work schedule written out. One week. No way could she find an apartment and move in one week. But Andrea had scheduled Baily's ceremony at a time when Mallory didn't have to be at the store.

It happened when she was eating her cereal. From outside, a ray of sun shot through the clouds and cut slabs of light in through the living room windows and onto the floor.

Mallory dropped her spoon. More sun spilled in through the kitchen, landing in glowing patches across the table and chairs. She grabbed her coat and pulled open the back door.

The stairs had been recently sprinkled with a fresh layer of snow that in the sunlight dazzled like thin mica scales. She shuffled through the fluff and stood at the edge of the deck, the trees still dressed in white. With her eyes closed she lifted her face to the sun.

Light, after being in the dark for so long, felt like a song, like laughter poured over her skin. It bathed her and soothed her and held her there in a space so bright and pure it was absent of all thought. It forgave her even as it revealed her sorrow, the rolling scent of its softness a reprieve. She felt giddy despite everything, vaguely exultant, somehow, at the thought of Shay. Because Mallory had been allowed to see her come out of those woods—the synchronicity of it felt ordained, all of it divinely arranged. When she thought of all the moments that led up to it, how else could it be explained? She was supposed to be with Andrea, should not have worked late, had wanted to be at a bonfire with Landon James. But instead she'd been two miles from her house in the middle of the night at the one spot in the woods where she could have seen Shay, and the moon had been full. The stillness of it, how surreal it had been to see her out there among the trees, bathed in moonlight, walking on snow.

Mallory opened her eyes. The sunlight caught itself in the silver nets in the tops of all the trees. She thought of her dad and how he had given her that eye patch; she thought of her grandfather and what he had said about feeling unworthy. She thought that she would never feel worthy as long as that darkness lived inside of her. She wished her grandfather would tell her what to do about that. She wondered if he struggled with the same thing, if that's why he had a fierce raven tattooed on his chest—to remind him that it was there, that it lived inside of him. When he came to her in that dream, what she had felt from him, more than anything, was love, as if he had wanted to right a wrong, to make amends. As if he were better at showing love from over there. And then she thought about Shay and how she'd come walking out of those woods.

Hope flashed small and distant as starlight.

Maybe she could help this girl. Maybe who she was and what she'd been through held significance for the people who crossed her path, if she were brave enough to walk forward in this life. She'd never told anyone the full truth of what had happened to her on the night that Jarrod took her to that party. If she could speak about it now, in the pure light of day; if she could finally admit it, what Jarrod had done, how she had let him, and why. If she could find a way to say what she had wanted to say while riding with Shay in the back of the truck. If she could help this girl change her mind about what she thought she deserved.

Across the snow, little animal prints lay like beaded necklaces strewn along the ground. The sunlight dazzled in the thin mica flakes and trees rose with their branches coated in ice, a filigreed majesty thrust into the pale blue air.

A winter blue. The most penitent blue.

PART

THREE

15

Jarrod had lived in a single-story two-bedroom on the outskirts of Sanders, not far from where Mallory grew up. Both houses were bordered by woods—stands of popple, maple, birch. Although he was two years older, he'd been only one grade ahead, and when she got on the school bus, its red lights flashing in the dark morning, the windowpanes pressed with sleepy heads, it was Jarrod's stop that came next. Sometimes he would sit with her and they would talk as the bus rolled through the dark.

More than an hour later they would be dropped off at school.

The night of the party was a Friday in January, and they were on winter break. By then she was fifteen, Jarrod seventeen. He no longer rode the school bus, but she still did.

A lot of older kids would be going to the party, kids from private schools in the cities of Minneapolis or Duluth. She didn't know them, but she pictured girls like Katelynn Arden, who went to their elementary but didn't go with them to the public high school because their parents had money and clout. On the basketball team, Mallory played against these girls, and she'd always felt this awareness of how she was different from them. If she had to say what it was, she'd have described material things—nicer clothes, newer cars, shinier hair. But it was more than that; it was something elemental inside of them. It was what they believed about themselves, who they thought they were and what they could do and become.

She was also pretty sure Jarrod wanted to have sex at the party. He had asked her if she was ready, and she'd said yes. They would be going with Trevor, who was eighteen, and his girlfriend, Ginny, who everyone called Gin, and she was twenty-one. "Wear a dress," Jarrod had told her. "Something nice." So she was nervous, and she'd told her mom that she was sleeping over at a friend's.

✳

The first time she saw Jarrod was at the elementary school, during orientation, when they brought in their supplies and got their pictures taken in the gym. Mallory and her sister braided their hair and wore dresses—to make a good first impression, their mother said. She got their dresses used, secondhand from the church bazaar, where you could fill up a grocery bag with clothes for five dollars as long as you didn't care about styles or brands. Their dresses were always long when everybody else's were short, or they were short when everybody else's were long, but they were clean and new for the two girls.

Jarrod's mother must have given her son the exact opposite advice about how to make a good first impression, because he never wore new-for-him shirts or jeans stiff from store shelves. Jarrod wore a hat. You weren't allowed to wear hats in school—they distracted from learning, the principal said—but orientation wasn't a real school day, so maybe that's why he got away with it. They were nice hats, usually fedoras, cream colored or black.

She had to say: Jarrod looked really excellent in those hats.

This and the fact that he wore concert tees in black and hard-worn jeans gave Mallory the impression that Jarrod was a renegade and that being with him would be more than a little fun.

The other thing about Jarrod happened during the early days out on the playground of the elementary school. She had found a frog stranded in the sand and was helping it off to safety, where it wouldn't get hurt. She had read a book about amphibians and knew that when she handled a frog she had to be careful; they have very sensitive skin. The other kids weren't paying attention to her frog, until they did.

"Let me hold it!" They swatted at it with their greasy, hot hands, fighting over who would hold it next. One boy caught it and the frog shot out the side of his fist, right near Katelynn Arden's head. "Oh my god!" she shrieked explosively, and all the boys laughed.

It became a game. They chased Katelynn Arden around, trying to squirt the frog into her hair.

"Don't touch it!" Mallory screamed at them. "Stop it! You're burning him! Stop it!"

But no one listened to her. They all thought it great fun, running around the playground squirting the frog while it writhed and squirmed and tried to get away. Mallory cried. She wailed, impassioned and unselfconscious, at the edge of the grass as spangles of heat burst vertiginously through her chest. She could feel the frog's burning, or thought she did, not as pain exactly but as a dizzy, spiraling sensation under each lung, on both sides of her chest.

The bell rang. The kids dropped the frog, limp and bruised, in the sand. It sat there with its eyes bulged and white throat pulsing. Mallory furiously wiped away her tears and watched while the frog died.

Jarrod knelt by her side. He didn't go line up with the other kids by the door.

"I'm sorry," he said. "Are you all right?"

She was not all right. She did not understand how kids could do that, how people could be so cruel. "I hate them," she said. "I hate everybody." She really did. Hot tears blotched her face.

"I know," he said. "But they didn't mean it." His voice gave her *the feeling*—she didn't know why. When he talked, his voice stroked the sides of her cheeks with the cool grit of a cut apple, sending shivers through her face, and that endeared this boy to her permanently and prematurely without her even realizing it. His voice would always do that to her. It tingled in her cheeks and vibrated through her skin, giving her the incontrovertible feeling that she was cared for, loved.

Jarrod looked at her with his liquid brown puppy eyes, "Here," he said, filling his hands with dirt. He put them together to make a bowl, and gently scooping and lifting the frog, he carried it off the playground and into the shade. "Nice toady," he said, setting it underneath the leaves of a bush. She didn't correct him and tell him it was a frog, or that it had already died. His voice shivered in her cheeks and that sweetness pooled in the back of her mouth and she saw that he didn't think himself above the frog, and they both shared that. Always would.

✳

They picked her up on the night of the party. Trevor drove and sat in the front with his girlfriend and Mallory got into the back next to Jarrod, tugging at her dress. She wanted to pull it down over her knees—the temperature that night was in the midtwenties, below freezing but warm for their area, so she didn't wear leggings, just ankle-high boots.

"What do you think?" She pulled her jacket down over her shoulders to show Jarrod the top of her dress. She'd used all her babysitting money so that she could buy it new and drove the sixty miles north to the mall in Duluth. It was a style all the girls were wearing, solid purple with asymmetrical seams and a sweetheart neckline. She'd liked the way it hugged her body, and the color brought out the depths of brown in her eyes. She'd also put on perfume and dangly gold hoop earrings. Her hair was lighter back then, and long, and she had curled it with a curling iron and pulled it up partway in a clip.

Jarrod's face tensed in the ash gray light. She should have seen it then—it was there on the replay in her mind. He wasn't looking at her with anticipation or anything resembling affection or love. He was anxious, nervous, weighing in.

But maybe she put that there afterwards, in the memory of it, to make sense of what had happened. Maybe it was she who was anxious, weighing in. The way she always checked herself in the mirror. *Am I satisfactory?* she always wondered. *Will I do?*

"Shut the door," Trevor said, and they careened away.

✳

The first time Jarrod got suspended was in elementary school. Mallory was eight or nine, in fourth grade. Jarrod had been called into the principal's office and Mallory was there, in the nurse's room. The sound of the principal's voice when he addressed Jarrod's mother had snagged her attention—he used the word "graffiti," which was a serious offense, but his tone had sounded amused.

Mallory jumped off the nurse's table to listen better. She had a slight fever but couldn't be picked up by her mom, so she'd been lying there alone, resting. The nurse was with another student, speaking in a low voice on the other side of a door in a private room. No one had noticed when she crept out into the hall.

They took Jarrod to the janitor's closet by the back door of the school, where he was given a mop bucket and a scrub brush before heading outside. She waited, slipping around to a different door on the other side. The bright sunlight split through her head and the fever glazed a sheen of sweat on her skin, but she found him at the back of the school. He stooped, dipping the brush. On the ground, right up next to the cement, splatters of paint stood out bright in the grass. Blue letters, sprayed right on the brick. Jarrod's graffiti, his act of vandalism:

I LOVE MY MOM

✲

"What did you tell your parents?" Jarrod's voice came to her from the dark backseat of the truck. It took twenty minutes of jostling west along unlit county roads before they got to the main artery heading north toward the Twin Ports. Club music blared from the speakers as they topped a rise, the city lights spreading out below them. Inside the truck, the divider between the front and back had a sliding window, and Trevor's girlfriend, Gin, passed a joint through it.

"I told my mom that I was sleeping over at Jayden's." Mallory's thighs spread out from under her dress and she worried that they were too large. They glowed in the dark of the cab, pressed against the upholstery and prickled with gooseflesh from the cold.

"She at home?" Jarrod rolled down his window a crack as smoke curled from his nose. His face had changed since middle school, thinned out, with dark stubble around the chin and jaws. The jag of his Adam's apple poked from his neck and his hair was buzzed short to his scalp, with nicks and scabs. In a certain light, she could see the scar from when the couch had fallen through the living room floor and his dad had beat him for it because he'd been sitting on it when it happened.

"No." Mallory shook her head, the earrings clattering against her neck. "She was already at work when I left." Her mom had gotten a new job waitressing at Julia's, a family restaurant in Sterling where she hardly earned anything other than tips, and her dad had redeployed.

From the front cab came muffled laughter. Trevor had said something to Ginny and Gin said something back that made him laugh. Jarrod's eyes flicked over to Mallory, as if they were in on a secret because they both knew how rare it was to hear Trevor laugh. Jarrod offered her the joint, but she shook her head no. She always said no; she was an athlete, and they had a game the next day. Jarrod never came to her games but he always offered her a cigarette, and she liked that he did. He also never wore a coat. He had sweatshirts layered over flannel shirts. And she'd never seen him play sports, not even as a kid. In order to play sports, you had to have a parent who would sign the permission slip, pay the activity fee, and drive you to practice and all the games. He passed the joint back, sliding the little window closed.

"It's a nice place," he said, his voice stroking her cheeks in the dark. "A real nice place, you'll see."

Without even thinking she said, "Nicer than Milo's?" It just came out, because Milo's was the nicest house she'd ever known. She didn't mean anything by it.

Jarrod pushed the smoke out with a voiced exhalation. His jaw jutted forward and tensed.

"Sorry," she said quickly, shifting her body closer to the door. In the dim light from the oncoming cars, the shadows scrolled across his face, and she saw what he would look like as an old man.

※

Jarrod had invited Mallory to one other party before, his birthday party during the summer after fourth grade. She was ten years old then and Dad had left for the Iraq War. The invitation was verbal, nothing written down.

"Do you want to go?" her mother had asked, when Mallory told her about it.

Oh, she really did. Jarrod was set to begin at the middle school. Laurel, who was only six, got invited to parties all the time for the kids in her class, but Mallory never did. Mallory was four years older and not cute. It's impossible to be cute when you're the oldest and always trying to be responsible without getting mad.

Jarrod's parents were both at the birthday party, along with uncles and cousins out smoking cigarettes on the front yard. The adults were skinny-looking in their worn jeans, heavy motorcycle boots, and black screen tees. They smiled with missing teeth and held out tumblers in grease-stained hands, all of them with visible tattoos, even the women. Mallory liked being among them; they accepted her without judgment. It was a soft summer day, with wind in the leaves and not much heat. Under the hood of a spindly charcoal grill, smoke from the hot dogs and burgers pillowed and burped, and the kids helped themselves to cans of cold Coke from a cooler filled with ice without even having to ask.

The best part, though, was taking turns on Jarrod's four-wheeler, going around and around in circles on the dirt track in the bare field next to his house. It was the feel of sitting behind him, her legs straddled over an engine, her arms wrapped tight around a boy for the first time in her life. It was being so close she could smell the musk of him in the folds of his soft sweatshirt hood. And it was the sound of his voice, *the feeling* as it tingled in her cheeks.

It was a good time—until Katelynn Arden arrived. Mallory should have seen it then; it was obvious from the look on his face. Jarrod felt for her what he would never feel for Mallory. To him, Katelynn Arden was like the stars or the moon. Mallory Moe was just another toad.

Katelynn got a ride on the four-wheeler without waiting in line. She sat behind Jarrod and circled her arms around his chest; they rode around and around. Mallory would always remember Katelynn's ride as being extra-long, a half hour or more. The adults pandered to Katelynn's mom, bringing her a cup of ice for her Coke and carrying Katelynn's present—a gift bag foaming with sea green tissue paper—into the house like some great prize.

Katelynn didn't come inside the house with the other kids when it was time to have cake. Instead, she had to go home. Thinking back on it later, Mallory thought that her mother probably didn't want Katelynn going into that house.

Jarrod's house wasn't just small; it was squalid and sad and bad things happened inside—she just knew. It was like those shabby bathrooms on the outside of gas station stores in poor, run-down towns: the door nicked, the knob loose, the latch broken, with a sink and toilet inside stained brown. Jarrod's house. The front steps listed and pulled back from the door, the gray-green siding with ruffled paint and rust discolorations dripped down from a sagging roof. Jarrod's house. Sheets hung over the windows instead of curtains, and in his bedroom they also served as doors. In five strides you could cross the living room where a TV always played, the carpet matted and worn. There was a new shag rug in the bathroom with a matching toilet tank cover in pink, fashion magazines stacked on the floor next to small items in plastic shopping bags, a curling iron plugged into the wall. Jarrod's house.

They ate their cake in the kitchen, iced blue cupcakes bought from the store. Everything in the kitchen had been scrubbed clean for the party—Formica countertops with half-moon stains, frayed at the edges with nicked-off chunks. The stove was dented, the cupboard doors scarred. Behind the purple sheet that hung lopsided over Jarrod's door, Mallory glimpsed a mattress on the floor.

It was a sad house, made even sadder by the fact of the house built right across from it, on the other side of the road. Jarrod's place sat on prime real estate, bordered by woods, on a three-acre lot with a partial view of Ashby Lake. But that view got obstructed during the summer Jarrod turned eight, when the Ardens built their three-story lakefront home to accommodate their burgeoning family.

Milo Arden, Katelynn's older brother, was the same age as Jarrod, and he rode the bus with them to the elementary school, but he didn't go to that party. He also wouldn't attend the public high school. He went to a private school thirty minutes away, where he was captain of the hockey team and excelled academically—beloved by teachers, everyone said. The Ardens had a backyard facing the lake, with playground equipment and an above-ground pool. Summers, Milo water-skied from the back of a speedboat; winters he loaded hockey equipment into the back of his mother's van. He went on school trips and family trips and lived in a ten-bedroom house that had real doors and a three-car garage, as well as a two-bedroom carriage house that had its own garage, on the same lot, for when the grandparents visited. He had new clothes ordered from catalogs and new snow pants every season, with a matching ski jacket and gloves and a hat.

Every winter, the Ardens staked and wrapped the row of juniper trees that served as a private hedge in front of their lot. Every winter, when the school bus rolled by, Mallory couldn't help but look at those hedges, wrapped so carefully in their burlap coats, and think about the boy who lived across the street and wonder how it was that those shrubs received more care and attention than he did.

She didn't think this was Milo's fault. She also didn't think it was Jarrod's.

But she wondered what it did to him, growing up across the street from the Ardens like that. How it felt to watch Milo, a boy his same age and height, coming home from school every day just like he did, but walking into that house, while Jarrod went shuffling off to his shack. How did that inform him, set him up for rest of his life, what his expectations were, what kind of man he would become and what he thought he deserved? Because in the beginning there was nothing wrong with Jarrod. He was a happy kid, decent and kind. He'd stayed out on the playground with her to move away the frog after it died. He'd been excited just like the rest of them on the first day of school.

He smiled at her from across the gym, out from under his hat.

❋

"So, I got you this." Jarrod passed her a small fuzzy box. They'd been driving in the dark for ninety minutes since leaving Sanders and were now headed northeast on Highway 61 winding alongside Lake Superior. The heater blasted through the truck but still it was cold, and she took her hands out from where they were pressed beneath her thighs and took the box.

"What is it?" she said stupidly. The box was a perfect square.

"Just open it."

The sweetness of his voice stroked her cheek, and just holding the box she felt pampered, beloved. It had stiff hinges, felt well made. She pried it open and touched the silky pillow inside, admiring the glittering fleck.

"It's real," he said, before she could ask. "That's fourteen-carat gold." He took the box, yanked out the ring. "I had to guess at the size."

"You got this for me?" Her cheeks tingled with a delicate flushing of saliva, the roughed sweetness of his voice stroking her like a kitten's tongue. She'd never had a boyfriend who bought her jewelry before, and she'd never had anything that was real diamonds or gold.

"Do you like it?"

She slid the ring over her finger and wiggled it. The diamond was the size of a flea, but it shimmered and she felt the weight of it.

"I can't believe it's real."

"It's real."

"It makes me feel royal."

"Good." Jarrod lit up a cigarette, cracked the window. "That's how I want you to feel."

The sharp hollow clacking of a semitruck thundered past. It vibrated in her collarbone and penetrated the base of her spine. She tensed and thought how now she would have to have sex. That was where her mind went. She felt conscious of the skin on her inner thighs spreading out under her dress and the soft cotton of her underwear and the weight of the gold diamond band as they rocketed through the dark.

❄

Jarrod owned a snowmobile, and during the winter Mallory turned thirteen, they would ride out together over the Solderlund fields, covered smooth by planes of snow. On that seat behind him, with the power of an engine thrumming between her legs and white wilderness flying past all around, she thought she was in love. That acceleration, the heart-thudding ecstasy born fresh during a wild ride, their connection to the ground and to each other—it made her feel invincible, alive.

They never wore snowmobile suits or insulated bibs or waterproof, windproof shells—they had their jeans and sometimes snow pants, with sweatshirts and jackets and knit winter hats, clothes handed down from older siblings or cousins or donated by the church. Her helmet was for a motorcycle, it wasn't insulated or ventilated, so the shield always fogged up in front of her face, and whenever they stopped she'd wipe it clear. Jarrod waited for her. He revved the engine, looked back to check that she had her helmet on, and sent them off again.

Usually they went to his uncle's place, where Jarrod had engines he was fixing, or they'd stop off at Bugsy's—the place where his mom tended bar—to get something to eat.

They weren't having sex, but sometimes they petted on his uncle's couch. They sat together until their bodies started rubbing, seemingly all on their own, and he'd pull her up onto his lap and they'd kiss, their tongues exploring the insides of each other's mouths. He mined for wonders under her sweater, and she rubbed against his knee until pulsing spasms between her legs turned her insides into a pool. At the time, she didn't know what that was. They'd had the sex talk at school. She'd talked with her sister and Mom about getting her period, and about safe sex, but nobody told her about orgasms. They felt forbidden, like something fattening or bad for you, like chocolate or drugs.

Afterwards, Jarrod would disappear upstairs, and he'd be gone for a little while before coming back down to the couch, where he would hold her and stroke her hair, and she felt like a person who mattered and like she belonged here on this earth in a way that she never did before or anywhere else but next to him, pressed against the heartbeat of his chest.

Jarrod's uncle lived in a clapboard rambler with cement stairs and an outdoor clothesline frosted white like an oversize eggbeater covered in snow. Jarrod lived there for a while, sleeping on the couch, but the first time he took Mallory over there she was only thirteen years old. They approached the house from out across a field of smooth polished snow, sailed in on the snowmobile and parked by the pole barn. He led her around to a side door, where an old Christmas tree canted, its needles paper-bag brown.

He held open the door for her. She would always remember the surprise of that, the moment he stood there waiting for her. She did not expect it. This was who he really was, she thought, and not who he had learned to be.

"Want a cooler?" he said, moving into the sunroom. She didn't know what a cooler was. "Sure," she said, even though she was already plenty cold.

They had to be quiet, he said, because his uncle was sleeping, even though it was the middle of the day. The house smelled of cat litter and sunlit dust. On every available surface, in corners and on tables and chairs, were stacked boxes and storage bins with trays of Christmas ornaments, sleeves of tinsel, bags of candy—gummy worms, Life Savers, Jolly Ranchers, all individually wrapped, some of the bags opened, others not.

"It's a twist-off," he said, handing her a raspberry Smirnoff Ice.

"Oh."

She held the bottle and followed him back outside, through the screen door and down the stairs. The snow had thickened, the air tinted orange. He led her over to the pole barn, a large building off to the side of the house, with a cement floor and a high, raftered ceiling. He pulled aside the door.

"These are my snowmobiles," he said, turning on a light. "I keep my main one stored in the garage at my dad's because it's brand new, but these belonged to my cousins. They're used, but still pretty good. They just need to be fixed up and then I can sell them."

Inside smelled of fuel and cold cement. She liked that he was showing her his private boy space and that he had plans for his future, a way to provide. She thought her dad would approve. But the smells of the room masked the feel of his voice, and the cooler wasn't as sweet as she would have liked. He tinkered with one of his machines while she stood drinking, the bubbles sharp objects on her tongue. She was looking at the bottle and not at the snowmobiles.

"Those are my aunt's," he said, speaking of the drinks. "She used to be really into wine coolers until they raised the tax on them, so now she gets these at Walmart because they're cheaper, but she still calls them coolers."

"Oh," she said. "Funny."

"Yeah. She won't notice they're gone. Honestly. She doesn't keep track."

"Okay."

"Seriously, it's like, I have two or three every day."

When they threw away their bottles before leaving, she heard the clink of glass hitting against other bottles and she waited to feel different, to feel buzzed, but mostly she just felt warm and relaxed, a feeling she thought she would have felt anyway.

He would take her there again as they got older, and Jarrod spent more time fixing engines for money. He taught her how to make minor repairs, and she discovered she was good at it—or maybe she wasn't, but she wanted to be good, to feel the warmth of Jarrod's breath when he leaned in close and cranked a lug nut or pulled out a wire and told her, "No, not this one," or when he was impressed because she'd done it right.

That fall, during Halloween, Mallory dressed up. Jarrod asked her to. He and Trevor got this idea to go trick-or-treating at the nice homes by the golf course in Sterling to score full-size candy bars, and they made her do it even though she was almost fourteen and too old to be dressing up. "You're short," he said. "No one will know." But *she* knew.

She disguised herself as a hobo, with dirt streaked on her cheeks, wearing baggy clothes and lugging a grimy pillowcase sack. They made her stay out until the sack was completely full and then they went back to Trevor's house by the railroad tracks to divvy it up. Trevor lived there with his grandma. They would go there a lot. The house was a slim two-story on the north end of Sanders, within walking distance of the bars.

"I want to get a job," she said to Jarrod that winter. "That way, I can *buy* you things."

"I buy you things."

"I know."

"If you get a job, we won't be able to hang out."

"Other people have jobs and they still hang out."

"There are other ways to make money, you know," Trevor had said.

Trevor was two years older than Jarrod. They were second cousins, although they didn't look alike. Trevor had a square face with a pug nose and nostrils that pointed up so you could always see how they were grossly filled. When he ate, he talked with his mouth full, bread clogging the crevices between his teeth. Trevor never finished high school, and he smelled like puppy chow, but he always worked some kind of job and he always had money.

"He's not stupid, you know," Jarrod said.

"Yeah, I know. You're not stupid, either."

"I know. That's why you should listen to me and do what I say." Sometimes Jarrod said things in what she knew was his dad's voice and not his own. Jarrod didn't like to sleep at home. He had three or four places where he could crash. There was always a couch, he said. "They're all my houses," he said, "but none of them are my home."

※

"At the party," Jarrod said, that night in the truck, "there's someone I want you to meet."

"Okay. Who?"

"It's his house, his party." He took out another cigarette and rolled down the window a crack. He had to talk louder now with the wind in the car. "He's an important guy; he has a lot of connections and stuff." The strap of her bra slid down over her shoulder and she pulled it up and tensed, as if that would keep the strap up. "His family owns a lot of vacation homes and resorts. They're a big construction company and, you know, he might get my dad a job."

"Oh. That's cool." She knew they were still in a recession and that finding work was hard. Her dad had gone back overseas. Jarrod's dad had just gotten his third DUI. Jarrod had his license and drove his dad's truck around town, to the auto parts store, to the Dollar General. He drove it with his dad and alone; Jarrod that winter seventeen years old.

"So just be nice to him, okay?"

"Okay, sure." She looked down at her new ring glinting in the dark. "What's he like?"

"Just do it for me, okay? It's a simple thing."

"Sorry."

"Do you like the ring?"

"I love it."

"I knew you would."

"I'm just surprised."

"Yeah?"

"Yeah. It must have cost a lot."

He exhaled and the smell of the smoke incensed the cab.

"It did."

❄

The winter she turned fourteen, Grandpa died. Nothing about her day-to-day life changed, but she felt his absence like a missing nutrient from her body.

Jarrod took her receipt shopping for the first time that January. The economy had just crashed and her dad couldn't find work and the restaurant in Sanders where her mom waitressed had closed. Just after the holidays, they drove north into Sterling, an hour away. They wouldn't do it at any of the stores near their town. "Don't shit where you live." Jarrod's father had taught him that. It was something he said.

"Look for the ones where people pay cash." They were outside a Walmart in a windchill of twenty below. "And make sure you check the carts."

Sterling was a smaller city than Duluth, but it was much easier not having to cross the bridge in the wintertime over the Saint Louis Bay. Brown sand and snow streaked the floor mats between the sliding glass doors, and Jarrod taught her to keep her hands in her pockets while checking the carts. People left their receipts inside of them, or they left receipts on top of overflowing garbage bins. Sometimes the receipts blew in front of her on the ground, sticking to the snow, and that was how she found that good one. It just appeared in front of her as if it wanted to be seen. "What's *she* doing here?" Trevor asked. They had reconvened at a table in the back of a Mickey D's. She blew into her hands, her skin chafed red from the cold.

"She's with me," Jarrod said. "She has a trustworthy face."

Mallory rubbed her hands and tried to look trustworthy. She'd already handed over her pile of receipts. Trevor groused about how she would get them all caught. He put five sugars and two creams into his coffee and his voice bumped against her like a cold metal box. You couldn't tell Trevor anything; he always had to know more than you did. But he also had a rough situation at home, much worse than hers or even Jarrod's, and these were her people, and with them was where she belonged.

"Holy shit, Mallory." Jarrod showed Trevor the receipt. Her face tingled with pride.

It was from Walmart, for two boxes of Nicorette gum. It was for just over a hundred dollars.

"Let Mallory do it then," Trevor said. "With her trustworthy face."

"She can't," Jarrod said. "She's not old enough. You have to be eighteen." He was protecting her, she thought.

"Yeah, to buy it," Trevor said. "Not to return it." He leaned over the table toward Mallory and said, "Listen to me and do everything I say." When he spoke, the bluntness of his voice raised the hairs on her arms and she felt uncomfortable the way you do when slightly cold. He showed her how to study the receipt for details—two-milligram or four-milligram, original flavor or fruit chill, 170 pieces, or only sixty. He showed her what the codes meant. "You have to get the right box off the shelf, and you got to do it right away," he said. "No fumbling around and shit. No looking up at the camera. And please god, whatever you do, don't go looking down at your receipt."

"Okay."

"You got to memorize it."

"I can do that."

"You have to know where the camera is at all times so they can't see your face."

"How will I know where the camera is?"

Trevor drew it out for her on the back of a different receipt—where the cameras were in the pharmacy aisle, in the pet food aisle, and the pocket near the goldfish tanks without any cameras at all. He had them memorized. "Wear a hat," he said. "Put that hair away."

They suited her up in one of Trevor's jackets, which swallowed her hands and half her legs. She wore a baseball cap with its brim tugged low over her forehead and her hair in a ponytail, tucked in under the collar of the coat. They sent her in and waited in the parking lot of the Dollar Store.

The door mats shined from melted clumps of snow, and a young disabled man with shriveled arms greeted her inside the store. She snagged a shopping basket, the empty Walmart bag with the receipt tucked under her arm. In the pharmacy aisle, she put a plain tube of toothpaste in her basket, then turned sideways and slid out the two boxes of Nicorette gum. She did everything Trevor said and she did it perfectly, until she got to the checkout and the clerk turned out to be someone she knew. It was too late to get in another line. The sight of her caused Mallory's heart to flutter, and the sound of this woman's voice made her want to sneeze—it was like her voice gave her an allergy.

"You look just like your mother," the clerk said, scanning the paste. Mallory's heart pounded and she nodded. Mrs. Frisbee had worked in the lunchroom at their elementary school, and she did have a particularly round head. Mallory tried not to sneeze as she handed over Jarrod's two rumpled bills, soft and moist as a used tea bag.

"I have a return," she croaked, and held up the bag. Inside were the two stolen boxes of Nicorette gum.

"Oh, sweetie." Mrs. Frisbee handed her three cents change. "You can't do that here." She pointed in the direction of the customer service counter, which Mallory already knew about, but doing it this way aroused less suspicion, Trevor said. She couldn't even say thank you because she sneezed.

Why did the clerk have to be someone she knew? The line for returns snaked out into the main corridor because of the holidays. Her sweaty hands clutched the plastic bags, the legitimate purchase in one and the stolen boxes in the other. She watched the demo video for a rentable rug cleaner that played in a giant red box against the wall. A coiffed lady strolled around with an appliance that looked like a vacuum cleaner and worked it strategically across a beige rug. She wore a skirt with a pair of high heels, and Mallory wondered who in the city of Sterling cleaned their rugs while wearing a skirt and heels.

Finally, it was her turn. "I'm returning this for my mom." She set the bag with the gum on the counter. "Nothing is wrong with it, she just got the wrong kind."

"Do you want to exchange it?" The clerk removed the boxes with his skinny arms and disappeared the bag. His septum piercing was sore-looking and infected, the skin around the metal ring red and crusted yellow. Nice guys, yellow.

"Yeah, no. She already got it," Mallory said. "She needed it right away." She felt proud of herself for improvising and adding details to make it seem real.

The clerk swiped away snot with one hand, his nostrils red and flaked with bits of dry skin, his forehead streaked with zits. He opened his register drawer, coughing into his arm, shot snot lugubriously to the back of his throat. He made no attempt to hide the fact that he was ill; the whites of his eyes were spiderwebbed and rheumy. She felt bad for him, having to work when he was sick, while here she was stealing and perfectly well.

"Feel better," she said magnanimously, after he'd counted out the bills and she was safely making her escape. The receipt checker on her stool sorted through the bags of a busy mom loaded down with potato chip boxes and three squawking kids. The doors slid open. Cool air refreshed her face.

"You should have seen yourself," Jarrod told her later, when they were alone, eating steak and lobster from to-go containers, sitting on his uncle's couch. "Coming out of that store like that, your pockets full of *cha-ching*." He sounded proud.

"It felt strange, seeing Mrs. Frisbee like that."

"I bet it felt good."

"She makes me want to sneeze."

"What did she say?"

"She said, 'Here's your change.'" Mallory lifted her arm and pretended to hand over three cents like they were the keys to the whole world.

He laughed. But the steak was tough and gristly and they dripped butter sauce on the upholstery. That night, lying alone in her own bedroom, Mallory couldn't escape the strange, smelly feeling she had from pretending that this was what she wanted because it was what she was told to want, when the truth was that it wasn't good for her. It wasn't good for any of them.

❄

They didn't go to the front door of the house; from the front, it didn't even look like anybody was home, except for the wreath wrapped in Christmas lights hung across the giant double doors. A driveway big enough for a semi and paved black wound around to the back. It was lined with cars from other people going to the party, and it was plowed, with not one speck of snow.

"Leave your coat and purse," Jarrod said.

"Why?"

"That way, you won't have to worry about it."

Mallory shrugged off her coat, pulling down her dress. She wanted to look nice and didn't question the decision to leave her coat. Her grandma used to leave her coat in the car all the time when they went to the shopping mall so that she didn't get too hot when they were inside. Jarrod lit a cigarette and left the truck, walking ahead. Trevor and his girlfriend went together around to the back of the house, but Jarrod walked in the other direction, away from it.

"Wait up!" She was already shivering, pulling her sleeves down over her hands and wobbling on legs spindly as a spotted deer. She wanted to hold on to him because her boots had heels, they were new, and she was still getting used to them. But the orange cinder flare of his cigarette bobbing in the dark only moved farther away.

❋

Jarrod's house burned down in a baleful rage on the hottest day of the summer. Jarrod was fourteen years old. Mallory and her sister were at Ashby Lake, sitting on the public dock with their scabby legs in murk-green water. Jarrod and Trevor rode past on bikes. They leaned forward, faces tense, and the *click-click* of their pedals in the static air sharpened against the knobs of her spine. The quality of light changed, her senses shifted into high gear, and she pulled her legs from the water and ran barefoot off the dock.

Feet slapping hot asphalt, she rounded the bend to confront a billowing stack of black smoke slicing into the blue marble of a summer sky.

Flames punched out the windows and blackened the front door. Only his mother cried. She stood across the street with arms outstretched, reaching for all she owned. People from the nearby houses held her shoulders, keeping her back. For a brief moment, seeing her like that, Mallory thought that Jarrod was trapped inside, the way she acted, shrieking and in a world all her own. But Jarrod stood there, behind her and off to one side. His face was expressionless, numb, his eyes glazed over, flat.

That small house was consumed by flames before the fire trucks even arrived. And when the fire was finally put out, all that remained were blackened beams in a circle of dead grass, the tree branches catching flakes of burned trash.

After that, his mother moved to another part of the state. Jarrod stayed with his father, living in the garage and sleeping on a cot in a cement-floored room heated with a woodstove. That winter, the winter Jarrod took her to the party, the heap of debris that had been his home still lay buried in the yard under layers of snow.

❄

"Is that the lake?" She finally caught up with him, standing by a rock wall. The wind blew back her carefully curled hair and the mineral scent of wet stone mingled with the smell of her hair spray and cheap perfume. The funneling rush of Lake Superior churned in the dark below. "Oh my god," she said, "look at the view."

A palatial vastness that was the largest body of freshwater in the country spread before them, a deep velvet hue. A single ore ship, with its lights burning, sat way out on the lake. It seemed not to move, both sinister and lost, and she watched its lights in the dark, feeling both nervous and displaced. Her home was two and a half hours away.

"Can we go inside now?" She shivered and danced in her boots, teeth clicking against each other in her mouth.

"What's your hurry?"

"I'm freezing."

Jarrod threw down his cigarette and turned away.

"Sorry," she said.

They headed away from the lake, toward the house, walking under a back deck that must have been recently built. It was so large and sweeping that they easily walked among the pillars. Mallory picked her way over rubble in her high-heeled boots. The ground underneath the deck was free of snow but uneven, mounded in hard frozen lumps. Jarrod in his flat shoes and warm clothes was several feet in front of her, blue lights strobing across his head as he neared the sliding glass door. A bassy dubstep thudded in the rubble beneath her feet.

Jarrod didn't look back when he got to the doors. Sliding them open, he slipped inside and left her standing out there, alone. Then he slid the door closed.

A plumb line dropped its weight from the top of her head down through her body—the dividing line, the moment when she knew she had done something wrong. No one in her family knew where she was; she'd lied about sleeping over at a friend's; she was freezing cold and standing alone under the back deck of a strange house more than a hundred miles from home. Why had she left her coat? It was annoyance with herself more than anything. She pressed her legs together, shivering, and thought, *Just leave.*

Later, much later, when she was older and able to look back with a clear eye on the time she had spent with Jarrod, that moment under the deck of that strange house—not even thirty seconds—would seem like a warning. The *ping* in her chest, the thought, *Just leave.* But she'd ignored it, brushed it off. Some part of her had known, but then, what could she have done? Walk out onto the highway, wave down a car, ask a total stranger for help? What if she saw someone she knew, or someone from the party? What if whoever found her wouldn't bring her home? She couldn't have done it, gone walking out on to that road alone.

❄

In the new year after the night of that party—the dividing line between the Mallory before and the Mallory after—she and Jarrod drifted apart, no longer friends. When Jarrod got suspended for missing too many days at school, when he got sent to juvie for beating up his dad in the parking lot of Bugsy's bar, she would hear about it secondhand. And she would remember how he had been suspended during elementary school. That memory clear as a bird singing in the rain, even during her fugue state. Blue letters. Graffiti on brick. I LOVE MY MOM.

His mom who went to orientation day with him, the two of them wearing concert tees in black. She had bought him, every year, a new hat. She always wore thick foundation caked over her pale skin. Mallory had always thought it was because his mom liked makeup, until the day she saw her at the grocery store. His mom, standing next to a store clerk, holding against her face a plastic bag filled with ice while behind it spread the dark tentacles of a bruise.

Mallory worked at that grocery store during the second year of her fugue state, her sophomore year, after she stopped playing basketball because of her grades.

Her junior year she heard that Jarrod was living with Trevor after being let out of juvie. Late one night in April she got a text: *See what I did for you.* She saw it on the news: he had set fire to the house belonging to Preston Rhodes. No one was home. But Jarrod had been the one to call 911. They found him outside—high on fentanyl-laced pot, it was later found—waiting for the fire trucks to come. He looked different in the mug shot posted online, the skin under his eyes paler than the rest of his skin, the color bluish chalk and rice paper thin. On his face was the same flat, defiant expression he had worn when he watched his own house burn.

The snow had melted; she could feel the approach of spring. She must have walked—her sneakers soaked and the grass matted brown. She approached the house where Jarrod had lived with Trevor and his grandmother, by the railroad tracks on the north end of town. Her face outside the lace-fringed windows, peeking in. No one home—at least, no boys. Maybe the grandmother was asleep, she thought.

She felt him, in the shadows of light and dark. How his body in its crushed flannel had moved across that soft filtered space between the table and the chair; his wooly brown puppy smell; the ache of his solitary ways; how he had looked at her across the dusty light of that kitchen, on just a regular afternoon, handing her a cooler with a timid, hopeful glance.

She had loved him, was the thing.

PART

FOUR

16

The male nurse in the ER referred to Mallory as "the good Samaritan" when she gave her name at Angel of Mercy on Tuesday morning. He led her down the corridor of a private ward behind locked doors and into a little room with chairs. He sat and opened his laptop, a laminated badge clipped to the pocket of his scrubs. She'd cultivated a corporate tough-girl look for the day, wearing her Speed Stop smock and an eye patch, holding the stuffed bear she'd bought for Shay. For sixty minutes she had driven in a rattling car through blowing snow, and now her foot pedaled rapidly on the balls of her toes.

"So, I'm Allan, an ER nurse with the psych consult service," he introduced himself. "We're basically a team of registered nurses and licensed social workers, and what we do is just get the story of what's going on." He had a very percussive mouth, almost dainty, the way he enunciated sounds. He seemed earnest and erudite and good at his job, but at the same time he didn't take himself too seriously. Mallory liked that he called it a "story." She gave the stuffed bear a light squeeze.

"Should we get started?" He typed as fast as she could speak, his fingers fluttering over the keys. He asked her questions about that night, referring to Shay as a vulnerable youth. He asked about guardianship—did Shay mention anything about family? Did she talk about her home life? Mallory told him what little she knew about the foster care situation and the brother in Bemidji. When he was done, Allan snapped the laptop closed and told her that she'd been a huge help.

"The police reports don't tell us crap," he said. "And sometimes it takes a while for a person in crisis to open up, so anytime we can get more information, we're super grateful." He stood and gestured toward the door.

"Can I see her now?" Mallory asked, holding the bear. She'd gotten the biggest one in the hospital gift shop—it was the size of a grocery store turkey.

"Oh," Allan seemed surprised. "I . . . don't know."

"Is she well enough? I mean, did she have a concussion?"

"I'm afraid I can't give out any medical information," he said. "HIPAA laws." He paused, shifting his laptop under his arm.

Mallory hugged the bear.

"But if you have time," Allan said, deciding something, "I can check in with her and see if she's up for a visit," he said. "Wait right here."

He ducked out of the room and Mallory the Good Samaritan waited. When she had first arrived, she'd parked on the street, clambering over the blackened mound of snow that was in the process of getting a fresh coat so that she could access the meter. She worried about the meter expiring and getting a ticket—a habit, she realized. She didn't care if she got a ticket; it would be worth it to see Shay.

There was an angel at the front entrance of the hospital, a statue set on a pedestal, inset in the wall. Looming and featureless, with a benevolent tilt to its head, it stood above a plaque that read, "Be ye at peace under the Angel of Mercy." She hadn't felt at peace when she passed beneath it, but she did remember Mrs. Champagne, the benevolent therapist who had given her a journal in eleventh grade. Mallory had been in trouble then. Her grades had fallen, she'd been kicked off the basketball team, and then gotten suspended for attacking another student in class. Her guidance counselor put in a request. That was the only reason Mallory had a therapist—her parents would never have been able to afford one otherwise. And it had been nice, having an adult in her life whose main focus was getting her to talk.

"Okay." Allan popped back in, moving quickly into the room. "Shay is awake and she's agreed to see you, so I think it's okay. Just follow me."

They moved back out into the corridor and went behind another set of double doors.

"Where are we?" Mallory asked. "Is this still the ER?"

"Shay's been cleared medically, so they moved her into our psych area, because there's always an issue with beds. We have an intern sitting outside because of her age, so we'll just have you keep the door open." He stopped outside a room with a young woman sitting out front. "She's right in here."

❋

Shay sat up in a bed, her dark hair mussed and spread out across the pillows. Her left arm sat outside of the blankets, wrapped in a hot-pink cast that ended several inches above her elbow, bent as if she were out on a jog. Where it cuffed her upper arm, she appeared thinner, more vulnerable. Restraint straps dangled from the edges of the bed.

"Hey." Mallory stood in the doorway of the small room. "Shay?"

The girl turned her head. For a moment it was as if she didn't recognize her; Shay's face was calcified, nonplussed. It was Tuesday, and they hadn't seen each other since the night of the blood moon.

"It's Mallory," she said. "I'm the one who found you."

"I know."

"Oh. I wasn't sure if you'd remember my name."

"They told me."

"Cool." The tiny pebble of Shay's voice had landed on her tongue, and Mallory had to get used to that again. "Thank you for seeing me. Mind if I come in?" There was no place to sit—the room bare, with not even a sink—but Allan briskly appeared with a chair. He also cleared away the remains of Shay's lunch, giving them both a nod as he whisked everything away.

"They let you order whatever you want," Shay said, seeing where Mallory's eyes went. It wasn't just that Shay had eaten everything; it was the smears on the plate as if wiped by fingers, and the cup of lime green Jell-O scraped clean. But if Shay cared about what she thought, that was encouraging.

"I'm glad you're feeling better," Mallory said. She took a seat and animated the stuffed bear, wagging its head as if it were nodding. Then, turning it toward her ear, she leaned in closer, as if the bear were speaking to her. "What's that?" Mallory asked the bear, like her dad used to do, holding imaginary conversations with their stuffed animals at night. Mallory nodded solemnly. "Oh, yeah." She turned to Shay. "Happy Bear hopes you're feeling better, too."

The bear nodded and clapped its stuffed paws.

The stony look Shay gave her reminded Mallory of her sister—mostly unimpressed and wholly embarrassed. Feeling like an idiot, Mallory put the bear on Shay's bed.

"At any rate, I got you this."

"Thanks."

"I didn't know what you would like." She wondered what she'd done with her gloves. "How are you feeling? Do you know when you'll get out of this place?"

Aside from the box bed, the only other thing in the room was a flat-screen TV mounted on the wall, its volume on low, screen protected under a shield of Plexiglas. Shay reached out and put a hand on the bear.

"It's so soft," she said.

"Yeah. That's why I picked it."

Mallory held herself erect in the chair, trying to make herself available for Shay, but the girl kept her face turned away. She still held herself in that regal way, a tiny, bright stud piercing one side of her nose. In profile, Mallory couldn't see the bruise on the other side of her head, but an abrasion spread out from under her chin, most likely from the fall out of the moving car. "So, how are things going for you?" Mallory asked. "Are they treating you okay?"

The show on the television was a nature program about a family of snow monkeys. Shay lifted her eyes to the screen, the thin black fronds of false eyelashes peeling slightly in one corner.

"I've been thinking about you," Mallory said after a moment. "You didn't deserve what happened to you. I want you to know that.

You did nothing wrong. And I'm proud of you for getting out of there and being so brave."

"Why you acting like that?" Shay said.

"Like what?"

"Like you know me."

"Sorry."

"You don't know shit about me."

Mallory shoved her hands into the pockets of her coat and tucked her feet under the chair. She tried to think how Mrs. Champagne had gotten her to talk when she was a teen. She'd been forced to meet with her during the in-school suspension. But by then two years had gone by. Two years during which she'd kept silent about what had happened to her on that night with Preston Rhodes. And then, when she did talk, she'd kept quiet about Jarrod's part in the whole thing. She had lied to protect him. A learned habit.

They watched the television while Shay mindlessly stroked the bear. A single white baboon moved alone through the trees. It slipped into a still pool, joining another monkey sitting in a hot spring.

"What's your favorite animal?" Mallory asked.

"A chicken."

"To eat?"

"No. I like chickens."

"What is there to like about a chicken?"

Shay looked at her.

"Sorry," Mallory said. "I don't get it."

"I like the way they move their head." Shay demonstrated by jerking her head in a chicken motion.

"Okay," Mallory laughed. "Now I get it."

"What's your favorite animal? A teddy bear?"

"No." Mallory sat up. "I like sea otters. They're super playful. Plus, they hold hands while they're swimming. "

"Figures."

"What?"

"You would be all sappy like that."

Someone from outside the room moaned. Mallory turned and saw two women in the hallway, one of them with wavy, tricolored hair. The daughter, presumably, holding the arm of the moaning woman she addressed as "Mom," moving slowly and with the grounded determination of a plow. The wide cuffs of her pants flopped as she shuffled patiently along, and Mallory couldn't hear the daughter's words, but the tone was kind. Their voices drifted away.

"I'm not a sap," Mallory said. "What's wrong with holding hands?" She still hadn't found her gloves. "Did you ever get ahold of your brother? The one in Bemidji?"

Shay swiveled her head. "You got a phone?"

"Yeah." Mallory lifted it from her back pocket. "It's fully charged."

"Can I have it?"

The directness of the question threw her. "You mean to make a call?"

"No," Shay said. "To find my brother. I just need it a few days."

"Oh, no, sorry." Mallory put her phone away. "I need my phone." She felt like she'd tripped on the stairs and couldn't figure out which foot to move next. Of course Shay didn't have a phone, and there wasn't a phone in this particular hospital room. "You understand," she said, overthinking it. She hadn't gotten her first phone until after high school, but kids these days expected it. Mallory felt bad. Maybe she should just give Shay her phone—what even *was* a phone? Just a hunk of metal. "It's just got all my pictures and contacts on it," she said, pushing her phone down into the back pocket of her work pants.

"You're gonna get butt cancer," Shay said.

"Maybe that will improve it," Mallory said. "Sorry, that was a terrible joke. Butt cancer is serious." Mallory fake-cleared her throat.

On the television, the program announcer talked about how clever the snow monkeys were. His voice made her drowsy. Mallory slouched against the chair. Maybe she should just leave. This wasn't going the way she thought it would.

"How did you know that?" Shay asked, her eyes still on the screen. "That stuff about where to pinch your nose?"

"Oh," Mallory sat up. "They just teach you that in basic. I served seven years. In the army."

"You went to boot camp?"

"Yeah."

"Did they yell at you?"

"Yes."

"I wouldn't like that."

"I didn't like it either," Mallory said. "But it toughened me up. I wasn't in the best shape when I joined. I was really afraid of having to run long distances and do push-ups and stuff. I wasn't that strong."

"That's cause you're a sap."

"Okay. Maybe I am."

Above them on the screen, snowflakes plunged into the water.

"Did you see the world?" Shay asked. "Like, Africa and shit?"

"I went to Kuwait."

"For real?"

"Yeah. It wasn't like what I thought it would be."

"What did you do?"

"When we first arrived, we were in the United Arab Emirates and during leave a bunch of us went to the shopping malls."

"They have malls?"

"It's the shopping capital of the world. We tried the camel milk—or, my friends did, I wasn't brave enough, I heard it was gross. But I did try the dates and figs. They were really good. And I have pictures of the tallest building in the world." She stole a glance and saw the girl was engaged, no longer watching the TV.

"In Kuwait we went to this topless beach. So many guys in speedos— and these were not attractive men—but it didn't matter because we were walking among all these people speaking in German, Russian, French, playing volleyball, sunbathing, and you think it will be awful going to the Middle East, but then you get there and you're in the middle of all this . . . this culturally rich amalgamation—" She stopped herself, looked at Shay. "Sorry, I'm talking too much."

"I don't care. What else did you do?"

Mallory told her how she worked as a mechanic, how she had long conversations with people from all over the world, debates about issues like abortion and women's rights while sitting together in the desert sand.

"The military did a lot to improve my body image," she said. "Before serving, I used to feel self-conscious all the time about my thighs, because they're so big. And then when I started running, I realized how strong they are, and I learned to appreciate them for their power."

"They're not that big," Shay said, appraising.

"Well, thank you."

"I don't think the military can help me with my nose." Shay put a hand to her face, cupping her nose. Her plastic ID bracelet bumped against the knob of her wrist bone.

"Why, what's wrong with your nose?"

"I'd be a ten if it weren't for my nose."

Mallory laughed, not expecting that. Shay smiled, showing her teeth.

That was when Allan came back into the room.

"Looks like we're having a good time." He held his laptop under his arm. "Just came in to check on you," he said to Shay. They had a nonverbal exchange that seemed private, so Mallory turned away. In her mind's eye, she saw again the small space between Shay's front teeth.

"Okay," Allan said. "I'm taking my lunch break now and Sara is right outside the room if you need anything."

"Oh," Mallory took out her phone, surprised it was lunchtime. She definitely had a parking ticket now. "I have to leave to go into work," she said. Was it just her imagination, or did Shay appear crestfallen? "But I can stay a little while longer," she added. It was only 1130.

"Okay," Allan said brightly. "I'll be back in twenty."

She was glad she'd worn her work clothes. She wouldn't have to drive all the way back to the cabin. It'd be a straight shot.

"He seems nice," Mallory said, filling the silence after the nurse left.

A family of snow monkeys was sitting together in the pool now in a perfectly uniform row. Only their heads and shoulders rose above the waterline, and the snow fell and steam rose in veils across their eyes.

"So I guess I feel this connection with you, Shay, because I had something like this happen to me when I was fifteen." Mallory lowered her eyes, tucked in her chin. "And I couldn't talk about it. It made me think less about myself for a long time, and I don't want that to happen to you." She glanced over at Shay. "You remember me mentioning my boyfriend, Jarrod, who brought me to a party?"

"Yeah," Shay said, eyes on the TV. The monkeys in the pool eerily watched the cameras that panned back and forth, the fur around their faces crusted with hoarfrost and gently fluttering in the wind.

"Yeah, well, he brought me to this guy's house and he told me to 'be nice' to the guy. So, I did. His name was Preston Rhodes. It was his house and his party."

"You went into his house?"

"Yeah. It was a really big house, but I never went upstairs."

"Why not?"

"The party was in the basement."

"Was it spooky?"

"No. It was clean and carpeted. It looked like a furniture warehouse, honestly, with random chairs still wrapped in plastic, sitting in these big, empty rooms. I didn't know the other kids. They sat in groups on the floor, with these shiny objects around them—mirrors, pipes, phones. Music blasted through the walls. It was so loud, we had to shout to be heard. Jarrod got me a drink and the alcohol hit and I started dancing with this girl."

She had forgotten about the girl.

"She had black and white–striped hair pulled up into two ponytails on the back of her head, with these black, thigh-high boots and eyeliner drawn around her eyes, all catlike and dramatic. And I thought she was the coolest, sexiest, most interesting woman I'd ever seen."

The edges of the room faded away and Mallory pressed her nails against her fingertips as she spoke.

"We were dancing, and it was like I dropped this weight I didn't even know I carried. The music so loud I couldn't hear the thoughts in my head, this blue strobe light flashing like it carried us all. And it felt like flying, you know? I felt free. And I thought how I could be anyone from anywhere and things at home didn't matter."

Her breathing became shallow, her fingers working compulsively, and she had the sensation that she was pressing a hard stick of butter into the bottom of a hot pan, the butter melting beneath her, sizzling, vibrating, a solid becoming liquid and steam. Any moment the butter would disappear and burn her hand. And yet she couldn't stop pressing.

"We were dancing," she'd never gone this far before, never said the words, "Preston and me and this girl. I was totally buzzed. And Jarrod looked at me and he gave me this nod that said, 'Go get him.' And in that moment, I knew what he was asking me to do, but I also *didn't* know, at the same time. I trusted him. I thought it was a party."

If the television was on, she couldn't hear it. If Shay was looking at her, she couldn't say.

"He fed me these pills, Preston did. He pushed them into my mouth with his fingers and thumb. He had this command, you know, from entitlement and wealth. I could smell the fabric of his new shirt and his expensive cologne and he had this easy way about him like he'd just stepped down off a private plane." Her face flushed. "I was lying on this bed, and it was so hot, I was just boiling in my head, and I saw this silver thing up on the wall in the corner of the room and I thought it was a sprinkler and I thought, god, I just wanted it to turn on."

She had become one giant talking head.

"He made a video of it. And then when I found out about it two years later and confronted Jarrod, he set fire to the guy's house."

"Pfft," Shay said, pushing air through her teeth.

"The police came to my house for questioning," Mallory said, an awareness of her surroundings creeping in. "They had found the video in his house, along with others—this guy had done it before, to other underage girls. My mom cried. She said, 'Why didn't you tell us you'd been raped?' And I felt shocked, hearing that word, because that wasn't how I had thought of it." Mallory felt self-conscious, but she was so far in, she just kept talking, pressing her fingernails, making indents on her skin. "I never told anyone, because I wanted to protect Jarrod. It was an instinct, you know? Rather than think less of him, I thought less of myself. I took responsibility for getting myself into that situation because it was easier to believe that about myself than to believe that about him."

From outside in the hallway voices intruded.

"All they have is cherry, Mom."

It was the daughter with the tricolored hair, coming back with her mom from the other direction. This time, Mallory could hear every word they said.

"I don't like cherry. Didn't they have grape?"

"No, Mom. If they'd had grape, I would have gotten you grape."

"I don't like cherry."

"I know. Should I throw it away?"

"No, no, it's all right. I guess cherry is okay."

The nature show ended. Credits rolled up the screen.

"I have to go." Mallory stood, feeling panicked and like she'd just undressed herself in a public space. "I shouldn't have told you all that." Heat flamed her face. "I can't find my gloves." Her feet tangled in the chair. "Sorry, I don't know what's wrong with me." Her gloves were lying on the floor. "I hope you feel better soon," she said. "See ya next time," she said.

17

Mallory strode out of the hospital with militant strides, barreling past doctors and nurses and passing through the sliding glass doors to the outside. Tears smeared down her face from the wind and the cold and she jaywalked out to her junk heap parked at its expired meter alongside the waist-high rubble of snow. Snatching the ticket out from under the wiper blade, she got in to start the car. It would have to warm up. Her nose ran, her eyes watered, the ends of her fingertips throbbed. The car coughed and the belt whined. It turned with a decrepit squeal, no matter what brand of belt she tried—and she'd tried them all, every kind, switching them out. And still it squealed.

Anger rose in her like a burning star.

She got out of the car and kicked at the tire turds caught by the wheel wells. Blocks of blackened ice dropped into the street. It was a mistake, to talk about all that for the first time in front of a vulnerable youth, a person in crisis, and in a psych ward for chrissakes. *What is wrong with you?* She had just wanted the girl to feel understood, to feel that she wasn't alone. It humiliated her that she got so emotional. She didn't know why. She didn't know why everything made her so angry. Sometimes it felt like she had always been angry, even before things with Jarrod went bad, like she'd been born this way. She'd never identified what, specifically, made her so mad. Anger so vast it obfuscated her. Anger occupying all the spaces in her skull until there was nothing left and no room to think. The only thing she could do was move her body to get it out.

She kicked and smashed until all the grimy ice blocks were obliterated. Another car went past, slushing up snow and ice. The cuffs of her work pants had soaked through, streaked with sand, and her hands were red and numb because she'd neglected to put on her gloves.

She was a little girl on a sidewalk with a chalk crayon, trying to make sense of things, and she didn't have the tools or the knowledge or the training.

When she'd worked with Mrs. Champagne, her therapist from high school, the woman always kept her voice the same. Nothing surprised her. Mrs. Champagne wore plastic-framed glasses on a beaded chain and didn't try to hide her age. When Mallory said she didn't want anyone's help, Mrs. Champagne took her glasses off and said, "Help isn't what you need, dear. What you need is mercy, and that is given unearned."

Mallory needed mercy because she had attacked another student in class. And she remembered Mrs. Champagne saying that, because she had never thought it *was* possible to receive anything unearned, let alone mercy. She'd been taught that to be deserving—of food, shelter, love—you had to earn it.

Maybe Shay believed the same thing. Maybe Shay didn't want anyone's help because she thought she didn't deserve it. Mallory could understand that. She got back in her car and drove the sixty minutes south toward Mire Lake.

❄

At the Speed Stop she parked in the back and walked in through the front to find the shelves picked clean and the aisles clogged with cartons and boxes. Asshole Craig hid in his office with the door half closed, doing who knows what—she honestly didn't want to know. The truck had come and made its delivery, but none of the back stock had been put out.

"Hey! Slappy Jake!" she barked at a coworker, a high school kid who played drums. They had two Jakes and someone—not her— had given him the nickname. "You guys get slammed this afternoon, or what? How come nobody did truck?" Alarm pulsed in his eyes before he shrugged and skittered away. In the reflection of a cooler glass door, she saw the image of herself in the eye patch, with her wet pants, her wispy red hair sticking out from under her hat. She looked deranged. It wasn't his fault that truck didn't get done; it was management. If Asshole Craig wasn't going to oversee it, then it was her responsibility as the guest service leader.

She went to her locker, hung up her coat, and tidied herself. She clocked in early at 0130 and tackled the job that should have been done, or at least started, before she arrived.

She'd always been different from other kids. When people asked what her favorite song was, her favorite movie, she honestly didn't know. She didn't think about those things. She didn't even get their jokes or laugh at what they found funny. Like in the movie *Ice Age*— why was it funny when the squirrel got hurt? When it got smashed and throttled until its eyes bulged? If someone accidentally bumped her in the hallway at school, she would shove them back ten times harder. If she detected the hint of a slight, even if the person only meant to tease, she'd return a cutting reply. She didn't mean to; it just came out of her.

She apologized to Slappy Jake and told him he could go home early.

For the next several hours she heaved and hauled and sorted and unloaded jars of spaghetti sauce, bags of rock salt. She pulled stuff out from the back shelves, checked expiration dates, rearranged, stacked, and shelved. The main responsibility of the day workers was doing truck, which meant rotating the stock from the back shelves to the front of the store so that when the truck came they had space for the new stock on the storage shelves. But it hadn't been done. The day workers must have been busy with customers, or Asshole Craig just didn't care. He'd been hired externally, not promoted from within. He'd gotten the job because he had known someone, or he'd graduated from a university that was well known. It was a safety hazard, having this many boxes in the aisles.

It was one of her teachers in elementary school who suggested sports. Mallory was restless, distracted. She had trouble sleeping and staying focused in class. She was short—she'd stopped growing for a few years when she was really young—and never particularly good at basketball, but the team played during winter, and her parents didn't have to buy a bunch of expensive gear, so they didn't object. She stayed after school so they didn't have to drive her back again, shooting hoops in the gym even though practice didn't start until six. The janitor must have felt sorry for her because she wasn't part of the after-school program, so he looked out for her. Standing out in the middle of all that empty space, launching the ball over and over and arcing it across the court, hearing the gentle *swish* of the net as the ball shot through—it gave her body something to do, and that soothed her.

"Mallory, I need you in my office." Asshole Craig's voice crackled over the headset into her ear. She startled and almost lost her balance on the ladder.

"I'm busy," she said, unmuting her mic. "Give me a minute." She was on the highest rung of a ladder with a box the size of a kid's coffin balanced on top, restocking sleeves of coffee cups on the highest storage room shelf.

"What are you doing?" he said.

"What?"

"What are you doing? I need you to come right away."

There were three other employees on duty that day, and they could all hear this exchange over their headsets. As guest service leader, she was the highest-ranking person on the floor, below Asshole Craig, and he had asked her, *"What are you doing?"*

"Are you coming, Mallory?" he said.

Jesus fucking Christ. She moved to climb down, the box shifted, she lunged a bit too aggressively, and a sleeve of coffee cups unloaded onto the floor, all two hundred and fifty cups spilling out in a brown and white cascade.

It was because she was a woman, because she was female and hadn't gone to college, Mallory thought. Asshole Craig wouldn't have asked Gavin, the other guest service leader who worked at that store and was studying at the U, what he was doing.

She kicked at the cups, clearing a space. Dropping to her knees and planking on her toes, she did a set of fifty wide-arm push-ups there on the floor.

Once, during middle school, in the heat of a basketball game, she'd accidentally elbowed another girl in the face while trying to reclaim the ball. It was a turning point; her team had regained momentum and scored. But the girl had been hurt. Mallory was benched on a foul. Nobody cared. Coach had clapped her hands. "I want to see more of that, Mallory," she had complimented her. "Let's get aggressive, girls!" After that, she was "Agro Girl."

"What is it?" Mallory stood in the doorway of the office and addressed Asshole Craig. Muscles cramped in her lower back, sweat lightly coated her skin, and when she rubbed a finger under her eye it came away smudged black.

Asshole Craig cooly looked up from his desk, with his bland, oily face, eyelids drooped and skin pink as canned tuna. "Oh, yeah, Mallory," he said, as if just remembering he'd called her in. "I need you to change out the main line of CO_2 for our soda fountain."

For a good fifteen seconds, she gave him the benefit of silence in which to amend his request. To change it to something that included a fire somewhere, or his gangrenous foot, to explain the urgency, the haste, why he had called her in "right away" via headset in front of the entire crew, undermining her and calling her instead of just doing it himself.

"Did you hear me?" he said.

"Is that it?"

"Is *what* it?"

"Is that the thing you needed me to do so urgently?"

He looked at her with the distracted concern northerners get when they suspect a wood tick might be crawling in their pants. "Well yeah," he said. "The soda is out. We need to change it for our guests. Right now, please."

Maybe it was about her home life, Mallory thought, kicking a path back through the spilled cups to the shelf with the CO_2 canisters. She humped one out to the floor, pried open the soda fountain, yanked out the old tank. She had been surprised when that came up with Shay. She'd had the realization in the hospital room that part of what had made that party so attractive had been this unconscious need to free herself from that weight—a weight she didn't even know she carried. She hauled and hefted and unloaded and re-stocked. It wasn't possible to talk about her family with Mrs. Champagne. Keeping the secret had been ingrained—it wasn't anybody's business, what went on at home. "Have you ever been tested for ADHD?" Mrs. Champagne had asked. Mallory's leg always pumping up and down, restless with the energy of all the things she could not say.

She kept her head down and stayed late to finish the unloading job, but the computer terminal punched her out with an automatic time stamp, despite the fact that she'd come in half an hour early and stayed a full hour late to take care of the back stock that should have already been done. The system didn't pay her for even one minute of overtime.

Meanwhile, as store manager, Asshole Craig—who did get paid overtime and could work as many hours as he wanted, and get paid for them—arrived and departed exactly on time.

❄

Moonlight spilled through the kitchen window. All the lights were off; no television. And no electricity—the lights, when she flipped the switches, didn't work. The high that day hadn't gotten above zero and the batteries had totally drained. On the stove and across the counter sat dirty pans and plates and cups and bowls stacked in dripping piles. No dinner. No dishes washed. But there was a note: *Shovel the roof.*

Back outside on the deck, she pulled at the cord of the generator, but it wouldn't start. Dragging the engine through the back door and into the kitchen, she left it on a towel to warm up and strapped on a headlamp. Maneuvering around the Baily memorabilia scattered around the living room—a photo album with puppy pictures, a giant trifold poster board, scissors, glue, doggie-paw stickers—she went into the bathroom and peed in the dark. The memorial for Baily was tomorrow afternoon—today, really, since it was almost midnight. It didn't seem real that Baily was gone. Mallory would forget, and then it would hit her again with a pang. She felt the absence of movement and sound in the cabin; no more clacking claws or jingling collar. No more greeting from someone who was always happy to see you no matter what kind of day you'd had. She washed her hands in the dark and whispered, "I'm so sorry, Baily Bales. I miss you."

In the bedroom she took off her eye patch and dug through her duffel bag, looking for snow pants. She couldn't find them—she had to take out every single item, they were all the way on the bottom, and she was so sick of digging through her duffel bag every time she needed clothes. At least she didn't have to be quiet. Andrea had gone to Ripley's, again.

In the dark of the living room the propane stove on its battery-powered, automatic timer flickered on, casting out heat with a wavering orange light. Mallory repacked and folded her clothes. When she was done, she laced up her boots, put on her gloves, and schlepped the generator back out to the deck. She pulled out the throttle, flipped on the switch, and yanked at the ripcord until the engine caught. Adjusting the throttle again, she flipped on the eco switch and plugged the cable into the charging bank. Around to the back of the house, she carried a shovel and an aluminum ladder through thigh-deep snow and climbed like the Michelin Man up and onto the roof.

Andrea was right. Mallory didn't have a clue about how to help Shay. She wasn't trained like Mrs. Champagne, a therapist with a voice that felt like her name—tiny bubbles breaking out across your skin. Mrs. Champagne, who listened while wearing her glasses printed with flowers like antique wallpaper, rocking them side to side when she maneuvered them onto her face. When she talked, she never looked at you with shock or disappointment or disgust. She never made you feel like you were *less than* because of what happened to you or how you responded or anything you thought or did.

"The survivor uses her skills to maintain equilibrium." Mrs. Champagne had said. "She learns how to endure, and that can make her look crazy to other people who are in normal environments. It can make her seem like she's gone mad."

Mallory had never thought of herself as a survivor before. She had, on several occasions, thought she was going mad. Once, in third grade, when her teacher had gotten called out, Mallory had stood and moved her desk to the far side of the room. She didn't know why she did it; she couldn't have explained her reason, just that she needed space. The teacher was gone a full ten minutes, and during that time Mallory kept moving things—chairs, bookshelves, even the teacher's desk. Eventually some of her classmates joined in; they thought it scandalous fun, piling all the furniture onto one side of the room.

On the roof, Mallory waded through a blanket of three-foot-deep snow, glossed lavender in the moonlight. The snow was totally unmarked, and she didn't know where to begin. It was so deep she could hardly lift her legs up out of it to drag herself through, making a path. She couldn't just shove the snow off the edge; the layers were thick and fastened with ice. So she cut through in slabs, shaving off the top layers and throwing shovelfuls off the roof. Her boots thudded hollowly as she moved.

Above her, the sky opened up in a rasher of stars.

❄

On the day she found out about the video, she was in the girl's bathroom. Someone showed it to her on their phone. "Is that you?" Two years had passed since the night of that party, and that's when it hit her: it had been a camera, not a sprinkler, in the corner of that basement room.

How Mallory got to her next class, she didn't know, but a dry-erase marker squeaked at the front of the room and someone next to her dropped a pencil. The boy bent to pick it up, leaned over, and showed his friend something playing on his phone. Smartphones were taking over the school; all the popular kids had them. It was the knowing smirk that slid across his face—

Mallory lunged and flipped over his desk, a red-hot fury burning in her chest.

❄

"What is wrong with you?" She was in the truck riding home, next to her dad—he'd been the one to pick her up. "Are you high? Are you on drugs?" He'd just gotten back from being deployed, his profile aquiline and the veins standing out in purple noodles along his arms. "What goes on in this house when I'm not around?" He folded his tongue between his teeth like a stick of chewing gum, his eyes wet steel as they watched the road.

Her parents started fighting the minute they got in the door. Her dad blamed her mom for the fact that Mallory had gotten suspended. He always blamed Mom, the receptacle that held his pain.

Mallory sat on her bed, tasting the imaginary scent of french fries and fresh lemons squeezed just under her eyes. Her legs trundled up and down. Laurel was away that week on a school trip to Chicago for her AP bio class, visiting museums and drinking bubble tea while Mallory sat on her hands and pedaled her knees. It was too much, listening to it. She was older now, she was seventeen.

Mallory strode into the living room and yanked out the cord of the freestanding lamp, picking it up, and swinging it around like a giant brass bat. "Stop it," she said, climbing onto the couch, standing on the cushions. "Just stop this right now!" She screamed at her dad and swung the lamp with all her fury. She hated him and everything he said, and they shouted at each other, circling through the room.

Mallory didn't remember how it happened or what she'd said, but somehow they ended up with their faces inches apart on either side of a window, the square panes on the back door. She was outside, he was in, still screaming at her, when a fist shot through the glass. Her fist. She didn't hit him, but she broke the glass, and the shock of it woke them both, the surprise arresting their faces. That's what she remembered most. In that elastic pocket of time, the two of them red-faced and heaving, silent, frozen, petrified in their recognition of each other in that same place at that same time on that night.

※

The roof had a clear patch now, the tar paper grit streaked with ice and powdered snow. Mallory had carved out a place where she could move. Around her, the snow was stacked like a wedding cake in layers that sparkled as she cut and served. She carried shovelfuls to the edge and heaved, one knee bent, both arms cocked, anchoring a leg so that she wouldn't fall off as she threw load after load over the side.

All her life she carried this weight, the burden, the responsibility of knowing what was going on at home and never being able to stop it. And maybe she should just surrender to her anger. Maybe there was no breaking the cycle. Maye a family was just like those flakes of snow with all their matching arms. She'd grown up this way, like a dendrite, matching exactly her parents' design.

It was funny, the way things that were important to your parents somehow became important to you, even if you didn't want them to be. Like the way she always reached for the cherry flavor—jam, Popsicles, candy—without even thinking, because it had always been her mom's favorite. How she picked the cooked peppers off her pizza. And she never took the first item of anything off the shelf— cereal, crackers, coffee. She always reached to the back for the one behind it, because that way, her dad said, you got the better one.

There were good things, too. It wasn't all bad. She'd learned discipline and perseverance, how to see a job through. She could stay up there all night, shoveling the roof.

❄

It must have been cold on that day when she broke the window, but she didn't go back for a coat. The spring thaw hadn't quite melted off all the snow and she had walked for miles through the woods that evening, eyes seeing nothing, the sun going down. She held her hand—it throbbed like it was on fire. The woods had gotten darker, but ahead of her a white gleaming shone through the trees.

A rising moon sat low over the lake. Ashby Lake, it must have been, the one that Milo Arden's house looked out over. The lake where Milo water-skied and Jet-Skied and swam from the dock jutting off the back of his three-story house—the house where his family picnicked and played, right across the street from where Jarrod had lived in a garage.

Mallory stood holding her fist. The lake that night had fully thawed, lit by a nearly full moon. The sight of all that open space stilled her as she breathed. Nose running, eyes streaming, she wiped her face on her sweater sleeves. She was seventeen, and this jumbled mass of confusion had landed inside of her too big to hold, and she did not know where to put it. All the times she had gone fishing with her dad—he had taught her how to hook a worm. All the summers swimming with her sister—splashing their mom at the lake. And she could never be that girl again. She could not imagine living in a world where she and that video existed at the same time.

Someone laughed. There was the *clink* of a glass bottle and a welter of voices as firelight crackled through the trees. A cry escaped from her throat. They were so near—how had she not heard them? A group of kids, gathered at a bonfire by the lake.

"Who is that?" a boy from the woods to her right called out.

Her shoes scraped back against the snow.

"Who's there?" The boy adjusted his pants; he'd gone off from the others to pee.

"Mallory?" another voice said. "Is that you?"

She turned quickly to leave, his voice giving her *the feeling* even as she ran, his presence by the firelight unmistakable at the edge of the woods.

"Mallory!" Jarrod called again. "Hey, wait up!"

She hurried, her sneakers slipping in the slush.

"Mallory!"

"Go away! I don't want to see you." It was darker going into the woods without the moonlight shining through.

"We need to talk!"

"No, we don't. I don't want to see you."

She was running and crying and protecting her hand. And then, like an idiot girl in every idiot movie, she tripped and fell. Her shin rammed into a log under the snow and the ground slammed up hard into her chest, her chin scraping against the slush. She held her shin and rolled over on the ground, blind with pain.

Jarrod kept the others away, their voices coming out from behind him, through the trees. He told them all to go away, to stay back, and they did.

"Mallory?" The feel of his voice on her skin as he leaned over and crouched down . . . They hadn't been this close to each other in eighteen months. "You all right?" The gentlest stroke of a kitten's tongue tingled across her cheeks. "What are you doing out here? Are you hurt?" He had been the only one who had stayed with her out on the playground that day when the frog had died. And it was never about a frog or a deer or anything else that might get hurt. It was only ever about her mom. Always it was about her mom.

"Go away." She lay curled up on the snow. "I can't talk about it." All the nights she had been certain that he was breaking her. All those years of hearing the thud of her mother's body slammed against the wall. She'd thought that he was killing her. And Mallory had stayed in bed.

Jarrod put a hand on her arm.

"Don't touch me," she jerked away. "Just go." She rolled onto her knees, brushing off chunks of wet snow.

"I heard about what happened at school," he said. "About the video. Everyone's talking about it." He was sloppy with his words; she could smell the beer on him and knew the only reason he was out here with her was because he was drunk.

She stood to face him, the sight of him—he'd changed. He was a man now, no longer a boy. He'd gotten bigger around his shoulders and arms, and he had a new way of holding his mouth, as if he held hot liquid in his cheeks, his lips pinched. It gave a look of permanent hostility to his face.

"I didn't know," he said. There was the smell of diesel oil and dry leaves in the folds of his sweatshirt with its fleece-lined hood. "I swear to you, Mal. I had no idea about the video." He still didn't wear a coat. She had always worried about his lack of a coat.

"I don't believe you," she said. "You're lying."

"It's true. I didn't know."

"Why don't you tell me what else you didn't know." She felt stronger than him now, strong because of all the weight she carried. She had changed, too. She'd become a woman.

❊

Mallory stabbed at the dense layers of snow and ice and carved off a block, digging hard with the shovel, breaking out pieces heavy as lead. It was connected, somehow, what Jarrod did and why she allowed it and how much she had wanted approval from her dad.

Her dad on the other side of that window glass when she'd almost punched him—her memory of his face filled with horror that over time had changed. At first, what she saw was his disappointment in her—she'd broken the window. It would be expensive to repair. Then she saw disappoint in himself—this was the daughter he had raised. She'd copied his design. But now, when she replayed the moment in her mind, she saw that he'd been surprised because, for the first time in her life, she hadn't done as she was told. When he said, 'Sit on your hands,' she sat on her hands. When he told her to stay in bed, she stayed in the bed. When he told her that she was making a big deal about nothing, that it wasn't that bad, or when he said it was her mother's fault that he behaved this way, that it was she who *made him* do these things, Mallory believed him and blamed her mom.

When she was young, Mallory had tried to help her mom. She had done as many things as possible so that Mom wouldn't get into trouble. For many years she did this, her daily routine: check the milk in the fridge, unscrew the cap, smell to make sure it hadn't gone sour; sort through the recycling to make sure nothing got put in there by mistake; make sure all the leftovers were properly stowed in the fridge, nothing left in the oven, no onion skins on the floor; make sure the beds were made; fix the towels in the bathroom so they don't look bunched. Every motion, every thought, her entire being bent toward the directive "Don't let Mom get hurt."

Then, when she became a teenager, she started to resent doing these things. It didn't seem to make any difference. Mom still got hurt. The fighting always came. The crying and the thumping were always the same.

Mom had stopped trying. It seemed like she didn't even care about getting it right, like she was trying on purpose to get it wrong. At some point, Mallory began to hate her. She saw her mom as weak and powerless, as someone who couldn't keep Dad happy. And so she hated her mom for ruining their family and turning her dad, whom she loved, into a monster.

And then Mallory hated herself for hating her mom, whom she also loved.

And Mallory became the monster.

18

Late day sunlight found her face-planted in the couch cushions at 1600 on Wednesday afternoon. When the back kitchen door popped open, Mallory shot up, startled awake. She still wore her Speed Stop smock and baggy work pants.

"What happened to you?" Andrea pulled off her hat. Her hair stood lopsidedly in short-bristled chunks, her cheeks were pinked, eyes a shade of liquid smoke. It was the first time they'd spoken since the night Baily died.

Mallory massaged her mandible with her fingertips until the tension in her jaw released and she could open her mouth to speak. "What day is it?" She'd had a few too many beers after shoveling the roof and could just imagine how she must look with her blood-filled eye and her skin creased with pattern lines from the couch. She wiggled her jaw, shuttling it forward and sideways as it clicked, working the tension out.

"I'm leaving for Baily's memorial service in one hour," Andrea said and disappeared into the bathroom. She closed the door. Outside the window a cyan sky stood quietly behind the trees. The rime ice had melted, all the crystals gone.

It was understood, ever since their fight, that Mallory was no longer welcome in Andrea's bed. It was an unspoken agreement that the bedroom belonged to Andrea even if she wasn't there to sleep in it. If Mallory didn't like being on the couch, she could just move out early.

"I was up late running the generator and shoveling the roof," Mallory explained, raising her voice so it would carry through the closed door. She moved aside the beer bottles and picked out the popcorn bits from her shirt and hair. A headache wrapped itself around her skull like an iron scarf. She didn't know why Andrea was taking so long in the bathroom—she could smell herself and needed to shower. She had wanted to visit Shay again before the memorial service, had been planning to get up early so that she didn't have to deal with Andrea until they were in a public place.

"Mimi fell into the dumpster again," Andrea said, opening the bathroom door. "Or, more accurately, she lost her can." Andrea turned on the TV to a news station then went back into the bathroom to preen in the mirror.

"Who's Mimi?"

"She's the eighty-year-old custodian we hired after Meller retired."

"At the lab?"

"Yeah, this tiny old woman with a dustpan and mop, but she said she wanted the job. She keeps tossing the garbage can in the dumpster because she's so slight it weighs more than she does, and so every time she loses her grip and in it goes. 'Oh Andrea,' she says, coming to get me, 'I dropped the can in there again.'" Andrea's voice when it mimicked Mimi shivered high and deliciously in Mallory's cheeks. On the news came a story about a man who shot a school bus driver on Interstate 35W.

"Can we change the channel, please?"

The man who shot the bus driver said that he had "overreacted" when the bus almost grazed his car.

"If you want to change the channel, do it yourself."

Mallory got up from the couch and changed the channel to a nature show about birds and then padded cautiously into the kitchen to make coffee.

"Clean that out with vinegar first," Andrea said.

"What?"

"The coffeemaker." Andrea was in the living room now, folding up Baily's sweater, and she came into the kitchen to get the leash. "You have to run it through with half vinegar, half water, once every six months."

"You want me to do that now?"

"Well, I'm not going to do it." She traipsed back out to the living room.

The nature show on the television was about cowbirds. Of course it was. Mallory lugged out the gallon vinegar jug. When she'd first moved in, Andrea had asked her to scrub the shower grout with vinegar, using a tiny little brush. And Mallory had done it—she'd wanted to contribute, to do her part. But now she wondered if maybe it was about something else.

"So, if I'm a cowbird," she said now, measuring out the vinegar, "what kind of bird are you?" These were the kinds of questions they had asked each other when they first started dating: *If you were a pizza topping, what would you be?* Andrea had said the controversial pineapple. They'd made pizza together with gluten-free dough, making a mess in the kitchen, the two of them air guitaring to Brandi Carlile's "The Story."

"Funny you should ask," Andrea said from the living room. "Ripley last night said that I reminded her of a Bohemian waxwing. At first I was flattered. I thought she was going to say, because of their grace and beauty." She gave a self-deprecating laugh. "They are stunning birds, a kind of dusky lavender—my kind of colors."

"What did she say?" Mallory asked.

"That they lack a true song.'"

Mallory switched on the coffeemaker, filled not with ground beans but with vinegar, encouraged that they were at least talking. The nature show on the television was soothing with its cheeps and wing flutters. "Why would she say that? You're a musician. You play saxophone."

"Yeah, I only played it because of my mom. She hated the sound of it, thought it loud and crass. That, more than anything, motivated me to practice. I got good out of pure spite."

It got quiet in the living room. Andrea packed up the Baily trifold display while Mallory plugged the sink and washed the dishes. On the television the commentator explained how in this one rain forest in Peru, biologists were perplexed to discover that mother birds left their nests intentionally, allowing cowbirds to deposit an egg, and then raising it with their other hatchlings. Later it was discovered that a parasite called the botfly had invaded these nests and used the baby birds for food by drilling holes into their stomachs. But the young cowbirds had a special ability to defeat the botfly, so by welcoming the cowbird hatchling, the mother was able to save her brood.

"I saw a cop car out patrolling on Riley Ridge Road," Andrea said. "You never see police cars out here. They must be investigating the cabin where you found that girl."

"Her name is Shay."

"You ever follow up with that?"

"Yeah. I went to go visit her."

"How was that?"

Mallory rinsed off the frying pan and laid it on the drainboard to dry. "It was okay." On the counter the coffeemaker gurgled. She thought about her mom, who started each day with a fistful of Advil for her constant headaches and recurring nosebleeds. Her mom who cried at night like a kitten getting slammed in a door, but never had obvious injuries, nothing that would impress a judge. "It's not that bad," her mother always said. And Mallory didn't have any way of knowing if this was true. The kitchen filled with the odor of acid.

"I don't know why this thing with Shay is affecting me so much," she said. "I can't stop thinking about Jarrod and my mom and my dad." She didn't know why she was saying this to Andrea. She transferred more dirty dishes into the sink. "I don't know what's going on. It's not like anything happened to me."

"But it did happen to you," Andrea said. "You were her witness."

❋

They drove in separate cars. The road in front of Mallory was white from the salt. *You were her witness.* That was the thing about

Andrea—she could be controlling and narcissistic, but she always listened and knew what to say.

Mallory found her in the hallway of the chapel, a place that did cremations for both humans and pets, setting up the memorial display.

"Andrea." Their call to presence.

"Mallory."

"I'm very sorry I broke your phone."

"Yeah, well, I got a new one with twice the storage space." A giant cream vase stood on the table between them, drooping with flower sprays. A murmur of voices came from a back-office room, followed by the soft tap of a closing door.

"I can help," Mallory said.

"I'm not going to stop you."

"Give me a job."

Andrea handed her a bag of dog biscuits.

Mallory opened them like they were potato chips at a party and filled a bowl, a parting gift from Baily for people who had dogs.

The memorial service lasted thirty minutes. It was a slideshow with puppy pictures and sappy music, followed by an opportunity for people to get up and speak. Afterwards, an employee from the chapel handed Andrea a gift bag covered in pawprints. It contained a certification of cremation, a copy of the poem "Rainbow Bridge," and a velvet drawstring bag with Baily's ashes. Andrea held the drawstring bag, palming its weight, while Ripley stood beside her, rubbing her back.

"Hey, so, I'm taking off." Mallory approached, and once again they stood by the giant flower vase. Ripley peeled off and went to talk with a group of women several feet away.

"Okay." Andrea busied herself packing up the Baily display. "Thank you for coming. And thank you for shoveling the roof."

"Oh, I didn't finish."

"Last guy I hired said it took a few days."

"I'll have it finished tomorrow."

"Just have it done before I leave."

"Leave?"

"I'm going to Mindo for two weeks." Andrea set down the trifold display. "We leave Saturday. I'm going with Ripley."

Behind her in the hallway laughter heckled out from the group of women who stood talking with Ripley. Mallory felt the *whomp-whomp*ing of her beleaguered heart. She had been feeling good, oddly vindicated by the discovery that cowbirds had a superpower. But now she felt jilted, which made no sense, with no idea where Mindo was, and she didn't want to be at the cabin alone.

"But you just had all that time off."

"I know." Andrea laughed and hefted the cloth shopping bag. "We bought the tickets a year ago—we got this really great deal. The best time to go is now, during the rainy season, when all the birds have migrated. We're staying at an Airbnb, in a cloud forest."

"A cloud forest?"

"It's a rain forest in the mountains—I thought you would love it. I was going to surprise you, buy Ripley's ticket from her, get you the time off from work. But now, given everything that's happened, I think it's best if I just go alone."

"But you're not going alone," Mallory felt the need to point out. "You're going with Ripley."

"So you're free to dote on Landon James."

"I don't understand how you can still think that what happened had anything to do with him."

"If it's not true, then it shouldn't bother you."

Ripley arrived. "You need help with anything?" Her voice chirped emetically. Ripley wore cargo pants and hiking boots and didn't do anything weird with her hair. It fell in softly brushed pleats around her plain, unadorned face. "Hello." She probably ate a wholesome breakfast that included fresh fruit. "You must be Mallory." Her eyes were bright and birdlike, noticing everything: Mallory's eye patch, her faded work pants half-tucked into battered boots.

"Fine." Mallory's face vibrated. "I'll get serious about looking for an apartment while you're gone."

"We're surprised you haven't already."

We're surprised? "It's only been three days."

"Better get busy, then." Andrea looked adoringly at Ripley. "Ready, babe?"

Ready, *babe*? They locked elbows, the two of them hip-checking each other as they jostled cozily down the hall, leaving Mallory alone in the lobby of the crematorium.

t's disgusting," she said to Noah that night at work. "It makes me want to barf." During the bewitching hours she told him about the breakup while leaving out a few key parts, namely the part where she ate food that had been touching a dead mouse. "It was just a big show of remorse. A pet memorial. Who even does that?" She felt raw and nauseous from her hangover, and embarrassingly, she was reeling from the fact that Andrea was with Ripley. She thought she'd wanted it to end, thought it would feel good to get out of this relationship, but it had given her at least some semblance of security. Andrea was the most stable thing in her life. "She can't be that broken up about it or she wouldn't be going off to Minot or whatever to go bird-watching with her girlfriend in a cloud fucking forest. I mean, seriously? She's mad at me for wanting to go to a bonfire with our neighbor? She still blames me. She still thinks I ran over her dog."

"Mindo," Noah's said, his voice coming in over the headset. "It's in Ecuador. Best bird-watching in the world."

"Of course it's in Ecuador."

"You don't want her to go?" He restocked the condiments for the breakfast sandwiches in the Hot Spot on the other side of the aisle while she tended to the coffee urns.

"No, because why should I care?" She drained out the old brew, dumped out the used pods, popped in the fresh ones, wiped down the machines, and did *not* run them through with fucking vinegar.

"Wait," Noah said. "I don't understand. You want her to stay with you?"

"I want her to go to hell." She would never drink Andrea's coffee again; she would just buy it from the Speed Stop when she came in. With all the coffeemakers going full tilt, a metallic hum filled the air, and if an angel was trying to get through to her, she did not want to hear it tonight. "It's just so fucking pathetic, the way she's carrying on." From the cupboards under the urns she pulled out the boxes of artificial sweeteners. "As if her mother had died. As if she was the one who walked Baily twice a day around the lake."

"Maybe she feels bad," Noah said.

"She'd better feel bad."

"Why does that make you mad? What else do you want her to do?"

"I want her to take responsibility for being manipulative and cruel. It's her fault I was out there in the first place. If she hadn't been acting like such a jealous freak, Baily would still be alive." It upset her that Noah didn't get it. She'd been waiting all day to talk to him, the one person who she thought understood her and would be on her side. She felt betrayed. They were speaking over headsets even though Noah was a few feet away. "And now she's going to Ecuador? Fucking Ecuador to bird-watch in a fucking cloud forest? I mean, what does all this even mean?"

The top of his acorn head disappeared through the kitchen door.

"Never mind!" she shouted to the back of his head, her voice also reverberating through the headset. "Just forget it. You don't understand." She inhaled, and the air like a bellows fanned the flames. "Fucking no one understands." She kicked the box of sweeteners to the end of the row to restock the station over there.

"That's not true, Mallory," his voice clicked back over the headset. "I'll be the first to admit when I don't understand something, because there's a lot of things I don't understand—I have to ask people all the time to explain what they mean. But I understand regret."

"What are you talking about?"

"Maybe Andrea wishes *she* was the last person to walk her dog."

The ringing had started, filling her entire head, a metallic hum at the same pitch as the brewing coffeepots.

"We don't all get the opportunity," Noah said, "to say good-bye to someone we love."

"What the fuck are you talking about?" She had stuffed the Cambros with Splenda and Equal, her fists now full of Sweet'n Low.

"You want me to feel bad for being the last person to walk Andrea's dog? You really don't get it, do you. This isn't about Andrea saying good-bye, it's about her trying to punish me. What she did was pure evil."

"I don't think Andrea is pure evil."

"You don't know her."

"I knew her before you did. She's the Muffin Monday Lady—"

"Oh my god so now you're an Andrea expert."

"No, I'm not saying that—"

"Of course not. Jesus freaking Christ, Noah, you don't fucking live with her."

"Yes, that's true. But I'm just saying, if you can hear me out, that it's hard to forgive yourself—"

"She should *not* forgive herself!" Heat popped to the top of her head as she burst through the swinging door. Noah swiveled his head. He stood across the kitchen by the ovens; she stood in the dish area by a stack of containers.

"You seem really mad."

"Why are you defending her? Baily is dead, Noah. She's *dead* and it's her fault! It's her fucking fault!"

"Okay."

"Not mine."

"Mallory, I think you need to relax."

"Do not fucking tell me to relax!"

It happened before she could think, before she even knew what she was doing—her hand shot out and threw one of the containers across the room. She aimed straight for his head. The Cambro smacked against the wall with a loud crack, missing him by an inch. It bounced and jackknifed across the stainless steel counter before sliding to the floor. The sound of it snapped her awake. Her eyes raised to his with the full shock of awareness—she had almost hit him in the head.

Noah's skin quivered like a poached egg. He looked at her from across the room and she felt the hurt emanating from him in waves. She could have seriously injured him. She'd wanted to. The Cambro lay cracked at his feet.

He waited for her to say something, to apologize like any decent person would. But she couldn't. It wasn't because she didn't feel bad, it wasn't because she would never, ever want to hurt him or anybody—she loved Noah, he was her best friend. It was because her whole life, every minute of her every day, every goddamned second, she was haunted by the feeling that she hadn't done enough, that things would never turn out right. All her life she'd carried this weight, this responsibility of constantly trying but being unable to make things right.

A timer went off for one of the ovens in the kitchen.

Noah picked up the tongs and took out a tray.

Mallory left. She went back out to the coffee station, and she and Noah did not speak to each other again for the rest of the night.

※

Long shots were her specialty. Mallory was short, but she had an 82 percent free throw rate. She practiced for hours after school. In the final moments of the game, if their team was down or the score was tied, they would pass her the ball. She'd crouch like a coiled spring and release the impossible from outside the three-point line. The moment she lived for, the moment they all held themselves suspended in this nugget of time, a three-second rush after the buzzer sounded and the ball soared past a hushed crowd with their eyes raised. They followed the trail of her ball like the arc of a comet as it scorched through the air, and when it swished through the net, the gym went wild.

Her balls always went in. And yet the Cambro hadn't hit Noah's head. She'd wanted to hit him but then hadn't hit him. Was that a line she wouldn't cross? Had some part of her at the last possible second moved her arm? Had she wrestled with her anger—and won?

She'd been proud of her decision to join the army—of all the things she could have done once Jarrod was sentenced for arson and Preston was charged. The original video had been taken down, but the digital copies would always remain. She'd had to learn how to live with that, knowing they were out there. Knowing that Preston was also at large, because there was no mandatory minimum, and his lawyer had gotten him a variance, so the five-year sentence was reduced to a handful of months. The army gave her an outlet for her rage. She'd passed a rigorous screening and extensive moral character review, got her medical exam, took her placement test, graduated her senior year, and left.

She thought leaving was how she would spare them, her sister and her mom. She thought it right not to remind them of what had happened, thought she was protecting them, showing them that she was strong.

Laurel was only thirteen that summer. And that's when Mom finally took care of herself and got Laurel out of that house. That's when she finally decided—after eighteen years of abuse—to go somewhere else.

They came to visit her three years later, when Mallory had received orders to ship out to Kuwait. Laurel and her mom, driving a rental, using coupon deals for cheap hotels and subsisting on free breakfasts and a cooler they packed with sandwiches and fruit. They'd arrived on base in Fort Worth, Texas, for family visiting day, knocking on her door on a Saturday in the a.m.

Mallory had answered in uniform, wearing a stiff pair of canvas fatigues and combat boots, hair bobby-pinned to the sides of her face.

"Oh, you're a soldier now," her mother had cried, squeezing and petting her arm. "I'm still not used to it." By then, Mallory had trained as a mechanic, graduating at the top of her class with a coin and a handshake; she'd attended lectures and classes, watched PowerPoints about terrorists and weapons of mass destruction. "It's so clean," her mother said, looking around the room. She looked even shorter because Mallory wore boots. Her mother in sandals and a new summer blouse—new for her—with ruffles instead of sleeves, blue jeans faded at the knees.

"I like your apartment." Laurel shouldered a purse the size of a Frisbee and waltzed right in. The dorm looked like an apartment building from outside. Mallory's room was a studio with a twin bed and a desk with a chair, connected to a bathroom she shared with a roommate on the other side of the wall. "Can I sit on your bed?"

"Sure, go ahead," Mallory said. "Make yourself at home."

Laurel gave Mallory's regulation-made bed a bounce, patting it with her hand. She'd filled out during the last three years, her body was a woman's now, and it was strange to see her little sister with hips and breasts.

"I like your hair," Mallory said.

Laurel smiled, cupping a hand under her bob in a goofy, mock beauty parlor way.

"Are you eating?" Mom said. "You look skinny."

"It's called getting in shape."

"I think she looks good." Laurel threw a pillow at her. It hit her arm and bounced to the floor. Mallory picked it up and pitched it back, beaning Laurel twice as hard.

"Ow!" Laurel cried and stood, batting the pillow clumsily back. It knocked into the desk lamp, sending it crashing sideways.

"Girls!" Mom's hands flew to her throat. "Stop that, please." She clutched at her chest and sank to the bed. "Please don't do that."

"Sorry, Mom." Mallory righted the lamp. "Look, it's fine. See? Not broken."

Her mom tugged agitatedly at her purse strap and patted her neck. Her skin stretched over her collarbone and was so thin that Mallory could see the ridges of her upper breastbone, lightly dampened from sweat. Her mother at twenty-one had already given birth to two babies. She still wore her eyeliner in the exact way she always had, with the black line drawn only halfway across her upper lid. Seeing that line there, how she had drawn it on that morning, Mallory imagined her mother peering into the bathroom mirror, preparing to see her estranged oldest daughter. And it hit her that they'd made the trip, her mother and sister, driving two days across the country in a late-October heat wave to get here for family visiting day. Mallory wanted her mom to feel glad they came. "Can I get you a drink?" she asked, offering them beverages from her mini fridge. "I have bottled water or OJ."

"Orange juice?" Laurel did an imitation of a begging dog. Mallory pulled out a bottle of Libby's and they all heard the pneumatic pop as Laurel snapped off the cap.

"Mom, do you want anything?"

"Actually, I thought you two girls might like to talk before we go to lunch." She stood and reengaged her purse strap over the ruffles of her sleeveless blouse. "Is there a place where I can go to get a coffee?"

"Yeah, of course." Mallory had reserved them a room at the hotel on base, where family members could stay, and she described the lounge where they had coffee and pastries set out. Her mom left not five minutes after she had come.

"So, do you like it here?" Laurel inspected her orange juice bottle, peeling thin white strips off the label from the circumference of the glass. "Is it weird, sharing a bathroom?"

"After basic, it feels like a luxury to have my own door."

"The bathrooms didn't have doors?"

"The showers were in a big open room with no curtains."

"Ew. I would not like that, everyone watching."

"Actually, it's not that bad. We only had a short amount of time, so everybody was just trying to get everything done."

Laurel piled the paper strips from the juice label on the blanket between them on the bed. The strips coiled and curved, making a delicate kind of nest.

"How about you? Are you excited for your senior year? I'm surprised Mom let you take time off from school."

"Mom wants me to tell you that I got into college. Early acceptance. I'm going to Colgate."

"Like the toothpaste?"

"No, silly," Laurel rolled her eyes. "It's a good school but far away. They have this program—I'm the first one in our family to go to college, so I got a scholarship and a grant."

The four-year age difference between them suddenly felt like a chasm, and she once again wondered about Laurel's life. Would she keep in touch with her high school friends? Would she chat with them on social media?

"I remember the day you were born," Mallory heard herself saying. She stood and went over to the mini fridge. "You came home from the hospital and all you did was sleep and eat. I wanted you to play. I can't believe you're going to college." Tugging open the door, she swiped out a water. "And with a scholarship—what an accomplishment. That must have taken a lot of discipline and hard work."

Laurel shrugged.

Mallory took a few swallows, retightened the cap. "Where is it?"

"New York."

"New York City?"

"Upstate, in the Finger Lakes region." She wiggled the fingers on one hand. "I can't believe I get to go." She bounced lightly on the bed.

"That's great," Mallory said. "I really am happy for you, and so proud." The words pilled in the back of her throat. She took another sip of water and swallowed it down hard. She wouldn't cry. Why would she cry? She turned toward the window that looked out over the parking lot and could see her reflection as she stood in her uniform. With her hair pulled back tight by her face, the light from the window shone through the thin cartilage of her ears, turning them a translucent pink.

From the door came a timid bump.

"I'm baa-ack," her mom said, bringing two coffees, one in each hand. The hallway smelled disgustingly of fried chicken. Mallory went over to help her mother close the door, touched that she had brought a coffee for her, but when she turned to get it, her mother was saying to Laurel, "They had the flavored creamers that you like."

"You drink coffee now?"

Laurel smiled, pleased that her sister had noticed.

"Did Laurel tell you her news?"

"She did."

"Did she tell you about the scholarship?"

Mallory nodded.

"It's merit-based. So between that and work study and the financial aid, we won't even have to take out a loan." Mom blew on her coffee and sipped. Her eyes flicked again to Laurel, who ever-so-slightly shook her head. Mom's shoulders tightened and her brows furrowed above her tense and pockmarked face. The greasy scent of fried chicken coated the still and quiet space.

"What?" Mallory swiped up all the shreds of the bottle wrapper off the bed and threw the strips into the trash. "What else haven't you told me?"

"Mallory, I'm going with Laurel. We're moving to Upstate New York."

The news landed like a brick through the glass window of her heart.

"It's something your sister and I talked about, and I think it will be good for both of us, you know, to get away and get a fresh start."

Laurel and her mom shared excited looks, lifting their two Styrofoam coffees in a toast. The edges of her mother's cup was lined with lipstick moons.

"We rented a U-Haul trailer. I was so nervous about driving it, but I figured it out—even backing up." She laughed, sliding Laurel a glance. "We brought all your stuff."

"Wait, what?"

"I had to pack up the apartment, Mallory. Your sister is going to finish up her senior year at a high school there."

"You already moved?"

"Don't worry, it's all labeled so you can easily find your things."

"You brought all my stuff *here*?" Mallory felt her voice tighten as it raised. "I thought this was family visiting day. I thought you were here about that, and for a tour of the base."

"We are. We did. Texas is not exactly on the way to Upstate New York."

"Mom, I'm shipping out next month. What am I supposed to do with all my stuff?"

"You'll find a storage space for it. The military offers support for these types of situations." She smiled nervously at Laurel. "Vella did fine in the car, even with the heat, didn't she?" Vella, their cat named after the mints. The cat they'd gotten the month after Mallory left—

when all growing up, she had begged for a pet. "We didn't know how she would do, but she rides along beautifully in the backseat with her litter box on the floor. I think she actually enjoys it."

"Are you finally divorcing Dad?" It came out sounding angry; it came out growled. He always said that cat dander was unhygienic.

"I don't know why you're always so mad," her mom whispered. "It was your decision to enlist. We kept thinking you would change your mind and come home, but I guess we were all wanting an adventure."

"Oh my god, it's not like that, Mom. They assign you places to go for training based on your tests, and then we go wherever it is they need us to go."

"Well, New York is where I needed to go."

Voices in the hall erupted into laughter, intensifying the fried chicken smell. Mallory turned toward the window, on the verge of jumping through it. But she was in uniform. She was a soldier now, and that meant something to her. "I'm happy for you, Mom." She would not cry in her army fatigues. "I'm glad you're finally doing something for yourself. That's really great. I'm so proud of you," she said.

Laurel set her coffee down and stood with her purse. "We brought you a present for when you're overseas." She glanced sideways at Mom and reached into her cream-colored purse. Mallory had never seen her sister with a purse. It looked new, like it came from the mall. "I hope you like it." She held out a fist-sized box wrapped in pink paper with yellow flowers and green buds. Girlish paper. Mallory hadn't felt like a girl in a long time.

"That's all right," she said. "You don't have to get me anything."

"Silly, we already got it," Laurel said, undeterred. "It's from Hallmark."

Grandma always said the best gifts came from Hallmark. Grandma drove them, she and Laurel, to peruse the carpeted aisles so they could surprise their mom for Mother's Day. The two of them in the gift store with their allowance money, carefully selecting their present, the scent of potpourri and artificial vanilla in the air. "You can open it now if you want," Laurel said, with her shiny hair and a new iPhone in its sparkly case. "You don't have to wait." Her younger sister, who looked for all the world like she belonged at college. She held out a present, and Mallory didn't take it.

"Mallory," her mom whispered. "Don't."

She wouldn't remember sitting with them at dinner or how they said their good-byes. She would remember how, in that moment, her mother had protected Laurel when she'd never been able to protect herself. She would remember coming back to her apartment alone and seeing that girly present wrapped and sitting there on the bed. And how she had picked it up and thrown it against the bedroom wall, shattering the contents inside without ever opening the box.

20

The ER nurses at Angel of Mercy were all busy when Mallory arrived, so she waited impatiently while the phones shivered in their cradles and squares of lights blinked off and on. Hot, hungry, overheating in her winter coat, she clutched a lime green bag of cherry sours because they had always been Laurel's favorite, and she'd forgone the eye patch because that day she didn't have to work. She'd be able to visit for as long as Shay wanted.

"Can I help you?" A blonde nurse with dark roots rapidly advancing finally lifted her head.

"Yes," Mallory said. "Is Allan here? From the psych team?" She set her bag of candy on the counter and removed her gloves.

"Oh. Is he expecting you?"

"No."

"I was gonna say, I don't think he's here today." This nurse was way too perky for someone delivering bad news. She scooted over in her roller chair and chattered her fingers over the computer keys. "At least I haven't seen him." She talked to herself and hummed, "Doot duh doot duh doot," flicking through different screens. "Yes," she congratulated herself for being right. "Allan has the day off."

Mallory hadn't considered this as a possibility. "I was hoping to visit one of his patients," she said. "I was just here the other day."

"What's the patient's name?"

"Shay."

"Last name?"

"I don't know."

"Date of birth?"

Mallory grimaced. A phone rang and the nurse pounced on it,

rolling sideways in her chair. Mallory rolled her eyes and turned away, feeling the *whomp-whomp*ing of her heart. After her fight with Noah, she'd hardly been able to sleep, and in her haste to get to the hospital, she hadn't eaten. Without Andrea cooking for her, she'd been subsisting on cereal and fakin'. She felt an emotional disturbance brewing. *Do not cry while in public.* An RN passed through the locked doorway that led to the private ward where, just the day before yesterday, she'd gone to visit Shay.

"So," the nurse said, returning, "I'm not finding a patient here by that name."

"Oh. Has she been released?"

"Are you a family member?"

"No," said Mallory. "I'm a friend. A good Samaritan." She bit down on the inside of her cheek. "I was able to visit with her last time. Was she moved?"

"I couldn't tell you," the nurse said. "Why don't you give me your name and I'll send someone out from PCS to talk with you."

Mallory thanked her and moved over to the chairs where there were no dweeping phones. In the army, she'd learned adaptation and flexibility, coping mechanisms for when her emotions overwhelmed her. But without the dog to walk, she hadn't exercised in three days. A bouquet of silver balloons bobbled down an open corridor and smells of antiseptic and boiled meat and microwaved popcorn competed for attention in the room.

A shrill, metallic ringing filled her left ear.

"Mallory Moe?" A woman in mouthwash-colored scrubs stood rubbing sanitizer on her hands, her stethoscope swung over one shoulder like an aviator's scarf.

The ringing in her ear gave her a heightened awareness of everything.

"Yeah, that's me." Mallory sprang from the chair. "So, I was here the other day, visiting with a patient named Shay. I'd like to see her again, if she's up for it, but I understand that Allan is not working today," she explained.

"This was Allan's case?" This nurse had one of those all-knowing hairdos, tactful and poufed. She pulled up a screen on a bumpered tablet, all business. "You said her name is Shay?"

"Yes."

"And you're her family?"

They're not my family, Shay had said.

"Are you related?" the nurse repeated.

"Oh, no, sorry. Just a friend."

"Okay. I can't give out any information about that patient." The nurse closed the screen. "Patient confidentiality, you understand." She kneaded her free hand against the small of her back, rolling around a fist.

Mallory prickled. She could have lied and said they were sisters, but she hadn't. "Oh. I understand." The ringing wouldn't stop. "I'm glad you're protecting her, but my name is on her chart."

Tiny fissures of concern appeared between the nurse's eyes.

"The form Allan filled out . . . The *story*?" Mallory pressed.

"You mean the progress report?"

"Yeah, that." Mallory didn't think it was necessary for her to condescend. "Can you just please check and see if he made a note about me? Please? My name is Mallory Moe. I don't mean to cause you trouble."

"Oh no, you're good," the nurse said, taking a few steps away. Mallory was not *good*. She was swirling down the drain. That was just a handy phrase well-adjusted people used when they knew you weren't getting what you wanted.

"I really need to see her," Mallory said. "Or at least know what happened to her. Please." An uncomfortable loosening was happening inside her chest, as if she were sliding off the center of herself. "I was just here the other day," she repeated. "Allan let me see her."

The nurse closed her tablet. "I'm glad you care about her, and it's nice that you want to visit, but you don't have any legal rights to private information about this patient."

The ringing cut out. Mallory was left standing alone, with her jaw sore from clenching, aware that she'd just behaved badly. She'd been watching herself while it happened, like she was an actor in a bad movie, unable to change her own behavior even though she'd been the one doing it.

"Yoo-hoo! Miss!" The first nurse, the one with the blonde hair, called out and waved. "You forgot your candy."

❆

In the car the belt hiccupped with squeals while the engine warmed up and Mallory obsessively scrolled through her phone, shoving candy in her mouth, searching for the number from the day when the psych department had called *her*. She wiped her eyes and nose, both running from the cold. She found the number, tapped it, then ended the call. She put down her phone. In front of her, the car exhaust from all the vehicles obscured the buildings alongside the street.

It would be weird if she called the hospital now, looking for Shay, and it would be weird even if she waited a few days. *You don't have any legal rights.* She'd given that nurse her full name. They were probably talking about her now, maybe even calling Allan on his day off. Mallory was mortified. She couldn't explain why the well-being of this girl she hardly knew was so important to her, how Shay lived like a sister inside her, like her own breath.

Loose sheets of snow skimmed across the street, the sky blanched white as the air. The male nurse Allen had told her that this happened all the time. He saw people in the ER during the worst crisis of their lives, he did everything he could to help them, and then he never got to see them again. He never got to find out if things turned out okay. They just disappeared back into their lives.

Mallory couldn't believe that her relationship with Shay was over. There had to be something more. She didn't want it to end. That other nurse probably thought she was a crazy person. Mallory thought again of what Mrs. Champagne had said about being a survivor.

Mallory had been around Shay's age when all that happened with Jarrod, and she'd never realized before how young she was. More importantly, she'd never acknowledged how much her situation at home had affected her, a situation that she could no longer convince herself "wasn't that bad." By focusing so much on this girl, Mallory hadn't been taking care of herself. She hadn't started packing or looking for an apartment. She hadn't apologized to Noah.

She hadn't talked with anybody in her family.

A small white car slid into the parking spot in front of hers. The driver got out, a young man of college age, with sandy hair, his jacket undone. He came out with a smile on his face as though in the middle of a reaction to something that had happened inside the car, and he was laughing, enjoying himself. As though it were not the middle of winter and the air not a granite wall of torpid cold. He got out, walked around, climbed up over the bulging bank of snow, and scanned the meter with his phone.

The passenger door was pushed open and hit against the snowbank with a metal *crunch*. A girl emerged, pink-cheeked and chubby, with long dark hair, also college age, wearing jeans and high-heeled booties. She squeezed herself out of the foreshortened wedge of space, shut the door, and stood hemmed in by the snowbank, tugging dubiously at her coat. The young man hurried over to help her, smiling, laughing even more, and that gesture—how he leaned across the snowbank and held out his hand, and how the girl reached and steadied herself, holding on to him, both of them laughing now—it was that *easy* between them, Mallory could tell. For them, this was their everyday.

Laurel probably had a boyfriend like that, someone who would come around to the other side of the car and give her a hand up. Mallory didn't know, but she hoped.

"Mallory? Is that really you?" Her voice hadn't changed.

"Hi, Laurel." Mallory sat in her car, holding her phone, watching the young couple make their way down the sidewalk, holding hands. "What are you doing?" She hadn't seen her sister in four years.

"I'm going to get food with my boyfriend. Oh my god, are you home?" Her voice rose excitedly, but then she sounded as though she'd dropped something—her voice went away. Mallory heard her say to someone, "If you take that class, I will dump you, and then I will kill what's left of you so that you die alone." A moment later she came back. "Mallory? Sorry, I got distracted. Where are you now?"

"I'm home. I'm working at a Speed Stop store and looking for an apartment."

"When did you get there? You never answered my text." Laurel sounded out of breath, like maybe she was exercising. Mallory pictured her, apple-cheeked in the upstate air. "I can only talk for a few minutes because I have to get to class."

"Okay. What class?"

"Peace Studies."

"Oh, wow. That sounds interesting."

"Ugh, it's not really. War is much more interesting. Peace is so boring!"

That made Mallory laugh. It was good to hear her voice. Laurel talked about her classes, her boyfriend.

"What are you doing in Wisconsin?" she said politely. "Are you going to get a job as a mechanic now?"

"Actually, one thing I learned while overseas is that I do not want to spend the rest of my life looking at the underside of cars."

Laurel didn't reply; something had distracted her again.

"Mallory?" She came back on. "I have to go. If I don't leave now, I won't make it to class on time."

"Okay, sure."

"Call me again when you have time!"

"Okay. Did you get to eat?"

"Wilhem brought me food. He made me a bagel!" She giggled, then said in a conspiratorial tone, "We eat avocados together in his room."

"Bye, Laurel."

"I love you!"

"I love you, too."

It hadn't gone anywhere. Laurel's love for her was still right there. It had begun to snow. The couple on the sidewalk was gone.

It had been a sixteen-hour flight to Kuwait. They'd lived in big industrial warehouses with bunks thrown in and showered in trailers with sinks and worked in tents where every day they sweated through their uniforms because the temperature inside the tents got to 110 degrees before noon.

But the bathrooms had private stalls, completely sealed. It was the best part about being overseas. And she thought about her sister, every time. How they always called bathroom stalls their apartments. How they dreamed of living together and going to college with each other. How they giggled while they peed.

She thought a lot about her family during those years. It was her first time being in a foreign country, on her own and working a job, with time to process what had happened, what she'd been through—not just with Jarrod but also at home. And what happened was, after hearing other people talk about their lives and hearing their stories and seeing how much they missed their families, how they had so many good memories, and then being asked about her life and her family, Mallory felt a terrible ache. She didn't know what to say. Even the good memories made her sad.

The first time she'd consciously realized that something was wrong had been in grade school, when she'd been at a friend's house for a sleepover. This friend also had a sister, and they were all in the kitchen while her friend's mom made pancakes. They were just hanging out, a Saturday morning, with cartoons playing in the background. And the dad cut into his stack of pancakes and raw batter oozed out. "Uh-oh, these aren't done." His chair had scraped back, and hearing that sound, Mallory launched herself to the stove, grabbing the pancake flipper from the mom and babbling frenetically, "I'm sorry, I'll fix it, let me do it," her heart hammering in her chest. It had been surreal, because the dad had come over and put his arm around the mom. "It's okay," he said amusedly. "We can just make some more." And he wasn't even mad. Mallory had looked at them and they had looked at her and she had not understood what was going on.

She understood it now. The snow landed on her windshield in tender curls.

It wasn't that she was jealous of her sister for going to college, or envious of her friend for having better circumstances growing up. It was this feeling that she'd lost herself, who she might have been. It was this weight. She felt denied, cheated, robbed of the opportunity to be who she really was, to develop her full potential, because of the weight she carried, this responsibility she shouldered.

All this time and worry and thought and resolve . . . Her entire childhood, her entire life up to this point, she'd wasted it by taking responsibility for and carrying the weight of a problem that was never hers to solve.

PART

FIVE

21

An arctic blast descended and plunged the Midwest into temperatures colder than the north pole. Schools and libraries and banks and credit unions closed. For three days buses didn't run. Twenty-six people died. A young college boy was found frozen outside his dorm, and a FedEx worker froze out in back by the delivery dock. These were the stories in the news.

Andrea left for her cloud forest in Mindo. She dragged a purple roller bag across the living room, whistling birdsongs. The earthy scent of her shampoo and conditioner hung in the room as she left, her car quietly sliding out of the garage. Noah traded shifts to avoid working with Mallory, and she kept her head down and tended to bakery. During her hours off, she went to the grocery store, bought things with green leaves, and put them in the refrigerator. She checked her phone regularly, still hoping for a call from the ER nurse Allan. She photographed snow-covered trees and learned how to make pouches of Bear Creek soup. She thought about her sister and her mom; she thought about Jarrod and her dad. She searched online for an apartment.

The first one she visited, in Sterling, had a red door in a stone-faced building that she thought from the outside looked cool. Located less than a half a mile from the lake at the north end of town, it shared the bottom floor with a tattoo parlor, and heavy metal music blasted through the walls.

She had forgotten that—how Jarrod's garage used to have that same music blasting every time they went over there, his dad working on some new engine or car. It was even in the pole barn where Jarrod worked, fixing his lawn mowers, snowmobiles, and later his own car. She had forgotten about that constant sound—the shouting, the screeching anger as the music throbbed and pulsed, circling the anger round and round.

The next place came cheap but smelled of cat urine, with wall-to-wall carpeting in mustard brown. It had a yard—that was what had attracted her—a fenced-in area with one tree and a dog. It had a view of an alley lined with dirty snow and disabled cars.

The third place, in a brownstone she would share with two college students, was a private bedroom at the end of a hall. Its window faced a park with a tree-lined perimeter. Kids bundled in snowsuits played out on the swings. Nearby, a cluster of chickadees gathered under a branch where suet hung. She thought maybe she could live there. She met with the building supervisor, paid an application fee, and filled out the forms online. The sun shimmered under cloud cover thin as skin over boiled milk.

It was a Tuesday evening, while Mallory was changing the water softener at work, that Gabby Stenberger called. An unknown number with a Duluth area code had popped up on her phone, and Mallory got a *ping* in her chest and knew it had to do with Shay.

"Not now, honey." The woman on the phone sounded hurried and breathless, like she was at a supermarket doing her grocery shopping while also taking care of a kid. "Silly goose, put that away," Gabby whispered congenially.

"Hello?" Mallory said.

"Oh! Sorry about that. Multitasking." She sang the word. Her voice buzzed in the top of Mallory's head. "I am *so sorry* to be calling you so late on a school night like this. This is Mallory Moe, right?"

"Yes. That's me." Asshole Craig was still in his office, the door ajar, so Mallory closed the locker room door and made sure her mic was muted. "Who is this?"

The woman introduced herself as a social worker from Carlton County. "The county has temporary custody of Shay and I'm her caseworker." When she heard the girl's name again, Mallory's heart did a little pirouette. It had been a full week since their last visit. "We have yet to track her guardian down, or anyone from her family, and that's been tough for Shay. She's at a temporary shelter and not very happy about it. Yesterday we were exploring different placement options and your name came up."

"Okay." Mallory's heart accelerated. More rustling sounds crackled over the phone, and she pictured Gabby opening and closing cooler doors, examining bags of frozen fruit.

"Shay mentioned that you had helped her, and that you had training. I'd like to set up a preliminary meeting to see if you might be interested in stepping in temporarily to serve as Shay's foster parent." Gabby whispered again, "No, honey, not those. You can choose between this one or these." Then, back to Mallory: "I can tell you more about it and what requirements you'd need to meet if you're open to discussing it."

"Yes." She had so many questions. "Can I see her?"

"Oh, Shay won't be at this meeting. But we could set up another one."

"Okay, thank you."

Ambient beeping came from a checkout counter.

"Shay would have to agree to it, but sure, if things check out, I don't see why not." More shuffling and rustling around. "I'll be in my office at the courthouse on Thursday, catching up on paperwork," she said. "If you don't mind me eating while we talk, I can fit you in at noon."

Mallory mentally checked her schedule. "I can do that." She would make it work.

"Great!" Gabby turned her attention to a transaction with the store clerk. "Okay, well, I look forward to meeting you. Just come by the Carlton County Government Services building, human resources, and check in at the front desk. See you at noon on Thursday. Bye-bye now."

She hung up and Mallory stared at her phone and looked all around. How had so much changed during a two-minute phone call? She didn't know what to think about this idea of fostering Shay, and she had no idea why Shay thought she had training in this area, but she was incredibly touched that Shay had thought of her.

Sliding her phone into her back pocket, she smiled, thinking about butt cancer, and put it in the pocket of her cardigan instead. But then she thought about thigh cancer and so she put it in her locker. All night she mulled the possibility of being a foster parent. What did it involve? What kind of training would she need? What if they did a background check? She had been convicted of shoplifting once—during her fugue state. She'd had to pay a $1,000 fine and do community service as part of a work squad, but that record was closed once she turned eighteen. The police had also questioned her during Jarrod's arson case, but she was never charged.

She'd have to get a bigger apartment, with a bedroom for Shay, she thought, someplace near the high school. St. Vincent's sold recycled furniture. The girl would need a bureau. Maybe they could get a cat. Mallory went through a mental checklist in her head while going through the checklist of duties for the store. Her mind was a teeter-totter all night long: up, down; hope, doubt.

Driving home out on the highway that night, she passed two deer that had gotten hit by a car, both of them lying together in the middle of the road. One of them was still sitting up, its long neck periscoping, its eyes wild and round. They glinted in the headlights of the oncoming cars, and it tried to get up, nudging the other deer. It was trying to help them both out of the middle of the road, but its legs had been too badly damaged, and it couldn't stand or run or do anything on broken legs.

❄

Wednesday, Mallory woke with her head thick and feverish and an appetite that reared with a vengeance. If she didn't eat, she thought she would perish. This was the way her body felt whenever she was getting sick.

She downed orange juice and heated up leftover soup, ate two bowls, then buttered some bread. By the time she drove to work, her sinuses had swollen hot in her head and she labored to breathe. Snot trickled into the back of her throat and she plugged one nostril with a corner of Kleenex—a trick she'd learned from her mom, which inexplicably made it easier to breath. In the rearview mirror she looked ridiculous, but the trick worked. Of course, at work she'd have to become a mouth breather and the back of her throat would get scratchy and dry.

"You should have called in sick," said Gavin, the other guest service leader. They were in the locker room; he was coming off his shift while she was coming on.

"No thanks," she said. "I'm not sick enough to stay in bed." One year from that January, a news story would report on a suburb in Wuhan, China, that was building a thousand-bed hospital in ten days for patients with a viral pneumonia of unknown cause, but that winter nobody thought about masks. She stowed her coat and clocked into the computer app and took out the binder and flipped through to the list of jobs.

Noah had switched his last two shifts to avoid working with her, but he was scheduled that night. She still hadn't apologized for throwing a Cambro at his head.

"Noah." She stood by the stainless steel counter next to him while he adjusted his hairnet. "I have to talk to you." It was the beginning of what would be a ten-hour shift.

"Get away from me." He pulled on the bright blue gloves, his eyes looking everywhere but at her, and yanked open the door to the walk-in cooler. He reappeared lugging a tote and sorted out the different bags of frozen soups and sandwich breads.

She sneezed and took out a tissue from the pocket of her sweater and blew her nose.

"You need to get out of my kitchen," he said. "A sneeze travels two hundred feet from your mouth."

"Sorry."

He galumphed back into the cooler, carrying the tote, was gone a few moments, then reappeared with another tote, full of vacuum-packed meat.

"What are you still doing here?"

"I'm sorry, Noah."

"Don't apologize. Just leave."

He unloaded the tote and went back into the cooler. The door buzzer sounded, indicating a valuable customer had come in, but Mallory was still standing there when he came back out.

"I'm sorry," she said again.

"You apologize for the little things"—he arranged his items on the counter—"but you never say you're sorry for the big things that matter."

"This is me apologizing for the big things that matter."

The door buzzed again.

"I'm sorry for . . . you know . . ." It was painful to admit. "For throwing that Cambro at your head."

"What about the other things?"

"What other things?"

"When you get into moods and say things and throw things around in the store, making everyone else feel tense and on edge." He put a bag of soup in the microwave, pressed the buttons, and started the cook cycle. "You are my friend, therefore I understand, but sometimes it's hard to be around you." He took the tote and stacked it in the corner with the other ones, preheated the oven, and opened a box of frozen corn dogs, laying them out on a lined baking sheet. "It's like you're two different Mallorys, and I never know which one I'm going to get to work with, the nice Mallory or the mean one." When the oven dinged, he hefted up the tray using the silver tongs and slid the corn dogs in.

Her face burned. He'd never said that about the two Mallorys before. "Noah, I'm sorry, okay? Really sorry. I've been having a hard time lately. I'm going through a thing."

"We're all going through a thing." He opened the microwave, flipped over the bag of soup, and restarted the cook cycle. "All of us all the time are going through things."

Again the door buzzer sounded.

"This is a big thing. I don't even know how to talk about it and it's messing with my head. Please, Noah. I could really use a friend." He clattered the baking trays and slapped down parchment paper sheets, lining them all. The door buzzer chimed again. "I have to go." She threw her wad of tissues away and popped a cough drop in her mouth. "This is going to be a long, sucky night if you don't talk to me."

The store got busy and she stayed out by the registers for the next several hours. She gave Noah space and took care of every customer who came in so he could stay alone in his kitchen. It bothered her, what he'd said about the two Mallorys. She didn't want it to be true, but because it bothered her, she knew it probably was true.

❄

At half past midnight Orange Juice Guy pulled up in an articulated Jennie-O Turkey truck, creaking and spewing alongside the pumps. He refueled and then entered the store, bouncing over to the fruit and veggie display. When he said hello to her and flashed his iridescent smile—he had stunningly white teeth—she felt the warmth of sand and imagined a tropical beach with palm trees swaying overhead. But then that ringing came back in her head.

"Orange Juice Guy is here." She spoke to Noah through the headset; she thought it would cheer him up. "Do you have a survey for me this week? I'll ask him."

His voice clicked brusquely into her ear: "How many turkey and cheese croissants do we have left?"

She glanced over at the Hot Spot. "Two."

"What happened to the ones I just brought out?"

"They're a hot ticket, what can I say?" She completed the Trendar purchase for Orange Juice Guy's fuel. "What does it mean when the ringing is in your right ear?" Noah didn't answer. His unspoken rule during their fight was to only speak about store logistics. He didn't share or report on his hygienic observations about life. The sound of the ringing in her ear practically glowed. "Noah?" she said. "The ringing is in my right ear. What does that mean?"

"I have that to-go order ready," he said. "I can't bring it out. I have too much to do."

The trucker came to her register with his easy smile and dizzying height.

"Good evening, mademoiselle." Those full lips caressing the susurrations of his words . . . She felt embraced by that perfect abrasion of sound, and the deliciousness of it made it impossible to feel bad, even with the ringing in her ear and her stuffed-up nose. "How are you doing today?" His eyes were so present, filled with liquid life, and she could marry him, she thought. And he really was asking her how she was.

"I'm having a rough day." She scanned his fruit juice and veggie tray. "I don't feel well, there's this ringing in my ear, plus I got into an argument with *my one true friend*." She pressed her mic for Noah so that he could hear that part, placing the items in a plastic shopping bag. "*Night*, I guess I should say—I'm having a bad night."

"I'm sorry to hear that." He slid his credit card into the chip reader slot. "Day, night, breakfast, dinner. I get all mixed up." He pronounced "dinner" as *deener*, with his deliciously sandy vowels. "My wife also was having a bad day. She does not understand the difference between American precooked and raw sausage. She continues to think they are all precooked because that is convenient." He smiled and removed his card.

Mallory laughed, not expecting that—not the part about the sausage or the part about his wife. "Will you be paying for gas tonight?" she asked, then remembered she'd already authorized his Trendar and he'd scanned his fleet card at the pump. "Oh, sorry." She blushed and slid over his grocery items in their bag. "My mistake. I'm a big, stupid idiot. I don't know what's wrong with me."

"No worries." He took his grocery bag. His vowels took care of her in an auditory way, like he was offering a hand or holding open the door. He smiled and gave her a look that made her feel seen. "You should be kinder to yourself," he said. "She knows what you are thinking about her." He tapped the side of his head.

She stared after him. *Had that just happened?* Had he just spoken to her about her subconscious in a Speed Stop store in the middle of the night?

She rang up a raspberry slushie and a pocket comb and ferried the to-go order. She thought about this other Mallory, the nice one who also lived in her head. She authorized the gas on pump three.

Orange Juice Guy was still sitting in the cab of his rig. "Go ahead on pump three." She used her lower register, in case he might hear. "We'll see you when you pay inside. Be sure to check out our fish sandwiches, on sale tonight in the Hot Spot for $2.99." She rang up a cup of chili, a box of crackers, and a container of mayonnaise. "See ya next time," she said, handing over the grocery items in their bag.

Orange Juice Guy had gotten out of his rig.

"Hey, Noah, you there?" she spoke into her mic. "I see five," she said, meaning there were five customers waiting in line. She rang up a thirty-two-ounce fountain soda and a Tex-Mex burrito and slid over the stepping stool to take down a carton of cigarettes.

"You need me to come out there?" Noah did not sound happy.

Outside at the pumps, Orange Juice Guy undid both front latches on the fenders and tilted back the giant hood of his Jennie-O Turkey rig. He peered and poked around, but it was clear he had no idea about what he was doing.

"Yeah, I do," she said to Noah. "Sorry." She rang up an apple, a yogurt, and a container of cut-up fruit. "We have a stalled truck." She waited until Noah logged in to the register at the far end of the counter before sliding the CLOSED sign in front of hers. "I'll just be outside a few minutes," she said to him.

In the locker room she pulled on the safety coat with its reflector tape, black and boxy, a one-size-fits-all that swallowed her up. She respected the fact that Orange Juice Guy was married—it gave her hope, to think that it might be possible to find a partner like him. She strode out while tugging on her gloves.

"Hey," she said to him. "What's going on with your rig?" The cold air refreshed her face and pinked her cheeks. His engine wasn't even running.

"It won't start." Even when apprehensive he remained congenial and polite, but it was clear he was in distress. He pressed the front of his temple with the tips of his fingers and lowered his head. "It is not the battery—the lights and radio come on. But when I turn the key, it makes a *pft, pft* sound and the engine is completely dead."

She always found it endearing when men mimicked the sounds of

204 • CAROL DUNBAR

their vehicles going wrong. They performed with such earnestness. "I used to be a mechanic," she said, not meaning to brag. "If you want to try and start her, I can listen and maybe help figure out what's going on."

"Really?" His surprise made her heart bounce. "That would be most magnificent. I would really appreciate, thank you." He loped around to the driver's door. "I don't want to call dispatch until I know what's going on because if it needs to be serviced that could cause many hours delay." He climbed up into his rig. His lights came on and a cover of Simon and Garfunkel's "America" blasted out through the truck's speakers. She heard her favorite line about the cigarette in the raincoat before he turned it off, and when his big brown eyes found hers again, they were worry-filled. "Should I turn it now?"

She bent over the engine and raised her hand. "Now." He turned the key and she heard the click of the piston firing forward, but it wasn't turning. "Do it again," she called out. He turned the engine over, and again it was dead.

"It's your starter, most likely," she said to him, coming over.

"My starter?"

"That's my best guess."

Other semis moved around them across the parking lot like humpback whales. "Safety is my number one concern," he said. "I don't want a mechanical failure to cause an accident to anyone while I'm out on the road. Etienné would never forgive that."

"Etienné is your wife?"

"She worry all of the times." He looked out over the white salted road. "We read to each other at night. I call her when I get to my stop and we pick up where we left off, at the chapter we agreed upon. It is how we stay connected while I'm on the road. All day I am listening to this audiobook, and I want to talk to her about what is happening, and when I call, we continue our story."

"That's really sweet," Mallory said, the wind tearing her uncovered eye. "If it's the starter, the worst thing that can happen is the engine won't start up for you the next time you turn it off." Her hair lifted from her shoulders in a diesel-scented gust. "If you have a flashlight, I can go under there and see if that's what it is. Might be something we can patch up to get you to your next stop."

"You want to go under there?" His voice cracked endearingly. "Under my truck?"

"I used to do it all the time."

Orange Juice Guy, whose real name was Augustin, had a trucker tool kit with everything in it brand new, purchased and packed by his thoughtful wife. Under the big rig, with her back on the cold pavement, she shined the flashlight around and found the starter—and the wire where one end of the plastic coating had frayed. Ripping the electrical tape with her teeth, she thought how, if Shay moved in, maybe she could teach her a few basic things about how to take care of a car, like how to change the oil, fix a flat. She wrapped the wire ends and shored up the connection and scooted back out and asked him try starting it again.

"Don't get your hopes up," she said. "It's just something to try."

The truck started immediately.

"Oh, thank you so much." He clasped her hand and festively pumped. "How did you learn to do that?"

"In the service."

"Like, in the military?"

"Yeah."

"Oh, okay. That's what I thought you meant."

"It will pay for college, but I don't know." She looked around at the parking lot of the Speed Stop store. "I feel too old for that now. Like it's too late. Everybody my age has already graduated or gotten married and started jobs."

"Oh, no. It's never too late for school," he said. "Someday, I hope to go back myself."

It was snowing now, small lake-effect flakes collecting on the cement. She couldn't wipe the grease from her hands or the smile from her face. She watched the articulated trailer of his Jennie-O truck turn out onto the highway and accelerate, a few puffs of gray smoke churning from the stack. Two bleats sounded from his horn.

She held up a hand, thinking of Augustin and Etienné reading to each other at night and how it was possible that two people could coexist together peaceably in a caring, supportive way. Back inside, removing the safety coat and gloves, she was still unable to wipe the smile off her face.

"Fourteen people," Noah said. "And one of them bought every kind of lottery ticket known to man. You owe me, Mallory Moe," he said, coming out from behind the register. "What happened to your face?"

"Nothing is wrong with my face," she said. "This is what it looks like when I'm happy."

"Oh," he said. "What I meant was that it's covered with grease."

❄

Thursday morning, she took three Tylenol and went to bed. If she wanted to meet with Gabby Stenberger, she'd only get two hours of sleep. She set an alarm and tried reading a book from Andrea's shelf. With bits of tissues rolled up and plugged into her already plugged nostril, she socked at her pillow and propped her head. Snot trickled down the back of her throat. The sheets smelled of Andrea, and the book was about a serial killer. She fell into an abortive sleep.

In her dreams she worked the whole time. Unloading boxes and totes, she got ready for the truck, hauling and emptying the stacked-up crates filled with squishy bags of milk. The sour residue of old milk trapped under the rubber flooring mats followed her into the dream as she sorted through the different kinds—one percent, two percent, skim.

The door was flung open and another Mallory came in. She walked backwards, pulling a dolly, and unloaded several crates of fruit.

This Mallory, who also had her hair dyed black and streaked bloodred, moved with an abruptness like her dad—squatting, pushing, unstacking the totes. She was short like her mom, but some part of her was neither of them. It surprised her, watching herself, how she didn't look on the outside the way she felt on the inside. This other Mallory pushed the dolly back out again, jacket unzipped, hair in wisps, one pant leg caught in the sock above her shoe. She had no awareness that this other Mallory even existed, and without even thinking, the first Mallory followed.

In the way of dreams, they walked out together, into a thick blizzard, foaming white. Other Mallory passed under the Speed Stop sign with her head down and her hood up, and she had this suspect way of being herself, as if she assumed at all times that she would do something wrong and so she tried always to preemptively correct herself. She stopped abruptly and looked around, apprehensive, then walked on, furtively keeping a lookout, as was her habit.

Watching her, Mallory felt in her chest a strange sensation that wanted to be love but couldn't quite. The sensation made her uncomfortable. She formed an impression of herself that was separate from her own imagined identity, and seemingly outside of time. And then she did feel it—not love but the gateway feeling of compassion for this young woman who was trying so hard to get it right while always assuming it was her fault when things went wrong.

Out across the parking lot, in a swirl of driving snow, a gas station marquee flashed an advertisement for the free condiment bar. "Help yourself!" the sign said.

And it was funny, because she did want to help herself. She wanted to tell this other Mallory that not everything was her fault, she was doing a lot of things right, and she was deserving of love, even if she couldn't yet give it to herself. And in the way of dreams the woman inside the swirling snow became the young girl Shay, and Mallory's feeling of compassion swelled to fill her entire being and she wanted to help this girl even more than she wanted to help herself.

And Mallory came awake with the knowledge that flashed inside her like a neon sign: *Helping her is helping yourself.*

22

The subconjunctival hemorrhage had almost healed, just like Noah said it would. Only a small patch of blood was left in one corner of her eye. After her shower, Mallory swung her hair back and forth to air dry it with her fingers before drawing black kohl around both eyes. She left her eye patch on the bathroom counter and drove the ninety miles northwest to the government services buildings in Carlton County, in the state adjacent to where she'd grown up.

A woman behind the Plexiglas spoke to Mallory through a hole the size of a baby's head. "Mrs. Stenberger will be out in just a moment to bring you to one of our conference rooms," she said. "Please have a seat."

Mallory stood, nervously leaning against the wall. A young adolescent sitting in the lobby kept his legs folded and face hiding in the shadows of a red sweatshirt hood; the way he sat, with his back curved and hands tucked in the sweatshirt pockets, reminded her of Jarrod. Next to him the father, presumably, stretched out his legs to occupy all the rest of the space. On the walls hung unemotional art, and the windows overlooked a parking lot lined with rubbled heaps of snow.

"Mallory Moe?" Gabby Stenberger stood with her hands folded, at the edge of the carpeted room, a woman of middle age with an abundance of fluffy hair. Brown slacks hugged muscled thighs, paired with a topaz blouse that Mallory rather liked.

"Hey." She jammed her hands in the pockets of her coat and came forward. She wore her black boots, sans the knife, black leggings, and her beanie hat.

"It was so good of you to come." Gabby lifted her shoulders and smiled. "If you'll follow me, I got us the couch room—it's the most comfortable, in my opinion." Gabby's dress boots thumped pertly down the hall. Mallory felt wired, jittery, overly sensitive to sound and nervous about what would be asked of her. She'd barely slept at all.

"Have a seat." Gabby closed the door. "I hope you don't mind my eating. Doctor's orders—no snacking, three square meals. This job can kill you if you let it."

Mallory's scalp tingled from the sound of her voice—it was more intense in the small room than it had been over the phone. White cinder block walls were hung with pages ripped from coloring books; the room was not more than a ten-by-ten space. She sat on the edge of the couch. A shelf crowded with precariously stacked board games stood against the wall across from her, not three feet away—Candy Land, Chutes and Ladders. The lids were split and patched with tape.

"I used to play those games with my sister," Mallory said, unexpectedly remembering. "We would play in the bathroom when she was learning to potty train." The memory was sharp and exact—she could smell the plastic training seat, feel the game piece in her hand.

"Sisters are the best." Gabby slid behind a table that served as a desk. "I'm one of three," she volunteered. "We get together every year for one week of skiing in the mountains. Just us girls. No husbands or kids."

Mallory nodded. She had never learned to ski—the equipment was too expensive. Gabby lifted a hand to brush hair out of her eyes; the makeup there was smudged and imperfect, with purple bags beneath.

"All righty, let's see." Gabby had her lunch things spread out next to a case file and a computer with a keyboard and mouse. "Mallory Moe, here to discuss foster parent options for Shay." She shoved a forkful of a pasta salad into her mouth and chewed unselfconsciously, adjusting her glasses to read from her computer screen.

When Mallory made the appointment, she'd looked up the requirements for fostering a minor. To get the licensing process started, she needed proof of employment and an address, and so she handed those things over now, explaining that she was in the process of getting a new apartment, and the social worker made copies, using a scanner that sat inside a desk drawer. While pulling it out and plugging it in, Gabby made small talk about the horrible winter, taking bites of her lunch and explaining how she had to leave in twenty minutes for an appointment across town. She sipped from a thermos cup and filed away the copies, turned off the scanner, and folded her hands.

"So, I know you're concerned about Shay, so let's start with that. She seems to be doing oh-kay." She pronounced the word with syllabic caution, tilting her head from side to side. "Her situation is tenuous, I'd say. We've been working to establish a routine, and this is usually the hardest part for these girls now, because they feel bored."

"Bored?"

"Once the threat of immediate danger is gone, they're left with having to deal with all their repressed feelings about what happened. We keep them to a very strict schedule: get up, eat, go to group, school, eat, go to group, sleep, and do it all again. No more exciting nightlife." An alarm went off, and Mallory startled like a peahen from the bush. Gabby noticed. "I do apologize," she said, tapping her phone. "I have to keep to a strict schedule, too."

Mallory nodded and repositioned herself on the couch, trying not to itch her scalp. On the wall, the hanging pages from the coloring books fluttered whenever she moved her legs.

"Why don't you tell me a little about yourself," Gabby said. "Tell me about your sister. Are you two close?"

"Um, yeah. She's going to college in Upstate New York, so it's been a while since I've seen her." She patted her jacket looking for her gloves; they were in the pockets. "I served in the army, stationed in Kuwait." It was the thing she most liked about herself. "My sister is younger than me by four, almost five years, so sometimes that's hard, you know, finding common ground." Her eyes shifted back to the colorings on the wall. A cowboy was colored in light purple crayon, painstakingly inside the lines, and right next to it was the same cowboy, this one scribbled over with hard, jagged lines. "Shay wanted to get ahold of her brother," Mallory said, remembering. "Did she tell you about that?"

"Yes, she did." Gabby nodded, chewing with one hand over her mouth. "A half brother in Bemidji who likes to fish. Unfortunately, he's on probation for drug charges." She scraped around the edges of the plastic container with a metal fork.

Mallory flinched. "What about her parents?" Her right leg pumped up and down. "I mean, why hasn't anyone from her family come forward?" She clasped her hands; she wanted to vigorously scratch all over her head. A door closed out in the hallway and Mallory jumped, her body rising slightly from the couch.

"Shay hasn't lived with her parents since she was five," Gabby said, screwing down her thermos cup. "While I'm still trying to track her guardian down, what I'm really hoping for is to get her connected with an organization that understands the tremendous challenges these girls face when getting out of the life."

"The life?"

"Drugs, prostitution, sex for money and things. You do understand what she's been through, right?"

A funny little squeak emitted from underneath the seal of Gabby's thermos cap. From behind the wall a cell phone chimed, and a thousand black ants marched insidiously across the top of Mallory's scalp. "Um, yeah. I was the one who found her that night." Her gloves fell out from the shallow pockets of her coat. "Shay told me that she didn't want to go back to her foster family. She said she would rather die."

Gabby gave a rueful smile and lifted her brows.

"She didn't think you or anyone would be able to help her," Mallory said, scooping up her gloves.

"They're groomed to think that," Gabby explained. "They're told by these men who make them feel special and loved that social services can't help them and that they don't belong in a square world. It's part of how they maintain their control. So much of it is psychological." Something on the computer screen caught Gabby's eye. She hastily wiped her fingertips with a napkin. "Oh, shoot," she said. "Excuse me, I have to tend to this. Just give me a sec." She clicked on the mouse and started typing furiously on her keyboard.

Mallory stood and paced the room. She wanted to do a set of burpees or run around the block, anything to alleviate the tingling on the top of her head and the building anxiety she felt about her ability to help Shay. Although her nose was stuffed up, she could still smell Gabby's lunch, the Italian herbs, the garlicky bits.

"Okay, I'm back," Gabby said. "So sorry about that." She screwed down the squeaking thermos cap. "Now, where were we?"

Mallory couldn't remember, because it occurred to her just then: she'd been here before, or someplace just like it, with her sister and mom, when she was young. She had the distinct memory of these same cinder block walls, her mother sitting in a plastic chair. The institutional smell of ammonia and crayon and mashed banana in the carpet.

"I think I've been here before." She stood by the door.

"Oh?"

"When I was a kid."

Gabby waited.

"I'm sorry," Mallory said.

"Did you have somewhere you want to go?"

"No. No, I was just thinking about my sister and my mom." Mallory sat back down on the couch, her right leg trundling. She rearranged her face. "I don't know anything about 'the life,'" she said. "To be honest, I'm feeling kind of foolish right now, for thinking that I ever understood anything about Shay." She coughed and put her hands on her knee to stop her leg from shaking. "I can't tell you how flattered I am that Shay spoke to you about me. And I'd like nothing more than to help her in any way I can, but I don't have the training—I don't know why Shay thought I did. And I'm still figuring out things in my own life."

"I think that's a good place to start," Gabby said. "So many people make assumptions about these girls, when what they really need is acceptance without being judged." She snapped on the Tupperware lid for her pasta salad and Mallory flinched. She couldn't stay seated. She sprang up again, agitated and itchy all over her skin. "Are you all right?" Gabby asked. "I apologize if my eating is making you uncomfortable."

"No, no, it's not that," Mallory said, having to pick up her gloves again. "It's just, I'm very sensitive to sound and I was up all night and that makes it worse. Sorry. I work overnights." She coughed again, clearing her throat.

Gabby waited.

"I probably have ADHD," Mallory said.

"Oh?"

"It's just something my therapist used to say." Mallory made a face. "Sorry," she said. "My teacher in third grade wanted to have me tested but my dad said no—he thought it was all a bunch of hooey." She clenched her hands into fists. "I'm just very sensitive to . . . everything. I sometimes have a hard time focusing, and I've always been hyperaware of sound, ever since I was a kid." She did not know why she was talking so much. "I'm not doing it on purpose," she said.

"Oh, I know that," Gabby said. "Our bodies have their own way of processing."

"Processing what?"

"Life experiences. What goes on at home." Gabby swiped a finger to move a few strands of hair away from her incredibly kind eyes. "I don't mean to pry," she said, "but did you and your sister have a rough situation at home? I'm only asking because it might be a bit of common ground for you and Shay."

Mallory met her eyes, and in the shared silence of that cinder block space, she offered the weight of the things she carried, arranged like items on a plate. "Our dad was physically and emotionally abusive," she heard herself say. She'd never used these words before and wondered where they had come from.

"That must have been very difficult," Gabby said.

"Oh, no, it didn't happen to me," Mallory said, reeling herself back. Her breathing came shallow and fast; she didn't know what to do with her hands. She had the strange sensation that her father was listening from somewhere in a nearby room. "He didn't hurt my sister or me," she said, her voice sounding excessively loud. "He just, you know, he got frustrated with our mom."

"And how long did this go on?"

"The first fifteen years of my life." Mallory was pressing the pads of her fingertips with the nails of her thumbs, alternating rapidly among fingers and pressing hard. "My dad deployed to Iraq after that, so for two years he was gone, except when he came home for the holidays, but then it was like he had never left, the tension was always in the room. I never understood why my mom stayed with him. Then, when she did leave , I was eighteen and out of the house."

"I see," Gabby said. "And did your therapist ever talk to you about PTSD?"

"Oh, no," Mallory said. "I didn't see much combat in Kuwait."

"No, I'm talking about from your childhood."

Mallory became aware of her cheeks, her heels, and the balls of her feet pressed to the bottom of her boots. The calloused pads on the ends of each fingertip swelled.

"A lot of the kids I work with have these same symptoms," the social worker said. "Girls like Shay who have been in the life, they have the same symptoms as combat veterans. They're jumpy, sensitive to light and sound, always on high alert." She looked at Mallory. "It's just something I'm trained to recognize—the difference between these symptoms, which are from child traumatic stress, and the symptoms of ADHD. And I'm not saying you don't have ADHD, but there's a lot of overlap."

"Okay."

"The symptoms can appear the same because they're identical— the reckless behavior, impulse control, anger issues—"

"Anger? That's part of it?"

"It's very common, yes. Continuous exposure to violent or abusive behavior—even if the violence wasn't done to you—rewires the brain." She placed her fork into a napkin and neatly rolled it up. "A lot of new studies are being done about this. A young, developing brain under constant distress will develop a smaller hippocampus, the area of the brain related to learning and memory formation, and an overdeveloped amygdala, the part of the brain that processes memory, emotions, and fear. So these kids will have an impaired ability to weigh options and make well-considered choices. Many of them find it difficult to connect socially, to fit in. They react more strongly to perceived threats, even if the threats aren't real, even if they're misinterpreted—their brain cannot be convinced.

"The good news is that while these experiences have the potential to be life altering, they don't have to be. We have the tools now to help these kids thrive and go on to achieve their full potential."

Mallory felt like an image on the other end of a lens that Gabby Stenberger, with her words, was refocusing. She sat down and listened and asked questions. They continued to talk as Gabby placed her lunch things into an insulated bag.

"Over ninety percent of exploited youth have experienced some form of violence or neglect in their home first," she said. "You can't ignore that. Shay needs a lot of support and people who will believe in her as she learns how to trust again and believe in a safe world. I think you can understand that." She zipped up her lunch box and loaded that and a few folders into a large butterscotch-colored bag.

"Does that mean you'll let me see her?"

"With the time we have left, why don't you tell me your thoughts about becoming Shay's foster parent. The training and licensing process can take a while, so it's a commitment."

"Okay." Mallory bowed her head. "The thought of it terrifies me, but in a good way. Since you called, I noticed that I'm spending less time obsessing over the past and more time imagining the future. If you think this could be a good thing for Shay, and if no one else comes forward, I'll do my best not to screw it up. I mean, it would be a privilege." She heard the rustle of paper as the social worker wrote something down while another alarm went off again on her phone.

"Please do not share this with anyone." She handed Mallory a slip of paper and turned off the alarm. "This is the youth hostel where she's staying temporarily until we find her a more permanent situation. I want to get her in someplace good like the Mirabi House or Casa del Sol. They teach these kids new skills and provide mentoring services, but they have waiting lists of two months or more. If she had someplace permanent to live, we'd be able to get her in sooner—and these programs have some of the highest recovery rates in the state."

"Thank you," Mallory said.

"You are very welcome." Gabby Stenberger stood. "I think this relationship could be a good thing for Shay. If she likes you, if she trusts you, it could be a way for her to reimagine her life outside of the world she's in."

Mallory looked down at the address in her hand. "She didn't tell me anything about the world she's in and I didn't ask."

"It's okay you didn't ask," Gabby said, putting on her coat and gloves and hat. "I think that's good. Tell her about your life and let her come to you. With these kids, it takes a while to earn their trust. I'd call the hostel and schedule a visit for the weekend. Saturdays are usually best." She went over the shelter rules while she shouldered the butterscotch bag and came out from behind the desk. She had an intimidating presence when she came out in all her coordinated winter gear, and it wasn't just because of the coat she wore or the way her hair spilled out clean and light from under her hat; it was her sense of purpose, her sense of self-worth.

"I do have one more question," Mallory said as they approached the door.

"Yes?"

"Is Shay safe? At this youth hostel, I mean. Is she safe from those men?"

Gabby adjusted the strap of her large shoulder bag. "The answer is yes. But what I worry about most isn't them finding Shay; it's Shay finding them." They moved together out into the hall. "I know it's hard to understand," Gabby said. "It's almost impossible to imagine a girl so desperate for affection and approval and a place where she feels like she belongs—"

"No," Mallory said. "No, it's not that hard to understand."

❄

Friday morning, in a coffee-induced haze with Muzak pumping through the walls, Mallory worked during the commuter rush, ringing up lattes and muffins, telling everyone to have a good night before remembering it was day. When a trucker was having trouble using the Trendar system, she went out to the pumps in the subzero wind and showed him how to use his fleet card for the first time, entering his password, waiting forever to get the approval. It didn't matter. Gabby Stenberger's words filled her like warm water that buoyed her chest. They gave her a new understanding of herself and the world.

Mallory had scheduled her visit at the youth shelter for that Saturday. In less than twenty-four hours, she would be reunited with Shay.

She rang up breakfast burritos and orange juice bottles and hard-boiled eggs, feeling strangely validated and more competent than she'd felt in a long time. When a young man came up to her register after the midmorning rush, asking for a money order, she didn't call one of her coworkers over to do the paperwork like she usually did; she tackled the job herself.

"The payee must be the US Department of Homeland Security, for the amount of $410, and it has to be signed by you, the issuing place, the financial place." He was very polite and had written the instructions down for himself in a neatly squared hand. He was a student at the rural technical college, trying to get his green card. "This must go through today," he said. "Or I am very screwed."

Mallory said she understood and processed his payment. Pulling up the instructions on her screen and going slow, she filled in the date and the amount on the form, double- and triple-checking herself before sending it through to the office printer. After it had printed—an impressive-looking document with keyed-in punches and vibrant colors on smooth cardstock paper—she called the manager on duty. Asshole Craig slid importantly behind the counter space, filled out the name and address of the store, signed his name as manager, and waved it around as if the ink had to dry before he handed it over.

She'd thought it had gone pretty well, until about two hours later, when she was in the automotive aisle, unloading jugs of wiper fluid, and the kid came back.

"Excuse me, please." He stood there trembling in his jeans. "There has been a mistake." His eyes shone and his fingers twitched over the money order in hand. "This has to be made out to the payee, to the issuing place. It has to go out today." She stood and looked over the document, her body flooded with instant shame. She couldn't focus on what he was saying, his distress something that she could feel, like a vertigo in her chest, but she understood that the money order had been filled out wrong. If the payment didn't go through, he wouldn't be able to stay in school.

"This is our mistake," she told him. "Wait here and I'll get it corrected for you right away." She assumed that she'd been the one to screw it up, until she paused outside Asshole Craig's office and saw that he'd written out the store address so large, it took up all the space, not leaving any room for the name and address of the payee.

"What is it?" he said, not even looking up. "I'm busy."

"Um, you filled this money order out wrong. We have to redo it." She stood in the doorway and heard the clicking of his mouse and the Muzak behind her playing "Shut Up and Dance."

"We can't redo it. It's a certified check."

She was sweating, her body trembling, her breath tight and high in her chest. She came into the small, cluttered room and showed him the document.

"That's ridiculous," he said. "I did it exactly the way you told me to do it."

"Well, it's wrong."

"Then that's his problem."

Her heart walloped in her chest.

"Craig, we need to write the address of—"

"I'm not doing it again." He wouldn't look at her; he stayed with the computer on his desk.

"But it's wrong."

"Tell him if he wants me to issue another check, he'll need to pay the money again."

"Are you serious?"

He stayed seated at his desk.

"But it's our mistake, Craig. You know he doesn't have another four hundred bucks."

"How would I know that? I don't know that." He licked his lips.

"You're assuming just from his appearance that he doesn't have the money. Ask him. If he wants another money order, that's the fastest way to get it done."

She went back out to the registers, a pulsing sensation everywhere under her skin. She couldn't think, couldn't read, couldn't hear anything other than words of self-recrimination in her head. But she was at work. If she wanted to help this person, and she did, then she had to focus and do her job. In the past she had always thought her issue had been ADHD, but what if that wasn't it? What if she just had an overdeveloped emotional brain?

Logging on to the computer at the front of the store, she breathed in through her nose and out through her mouth. She pulled up the history for the money order, aware that the kid stood by the doughnut display, watching. She tried to go in and reprint the document, to reissue another one, but Asshole Craig was right. There was no way to reissue the check unless she processed another payment.

"You wouldn't happen to have another four hundred bucks on you," she asked him dryly, "would you?"

He got upset then. His hands flew up and raked over the hair on his head. "I knew it," he said. "I knew I would get screwed. I always do it wrong."

"You didn't do it wrong."

"I can't pay for it all over again!"

His panic had the strange effect of calming her. "It's okay," Mallory told him. "This isn't your fault." He was barely keeping it together. "We'll figure this out." *This isn't your fault.* She searched online for information about money orders and read through an article on the computer screen five times before the information clicked and she turned the money order over and saw the phone number printed on the back. She called it, waiting on hold, pressing the pads of her fingers against the nail of her thumb in a repeated pattern until her fingertips were dented and red. But it calmed her, kept her from sliding off into despair. By the time she finally got through to someone who let her explain the situation, Asshole Craig had strolled magnanimously onto the floor. When he stopped by a display to straighten out a few boxes of baked goods, she waved him over.

"I've got them on the phone," she said. "They want to talk to the store manager about the money order."

He frowned and flapped his hand; she gave him the receiver.

"Yes, this is the manager of the store." His brow pinched and he patted his stomach. "Yes, I signed the money order." He paused, and his voice changed from defensive to congenial. "Yes, that is correct—my associate filled out the form." Craig shot her a look and Mallory busied herself behind a register, rubbing at a spot on the banana scale. She knew the only way to get the mistake corrected was to save Craig's ego and admit to filling in the store address herself. "Yes, yes, I see," she heard him saying. "Yes, all right, we can do that. Thank you," he said.

Asshole Craig hung up the phone and logged on to the computer terminal next to her without saying a word, working at the screen several moments before disappearing into his back office. A few minutes later, he came back out and handed the young man a newly reissued check.

Mallory rang up a hot coffee and a cheeseburger wrapped in wax paper. "See ya next time," she said. And it would take a while for her body to calm down, but she had an explanation now, a reason for why she behaved the way she did. Instead of hating on herself all the time, she could understand. Instead of doubting herself, she could give a little space. Her body was not always living in present-day reality. Her brain and central nervous system were still wired as if she were living in constant fear for the people she loved.

Because for the first fifteen years of her life, she had.

23

The youth shelter sat on a residential street in a row of apartment rentals and single-family dwellings. Black snow walled the edges of the street, the snow cavities pitted and decayed and mounded so high on the corners they blocked the view of oncoming cars. Saturday morning, just before 0900, Mallory parked there on the street. Her wheels bumped over the hard blocks of snow dropped from the wheel wells of previous cars as she centered her vehicle, turned off the engine, and palmed the keys.

She'd accepted the fact of her cold now. The rims of her nostrils were sore-looking and red, but she'd slept the night through, her hives were starting to clear up, and she felt ready to see Shay. Popping a cough drop and locking the car, she left the hood of her coat down, not hiding her face.

Gabby Stenberger had suggested a visit on Saturday morning because that's when they scheduled outings for the residents. She'd have more privacy with Shay that way. They hadn't seen each other in ten days, and it had been almost two weeks since they met on the night of the blood moon. The diamond-shaped window glass shivered slightly under Mallory's gloved fist when she knocked. A car sat running ominously behind her, across the street, its exhaust soiling the air. A woman with a small, fox-shaped face fringed by ash-blonde hair answered the door.

"I'm here to see Shay," Mallory said. She gave the woman her name.

The woman nodded without saying anything and, wrapping a cardigan around herself, led Mallory into a foyer that smelled of fried potatoes. Before letting her in through the second, inner door, the woman took out a key and unlocked a metal box sitting on a pedestal outside the door.

"Phone," she whispered, as though it pained her to talk.

"Oh." Mallory removed her phone and dropped it into the box, remembering what the social worker had said about the strict no–cell phone rules. She had felt so bad about not giving Shay her phone, and it was a relief to know that she'd done nothing wrong.

The fox-faced woman proceeded through the living room and into an apartment space that contained a collection of mismatched bean bags and chairs around a single TV. A giant whiteboard on wheels dominated the other end. The board was divided neatly into colored squares—a chore chart marked with names. Like a parent searching for their child's artwork, Mallory scanned the list until she found Shay's name, written in blue letters in the column marked "Recycling."

"Wait," the woman whispered with her wounded, graveled throat. They were in the dining room now, filled with a small hutch and a table with chairs, two doorways offering views of the kitchen and stairs. Mallory thought about how they might share the domestic chores, she and Shay, pictured them washing the dishes together, but not on a school night, or if Shay had to study for a test. Mallory started to worry about helping Shay with her homework but stopped herself. The woman slowly ascended the stairs, as though to move any faster would cause her pain.

On the back of a wooden chair, Mallory quietly hung her coat, plucking off her gloves and stuffing them in the coat sleeves. She had smelled cigarette smoke in the woman's clothes and got the feeling she was in a protected space among very fragile and breakable things. She moved slowly, taking a seat at a lacquered wood table in the middle of the room. A dream catcher made of bent willow switches hung behind the door in one corner, above a boiler painted white. On the other side of the doorway, a pet carrier sat wedged between the wall and a china hutch. Instead of dishes behind the glass doors, the hutch stowed craft supplies—plastic containers of pom-poms, feathers, googly eyes. Labels adhered to the drawers boasted of acrylic paint, markers, and colored pens.

Shay descended the stairs. She moved languidly in fleece-lined

boots made of faux suede, with soft gray sweatpants and a matching
sweatshirt, no hood. Her hair, clean and brushed, hung smooth and
straight by the sides of her face. It covered the area where the bruise
had mostly healed, her skin there a yellowish green. Her eyes were
clear and bright. They swept across Mallory as she slid into her seat,
her left arm traveling in its cast. The first thing Shay did was push
an envelope out to the center of the table.

"What's this?" Mallory said.

Shay shrugged.

Mallory pulled the envelope in. Doodles of farmyard chickens
and hatchlings decorated the outer edges of the envelope. Dots of
colored pen in yellow, brown, and red, representing chicken feet and
beaks, even the rooster comb.

"That's great," Mallory smiled, keeping her voice hushed. "You've
really got a talent for rendering chickens."

Shay lowered her eyes, and the stud in her nose shyly glimmered.

The envelope hadn't been sealed, so Mallory fit a finger in to
pull out the flap. Inside was a bracelet made of yellow and white
beads. Plastic prisms cut into five-pointed stars were interspersed
with smaller beads the size of rice. "This is beautiful." She felt its
cool weight, the pleasant heaviness on her skin. The beads, strung
along a band of elastic, easily rolled over her hand and onto her
wrist. "Wow." Mallory did not know what to say. "This is so nice.
Thank you."

"We had to make it."

That small pebble had landed inside her mouth with its cool, hollow weight.

"I love it. Now, whenever I see it, I'll think of you."

Shay drew in her shoulders as if to ward off the praise.

"You know, I went to the hospital again to visit you," Mallory
said, "and they wouldn't tell me anything about where you'd gone. I
thought I was never going to see you again."

Shay inspected the ends of her hair.

"So how are you doing? Are things going okay?"

"I guess."

"What do you do here all day, besides making beautiful brace-lets?"

"We go to school."

"Where?"

"At the school."

Mallory took her hands off the table. Maybe she had made too big of a deal about the bracelet. Maybe she needed to dial it back. Her right leg trundled under the table, and she sat up straighter and fingered her own hair. Lifting it off from the side of her face, she tucked it—very deliberately and for the first time in ten years—behind one ear.

"I met with your social worker," Mallory said. "What do you think of her?"

"She's okay."

"I like her. I think she's good. She let me see you."

Shay shrugged and started picking at the lacquer on the wood table with a fingernail. Behind her, through the archway, the woman who had let Mallory in moved quietly around a kitchen. It was clean, all the counters wiped down and dishes put away, with no school drawings or pictures hung up with magnets on the fridge.

"How is your arm?"

Shay pushed out her lips and shrugged.

"When do you get your cast off?"

"I don't know."

"Few weeks?"

"Prolly."

"Cool."

Mallory had thought about what Gabby Stenberger had said, to tell Shay about her life. But now, in front of the girl and with this woman in the kitchen, Mallory didn't know how to start. Snot trick-led into the back of her throat and she coughed. A little furrow of scraped-off lacquer had built up beside Shay's finger.

"So," Mallory tried again. "I started the process to get my foster parent license."

Shay lifted a brow.

"I don't know if I'll be any good at it, and I'm no cook, but I'm willing to give it a try if you like the idea." She swallowed hard and waited.

"Yeah, okay."

"Okay. Do you have anything you want to ask me?"

"Like what?"

"I don't know. Just, anything."

Shay glanced up. "Why did you tell me all that stuff at the hospital last time?"

"Yeah, about that." Mallory reached out a finger and also scratched at the lacquered wood. "I'd never told anybody the whole thing before, and once I got going, it just sort of took over and came out. I didn't mean to dump on you." The air dried up in her mouth, with the sharp taste of menthol. "I just wanted you to know that you aren't alone, that you're more than just who you are to some guy in a relationship, and when you're ready to talk, I'm here, and I won't judge."

From the kitchen, Mallory heard the crinkling of a cigarette pack, and the woman who had let her in slipped out through a back door. A waft of cold air snaked into the dining room with the soft percussive closing of the door. It was a back door that led out to an alleyway at the rear of the house, where any car that wanted to could roll in from off the street.

"Do you feel safe here?" Mallory said.

Shay teeth-sucked air. "I don't know why I'm here." She sounded annoyed.

"You really don't know?"

"They put *you* in a safe house?"

"No. Nobody knew what my boyfriend did."

"He hit you?"

"He bought me a ring."

"J.T. got me a case of orange pop—a whole case all to myself." Her eyes dipped coyly. "He didn't want any for himself."

"That your favorite?"

"I like orange things."

The loud rattle of a metal lawn chair banged from outside and both girls jumped in their seats. Their eyes met, both their startle reflexes heightened, and that meant something to Mallory now.

"It's like a spider is going to get me," Mallory said. Turning her hand into a tarantula, she scrabbled it across the table and mock-shrieked quietly, "Ah!"

Shay mock-jumped. "Get that thing away from me!"

Both girls smiled knowingly as Mallory put her spider hand away. No more loud noises came from outside.

"My boyfriend, Jarrod, got aggressive sometimes when he got mad," Mallory said, admitting this for the first time. "If he got frustrated, you know, and I said something he didn't like, he would yell at me or throw things or kick the dog." She brought her hand out again and peeled off another thin curl of the lacquer with a fingernail. It was oddly satisfying. "It bothered me, and I always thought it was my fault, you know? I thought it was normal, to be afraid around the people you love."

She paused, hoping Shay would share something in return. When she didn't, Mallory continued, scraping up the tiny, opaque curls, keeping her voice steady and low.

"I thought this because of the way my parents would fight. And I know I was lucky to have both a mom and a dad. I know that everybody fights. So, we just did what we were told."

She was pushing out steady strips of curls now with the end of her nail, avoiding Shay's eyes, just staying with the sensation of gentle pressure on the tips of her fingers.

"It took me a while to understand that she didn't deserve it. I thought my mom kept screwing up, and I just wanted her to stop screwing up. I'm only figuring it out now. Like, my mind couldn't process it at the time, so I dissociated. So much was happening, I split into two, and now I'm reconnecting with myself, and all these memories keep coming up. I can't stop replaying them, you know? They're like movies in my head." She looked at Shay. "Do you ever do that? Your social worker said it was called *trauma reenactment*. Like, you can't stop thinking about it over and over even though you hate it?"

"Yeah," Shay said. "I got that."

The back door screeched open and the woman came back in. The scent of cigarette smoke reappeared briefly on a swath of cold air and Mallory heard the scrape of slippers on the linoleum and the clipped pop of an opening cupboard door.

Water gushed into a teapot, followed by the rattle of spoons in a drawer. From outside on the street a car sloshed through snow.

"I keep having this one whenever someone buys milk at the Speed Stop store," Mallory said, going first, her tone level and detached. "The milk triggers it, I think, and it's like I'm there again, watching it.

"I'm a kid standing in a nightgown with my feet freezing cold. My mom has her head bent over the kitchen sink and my dad is holding her by the hair. She let the milk go sour in the fridge again so he's making her drink it. He's pouring milk into her mouth, yelling at her to drink it, and she's trying to but also choking and crying. I can see the curdled chunks in her face and hair; I can see the tears on her cheeks. But I'm standing there, I don't do anything. I don't try to stop it because I know if I do it will only make it worse, so I'm just watching and listening." *You were her witness.* Mallory raised her eyes. "It's very confusing to watch someone you love hurting someone you love."

Shay didn't look up. Her finger picked at the lacquer, the veins on the inside of her wrist a cold winter blue. "Angie stabbed my brother."

Mallory waited.

"My stepmom." Shay didn't raise her eyes. "In the kitchen. They were fighting and she turns around and stabs him with a steak knife in the stomach. I see her do it. I see the blade go in through his clothes. I get my phone and I'm calling the police. I'm outside when they come, because it's like I'm puking tears and the officer keeps telling me to calm down like I'm acting wrong. And my stepmom is yelling at me from the window, 'Get yourself back in here,' and she's acting like nothing happened and everything is fine, and she tells the police that I'm lying. And they put me in the cop car. And

I can't calm down now because I know they don't believe me and I'm trying to call my brother but he isn't answering his phone." Her breathing had changed and a light sheen of perspiration stood out on her brow. Between the two of them, the flecks of table lacquer had piled up like dandruff flakes of snow.

"I'm sorry, Shay."

"What for?"

"For what happened."

Shay teeth-sucked more air. "They don't care."

"I care."

The teapot in the kitchen shrieked. Shay's body stiffened and she looked away, face expressionless, as if pretending she didn't exist, and in that reaction Mallory saw herself, as if she were looking in a mirror.

"Do you want to get a dog?" Mallory asked. "Or a cat? Maybe a goldfish. A snake?"

"I do not want a snake."

"Tarantula." She brought out her spider hand again and crawled it toward Shay.

"Stop that!" The girl smiled, and Mallory saw that little gap between her front teeth. It felt nice between them, good and right. It felt like the true beginnings of their solidarity.

24

For the first time since she'd gotten back from Kuwait, Mallory dug joyfully through her duffel bag, looking for her running clothes. She thought about how they could decorate Shay's room—they could order cute things like decorative pillows and white lights, maybe get a houseplant. She didn't have to work until late that night, and the temperature outside had finally risen above ten degrees. By the time she got to the lake she had warmed and felt the power and strength of her own muscles, how they carried her. The positively flowing endorphins must have given her the gumption, because when she saw Landon James outside in his backyard, gathering firewood, she called out with gusto and waved.

"Hey! I have news about Shay!" She took her earbuds out and bounded up. "She's doing much better. I just came back from visiting her." The gaiter around her neck had beaded from her breath and her nose wouldn't stop running. Odin hurtled through the snow to greet her, wagging and pushing into her legs.

"That's great," Landon said. "How wonderful." His arms, loaded down with firewood, looked pumped even under his woolen flannel, and he hadn't shaved, the golden stubble thick on his neck and chin, threaded with glints of silvery gray. A pair of reading glasses perched lopsidedly on his head, and he wore gloves but no coat.

"I was just out getting wood," he said sheepishly. "Do you want to come in?"

She hesitated, rubbing Odin behind the ears.

"Or maybe I shouldn't interrupt your run," he said.

"No, it's fine," she said. "I have time."

"You saw her today?" He held open the back door leading into the kitchen, the same door where she had arrived with Shay. Odin pushed himself in first and Mallory followed, grateful for the rush of warmth. She removed her gaiter and gloves.

"Yeah, just this morning. I went to the youth hostel where she's staying and we talked." She followed Landon into the living room and told him about the visit, about how well Shay had looked, how she was going to school and was on a wait list for a good program her social worker was trying to get her into. Landon James knelt by the woodstove and built up his fire.

"How long is the wait list?"

"Uh, a few months I think."

Landon winced, poking at the logs.

"I know. But these are the best programs in the state, and if they can find housing for Shay that's not at the shelter, then she might get in sooner."

Landon fed another log to the crackling flames.

"I'm applying to be her foster parent. Just temporarily; just if no one else from her family comes through."

He turned at looked at her. "Are you up for that?"

"Yeah, I think so." She got nervous. "You don't think I can do it?" She felt herself get defensive and a little peevish.

"No, it's not that," he said. "It's just a big responsibility." He cranked down the venting shafts and shut the cast iron doors.

"How did you know all that, about safe harbor states?"

He stood, brushing wood detritus from his sleeves. "Can I get you anything? Coffee, tea, or a water?"

"Oh, no thanks." She watched him whisk around a mini dustpan and broom, apparently ignoring her question. On the reading chair by the window, a fleece blanket was coiled next to a book and a coffee cup perched neatly on its moose coaster. She hadn't stood outside watching his house in almost three weeks.

"I didn't know I'd be seeing you or I would have brought back your things," she said.

"What things?" He hung the sweep kit back on the wall.

"Your duffle coat and shoes?"

"Oh, don't worry about those, they're so old. Give them to Good-will or— Hey, I almost forgot." His face brightened. "I have some-thing for you downstairs. You said you have a few minutes?"

"I do."

"It's in the darkroom."

She followed him into the kitchen, where he flicked on the light at the top of the basement stairs and trotted down in front of her.

"I've never been in a darkroom before," she said, hesitating at the top. She wasn't exactly fond of basements. But she'd known Landon was a photographer since the first day they met, back in August, when the sky held clouds of Jiffy Pop and sun rays unfolded without ob-struction. She'd been out walking Baily and had found Landon in the middle of the road, crouched behind a tripod, the sky a tender shade of pink.

"I think I got it," he had said. "The sunsets are the best. With the sunrises you're always waiting for it to get more beautiful, so you miss the perfect shot." He grinned. "Or I do, at any rate."

She held on to the railing now and took the steps slow. Landon had already turned on another light and was going through boxes.

"Holy shit," she said, the walls coming into view. "You take a lot of pictures."

He laughed. "Got to. It takes a lot of bad ones to get the one that's good."

She stood a moment at the bottom step, taking it all in. The bare bulb cast its light along the walls of a space different from any she'd ever seen before. Pictures were everywhere—taped, tacked, hung, strung; large and small, eleven by fourteen, six by eight, framed and unframed, even miniature ones with the edges of the photopaper artfully torn; some black-and-white, others full color or sepia-toned in gilded frames; prints professionally matted behind glass; sketches on notebook paper, charcoal drawings, other artwork he must have done, tacked to the white cinder block walls; a whole series of eight-by-ten photographs of ships coming in to dock on Lake Superior hung from a piece of twine, pegged like clothes on a line. Bottles and jugs of fluids lined the shelves of a long worktable covered in large, shallow trays, taking up the entire wall under the basement windows.

"Go ahead, take a look around," Landon said, noticing she was still standing in one place. "It's not every day I get a visitor down here, so please excuse the mess." He'd ducked again under the stairs to sort through cardboard cartons, removing the lids.

"Do you develop all your photos the old way?"

"No. I own a few digital cameras—got to, to compete. But it's how I prefer to work."

"Why do I smell hamburger pickles?"

"That's the stop bath solution. My sister says it smells like salt-vinegar chips."

"Oh my god." She grinned. "That's what that is! I've always wondered what that smell was in your clothes."

"Yeah?" He hopped behind another stack of cartons and pulled on another string, turning on a light under the stairs. "Best smell in the world."

A framed photo caught her eye then, of a young girl, early teens, with dark hair and a slight build, standing on a rock overlooking a lake. It was the way it'd been shot and then developed to accentuate the sharply contrasting shadows, the way the water brooded, its folding musculature, and how the girl stood—Mallory could feel her anger, raw and heavy.

"I think this is my favorite one," she said. "It's so emotional. I don't know how you did it."

Landon turned his head. "You have a good eye," he said. "That photograph won me a major prize and led to my first job with *National Geographic*." He clamped his hands on his hips and went back to his search. "I thought I put it in one of these boxes. Sometimes I can be a real neatnik when it comes to my cameras."

The girl in the photo had her back to the camera, you could only see the side of her face, and yet Mallory thought of Landon James. She couldn't say why—something in the girl's build and the way she held herself. And Mallory remembered the conversation they'd had in the truck, about a father looking for a daughter he thought was dead.

"You have a daughter," she said.

He shuffled a cardboard flap. "I do."

"I didn't know you were married."

"I'm not. Just a father, and a poor one at that." He stood with his head bowed over another box, his face in shadow under the bald light. "Of course, my daughter hates that photo." He moved to another shelf, pulling down another lidded box.

"I don't know why," Mallory said. "All a daughter ever wants is to be seen by her dad." She said this and a prickle broke out across her skin. With the sweat drying in the cool air under her clothes, she suddenly shuddered. "Sorry," she said.

"Why are you sorry?"

"I don't know."

He looked at her, seeing her in that way he had, and the moment swung precipitously, as if time were a pendulum and they had come to a stop on the top of a swing in the half-second before its fall back the other way. "What I said earlier about the responsibility of being a parent wasn't about you," he said. "It was about me. I'm sure you'll do great."

She held her breath, waiting for the pendulum to drop, the praise suspended inside her.

"When I was your age and living in LA, my girlfriend got pregnant and we had a daughter named Kierra. She was bright and curious, but I wouldn't let her into my studio. I thought art was all that mattered. I moved out when Kierra was eight."

"I'm sure you had your reasons."

"No." He shook his head. "I didn't know what I was doing. Her mother had a drug problem that I was too self-absorbed to see. She was in the entertainment industry; she took pills to stay thin. When she wasn't on the pills, she was difficult to be around, because she wouldn't eat, and I couldn't handle the drama of it all and it was affecting my health. But Kierra refused to come with me. She stayed to take care of her mom and then became addicted herself. I spent the better part of my thirties in limbo, searching for her. Last I heard, Kierra was living with a crackhead boyfriend and working in a gentleman's club."

Mallory didn't know what to say. A quarrel of energies had filled her, she felt wildly defensive of Landon, and yet, he'd fallen off her pedestal.

"Aha! Found it." He turned around. "First digital camera I ever owned." He rubbed a thumb across the screen, then wiped it with a rag and brought it over to her. "It's old technology but still works. I'm not using it anymore and I thought, 'Mallory should have this.'" He put the camera in her hands. "It's yours to keep, if you're interested."

She held the bulk of its mechanisms and tasted the cold metal that had filled her nose. "My dad left," she said. "I would give anything for him to come looking for me." She set the camera down.

Landon pulled a camera lens from the box. "It's none of my beeswax," he said, "but I'm sure his leaving had nothing to do with you." He took the camera, snapped off the lens, replaced it with a macro, and gave it back to her. "Sometimes we convince ourselves that the only way to help someone who is hurting is by hurting right along with them. But that doesn't work and it never will. Becoming less doesn't help anyone to become more."

She set the camera down again and very slowly backed away. "I have to go." She bumped into the bare bulb above the shelf, sending crazy shadow lines swinging across the space.

"Mallory?"

She headed up the stairs.

"I didn't mean to upset you," he said, calling out behind her. "Don't listen to me. I'm just a nosy Nancy."

She tripped over the dog.

"Honestly, Mallory, I say whatever comes into my head."

And she was gone, out the door, running past his house and into the road, with the cold ripping the water back from her hot and bewildered face.

25

The last person to run the floor washer hadn't changed out the detergent. Mallory dumped the stagnant water in the mop bucket sink and the chemical smell of ammonia and mildew filled her nose. She ran fresh water, scrubbing out the tank, and thought again of being in the basement with Landon James. A welter of spirals jumbled in her chest. She measured the detergent solution, refilling the tank with fresh suds. It was just after 0230 during her Saturday night shift, the last two hours had crawled by, and she would die if Noah didn't talk to her now. She unmuted the mic on her headset.

"Noah, you there?"

He didn't say anything. He'd been barely civil all night.

"Landon invited me down into his darkroom." She waited, held her breath.

"Good for you."

Oh thank god, she thought, and exhaled. "No, it wasn't good. It was totally uncomfortable, because it turns out he's a dad. He has a daughter whose probably around my age and she's missing." The words poured from her mouth while water poured into the tank. "And he was trying to give me this camera, a totally kind thing, a really great camera, which I totally wanted, but then I started thinking about my dad and I started wondering, did he have hobbies? What else did he want to do other than work? And I left without taking the camera."

She turned the water valve under the washer to the horizontal *On* position.

"I don't know why, but I've never thought of my dad as a regular person before, as someone outside of his role as *my dad*. I always thought of him as God." She checked the water-level gage, but it still hadn't filled. "Noah?"

"We all have to face this," he said. "Everyone comes to the realization that parents are just people trying to figure things out and sometimes, they make mistakes."

"Yeah, well, I never thought of it that way before. I mean, I guess I felt entitled to a safe environment as a kid and then felt sorry for myself when I didn't get that."

"Yeah. And I felt sorry for myself because my dad never bought life insurance."

She turned off the hot water.

"Great. So, here we are."

"My mom told me, 'You can blame anyone you want to for your shitty life, but in the end, you're still the one who has to live it.'"

Mallory refit cap to the water tank. "Your mom used the word shitty?"

"She taught English. She wanted me to have access to all the tools."

Mallory inserted the key and turned the washer on. "I really want to go back and get that camera, but I have to do it before Andrea gets home or she'll ask me where it came from."

"Why? I thought you two broke up."

"We did, but I'm still living with her until I find an apartment." She disengaged the back pedal, lowering the pad driver to the floor. "She doesn't get back until tomorrow night." Mallory tried to lower the squeegee but it was stuck.

"You mean Monday night?"

"No, she gets back Sunday night."

"That's today."

"Shit." She aggressively torked the lever but the squeegee still wouldn't lower. Fearing she might break it, Mallory stepped away. The fluorescent lights hummed in the ceiling and a Phil Collins song crooned overhead. The week had gone by so fast, and the apartment she'd applied for had fallen through. She didn't know why it had fallen through—she'd just received a form rejection via e-mail, saying the unit had been rented and to try again. Had they done a background check? Found her image on the dark web?

"I was supposed to be moved out by the end of this week," she said, "and I haven't been able to find an apartment." She knelt to examine the crank handle, gently jiggled it around. "I don't know why this is so hard." Finally, it released, and the mechanism lowered to the floor. She pressed the brush button and moved the washer out through the locker room door. "Do you know anybody looking for a roommate? Someone who wouldn't mind living with a Jekyll and Dr. Hyde?"

"It's Dr. Jekyll and Mr. Hyde."

"Thanks for the clearing that up."

"You want my heart to bleed for you?"

"No, that's all right. I already hear you quietly judging me." She walked behind the washer as it slowly polished the floor. It was like pushing a large, sleepy lawnmower with scrubbers instead of blades. "You're the one person who I can talk to, Noah, and I've got a lot going on."

"You think you're the only one with stuff going on?"

"No." She maneuvered the washer around the end cap of an aisle. "I'm sorry, Noah. What's going on with you?"

"You gave me your cold." His voice in her ear did sound congested. "I think it's turning into a sinus infection, or maybe walking pneumonia."

"That bad?"

"Also, I have to micturate."

He came out from the kitchen wearing a surgical mask, with a village of boxed chicken tenders on his tray. That was Noah—ahead of the curve. He'd always been concerned with germs, even as a little kid. His mother kept a domed lid for him, from an old wok, and used it to cover his food at the dinner table in case one of his brothers sneezed. His uncle who worked in a hospital kept him supplied with masks. Noah restocked the Hot Spot and left through the swinging kitchen doors.

She pushed the floor washer alone down another empty aisle.

"Noah?" she spoke into the headset. "Are you going to micturate now?" She'd had to ask him what that was, the first time he'd used the word to ask for a bathroom break.

"No. I have to wait until my waffle fries are done."

"Okay. Because I want to apologize to you." She walked past the peanut and sunflower seed display. "I'm sorry for giving you my cold. And for yelling at you when you were only trying to help. Most of all, I'm sorry for throwing that Cambro at your head and being an angry asshole all the time." She turned the floor washer around and went down the next aisle. "I don't want to be. I swear to god I never want to be." She didn't like that it had taken her so long to say this, but she actually felt sorry now—unlike last time, when she knew she should but didn't.

"I forgive you," Noah said.

She was glad that he'd forgiven her but sad that he'd had to.

"Do you think I make things harder than they need to be?" The floor washer hummed and the Muzak bopped and time swung on its pendulum and came, during that brief period in the dead zone in the middle of the night, to a rest. "It's like there's this darkness inside of me that I can't get rid of, and I don't know how much if it is real and how much of it is imagined. Sometimes, I can't stop thinking bad things in my head." She turned the floor washer around again.

"Dark matter makes up 27 percent of the universe," he said, "and dark energy accounts for 68 percent; therefore, we need the darkness, or the universe would fall apart."

One of his oven timers went off.

"Dark stuff holds us together," he said, clarifyingly. "We need it."

"Thank you, Noah." She didn't know what to say. A strange kind of emotion swung through her chest. "How'd you get so smart?" She wasn't really asking, but he took it that way.

"My mom used to read books to me all the time when I was a kid."

"Oh yeah?" She pushed the floor washer down another empty aisle. "Like *Einstein's Theory of Relativity, the Deluxe Edition*?"

"No, we read normal bedtime stories. Like *Goodnight Moon* and *The Little Prince*."

"Oh, that explains it."

"Explains what?"

"My dark matter. My mom used to tell us stories that started with 'Once upon a time in the deepest darkest woods . . .'"

"She never read to you from books?"

"No, she did, but we read the wrong books. We read *Bad Night Moon* and *The Little Shit*."

Noah opened another oven door and took something out. *"The Very Angry Caterpillar,"* he said.

"Harold and the Black Crayon."

"Where the Wild Things Aren't."

"The Taking Tree."

"The Little Engine that Would Not."

"Winnie-the-Screw-You."

By the end of it they were laughing so hard the tears had washed the black kohl from under her eyes.

26

Mallory got the call at 0700 that morning. The youth hostel had called Gabby Stenberger on Saturday night. Sunday morning, Gabby called her.

"Mallory Moe?" She sounded breathless and focused.

"That's me." Mallory had changed into sweats and was in the kitchen, getting down a soup pouch.

"Thank goodness you're up early. I'm in crisis mode about one of my girls. I'm calling to ask if you've seen or heard anything from Shay."

Mallory opened the fridge to get out the milk. "Sure, I just saw her." The wolf wailed down its lonesome call.

"Where? When?"

"Today. I mean yesterday. At the shelter."

"Tell me exactly when."

"I saw her on Saturday like we talked about."

"Morning or afternoon?"

"Morning." Mallory set the milk on the counter, tingles dancing in the top of her head. "I got there around nine a.m. I thought our first meeting went really well. She made me a bracelet."

"What else can you tell me? How did she seem?"

Something was different about Gabby Stenberger's voice. "What's going on?"

"It's a long shot," Gabby said. "I'm calling everyone I can think of. I thought maybe you might know where she is."

"She's not at the shelter?"

"No. She left there last night and didn't come back. Broke her curfew and about ten different rules."

Mallory felt emotionally kneecapped and had to sit down.

"She could still show up for school on Monday, and I'm reaching out to a few other places, but the shelter called to see where else she might have gone, and I'm just following up with everything I have."

"Could she have gone to Bemidji?"

"Maybe."

"How would she get there?"

"She would hitch. Unless these girls have a phone, that's usually their best option. I'll be calling all my contacts up there."

Mallory thought about how she had almost given Shay her phone. "Do you think she somehow got a phone?"

"Oh, I'm sure she did. Kids these days always seem to be able to get a hold of a phone no matter how many protocols we have in place. It's how these men control these girls, how they lure them back in. It's how they do everything."

"I don't understand." Mallory was pacing now. "Why would she go back? Things were going so well!"

"I know. Most people don't understand. Most people would find it inconceivable to understand the amount of psychological control these guys have over these young girls. They think it's about the physical control, the beatings and abuse, and that is part of it, but it's the psychological chains that are so much stronger."

"What can we do?" Mallory said. "Do we call the police?"

"And tell them what? Shay left of her own free will. We only ever had temporary custody."

"But she's just a kid." Mallory halted in the middle of the room. "Was it something I said? Or did? Was there something else I could have done?"

"Don't even go there," Gabby said. "That's always the tendency, the first time it happens."

"The first time?"

"Usually it takes three or four times before these girls are able to break free. I know it's heartbreaking. The pull to go back to what

you know, bad as it is, will always be more appealing than the difficult and unknown path that lies ahead."

"So, what do we do now?"

"Now, we hope."

❄

Her body had begun to move before she could even think. It put
on her coat and hat and winter boots. It yanked on her gloves and
pulled open the back kitchen door. It stumbled down the cedar
decking stairs.

A streaked and snow-covered road led the way in the pale cold
light. Bands of pink and yellow colored the sky. Her breath churned
whitecaps as she strode out into the quiet of an early morning, where
trees stood multitudinous all around.

Sound came from her throat—low, guttural bursts. She could
not keep it inside, the groans. They escaped through her jaw, primal
grunts, obscene and gruff.

At the intersection where Riley Ridge branched out to meet the road
that looped around the lake, she pressed on, going down the middle of
the road, straight. Sound vibrated in her throat, fluttered her lips. She
could not keep it in.

Mallory stopped in the road and let out a cry. Shaking her head,
she scavenged for breath, walked on.

She continued until she came to the deer carcass, left clean and
picked over on top of the snow. Hollow archways of rib bones flocked
with ice sparkled absurdly in the morning light. The sickle of a morning moon hung low and bright just over the tree line, and Mallory
climbed up over the embankment, her gloved hands scraping across
the snowbank. She scrambled to her feet, stood unsteadily, and skated
out across the planes of polished snow.

Holding her hands out to either side, she wanted to walk where
Shay had walked, breathe where Shay had breathed, skate out across
the three-foot-deep snow.

But Mallory's boot punched down, her leg dropping all the way
past the knee, and she fell, losing her balance. "Motherfucker,"

she said. "Motherfucker, motherfucker, motherfucker!" She yelled into the woods toward the cabin where Shay had once been. She cursed and flailed and lifted out her legs, but over and over her boots punched down. The conditions that had allowed Shay to walk across the snow had changed, and Mallory never saw the other cabin, never heard or saw another human soul. Fighting and straining, she went on anyway, lungs burning, eyes stinging, nose running against the cold. She howled and fell and cried and wailed, keeping nothing in. She got out all her rage. All the things she wanted to say but didn't know how. Her confusion and loss, her sorrow and shame, her guilt and the ways she had failed, her pride and the ways she had loved.

The woods as she had known them had always been her safe haven, a quiet place. And on that day, the woods did not let her down. The trees stood in the preternatural quiet of a winter morning, with only the tops of their branches glowing brilliant in the light. They listened and said nothing back. They did not argue. They did not tell her that she was wrong. They took it from her and held her pain. They listened and absorbed her rage.

And the woods remained unchanged.

A large raven broke loose from the arrowed point of a nearby spruce, the bird so close that Mallory felt the displaced air against her cheeks. It soared through the trees, calling three times, *gronk, gronk, gronk,* rising upward with voluminous sweeps.

It came to her like the nod of an acknowledgment—not a good feeling like an epiphany or a revelation but simply the fact of how it was. The bird moved away on silent wings and Mallory understood now why she could no longer fly in her dreams, the force that was holding her back—what prevented her from succeeding, from going forward in this life. It was never outside of her. It was never them or anyone else. It was her.

It was only ever her.

PART

SIX

27

Andrea's headlights scoped across the walls, the light skittering through the window glass as the car turned into the driveway. In the living room, Mallory's heart drummed as she repositioned the couch pillows. After getting the call Sunday morning from the social worker and going on that walk in the woods, she hadn't been able to sleep. She'd tossed and turned and finally got up to clean and prepare the house. She'd stripped the slipcovers from the sofa, treating the stains, washing and drying and putting the covers back on. She'd vacuumed in all the crevices, sucking up dog hair and popcorn, steam cleaning the carpet, shaking out the rugs. The electric hum of the generator on the back deck vibrated as the sun rose and set.

"Hey, welcome home." Mallory held open the door. Sweat stood out in the fine hairs around her ears and along the back of her neck. She'd been aware of her rising anxiety for the last several hours. She was hot and cold, expectant and scared. It was just Andrea coming home, but it felt the same to her as it had when her dad returned after a long deployment, and her body could not be calmed.

"Hola, chica." Andrea maneuvered her purple suitcase over the threshold and rolled it through. White alpacas marched across a new fleece hoodie. She smelled of sunlight and rain.

"You look refreshed."

"It was an incredible trip." Andrea rolled the suitcase through the living room. "I have a whole new respect for birds." In the bedroom, she flicked on the light. "You cleaned!" Even from halfway across the house her voice tingled in Mallory's cheeks.

"Yeah, I also made soup." She'd opened a pouch, added milk. "It's homemade."

"I'm starved," Andrea said, returning without her coat. "Eat with me? One last supper?" The *whomp-whomp*ing of Mallory's heart beat harder, the vibrations quivering in her throat.

"Yean, I have time." She was already dressed in her faded work pants and blue smock.

Andrea pulled the handle of the fridge. "You want a vitamin water?"

"No, thanks." Mallory stood at the stove ladling the soup. The sound of the lonesome wolf poured sugar down her back and her heart thunked louder in her chest. But she understood it now, she knew the reasons why.

"Which store are you working at tonight?" Andrea said.

"I'm still out here. I don't start at the store in Sterling until the nineteenth of February." She set the soup bowl down carefully so that the liquid didn't overspill the rim. She stood back, with her hands laced behind her back. "Do you want soda crackers or bread?" Sweat coated her brow and the inside of her palms and she could smell herself, the stress hormone that her body—without her permission— continued to secrete because it thought she was in danger right now. She rubbed her hands on her pants and stood at the table like her mom had always done, smelling the acuity of her fear.

"Just the soup," Andrea said, having no idea.

At the stove, Mallory ladled her own bowl, back straight, neck tight, alert and attuned to every little sound—the dip and scrape of Andrea's spoon, the clearing of her throat, every shift and creak of her chair.

"How is it?" Mallory almost winced from the sound of her own voice. She brought down the box of crackers and sat, but the minute her butt hit the chair she sprang up again. She'd forgotten salt and pepper—the unforgivable sin. Grabbing them from the stovetop, plucking off a ream of extra napkins, she sat back down, perched on the edge of her chair, and told herself that everything was all right. Hair pulled back, ears sticking out on either side of her head, she spread the paper napkin on her lap.

"Mmm," Andrea said, drawing liquid into her mouth.

"It's all right?"

"It's great."

"Does it need salt?"

"No, it's very good. Why are you watching me like that? You're making me nervous."

"Sorry."

"You're sweating."

"Yeah, I was cleaning." Mallory picked up her spoon. It'd been twelve hours since she'd received the phone call from the social worker. She'd spent the entire day cleaning in anticipation of Andrea coming home, but instead of feeling a sense of accomplishment and release, she'd felt a persistent nausea and rising despair. Between laundry cycles and while washing dishes, she'd listened to a podcast about survivor's guilt—a symptom of PTSD she hadn't even known she had.

"Andrea," she said, putting down the spoon.

"Mallory."

"I think that I have post-traumatic stress from living with my dad." Again, she got the feeling that he might be listening. She shifted uncomfortably in her seat.

"Makes sense."

"Does it? I always thought it didn't happen to me, you know. It happened to my mom."

"It happened to all of you. By not leaving, she put you in an impossible situation where all you could do was stand by and watch." Andrea continued eating her soup. "That's a special kind of torture called *inescapable shock*."

"Okay."

"Haven't you heard of it?"

"No."

"Pavlov discovered it when his lab flooded and he had all these dogs locked in cages and the poor things were trapped overnight in freezing, rising water. None of them died, but the experience totally changed their personalities. These once happy, friendly, playful dogs were suddenly aggressive and despondent. Pavlov attributed it to a system breakdown: their fight-or-flight responses were firing big-time but the dogs had nowhere to go."

Mallory stood, crossed the kitchen, got the butter dish from the counter, along with a plate and the bag of bread. She sat back down. Andrea the trauma expert made delicate slurping sounds.

"I've been having flashbacks all winter," Mallory said, buttering her bread. The round, velvety scent filled her nose. "I guess because I'm finally in a stable place, you know, not moving around or living overseas. I'm remembering things." Their utensils clinked lightly against the crockery, and the scent of lemon cleaner lingered in the air. "I'm struggling all the time for emotional stability. And I'm not always living in the present." Mallory picked up her spoon, willing herself to believe that things were okay. She could taste the lemon cleaner, or thought she did.

"Look at you, coming out of the trauma closet." Andrea smirked, rattling and crinkling the cracker box sleeve. "I can give you the name of a good therapist." She bit into a cracker, the sound of her chewing megaphoned in Mallory's ear. "Sometimes it takes a few tries to find one you like."

"Oh, um," Mallory set down her spoon.

"What, you don't think you can deal with this alone, do you?"

"No. It's just," she swallowed. "I don't know if talking about it helps, you know? It just recycles the pain."

"That's why you need to work with someone who specializes in healing trauma. They have new treatments—EEG neurofeedback, EMDR therapy, yoga, somatics—ways to help you release it from the body." Andrea snapped into another cracker. "There's been a lot of groundbreaking work done in this area. Doctors are calling adverse childhood experiences the greatest undiagnosed health threat in America. People are starting to get it—we're all walking around traumatized and not dealing with it, and so we keep hurting each other."

"Okay." Mallory nodded stiffly. "That's good advice."

"You might also ask them to prescribe you some Prozac," Andrea said, reaching for a handful of crackers now. "Seriously, I think the serotonin boost could really help you relax." She crumbled the crackers over her soup, the crumbs sifting down like snow.

"Can we talk about something else now?" Mallory said.

"Enough about you; let's talk about me."

"How was your trip?"

"I could tell you about the birds."

"Okay." It was good soup. "Tell me about the birds." It was just a package mix.

Andrea launched into a diatribe about a man named Angel Paz. "His name literally means 'Angel of Peace,' and you know how I have a thing for angels." Andrea dunked her crackers and stirred the soup, explaining how they had to get up at the crack of dawn to go birding. She spoke freely and unselfconsciously, and that allowed Mallory to settle and relax. She tried to pay attention and stay in the moment.

"He takes you out to this place in the forest," Andrea said excitedly, "and he calls to the birds by name. 'Good morning, Pepito,' he'll say. *Knee-knee-knee.'* And then we all hear from way back in the mist this little bird cheeping, *'Knee-knee-knee.'* And it takes, like, twenty minutes of this back-and-forth *cheep*ing and *knee-knee*ing, and then little Pepito comes hopping out and it's so fucking cute—this little yellow antpitta on tiny toothpick legs. I swear it looked just like my dad with his stick legs and belly paunch." Andrea laughed and Mallory smiled.

"They call him the Bird Whisperer," Andrea continued. "They eat right out of his hand. And I never realized that even within the same species, each bird has a different voice."

Mallory listened and watched as Andrea became animated again, imitating the birdsong of the Choco toucans, squawking and throwing back her head. Mallory was laughing now, and this was the Andrea she had fallen in love with when she'd first moved in. And she didn't want this to end. She didn't want to live alone. What she feared most was that she didn't know how to build her own nest.

"You don't really give a shit about the birds, do you?" Andrea said.

"No, no, I do. It's just . . ." Her eyes went to the windowpane reflecting back the ghost of another Mallory. "I'm thinking about how you're with Ripley now."

"Actually, I'm not." Andrea lowered her head, sifting her fingers over her napkin.

"What happened?"

"Nothing I want to get into right now."

They both scraped around in their soup bowls.

"You can keep talking about the birds," Mallory said.

"No. I'm done."

"I didn't know you had such a thing for them."

"My parents were not at all supportive when I went into environmental studies. Being a chemist was a compromise; it was the only way they would pay for my degree. I wanted to major in biology." She finished her vitamin water. "But there's no money in that. I mean, who knew about the Bird Whisperer?" She smirked, Andrea with her lopsided grin and liquid smoke eyes.

Mallory stood with her bowl. "Do you want more soup?"

"I'm satisfied, thank you." Andrea put her feet up on the empty chair while Mallory ran the warm water and squirted dish soap into the sink. "Did you find an apartment yet?" Andrea asked.

"I did, but it fell through." She plunged her hands into the suds. "I have appointments to look at more on my days off."

"When's that?"

"Tomorrow and all day Tuesday." She washed and stacked the bowls. "Three in Sterling, two in Duluth."

Behind her, Andrea got quiet. A few moments later, from the bedroom, came the spiky hum of a zipper travelling around three sides of a case.

Mallory thought about how when they'd first started dating, one night at a bar, some guy was telling a joke while Mallory stood there waiting for drinks. "Why do husbands beat their wives?" And that had snagged her attention. He delivered the punch line with a meaty smack of his fist in a mock angry voice: "Because they just don't listen!" And all his buddies had laughed.

"That's not funny," Mallory had said. The men swiveled their heads. The one who delivered the joke had a hamburger meat nose, his body twice her size, three times her weight. "You need to stop telling that joke," she told him. "It's crass and insensitive."

The man ran his tongue along the gumline of his teeth and said something along the lines of "You gonna make me?"

And Andrea had been there, rolling up her sleeves, angels blazing along both arms. "You boys sure you want to tangle with two angry bitches?"

"I have a huge favor to ask you," Andrea said now. Her tone had darkened, the vibration of that bass cello voice tingling in Mallory's cheeks. Mallory used to get drunk with it, inebriated by the feeling of being cared for and loved.

"I've been working on this list." Andrea held out a piece of paper and stood by the sink. "Every time I think of something, I write it down. These are all the things I can't live without that are still at my old house."

"Your place in Duluth?" Mallory scanned the items from the list. "A bug board? Is that what I think it is?"

"I was afraid of bugs, so I took a class." Andrea left the list on the counter and sat back down.

"The complete works of William Shakespeare?"

"My brother gave me that." She mocked a Shakespearean accent: "He thought it would improve my vocabulary."

"A Hello Kitty alarm clock?"

"You don't have to read everything out loud." Andrea folded up the cellophane wrapper of the cracker sleeve. "I'd do it myself, Mal, but I just can't go back there, and the guys are coming at the end of the month to paint and clean. My agent wants to get it listed to start showing by the first of March. Do you think you could stop over there and pick this stuff up? It would mean a lot."

"Sure." Mallory washed out a spoon and a cup. "So, you're selling?"

"I am."

"What about the rest of the furniture?"

"It's not much, and nothing I miss. St. Vincent's is picking it all up on Friday."

Mallory thought about how she'd been planning to fix up the apartment for Shay.

"Also, I got you a small souvenir," Andrea said. "They didn't have any cowbirds."

Mallory rinsed off and dried her soapy hands. On the table was the figurine of a bright red bird attached to a silver key ring.

"It's called the cock on the rock," Andrea said.

"Are you flirting with me?"

"It reminded me of you. Small but strong."

Mallory picked up the bird.

"And I stopped by my PO box on the way home. This came for you." It was an eight-by-ten yellow envelope, addressed to Mallory Moe. "You got the big one," Andrea said. "That's a good sign."

Mallory's stomach wobbled. The envelope was from the university where she had applied. She stood holding onto the little bird key chain. "I can't open that right now."

"Okay. Want me to do it for you?"

"No. I'll do it later."

"Are you afraid of getting in? Or *not* getting in?"

Mallory looked down at the bird in her hand. "Do you really think I'm strong?"

A brief quiet moved between them, the emotional equivalent of a rock in a shoe.

"I don't regret it, you know. Us," Andrea said. "We've been to some dark places, you and me. I've told you things I've never been able to tell anybody, and I thought the same was also true for you."

"It was."

"But I'm an adrenaline addict, a junkie. If I can't get it through substances, I create it through drama. I need to be with someone who can handle that." Her voice tenderly stroked Mallory's cheek. "It's been a while since I've lived on my own. My plan is to get a dog and find my own song."

Mallory put the bird down on the table and went back to scrubbing dishes in the sink.

Andrea put away the crackers and the bread. "What are you going to do if this envelope here says you're going to college?"

"I don't have to go."

"Why wouldn't you go?"

She didn't want to talk about college or her family or Shay. She suddenly and furiously wanted to be left alone.

"Mallory?"

"Maybe college isn't for me."

"Why would you say that?"

"I don't know. Why can't we live together and just be friends? Why can't you find your song with me around? We're just starting to figure things out."

"Mal."

"What? I don't understand. You say you want to take care of me, you say you want me to confront my trauma. Well, I'm doing all of these things and realizing all of this stuff and still it's not enough."

"This is me taking care of you. I'm sorry if you can't see that."

Mallory rinsed and rattled the dishes, cramming them onto the drainboard and rinsing out the sink. She knew that she was clinging to a failed relationship because it was familiar. She knew it was irrational and emotional that she was still reeling from the loss of Shay. It was a pattern she went sliding back into, a habit that she had learned—if Shay didn't have a chance at a future, then Mallory didn't want one either. She understood now what Landon had said. She'd been doing this unconsciously her entire life.

Becoming less doesn't help anyone to become more.

28

The customers came and went. Mallory checked off the items on the work list, blasting the pressure cleaner to loosen grime out of the grout, polishing the stainless steel coolers, and restocking the paper products on the back shelves. Eventually, things slowed and she was left alone in the store with a hollow, hopeless feeling in the depths of her bones. She sat on a high stool behind the register with a label maker in hand and she wanted to cry, to sleep for a million years. She wanted to crawl back into that hole inside of herself and hide there until all the snow had melted and the soil had warmed.

"Wakey-wakey," Noah said.

She jerked awake, pulling a hand from under chin, her stool clattering to the floor. "Oh my god, I am so tired," she said, righting the stool. "I just fell asleep sitting up."

"You should sleep all day after your shift." Noah spoke to her through the headset even though he was out on the floor. "Don't even try to get stuff done. And don't look at your phone." His hairnetted head bobbed along at the Hot Spot, unloading sandwiches from his tray.

"Can't. I have shitty apartments to look at."

He emptied his tray and went back through the swinging kitchen door. A few minutes later his voice came over the headset and into her ear.

"Hey, Mallory, I have a hot tip for you."

"What?"

"When you blink, *cherish* it."

She slapped another REDUCED label on a bakery box. That was another loss: she'd no longer get to work with Noah, at the store in Sterling. His survey that night had been "Do you shave the tops of your toes?"

She'd finally told him about Shay. He'd remembered the night Mallory had shown up at the Speed Stop in the banana-yellow truck to get road snacks in the middle of the night. His Spidey sense had been tingling—he knew something was going on. She told him the whole saga, about how she had tried to help Shay and was finally starting to make progress, had even begun the process of applying to become her foster parent, when Shay ran away.

"Noah, you there?" The truckers had come and gone. The Guzzler had slammed another can of Twisted Tea. It was the bewitching hour in the middle of the night. She sat on a low stool behind the registers, restocking the cigarettes and cherishing her blinks.

"Yeah. Where else would I be?" The congestion in his nose was still something she could hear, even though he did seem to have a little more energy.

"I can't stop thinking about Shay."

"What are you thinking?"

"That the guy she's with was probably once someone like Jarrod." She sliced through the tape on another box with the X-Acto knife, feeling the specificity of its blade.

"Jarrod your boyfriend from high school who burned that guy's house down?"

"Yeah, him." She pulled back the flaps and took out a carton of cigarettes. "Sometimes I wonder what would happen to the problems we're facing as a society if we did more to nurture our boys and young men."

Noah didn't say anything, but she heard the rattle of his congested breath and the bright slap of a metal tray.

"Jarrod had it much rougher than I did at home. I grew up right down the street from him. We both went to the same schools, took the same classes. We both did things I'm not proud of. But Jarrod got time in prison after being sent to juvie, while I got a therapist who gave me a journal so that I could write my feelings down."

"He set somebody's house on fire."

"I know what he did." She stood from her stool, gathered a handful of packs, and stepped up to reach the higher shelf. "Never mind.

You don't understand. Not everyone grows up with parents who just want you to be yourself."

"My dad died when I was seven and my mom was left with three kids to raise. We weren't thinking about being ourselves, we were just trying to survive, but that doesn't give me the right to be an asshole or a criminal."

"I'm not saying that what Jarrod did was right; I'm saying that we've normalized violence for boys." She got down off the stool, moved it over, stepped back up. "I'll tell you something the social worker told me: Girls tend to turn their pain inward. They act out against themselves. They cut, refuse to eat, or eat too much. Boys turn the pain outward. They punch. They fight. They rape. Same pain, just put in a different place."

"It's not your fault he's in prison, Mallory."

"I know."

"So why are you making excuses for him?"

An oven timer went off. Mallory broke down the empty cartons.

"It's not okay to treat people that way," Noah said. "You know that, right?"

She tossed the last flattened carton into the corner where she'd started a stack.

"We all have to be accountable for our actions. There has to be a moral line inside yourself that you just don't cross."

"Says you who never saw your parents cross that line." She sat on her stool and ripped open another box. "There was this blue jay that got into the pole barn once. We were working on the snowmobiles, Jarrod and his uncle and me. And this blue jay got in. It was beautiful, with a delicate black circle around its blue capped head. You think you know what blue is until you see it up close on a creature in the wild, and then it's just blue on a whole different level." She sat with her knees tucked under the stool, bent over, restocking the lower shelves. "Jarrod and I were trying to help it; we were shooing it out with a broom. But his uncle kept yelling at us because we were letting in the cold air, and the bird wouldn't go out. So he gave Jarrod his pistol. 'Just shoot it,' he said. 'Kill that damn devil bird.'" She sat up and tossed out an empty box. "And Jarrod didn't want to do it. He was not the kind of boy who wanted to kill a bird. But he had to shut that down and cross that line, and I saw him do it. Jarrod became someone else because that's what was expected of him. It was the only way to get approval from the men in his life. That's all I'm trying to say." She went back to plugging in the lower slots.

"This is an old argument, Mallory," Noah said. "Nature versus nurture."

"Says you, who got the nurture."

"Why do you keep bringing my parents into it?"

"Because you don't understand."

"Because I had nice parents?"

"I don't know how to explain."

"Well, you don't have to attack me."

"I'm not attacking you, I just want you to understand that for some of us growing up is a process of becoming less yourself." She opened another carton of cigarettes.

Another oven timer went off. Through the headset she heard Noah take out one of the large industrial trays using the metal tongs. She didn't know why she was talking about all this when he was sick and not feeling well and it was the middle of the night.

"Sorry," she said, arms full of cigarettes. "I didn't mean to make you feel attacked."

"It's all right. I'm used to it." Phlegm gurgled in the back of his throat. "My best friend in middle school used to attack me all the time. He made fun of my last name—called me 'the quaky bush' whenever I disagreed with him, because my last name is Quakenbush, and sometimes my voice would break. If I made something I was proud of, he would put it down. If I said something funny, he would just turn on me and get really mad. And I never knew why. I thought we were friends. I thought it was something I wasn't understanding because of my Asperger's."

"He probably felt bad about it afterward."

"No, he didn't."

"Did he have a good situation at home?"

"His dad was a super asshole."

"There you go—he was probably jealous of you."

"His family had a ton of money though."

"Having money doesn't help you find yourself. It's like playing video games with the cheat code." She stood on the stool to plug in the brands on the top slots.

"You should consider social justice issues when you go to college," Noah said. "You know, social work or juvenile law. You'd be really good."

She heard what he said and stepped down off the stool. There, in the empty box that once held cigarette cartons, sat a feather. It lay there perfectly in the center at the bottom of the box, as if it had been placed there, as if it had been put there by a divine hand at this exact moment in time. It wasn't crushed or flattened. It wasn't small like an errant piece of fluff. It was a big, tall feather, long as a toothbrush, with all its ribs fanned and intact.

"Noah?" She could have sworn it wasn't in there before. She would have noticed it, wouldn't she? "I just found this giant feather in the bottom of the cigarette carton box."

"That's nice."

"It is, it's very nice, and I don't know how it got there." She looked up and around at the store.

"What color is it?"

"Black."

"Interesting."

"Why?"

"Probably nothing."

"What?"

"My mother would tell you—" He coughed and blew his nose. "A black feather means disaster averted."

"What disaster?"

"I don't know. *You're* supposed to know."

"I don't know."

"Maybe it'll come to you. Or maybe it just blew in there when the cigarette company was packing up the box. You pick."

She picked up the feather and thought of her grandfather. She saw in her mind's eye the black ink of his tattoo and the wink of snow-melt dripping in the sun.

"What am I supposed to do with it?" she asked.

"With what?"

"The feather." She was absurdly moved.

"Nothing. Just say thank you."

"Thank you."

"Not to me."

"I know." Her chest filled with something like helium. Was that love? Love for whom? "Does your dad send you feathers?"

"My mom thinks he does. White feathers means that someone from the other side is thinking of you, but our couch cushions are filled with down, so these little white feathers come poking out all the time."

Mallory put the feather in her back pocket, behind her phone, where it would stay protected. Outside, the gas pumps stood empty, the asphalt white and dry as salt.

Noah popped through the kitchen doors with bundles of wrapped sandwiches on a yellow tray. He unloaded them at the Hot Spot and spoke through the headset even though she was ten feet away. "Did you hear back from that school yet?"

She still hadn't opened the envelope.

"They're sending out early decision letters now," he said. "I just got mine from Harvard." Noah disappeared back through the swinging kitchen door.

"Wait, what?" She sat up and adjusted her headset. "Why did you get a letter from Harvard?"

"Because I applied there."

"When?"

"Last fall."

"And you're telling me *now*?" She stood and cuffed aside several cartons. "And?"

"I got in."

She shambled through the doorway of the kitchen. Noah lifted his head.

"Congratu-fucking-lations!" She raised a fist over her head. Noah didn't like to be touched or hugged, so she thought he'd appreciate a fist bump instead.

"Yeah, thank you." He wiped his hands on his apron, muted his mic, and came over to her, holding his hands out under her fist. He held them cupped in the shape of a bowl, as if she were about to drop coins from her hand. He stood there quite earnestly.

"Noah, what are you doing?"

He startled. "Oh, I forgot."

"You forgot what a fist bump is?"

"I know what it is." He awkwardly bumped her hand.

"You got into Harvard but forgot how to fist bump?" She held up her other hand for a high five. "How about this?"

"I know that one, too." He pressed his palm with hers.

"I'm just looking out for you," she said, raising her other fist. "Let's try this again."

He gave her a slightly more confident fist bump.

"That's good. How about sideways?"

"We don't have to practice."

"I think that we do." She held out her fist and he bumped it sideways on his way to grabbing the box of parchment paper. "Give me some skin." He swiped her palm on his way back to the trays. "When do you leave?" She got down on her hands and knees.

"I don't know." He lined the trays with the parchment sheets placing the egg pucks on top and another tray with the English muffins, sliding them into the microwaves while she did a set of diamond push-ups there on the kitchen floor. "I don't start until fall semester, but being somewhere new makes me wig, and there's no way I can live in a dorm with my hygiene issues. So I want to get out there early, like June, so I can find an apartment and a job. It's crazy expensive if you want to live alone." When the microwave beeped, he stacked the slices of cheese on top of the egg pucks and muffins, rolling them up in yellow paper, sealed with a sticker.

"What about your mom?" Mallory inquired, slightly out of breath. "Was she happy when you got in?"

"She cried."

"Happy tears."

"I don't know."

Mallory sprang to her feet and held open the door for him, following him back out onto the floor.

"Maybe you and your mom were keeping each other stuck," Mallory said into the headset, sliding into her station, watching as Noah's head disappeared back through the kitchen door. "Maybe she was your excuse for not going on with your life. Because it's easier to stay where it's safe. But you won't ever find out what you're capable of if you keep playing it safe."

She heard the microwave beep.

"It feels wrong to leave her," he said.

"I'll check up on her for you, if you want."

"You would do that?"

"Of course. I'm going to be working right in Sterling, so it'll be easy."

"Thanks."

Through the headset she heard another oven timer as she broke down the empty boxes and cartons for the recycling bins.

"You know how to do nice things for other people," Noah said, through the headset in the middle of the night. "But you don't know how to do them for yourself."

✳

Mallory sat in her car in front of the youth shelter, with the heater blasting and the serpentine belt squealing. A plastic grocery bag had caught itself in the iron grillwork of the front stair rail. It swelled with air, bobbed and thrashed, but still it clung to the rail. Mallory turned off the engine and watched the bag fidget and bounce. The light behind clouds cast graded shadows in the slow gyrations of a winter afternoon.

After looking at apartments in Sterling she had driven across the bridge to climb the streets of Duluth, thinking about what the social worker had said—that Shay might turn up at the school. When she turned off the engine, she still felt its vibratory buzz in her body.

She thought about the other things that had stayed in her body, and how young she'd been when those things had happened. She took the feather out of her back pocket, turned it around, then put it back. She waited, drifting in and out of sleep. When the air in the car got so cold she could see her breath, she started the engine again.

Just after 1530, a large school bus in nice guys yellow came chugging up the hill at the end of the street. It opened its doors and a row of youths filed out, different sizes and shapes, with different-colored heads—including blue and pink. They all had young faces, soft and slightly plump, and all carried backpacks, their jackets unzipped. They filed out to the sidewalk and separated, a handful of them heading down the sidewalk toward the youth hostel. The fox-faced woman who smoked cigarettes stood in the doorway of the house now, watching.

Young and displaced, without homes of their own, they made their way together along the sidewalk until they got to the front stoop. They filed inside, huddled in a loose group. The door closed and the street returned to an everyday quiet.

None of them had been Shay. Or maybe all of them had been Shay. A shrill ringing landed in her ear.

Mallory looked around. No one saw her and she saw no one. The door to the hostel remained closed. She texted Noah even though she thought he was probably asleep. *What does it mean when the ringing is in the right ear?*

Miraculously, he texted back. *It means you're supposed to pay attention.*

She sat up and looked around at the tree-lined street with its two-story houses and the sidewalk and steel gray sky. There was literally nothing at all happening on the street, in the air, or in the branches of the trees. She texted back, *Pay attention to what?*

He responded, *To the fact that you need to see a doctor.*

29

The next morning Mallory got up earlier than she needed to; her first appointment was not until 0900. She shoveled the snow out from behind her car and drove north again in her rattling junker. In the industrial town of Sterling, she motored past bars and Speed Stops and streetlamps hung with large plastic snowflakes covered in twinkle lights. The smokestacks from the refinery churned in the distance and the lights from the city faded as the sky grew bright.

A crossing guard with blowing gray hair, dressed in reflective gear, held out a STOP sign and waved a hand. Mallory came to a halt and watched as a group of kids crossed in front of her, buffeted by the wind. They clutched their backpacks and instruments, wearing heavy boots, the woman guarding over them, arms windmilling, making sure the other cars had stopped, and they had. Mallory felt a surge of affection for this rundown town, for the people and families who lived on this side of the bridge. They didn't have the nicest cars or newest homes or the best schools. They weren't perfect or shiny or doing everything right. But they took care of each other. They did what they could. They saw each other through.

As she crossed the bridge into the sister city of Duluth, snow unraveled from the roofs of passing semis and cars in twisting ribbons that blew across the lanes. Below them, the frozen arm of the bay wrapped itself around the strip of land that rose shining on the hill, and Mallory turned off the highway and climbed up the steep residential streets until she got to the one with the youth hostel where Shay had lived. The tires crackled over the hardened ice and rubble that had frozen overnight, and she parked across the street and sat in her car.

The door popped open just after 0800, a row of heads filing out. They wore skinny jeans with sneakers even though it was winter, and backpacks that rose like humps on their backs. One of them pulled up her sweatshirt hood. The fox-faced woman who smoked cigarettes stood in the doorway watching as the young girls followed the sidewalk to the bus stop near a mound of snow at the end of the street. Mallory didn't hide her face. She waited, and the woman smoking the cigarettes noticed, their eyes meeting from across the street with a shared knowledge hard as ice. The bus appeared, the STOP sign flipped out, and the doors shuttered open. The kids climbed on board; the bus swallowed them whole, then labored up the hill and disappeared. No other vehicles came from either direction in the street. The fox-faced woman went back into the house.

It had gotten cold, but Mallory didn't leave. She started her car and sat alone, staring at the leafless trees.

Another door opened, on a house across the street, and a woman with rich glossy hair spilling from under her hat came out, wearing a baby in a front carrier and holding the hand of a little girl in a pink snowsuit with a pom-pom on her hat. An older boy with long legs and a Spider-Man backpack strode ahead. The girl toddled beside her mom and hurried to keep up with her brother while still holding her mother's hand, but at one point along the sidewalk she stopped. Something in the snowbank had caught her eye—a piece of trash, the glint of something shiny. The girl with the pom-pom hat let go of her mother's hand. She crouched and poked at whatever it was, and then, finding it not that interesting after all, she stood and held out her hand.

The way she did it—not even looking to see if anybody was there but just sticking her hand up, confident that her mom would be there. And she was. The mom had paused and come back, and she took her daughter's hand, and on they went, walking to the end of the street. When the bus came and the older brother got on, the little girl and her mother waved.

Mallory turned off her car. It was an hour later there. She called, even though it had been four years. And her mother was there.

"Mallory? Is that really you?" She answered before the third ring. She sounded happy.

Mallory's throat seized up and her voice cracked. "Yeah. It's me."

"Oh my goodness, sweetheart, where are you? Are you stateside? We haven't heard from you in ages." A disturbance in the background. "Oh, hold on a second." Voices muffled, a male voice not her dad, followed by some laughing. Her mom, laughing?

"Is this a bad time?" Mallory asked. "If I'm interrupting something I can call back."

"Oh no, it's fine. I just had to get myself untangled from the sheets."

"Oh my god, I'll call back."

"It's not that!" Her mom laughing, again.

"You're still in bed?"

"It's only just after nine."

"Don't you have to be at work?"

"Listen to you!" Mallory heard the running of water and the clink of ceramic mugs. "My shift doesn't start until eleven. Plenty of time to talk while I have my coffee." Rather than brewing a new pot in the morning, her mom always reheated the old coffee, claiming it tasted better that way. As a girl Mallory had believed her, but at the Speed Stop they drained out the old coffee and threw it away.

"Where are you working, Mom?"

"Oh, the most wonderful place. It's the Student Union bookstore here in town. They don't just sell books; they sell other things— spirit wear, jewelry, the most beautiful journals. I walk to work every day, the winters here are so mild, we hardly ever see temperatures below zero, and the streets are lined with these big old trees." She didn't sound like the mom Mallory knew growing up. She sounded like a different person—confident, expressive, her voice a gentle buzz that misted Mallory's face.

"That's great, Mom. I'm really happy for you." Always she had feared when the spring would cock, when the anger would unload. She never knew, growing up, when her dad would explode. *But it did happen to you. You were her witness.* "Is Laurel living there with you?"

"Oh heavens, no. Laurel's a senior now and living off campus with friends. She has a boyfriend. Aren't you getting my letters?"

She couldn't open them; it was too painful. Just seeing the careful scrawl of her mother's handwriting would trigger flashbacks, memories, sounds.

"How is she liking—"

"They're going abroad—"

They both spoke at the same time.

"Oh, you go ahead," her mother said.

"No, tell me about Laurel."

"Well, she and her boyfriend got into a study abroad program together, so they'll be traveling all summer."

Mallory sat in the car that had gotten cold and held herself together in her coat, listening to her mom talk about Laurel and her boyfriend and how they were going to travel to Denmark, Sweden, Amsterdam, France. Outside, the wind rocked the branches in the trees and scarves of snow gathered across a snow-covered yard.

"She's applying for internships and looking at grad schools," her mother said. "And they plan to stay on the east coast after they graduate. They're looking at schools in the Boston area."

"Will Dad be at her graduation?"

"Oh, Mallory," her mother said, her enthusiasm dampened. "It's too early for this. I haven't had my coffee yet."

"Are you still heating up the old stuff?"

"No," she sounded confused. "I always brew a fresh pot."

"I'm glad you're finally letting yourself have a good cup of coffee."

"What are you talking about?" She laughed. "What a strange thing to say." It was a nervous laugh, and in it Mallory recognized the mother she had known, the woman she had grown up with.

"It's one of my childhood memories," Mallory said.

"Well, I hope you have some good memories, too." The man who lived with her mother said something softly and her mother responded to him. "I can tell you this," her mother said, alone now and in a different room. "Your father is finally doing something for himself. He thinks we're better off without him in our lives. Sometimes, desertion is an act of grace."

Mallory laughed. It was unkind.

"I just don't understand why you're always so angry." Her mother sighed. "You girls had so much more than I ever did, plenty of food and nice clothes. You had opportunities that I never got—you had your basketball, Laurel had speech. We always made sure you had outdoor experiences and camping trips. We did the best we could."

"I know, Mom."

"If you know, then why are you so mad?"

It had started to snow. Mallory didn't notice when, but large white flakes clutched each other as they fell down, dangling like the solar systems she'd made from Styrofoam balls as a kid. "I used to think," she said, "that if I suffered enough every day, if I denied myself things that I really wanted, if I scraped myself or reinjured a bruise, poked at a cut, peeled at a scab, made myself bleed, that you would get hurt less."

The snow covered up all the dirty patches in the street.

"I'm angry because it was your job to protect me, and instead it was me who was trying to protect you. And I always failed."

It fell on the window glass, it lined the branches of the trees, a thick and fuzzy snow with clusters of flakes.

"Oh, Mallory," her mother whispered. "Things weren't that bad."

"I thought he was killing you."

"There will always be people who have it better and people who have it worse. That's what I've learned."

Flakes like asterisks punctuating the air.

"I did try to leave once," her mother admitted. "After this one night when I got scared. I went to a few meetings and I prayed, but the women who left seemed no better off to me, and they always went back."

Mallory had the flashback of a room with cinder block walls and women crying in chairs; she and her sister playing on the floor with mashed banana in the carpet.

"We stayed with your grandparents that summer. Do you remember? They loved you girls very much."

The snowflakes coated the sides of her windows and windshield, collecting on the edges but melting in the middle where it was still warm.

"I just wasn't equipped to leave," her mother said. "I had no job, no money, and two babies to take care of. My father had just died, and my mother lived far away."

"I remember when your father died."

"And I didn't want to raise my children in a broken home. That was very important to me. Your father always provided. He did whatever it took to take care of you girls. He wanted to give you better than what he had, and that's what he did."

Mallory closed her eyes. She could no longer feel her fingers or nose, but she could feel that disturbance in her, that anger brewing low in her gut. "I was planning to reenlist," she said, shivering. "Serve another eight years. I came home because I wanted to talk to Dad." She tightened her coat. If she started the car, the serpentine belt would squeal.

"That breaks my heart, Mallory."

"Why? I'm proud to serve my country."

"It's not that."

"What, then?"

"I never imagined this for you. You were always my sweet girl, so sensitive and soft-spoken and kind."

"What? When?"

"Always. It was your sister who I worried about, your sister who I thought needed discipline and military training."

"Laurel? You were worried about Laurel?"

"Oh, you girls were polar opposites. Laurel could be so devious and sneaky—she would take advantage of you in a heartbeat to get what she wanted. But you were just so nice and understanding; you never seemed to mind."

"I'm surprised you remember that."

"Why? You were my girls. I remember everything."

"I remember everything, too." On her window glass, a perfect snowflake with six identical arms. "Do you remember the Speed Stop store in Sanders where we used to go for shakes?" She thought of her mom on tiptoe, peeking in while the machine was blending their ice cream. "Those stores are all over the place now."

"Yes, I remember those stores. They don't have them out here. They have Turkey Hill."

"I started working there, overnights. Usually, I sleep during the days."

"Oh. I was wondering why you hadn't called. Laurel told me you were back."

The hurt in her mother's voice settled like a fog over her mind and Mallory once again closed her eyes. It was quiet in the car, the snow sealing her in a kind of cocoon.

"I pray for your father every day," her mother said. "He had a difficult time growing up. I don't want to say bad things about the dead, but his mother did things to him, and what he did to survive shamed him. That, more than anything, is what haunted the deepest darkest parts of his mind."

A thousand tiny fissures opened on her skin, each pore sharpened, then closed back in. Mallory felt those tiny dendritic arms reaching inside herself, searching for the love that she had withheld, and all at once the coldness of her anger and the truth of her mother's words alchemized inside of her. She forgave them, as if there was nothing to forgive. The darkness in her turned to ice like the hard rime in the woods during wintertime. She saw it clearly: the futility of harboring hatred for people who were only doing the best they could.

Mallory opened her eyes. White feathers of ice scrolled along the inside of her windshield.

The man who lived with her mother must have come back into the room, because her mom was speaking to him now. "Yes darling, thank you." And then to Mallory she said, "Arthur is making us breakfast. I'll have to go here in a minute. Did you have anything else you wanted to ask me?"

"What changed?" Mallory asked. "After all those years, why did you finally leave?"

"I left because of you."

Her mother's voice, stacking crystals of white.

"It was seeing you join the army like that, going off to all those faraway places, learning combat, firing weapons—it was so brave, after everything you'd been through, so brave. And I thought, if my girl can do that, then I must have done something right. It gave me such courage. It gave me hope. And I finally had the strength to leave."

30

Mallory singed the lease for her new apartment on that Wednesday. She did some packing in the morning, including the camera Landon had left for her at the back door, along with a copy of the novel *About Grace*. She drove into Duluth, stopping at the youth hostel afterwards to wait for the school bus. When it came and its doors shuttered open, Mallory watched from her car as first one girl and then another stepped down, but none of them were Shay. The bus left, the girls walked along the sidewalk, and then they disappeared into the youth hostel as if they had never been there at all.

Mallory started her car. She would never see Shay again.

Andrea had given her the key to her old house in West End, so Mallory drove there, taking the highway. She texted Andrea after she'd parked and turned off the car. *I'm here.* She took a picture of the house. Snow had drifted across the front stoop, and one of the windows had a plywood board nailed over the front. But the sidewalk and walkway had been shoveled and sprinkled with rock salt.

She parked on the street as she'd been instructed, approached the front door, fit the key into the lock. Inside, the smell of rodent feces hit her, followed by the cold and other smells—rotting food, wet sand. The heat and water had been turned off, the interior washed in a stark light. Mallory stood in her coat and hat in the middle of the living room and looked around.

It wasn't just the electrical cords dangling from the walls where her speakers and television had been, or the garbage strewn across the floor, the butter wrappers, pizza boxes, the empty soda cans. It wasn't the other side of the boarded-up broken window to the left of the door or the signs of rodent droppings everywhere. It was the word "DYKE" spray-painted in crude red letters across the largest wall, and the way the paint had bled.

Of course, Mallory thought. It all made sense then. She exhaled and her breath plumed white into the room. Of course there would be this. The feeling dropped into her like a bird to a lower branch. She knew about the vandalism, the robbery, but those were just words, not the experience of the thing itself. She stood in that room with a new understanding of how Andrea had been living with this room in her head all winter.

A sound came from the back of the house, a *harrumph*ing, with flutters in spasms of three: *Harrumph, rumph, rumph. Harrumph, rumph, rumph.* A flopping sound, disorganized and frenetic. In a three-season sunroom sealed off from the rest of the house, a few windows had been left open during warmer days. One of the screens had ripped, Mallory noticed, and a bird had gotten in and was unable to find the opening back out. Mallory stood in the doorway while the bird hopped and bounced across the screens, fruitlessly beating its wings.

She went over to one of the windows to open the screen, but it was rusted and stuck shut. She tried several of the screens but couldn't get any of them to budge, and her presence only served to further agitate the bird. It seemed convinced that the opening to get back out was on one side of the room, when in reality it was on the other. Over and over it battered its wings against the screen before stopping to recover and rest. Mallory could see the throbbing in its panicked breast, and she thought about texting Andrea, but decided to just look for the items on the list.

Moving through the rooms, she gathered up books, photographs, and the Hello Kitty clock. Andrea's bug board surprised her—the insect wings in jeweled tones were carefully fanned and tacked. Mallory spoke to the bird whenever she came near the sunroom. "It's all right, little fella," she said. "You'll be free soon." Eventually it sheltered itself on the far side of the space.

After she had secured all the items inside boxes that she loaded into the car, Mallory went one last time into the vacant house. "I can help you get out," she said to the bird, "if you can trust me." It wasn't any kind of bird that she had ever seen before, its wings edged in iridescent green, its beak a ruddy yet delicate maroon. She thought of the Bird Whisperer and kept her voice soft and low. "It's all right," she told the bird. "I'm here to help." She thought of Shay riding in the back of the truck.

The bird went still and seemed to listen. Mallory approached, still wearing her winter gloves. "It's okay. It's all right." The bird trembled and turned away from her as if wincing, as if it couldn't bear to look. It tucked its thin ruby beak into the crook of its wing and didn't move.

Mallory took the opportunity to gently cup her hands around it, making a loose shelter. "Good job, little bird," Mallory stood. "I got you." She stepped carefully through the house, back to the open front door, with the bird trembling in the dark pocket of her gloved hands.

She was proud of the bird for trusting her and proud of herself for being able to help. When she stepped outside, she opened her hands.

The little bird looked up and flew free.

31

On her last night at the rural Speed Stop, Mallory Moe restocked the plastic spoons and ketchup packs at the fixin's bar while Noah Quakenbush in the kitchen made the sandwiches for the Hot Spot. He came out with his acorn-shaped head in its black hairnet, wearing the Smurf-blue gloves and holding the sandwiches on a yellow tray. He unloaded the bundles of salty, cheesy food, bobbing his head, new wireless earbuds curled under the muff of his headset.

"Christmas music completely ruins Bach," he said, his mic unmuted. He finished unloading his tray and swished back through the kitchen door.

"You know it's February fifteenth, right?" Mallory knew this because after work she'd be moving into her new apartment. She scrubbed at the dried ketchup hardened and caked around the Cambro's rim. It had been three weeks and four days since she had seen Shay walking out of those woods.

"It soothes me," Noah said of the music.

The buzzer sounded, indicating a valuable customer had come in. Wiping down the stainless steel containers with her rag, she saw from the corner of her eye the ginger-haired trucker in a plaid wool coat. Over it he wore a neon yellow construction worker's vest with reflector tape in large white stripes—not a very good costume for a burglar. She moved around the condiment island while he moved down the aisles, dirty snow dripping from his boots.

"Noah," she said over the headset. "The Guzzler is here. I've got eyes."

"What's he doing?"

"He's entering the beer cave."

"Are there any cops in the parking lot?"

"Negative."

"What are you going to do?"

"I'm going to follow him." She hastily shoved the cartons of ketchup packs and plastic spoons under the cabinet and slid around the condiment island so that she had a better view of the beer cooler, but he'd already gone inside. When he came out, they collided.

"Oh, excuse me, sir," she mumbled, passing inside. He wasn't as old as she had thought. Without his beard, he could have maybe been twenty-five. Pointlessly she arranged the six-packs of Bud Light, peeking out through the glass windows and monitoring the Guzzler's progress as he headed toward the restroom corridor. "Shit," she said to Noah. "He's going toward the bathrooms." She came out of the beer cooler clutching cardboard cartons.

The Guzzler cleared phlegm from the back of his throat. He'd planted himself at the last cooler before the restroom doors, perusing their selection of iced tea. Mallory whizzed past and broke down the cardboard in the corridor between the ladies' and men's restroom doors, stomping and stamping while the Guzzler opened another cooler door. She heard the clipped pop of a pneumatic suck and got a flash of herself, reflected there in the cooler door. A pale hand, the faint moon of her face, the rest of her body in shadow. And she had the strange, existential, middle-of-the-night thought that maybe she'd been the Guzzler all along. As if there really were two Mallorys and one of them didn't know what the other one was doing; as if that winter had many timelines with multiple possibilities that existed simultaneously; as if she could have made different choices, met different people, or no people at all, and things could have ended up going other ways. She thought of the black feather, *disaster averted*. The trucker closed the cooler door and the illusion disappeared.

"Will that be all for you today, sir?" She slid away the CLOSED sign at her register and rang up his items: a squirt bottle of mustard, a card, and a regular bottle of unsweetened iced tea. No beer. No Twisted Tea.

"Don't call me 'sir,'" the Guzzler said. "That's for my dad."

She peeled open a plastic bag. "You'd be surprised by the number of times I hear that."

He asked her for a Powerball ticket, just one.

"It's at $80 million," she said. "Sure you don't want two?"

"Yeah, no," he said, in that habit young people had of agreeing with you and correcting you at the same time. "I'm not a gambler."

She rang it up and printed it off and gave him his ticket along with the total for his groceries and gas. He paid with a debit card, the pads of his fingers calloused and puffy in a pair of fingerless knit gloves.

"See ya next time," she said, closing her register drawer. He took his bag, their eyes never meeting, and his wide padded back slumped out into the cold gusting lot, the wind rippling in his grocery bag. She wondered about him, who he was as a kid, a small boy—who he had been, who he'd learned to be, and what he was still deciding.

"The Guzzler just bought a card," she said to Noah over the headset, after the truck had left the parking lot.

"What kind of card?"

"Happy Birthday." She imagined the Guzzler signing the card and wondered who it was for. "He also bought a Powerball ticket. I think he's going to put it in the card."

"Nice," Noah said.

"He didn't buy any beer."

"Twisted Tea?"

"Just a regular iced tea. Unsweetened. And he never even went into the restroom." She could have become the Guzzler, could have easily smuggled beer or Twisted Tea into the restrooms to drink during the dead zone in the middle of the night. If she hadn't had Noah to talk with, if she'd stayed in that relationship with Andrea, if no one had come walking out of those woods.

"Maybe he's not the Guzzler," Noah said.

"No, I think he was."

"Maybe you scared him off."

"Maybe he's going to AA."

"Guess we'll never know."

"People change."

"My how the turns have tabled."

"Did you say that wrong on purpose?"

"I won't even dignify that with a response."

⁕

Noah had found an off-campus apartment in Cambridge. His uncle owned a building and was renting him a basement room at a rate that he could afford. Noah would work three more months at the rural Speed Stop before driving out with his car loaded down with new sheets and a window fan. Mallory would be taking the next few days off to move into her new apartment in Sterling before starting back full-time at her old store, where she would stay until August. Then she'd be going to college. She'd gotten in. A university in southwestern Wisconsin had accepted her and she'd accepted the opportunity. They would never work together at this store again.

"Mallory, you there?" It was the bewitching hour in the middle of the night.

"Of course I'm here. Where else would I be?" She grabbed the spray bottle of disinfectant along with a stepladder and rags and headed over to the condiment island. "Noah?" she spoke into the headset. "You okay?"

"I'm very uncomfortable with this idea of going to Harvard," he said. "I won't know anybody there. Everyone will have more money than me. It's one thousand two hundred and forty-two miles away. What if I fail?"

"You won't fail. You're the smartest person I know." She sprayed down the plastic shield over the top of the condiment bar, stepped up onto the ladder, picked up her rag, and wiped off the dust and grime on that side of the island. "Anybody who gets to know you will come to love you and consider themselves lucky to call you a friend."

"I could say the same thing about you."

"You could, but you won't." She stepped down off her ladder, dragged it to another side, and climbed back up. "I'm actually nervous, too. It's been a long time since I thought of myself as a college student. I'm afraid I won't belong."

"If you want to be there, then you belong."

"So will you."

"But, Mallory, there is a very real probability that I will fail, that I will flop socially and have some kind of episode and have to leave school."

An oven timer went off; she heard the dinging through her headset, and that reminded her.

"Hey, I finally went to the doctor about that ringing in my ear," she said. "And guess what? I don't have a brain tumor."

"That's cheery news."

"I know, right? I learned that, at night, when we sleep, these little hairs inside our inner ears called cilia move back and forth to move out the earwax that accumulates there during the day. And when you wear earplugs all the time like I do, that wax isn't able to move out, and so it builds up, and that can cause a ringing in your ear." She got off the stepladder, dragged it around to the fourth and final side, climbed back up, and sprayed down the Plexiglas. "All I have to do now is stop wearing earplugs and rub a little olive oil into my ear. She even said my wax buildup isn't that bad, considering."

"Neato."

"I thought you would want to know." She folded up the ladder with one arm and stowed the cleaning products behind a bottom cabinet door. "But, to be honest, I liked your mother's explanation better. About the angels."

"I don't believe in angels."

"I know."

"I think we have to take care of each other."

"You're not responsible for your mother, Noah."

She heard him fumbling with the metal baking sheets.

"Noah?"

"I promised my dad," he said. "I told him we would take care of her."

"And you did. But now you have to take care of yourself. You have an obligation to fulfill your potential. If you don't, you'll become an angry asshole. Trust me; I know." She sorted through the bubble pack of bakery goods on the table display, checking the freshness dates and slashing the prices. "You can still call her every Sunday. Plus, you're not the only angel she has."

"But you're leaving in August."

"I'll only be four hours away. I'm planning to come back to work at my old store on certain weekends and holidays, so I'll stop in to visit her whenever I can."

"You would do that?"

"I said I would."

Noah came out of the kitchen, holding a tray. "All right. I'll say it now."

"Say what?"

"Anyone who gets to know you will be lucky to call you a friend."

She looked at him, the two of them wearing hairnets and blue gloves in a gas station store in the middle of the night. And all the things they had said to each other during that long, dark winter were still there— the understanding, the affection, the vulnerability, and the pain—it was right there between them. And it would always be there, even if she never saw him again.

They passed the night. When it was over and the gas truck came to refill the underground tanks and the new team members logged on, Mallory and Noah stood in the locker room putting on their coats.

"Goodbye, Noah Quakenbush." She unclipped her nametag from her shirt and freed her hair from under the collar of her coat. "Come and visit me at my old store whenever you're in town." She tucked a piece of hair behind her ear, letting him see her face.

"You won't be working there long, Mallory Moe."

PART

SEVEN

32

The first time Mallory saw the boy who would become her son, she didn't hear his voice because she was on the fifth floor of the government services building and Hainy was outside in the parking lot. He couldn't have been more than four—his body small and thin, with a shock of dark hair. It could have just been dirty. The police had called social services that morning. A woman had found a vehicle that had gone off the road and into the woods, the two adults inside dead from a drug overdose, and a boy strapped to his car seat in the back.

Mallory didn't know what made her look out the window at the parking lot—it certainly wasn't the view. They had already chosen their cases for the day, and Mallory was checking her e-mails. She stood to get more coffee, and once she looked, Mallory couldn't turn away, because of the drama unfolding below.

This boy would not hold the social worker's hand. Even through the window glass and with five floors between them she understood his body language. He pulled away, hugged himself, and sat down between the parked cars, his backpack looming high over a shaggy dark head.

The social worker in charge conferred with her colleagues and a police officer who came over to help. There were several adults standing around in the parking lot that morning, most of them in business attire, the wind rippling through their thin synthetic pants. It had to have been below freezing, with mounds of sooty snow piled in the corners of the lot. None of them were a match for this boy. He stood, wearing a thin beige jacket and facing the hood of the car that had brought him. Police vehicles came and went—it was a safety issue, getting him into the building, since the offices were centrally located downtown, alongside a busy street. A gust from a city bus could have knocked him over, but he sat gripping his bony shoulders as though they were knobs, instead of taking the social worker's hand. When she tried lifting him, he went noodle-legged, refusing to stand. When the police officer came over, preparing to heft the boy over his shoulder, the boy escaped by rolling underneath a parked car.

Mallory had to laugh then. She knew exactly what he was looking at under there, the smelly undercarriage of bent metal, the oil-soaked asphalt, the freezing cold leeching through his thin jacket and pants. But he stayed under the car and didn't come out.

Mallory took her coffee and went downstairs.

She had a meeting to prepare for, and this boy was not her case, so she focused on setting up the room. She'd earned a bachelor's in psychology and a master's in family crisis and now worked as a social worker for the Department of Human Services in downtown Sterling. A good ten minutes passed. Mallory had the door open to the room in anticipation of her appointment, and so she heard the commotion when they finally brought him in through the double front doors. She didn't see it but she could imagine the knot of adults gingerly carrying a kicking, screaming boy. He yelled—not words but unintelligible sounds.

It happened then.

The sound of his voice placed a hollow pebble on the middle of her tongue.

A frisson of energy lit across her skin—a sensation as if she'd been highlighted. Her body went utterly still and she felt herself glowing. She hadn't felt a voice like that since Shay. It had been ten years, and she tried to imagine Shay as a mother, to picture her at twenty-five. There were other sounds: the adults trying to sooth him and the banging from the entrance doors. But his voice. It was clear.

※

It was spring now, a warm June night, and the county had just tarred the road to seal up the winter cracks. Strips of what looked like toilet paper clung to the asphalt and flapped in the headlights like a flock of run-down birds. She rolled down the window to smell the new earth, driving home.

Of the two adults in the car that had crashed into the woods, one of them had been Hainy's father, the other, a girlfriend. Mallory wanted to believe that Shay was still alive, but no other family members had come forward. There was no way to know for sure if Hainy was her son, but that didn't matter. Mallory had made her decision and completed the process she'd started more than ten years earlier. Her husband, Stewart, was in full support. It was harder than they had imagined, but mothering Hainy had come naturally to her; she followed her instincts and always knew what he needed. For the first three months after they'd become foster parents, Hainy wouldn't speak. They couldn't leave him alone, not even to go to the bathroom, and he still had nightmares and wet the bed. That had been four years ago. He was seven now and learning to read.

Whenever kids asked her, "Why do bad things have to happen?" Mallory had an answer now. It was a simple answer, but one she had earned. "Bad things happen so that we can know things we wouldn't otherwise have any way of knowing." She might also tell them that there was more help available to them than they could possibly know, and that sometimes other people got things wrong so that we could get them right.

She slowed the car and came around a wooded bend. Their house sat on a ten-acre lot fifteen minutes outside of Sterling. This time of year, the peepers were singing in the bogs and the swamp cotton and lily pads had bloomed. Each time the car approached one of the ponds, the croaking of the frogs became louder, until she drove past in a jangling climax that became a decrescendo as she wound away. She ran on these roads, knew every pond and bog, every pothole and bend.

Sometimes she resented the fact that she had to pound out miles of pavement every week in order to stay clearheaded and sane, but she was learning, still, how to rewire her brain. Hainy and Stewart were teaching her. Because if you loved someone long enough and true enough, they would show you how to be enough.

❄

That day in the conference room, when she first heard the sound of Hainy's voice, Mallory had stood frozen in place, unable to move. And it wasn't a big room—it was the one with the couch, next to a desk with a computer and a chair. She stood holding a cup of coffee, feeling that concave depression in the middle of her tongue. All the things she had wanted to say to Shay but never had the chance, what she had wished she had done, and the things that she didn't know then that she knew now. It didn't even register to her that this little boy had gone running down the hall.

Suddenly, he was just there, with her in the room.

He stood eight feet away with his back to Mallory and had no idea that anyone else was in there. Both hands pressed against the door, his breathing so hard the backpack rose and fell. His exhalations shook his chest, and with one swift motion, he cleverly clicked the lock.

The social worker on the other side wiggled the knob. "Hainy," she said, her Minnesota accent thick as wild rice soup. "I know you're in there, honey bun. Now let me in."

Hainy said nothing.

"Hainy, can you please let me in? All we want to do is help you." Other voices in the hall overlapped, and the discussion that ensued sounded somewhat humorous from Mallory's vantage point inside the room.

"He locked the door."

"Well, I can see that."

"Why do these doors have locks?"

"I never knew they did."

"Send someone for the key."

"Do we even *have* a key?"

Hainy backed away, tugging at his backpack straps. He pulled at them compulsively and in a private rhythm of gripping and squeezing. He turned to pace, pulsing his fists, still believing he was alone in the room—until he saw her.

His body stiffened like a thunder sheet, eyes big and round as a baby Yoda.

Mallory said not one word. She still wore black boots but with cargo pants because of their deep pockets, and because jeans were not allowed. Her hair had grown out, no longer dyed black and red but her own color now, a shy, frizzy brown. She lowered herself, slowly but carefully, to the carpeted floor, setting her coffee cup down.

Hainy watched, his little chest pumping, not yet recovered from the exertion of getting from the parking lot to the hall. His thin arms, threaded through the nylon straps of the pack, were festooned with scabs, partially healed. His khaki pants fluttered inches above his ankles, which disappeared into worn canvas shoes, and he smelled, even from across the room, like an untended aquarium. He'd been fending largely for himself, but it was clear that someone had once loved him—his backpack was sewn with his name in red letters, and his T-shirt, avocado green, had a faded yellow font that boasted "Superstar!"

The commotion at the door returned. Hainy turned his head. He held the pack's straps and squeezed his tiny fists, pulsing them in sequences that seemed to be self-soothing, a subconscious, self-protective moment of autonomy that she understood. And in that moment, without her even knowing, he became endeared to her, prematurely and permanently. This boy, he had already won her heart.

They were trying different keys, fitting them in. It wouldn't be long now. He had to decide whether to trust her.

Hainy eyes darted from the door to Mallory and back again, his face flushed and sweaty. He squeezed and pulsed, the fringes of his hair soaked into peaks, and up close she saw the thin scratches on his cheeks, red lines fine as whiskers. His lower lip quivered; his chin crinkled and shook.

Mallory opened her arms.

When they came in through that door, they found Hainy curled up with his backpack facing up like a protective turtle shell while he burrowed against her chest.

❄

She turned left onto their street. Their house in the darkening twilight came into view: a path leading up to a front door, a porch light that glowed, a little red plastic car designed for a child, with its door flung open because Hainy had been in such a rush to get inside. Stewart, her husband, worked from home, so he was there every day when the yellow bus dropped Hainy off from school.

Stewart had been one of the field instructors during her internship for grad school. The first time she agreed to meet him outside of work, he was twenty-nine and had just lost his job due to lack of funding. Yet when she entered the café, she spied him bent over at a stranger's table, picking up a dropped cardigan. The sweater had slipped off the back of an elderly woman's chair, and he hung it back up for her, smiling, wishing her a good day. Stewart was almost infuriatingly kind, so much so that it sometimes relieved her when he got mad. Not that they ever argued about Hainy. Stewart knew he wanted to have kids and watching him rise to the occasion of fatherhood had been one of the greatest joys of her life.

The last time Mallory saw her own father had been during the pandemic. He'd agreed to Zoom after he'd gotten sick and they were all afraid the world would end. Mallory's family had appeared in separate squares on her laptop: first her mom and Arthur, then her sister with her then-boyfriend and now husband, Wilhem. The last to arrive: Dad. Once their faces had all populated on his screen, Dad had smiled in a delayed response, then froze due to an unstable connection. He still had his military crewcut, his eyes glassy, face gaunt. He still had too much cartilage in the concha of his ears, which had pulled them away from his head. When the connection timed out, he disappeared.

The sky behind the tree line flushed a violent tangerine as Mallory slowed the car in front of her house. That Zoom session had been nine years ago, and she'd been surprised to find herself holding so much love. She didn't know where to put it. Stewart had told her to give that love to herself. She was trying, and still she hoped . . .

Hainy's dear head ran past the big picture window—he wore his footie pajamas, the ones with the dinosaurs. The dog followed, his tail raised like a white flag. Her husband's stooped back appeared next, calling Hainy's name. Just the sight of him speaking buzzed lovingly across the tops of her feet, the area between her toes and ankles, which shivered at the imagined tenor of his voice.

She turned off her headlights, let the car roll to a stop. Soon she would pull into the driveway, but not yet.

Hainy climbed into the reading chair and settled into his father's lap. The two of them sat by the front window with their heads bent together, looking over a book; her husband reading out loud even though he was tired, Hainy carefully turning the pages, his hair still damp from a bath. She could tell by the dignified tilt of Hainy's head that he was following along, examining the pictures, pointing every time there was a dog.

Soon she would pull into the driveway, open the garage door, and go in. But she couldn't do it now, not yet. She had to go slow to take it all in, this picture at the end of her day.

One house, one chair, one dog. A light on in the window. Trees like wardens all around. Nothing hidden between her and her spouse, no secrets kept, no love withheld. Why wasn't this enough? Why wasn't this everything?

Domestic tranquility.

She knew of nothing more beautiful created by man on this earth.

ACKNOWLEDGMENTS

I'd like to thank the following authors and individuals who shared with me their personal narratives, research, and expertise during the writing of this fictional work: Lindsay Sauer, MSW, LGSW, child protection social worker; Staff Sergeant Sabrina Kanyi; Staff Sergeant Jacklyn Lockwood; Jeremy Kershaw, RN; Tarra Lind, youth advocate and Native American descendant of the Fond du Lac Band of Ojibwe; Rachel Lloyd, founder of Girls Educational and Mentoring Services (GEMS) and author of *Girls Like Us*; Rachel Louise Snyder, author of *No Visible Bruises*; and Dr. Bessel van der Kolk, author of *The Body Keeps the Score*.

Huge tankards of thanks to my agent, Abby Saul, my editor, Robert Davis, and the team at Forge who took such beautiful care with this book: Jessica Katz, Troix Jackson, Jacqueline Huber-Rodriguez, Heather Saunders, Russell Trakhtenberg, Jennifer McClelland-Smith, Ashley Spruill, Todd Manza, and Lauren Hougen.

Much gratitude to Diane Wilson and the writers at the Grand Marais Art Colony for being my early champions: Lin Salisbury, Pat Henderson, Cindy Selnes, Joan Farnam, BJ Justice-Kamp, Lavonne Schuldt, Kathleen, and Kelsey Young.

And to the individuals who lifted me up during the many drafts and dark nights with long and thoughtful conversations: Daniel Dunbar, Michelle Greene, Juli Patty, Avesa Rockwell, Tina Higgins-Wussow, Lorraine Butler, Rae Dunbar, Andrew Miller, Lilly Glenn, Sawyer Dunbar, Gail Towbridge, Eric Chandler, and Felicia Schneiderhan.

Lastly, I want to pay tribute to my dear friend Helgi, the giant Alaskan malamute who passed away during the writing of this book. Helgi had a stroke on Christmas day, and six weeks later, Juno came into our lives, a Great Pyrenees with PTSD whose symptoms further deepened my understanding of the subject matter in this book. Many blessings to the good folks at the Chequamegon Humane Association for the love and kindness they give to all creatures great and small.

RESOURCES

The National Human Trafficking Hotline
   1-888-373-7888
   help@humantraffickinghotline.org
   Text HELP to 233733 (BEFREE)
   www.humantraffickinghotline.org

The Center Against Sexual and Domestic Abuse (CASDA)
   1-800-649-2921 or (715) 392-3136
   info@casda.org
   www.casda.org

The National Domestic Violence Hotline
   1-800-799-7233 (SAFE)
   www.thehotline.org

Love is Respect
   1-866-331-9474
   www.loveisrespect.org

The National Health Resource Center on Domestic Violence
   (415) 678-5500
   info@futureswithoutviolence.org
   www.futureswithoutviolence.org

National Center on Domestic Violence, Trauma & Mental Health
   1-312-726-7020 ext. 2011
   www.nationalcenterdvtraumamh.org

The Childhelp National Child Abuse Hotline
   1-800-4-A-CHILD (1-800-422-4453)
   www.childhelphotline.org